RIVER DEEP

Also by Rowan Coleman

Growing Up Twice
After Ever After

RIVER DEEP

Rowan Coleman

C

Century · London

Published by Century in 2004

1 3 5 7 9 10 8 6 4 2

Copyright © Rowan Coleman 2004

First published in the United Kingdom in 2004 by Century

The Random House Group Limited
20 Vauxhall Bridge Road, London, SW1V 2SA

Random House Australia (Pty) Limited
20 Alfred Street, Milsons Point, Sydney,
New South Wales 2061, Australia

Random House New Zealand Limited
18 Poland Road, Glenfield
Auckland 10, New Zealand

Random House (Pty) Limited
Endulini, 5a Jubilee Road, Parktown 2193, South Africa

The Random House Group Limited Reg. No. 954009

www.randomhouse.co.uk

A CIP catalogue record for this book
is available from the British Library

Papers used by Random House
are natural, recyclable products made from wood grown in
sustainable forests. The manufacturing processes conform to
the environmental regulations of the country of origin

ISBN 1 8441 3391 5

Typeset by SX Composing DTP, Rayleigh, Essex
Printed and bound in Great Britain by
Mackays of Chatham plc, Chatham, Kent

For Erol and Lily, always

Acknowledgements

Writing this book has been one of the most pleasurable and joyful experiences of my life so far. This has been in no small part due to the continued support and dedication of my always inspirational editor Kate Elton, for which I am ever grateful – thank you so much, Kate.

Thank you to the excellent editorial department at Arrow, especially Georgina Hawtrey-Woore and Juliet Van Oss. Also thanks to the entire sales, marketing and publicity teams at Random House for all their hard work and commitment. It really means a lot to me because I know exactly how hard you all work.

Good friends continue to provide unfailing encouragement and support so thank you especially to Clare Winter, Jenny Mathews, Rosie Wooley, Natalie Jerome, Cathy Carter, Sarah Boswell, Amanda Hamilton and Lynne and Rosie Smith.

Since I have known her my wonderful agent Lizzy Kremer has always been on hand with advice, support and excellent ideas. Lizzy what would I do without you?

Finally, thank you to my family. To Erol, whose love and faith in me keeps me going and to Lily for just being my perfect non-stop-all-singing-all-dancing light of my life!

Prologue

St Albans, July 20th

'Did you hear what I said? Maggie?'

Maggie opened her eyes and was momentarily dazzled by the rush of morning light that swam dizzily on the smoked glass coffee table. She screwed her eyes shut as she pulled herself into a sitting position, trying to make sense of the situation. Gradually the edge of the coffee table came into focus and beyond it sat Christian, his hair unkempt, his face dark with stubble, his eyes rimmed with red. Maggie smiled at him.

'Oh, you're back!' She looked around her and down briefly at her crumpled shirt. 'I can't believe I slept all night on the sofa waiting for you to get home!' She touched her face, aware that her skin would be red and creased with sleep, and pushed her tangled hair behind her ear. 'You must have been hard at it all night?' She gave a small laugh but there was something, some sixth sense, which stopped her just short of crossing the room to fling herself into his arms as she had done so many times before. As Christian listened to her she noticed his face crumble slightly. He dropped his chin and looked away.

She looked at the wall clock. Five forty-five a.m. 'God, it's still the middle of the night! I know, I'll make us some coffee and we can take it to bed?' She raised her eyebrows playfully. Hopefully.

'I said – that it's over. It's over, Maggie. I'm so sorry. I didn't plan it this way, I never dreamt things would end like this, but they have. You have to believe me, I'd do anything not to hurt you like this. I'd . . . I'm sorry.'

Maggie stared at him, rooted to the spot. She felt panic constrict her chest, and as she looked at him she felt the same love, the same passion she had always felt ignite into an uncontrollable storm that raged behind the stupidly calm façade of her face.

'You mean the business, don't you?' she asked him, knowing that he didn't. 'But listen, listen to me. It's OK, because . . . It will be OK. I've been thinking, we might have overstretched ourselves opening a London branch now, I think maybe we needed more time, maybe we were going too fast.' She paused as he lifted his gaze to meet hers, saw tears in his eyes, and felt fear and hope all at once. 'Because it doesn't matter. We're in good shape here, we might have to let a couple of people go, which is a shame, but I made sure when we started this . . . I made sure that if the London branch didn't work out it wouldn't be the end of us, of Fresh Talent, I mean. It wouldn't be the *end* of us. I know we'd have to start again, but we can, we built this up from nothing once, and look how far we've come. If we have to do it again it'll be better, much better, this time.'

Without realising it Maggie had crossed the room and sunk to her knees at Christian's feet; unclenching his stiff fingers and holding them in hers, she looked up into his eyes and shook her head. 'It doesn't have to be over, Christian,' she said again. 'It doesn't have to be.'

As she looked up at him, she felt that the whole of her life, everything she had given to make things work with Christian, was balancing on a cliff edge. Christian disengaged his fingers from hers and ran them through his hair, shaking his head, and Maggie knew she was falling.

'Please, Mags, please. Listen to me. I don't mean the business,

I . . .' He stopped, and it seemed as if he had entirely deflated. 'I mean *us*, Maggie. We are over. You and me. I'm in love with someone else.'

Maggie felt the sudden shocking calm of a drowned woman.

Leeds, later the same morning

The first thing Pete saw as he opened his eyes was the curve of Stella's bottom, like luminescent marble, smooth and firm. She was sitting on the edge of the bed, her back to him, perfectly still, thinking. For the millionth time Pete marvelled at her waist-length hair which somehow managed to be all kinds of blonde and curly and straight all at once. Occasionally, when he ventured to compliment her about it, she'd laugh and mention something about it being out of a bottle, but Pete preferred the wonder of it as a mystery. In fact, Pete preferred the whole wonder of Stella as a mystery, an insoluble enigma that he couldn't hope to understand but could only marvel at. Stella was the universe encapsulated in a single small but perfectly curvy body.

Not realising he was awake, Stella lifted her bottom gently off the bed and walked over to the mantlepiece of their bedroom. She eyed herself in the mirror for a moment, turned her body a little to examine her profile, and Pete felt the familiar surge of desire for her as he watched her watch herself. That was the wonderful thing about Stella. When Pete had first met her five years ago, she wasn't like so many of the girls he'd encountered in the past. She wasn't born half empty, always looking for a fix or a cure in the shape of a man. She wasn't the type to try and rush relationships to some premature conclusion. If anything, Stella liked to keep the emotional side of things in a kind of suspended animation, and commitment was something she'd only hint at just when you thought all hope might be lost.

Pete smiled to himself and let out a small breath. It had been

3

like that with him and Stella not so long ago. She'd come and go, and he'd be waiting for her latest fad or fling to fade until she came back to him, and she always did. But for the last year almost, eight months anyhow, there had been no one else, he was sure of it. In the last few months she'd started to call Pete's flat 'ours' and she'd make plans with him for the weekend as early as Wednesday night. Pete was certain, he was *sure*, that his persistence had finally won her. She'd stopped searching for a more promising alternative. She was finally his.

He found it hard to prevent himself from laughing with pure joy as he watched her bend over to rifle through the contents of their bottom drawer, but just as he was about to call out and ask her to get back into bed, Stella straightened and looked at herself in the mirror again. Pete caught sight of her reflection. In her right hand was her passport.

Pete closed his eyes abruptly, his mind racing. 'Idiot. Stupid bloody idiot,' he cursed himself silently. 'Haven't you learned that tempting fate always, always ends in tears?'

He opened his eyes just a crack to see Stella, still naked, zipping the passport into her backpack and stuffing summer dresses on top of it. He'd lulled himself into a false sense of security and now, on the very morning he'd been con-gratulating himself on being able to keep her, she was leaving. Only this time he wasn't going to let her go.

Desperate and determined, Pete formulated the only plan to make her stay that he could conjure up in those few split seconds. It was pretty extreme, sort of Bruce-Willis-on-top-of-a-skyscraper-full-of-terrorists-with-a-nuke extreme – but needs must.

'I've got a surprise for you tonight,' he said, sitting up quickly.

Stella jumped and dropped a selection of near translucent thongs on the floor.

'Bloody hell,' she laughed, and then, gesturing to the bag. 'I was just sorting out the washing.' They looked at each other. They both knew she was lying.

'Reservations at that place you're always banging on about . . .' Pete struggled for the name.

'Hugo's?' Stella gave a little jump and Pete groaned inwardly, trying to keep his mind off her breasts and on the plan.

'Yeah, there, I've got reservations for tonight at eight. You'll be there, won't you?'

Stella looked at the bag. Suddenly she reached for her dressing gown and put it on, wrapping it tightly around her.

'Of course I will,' she said with quiet uncertainty.

Pete ploughed on. 'Because I've got to go out today, I've got a few things to organise, some surprises for you and stuff . . . and you won't go anywhere, will you, Stella? Promise me you won't do anything until after tonight, until then, will you, Stella?'

Stella examined the ends of her dressing gown cords for a long moment before meeting his eyes with a smile.

'No, I won't. I promise I won't, but Pete . . .'

Pete knew that his plan, his last stand, was about as clear as glass and he knew that Stella could see what was coming a mile off.

'Look, Stella, please. All I'm asking is that you come tonight and just see. Just see how you feel after tonight? I've arranged it especially for you.'

Stella scooped the fallen thongs up from the floor and stuffed them, temporarily at least, back into the drawer. The passport, he noticed, stayed where it was.

'Of course,' she said with half a smile, and turned on the TV.

'Well,' thought Pete, high on the terror inspired by the thought that he was going to have to get a diamond big enough to keep her and what's more a reservation at the most exclusive place in town – by eight o'clock tonight. 'It's about time I took the plunge.'

5

Chapter One

'Right, Mrs Billingham.' Sarah looked at the reflection of the woman in her seventies seated before her, and then at the picture of Cameron Diaz clipped neatly from *Hello!* that she held in her hand. 'You want ash blonde with honey lowlights and an elfin tousled cut, is that right?' She raised her voice just a little for Mrs Billingham's benefit.

'Yes, dear, I thought a change would be nice, don't you?'

Sarah cast an eye over Mrs Billingham's fine hair, drained and thinned by years of colour and permanent curls, and wondered if it could stand a semi-permanent colour wash let alone anything more spectacular. She leaned over the back of the chair, bringing her cheek level with Mrs Billingham's and, lowering her voice a little, caught her gaze in the mirror. 'The thing is, love, these colours aren't included in the pensioner's special. I mean, you're right, you'd look a treat, but the colours alone would set you back fifty quid. If you've got that to spare then fine, otherwise I can do a nice set and colour rinse for a fiver. What do you say?'

Mrs Billingham's face fell. 'It's a terrible thing being old and impoverished, dear. Fifty years I worked, and for what? Don't even see my son any more.' She shook her head sadly. 'Go on then, a nice set and colour rinse will have to do.'

Sarah bit her lip, feeling a pang of guilt even though she'd knocked three quid off her usual pensioner rates.

'Mum! Phone!' Sarah turned to reply to her fourteen-year-old daughter only to find she had already headed back to the flat upstairs, leaving the door marked 'Private' swinging in her wake. Good morning, Becca, and how *are* you? she mumbled under her breath.

'Luce!'

The junior raised her head from the five-minute job of sorting the colours that she had so far managed to make last all morning. 'Get Mrs Billingham washed, all right?' Sarah asked her, and headed for the stairs up to her flat. She couldn't think who would be calling her on the flat number during the day. Everyone knew she'd be working. It must be creditors or her mother or someone else equally terrifying. Becca had tossed the handset onto the sofa and returned to her bedroom, leaving the TV blaring to an empty room.

'Hello?' Sarah waited for the reply and then realised who it was. '*Maggie! Hello!*' she bellowed, picturing her friend jumping out of her reverie at the other end of the line. 'I'm at work, you should have called me in the shop.'

'I'm sorry,' Maggie said at her end. 'I forgot. What's Becca doing at home, anyway? It is a Wednesday, isn't it? Or have I totally lost it?'

Sarah listened carefully to the tone of her voice. She seemed reasonably composed: calm, if mildly distracted.

'Summer holidays, or Purgatory for Parents as I like to call it. So, um, what can I do for you? It's just that I've got Mrs—' Maggie's sob tore down the phone line and battered Sarah's ear drum before she could pull it away.

'It's just . . . I can't stand it! I can't stand any of it, Sarah. This bloody pub, Mum and Dad, my stupid bloody brother and the . . . and the . . . the fact that he's gone. Christen's gone and I just can't . . . can you come over? Now?'

7

Sarah thought about her pensioners, her Wednesday morning bread and butter, and wondered if Jackie and Luce could cope by themselves. And then she realised they'd have to. In all the years they'd known each other, Maggie had always come to her when she'd got in a mess, across the country sometimes and in the middle of the night. The very least she could do was get across town.

'I'll be there in twenty minutes, all right?'

Maggie continued to sob regardless.

'OK, well, I'm hanging up now, so I'll be there in twenty minutes.' She paused for a moment. 'You can put the phone down now,' she added.

As she picked up her car keys, Sarah gave a cursory knock on her daughter's door before opening it.

'Mum!' Becca squealed a generic protest.

'I'm going out, all right. Keep an eye on your brother.'

Becca looked as though she'd just been handed a death sentence. 'But I'm going out . . .' she began.

'It's an emergency, OK? You want to be treated as an adult, then act like one.' Sarah winced as she heard herself trot out the same words her mother used to bludgeon her with as a girl, and which she had sworn she would never use on her own kids.

'Aunty Maggie blubbing is *not* an emergency,' Becca said blithely, turning her face away as her mother tried to kiss her. 'It's been a daily bloody occurrence for the last two weeks. I don't know why it's taking her so long to pull herself together. I wouldn't let that old git Christian make me so bloody sad all the time!'

In the back of her mind Sarah knew Becca was unleashing her level-two swearing to try and keep her there for a few minutes longer, even if it was just for a fight. For once she'd have to let her get away with it.

'It *is* bloody sad,' she said to Becca as she shut the flat door and headed down into the salon. 'Bloody fucking sad.'

'My God, this is the Blue Peter time capsule.' Sarah looked around her at Maggie's old bedroom. The only room on the top floor of her parents' pub, it was small, with a sloping ceiling in which a dormer window was set. The narrow single bed on which Maggie was currently huddled was pushed up against a wall papered in pink and patterned with white love hearts. Sarah smiled to herself remembering the day Maggie had dragged her up the many stairs to look at her new decor.

'Finally, Mum and Dad have let me have something modern,' Maggie had said proudly. 'It's skill, isn't it?'

How old were they then? Eleven maybe? Twelve at the oldest. Layered over the paper was poster after poster, ranging from A-ha to Bon Jovi to Take That.

'Ha! Take That! Do you remember us pretending to fancy them ironically, but actually we fancied them totally and screamed like babies when we went to see them? How old were we then? Twenty-three?'

Sarah looked at Maggie, whose head was buried between her knees, and realised that maybe now wasn't the best time to be talking over old times. She sat down on the bed and took hold of Maggie's hand. The summer had arrived with full force the day that Maggie and Christian had split up. For two weeks there hadn't been even a hint of rain, and the room felt like an oven. Sarah longed to open the window, but instead she spoke soothingly to Maggie.

'Come on, baby,' she said, remembering how she used to soothe Becca before Becca grew prickles and became allergic to her mother's touch. She pulled Maggie into her arms. 'Come on, talk to me.'

Maggie lifted her head and roughly wiped her tears away with the heel of her hand. Her large brown eyes were bloodshot, and ringed darkly with grey, which made a stark contrast against her pale skin.

'I'm sorry, I'm sorry . . .' Maggie began. As she talked, she felt her breathing slowly begin to even out and the edges of the room creep back into focus. 'It's just everything, you know? It's this bloody time-capsule room where everything, including my life, stands still, it's Mum and Dad always looking at me and Mum trying to talk to me, and I know she means well but if she thinks bloody ylang-ylang and positive affirmations are going to help . . .' Maggie felt her voice rise hysterically and she took a deep breath. 'It's not having anything to do, not really. I mean, Mum said I could work in the bar, but Jesus, I did that for pin money when I was a student.'

'You'll find another job in no time, with your experience,' Sarah tried to console her.

'I know, I know I could find a job, but then if I did it'd be in catering and I know everyone in catering, and they'll all know what's happened, and anyway, even if that didn't matter, it wouldn't be the same, would it? It wouldn't be the same as running my own business. Building something up from scratch. With someone I love.'

Maggie uncurled herself and leaned her back against the wall. 'Fuck,' she said simply. 'I'm fucked, and that's all there is to it.'

Sarah leaned back next to her.

'I know, shall we smoke a fag out of the window?' she said, nudging Maggie gently in the ribs, dying for a breath of smoke-polluted fresh air. 'I mean, I know we're thirty-two and can smoke where we like, but as it's permanently 1987 in here, out of the window would be more, you know, nostalgic.' She proffered Maggie the packet, more for a joke than anything else, and then covered her surprise as her non-smoking friend took a cigarette, lit it, hauled herself off the bed and opened the window.

'You know,' Maggie said over her shoulder as she leaned out, 'it wasn't because I was worried about Mum and Dad catching us that I made us smoke out of the window – they'd have been "cool" with it. It was because I thought they were so embarrassing with all their bloody "permissive" parenting. I wanted them to be more like your mum, you know, the kind of parents that forced you to hide your disco clothes in a Tesco bag until you got half a mile down the road. Not the sort that had sex in the middle of a muddy field with a few thousand other people. When I was a kid I used to pray to be sent to a boarding school, like Trebizon or Mallory Towers or something. I couldn't stand it here, couldn't wait to get out of here and make my own life, get married, have my own kids. Force them to brush their teeth and do their homework instead of saying, "life is full of choices, Maggie, and they are all yours to make." '

She stubbed the half-smoked cigarette out in an empty coffee cup – something which, in a woman who was almost compulsively tidy and neat, Sarah considered to be borderline psychosis – and continued. 'Which is bloody bollocks, anyhow, because I didn't *choose* to be back here in my parents' pub, with my as-good-as-useless brother still living off them, still wandering about like an aimless halfwit. I didn't *choose* for Christian to leave me. I didn't *choose* any of this, but I've got it and I just can't see where I go from here, Sarah. I just can't see what to do.'

'Listen.' Sarah crossed the small room and stood in the square pool of sunlit warmth. 'I know that right now things seem as if they'll never get better – believe me, I've been there more times than I care to mention – but things will get better. It's only been a couple of weeks. You haven't had a chance to sort things out

11

yet, you haven't let it all sink in. And what you were saying about my mum . . . Have you forgotten she threw me out at eighteen because she wouldn't have a pregnant girl bringing shame on the house? I never see her, I never speak to her and she lives two miles away. At least your parents are here for you. They *love* you, Mags, even if they are a bit flaky. And at least you've got a roof over your head and a way of earning some cash until you get back on your feet.'

Sarah reached out and tucked her friend's dark hair behind one ear.

'What you need, apart from some coppertone lowlights and some *really* good concealer is a plan. You need to get some direction, move things on a bit.' Sarah paused cautiously. 'You need to see Christian, Mags. You've got money in that business and in the flat. You have to be practical, get what's yours and move on. It's the only way, mate, trust me.'

Maggie rubbed her hands across her face and ran them anxiously through her hair. 'I know,' she said. 'I know. He keeps leaving me messages on my mobile saying we've got to sort out the practicalities, but he sounds so normal, he sounds as if he's ordering vegetables. Like *this* hasn't touched him at all. I want to see him, but not like this . . .' She stopped. 'But I know, I know I have to.'

Sarah nodded and checked her watch.

'Mate, I've got to go, I've got a full head of colour in twenty minutes. Listen, I'll come with you when you see him, if you like. I could thump him for you, kick him in the bollocks? Or make derogatory remarks about his sexual prowess?'

Maggie half laughed before suffering a split-second but entirely vivid memory of Christian making love to her. She forced the image out of her mind with a small shake of her head.

'No, don't worry, I'll do it on my own.' She didn't want to tell Sarah that the last thing she wanted was someone there to keep her together. She didn't want to be together, she wanted him to see what he'd done, to realise how wrong he was. She wanted a chance to change his mind.

Sarah scrutinised her briefly and then nodded.

'All right then, but if I remember rightly, the appropriate time-capsule way of dealing with a broken heart is two extra-large slabs of Dairy Milk and two bottles of Blue Nun before a night on the town. My nan's got the kids on Friday, so you and me are going out, and we'll go shopping in my lunch hour and I'll do your hair first, no arguments. Agreed?' Sarah ignored Maggie's terrified look. 'No arguments.' She grinned at Maggie as she left. 'You just have to think of this as a beginning, not an end, OK?'

'OK,' Maggie agreed weakly, but what little resolve she mustered had vanished by the time Sarah had shut the bedroom door.

Chapter Two

Every time Pete thought of that evening, of that whole day really, it was always the same. He felt a sharp pang somewhere in the location of his heart, followed by a knotted feeling in his stomach. They were always brutally physical, his reactions to Stella, as if the emotions she engendered in him had seeped into each molecule of his body; as if it was only loving her that had made him three-dimensional at all.

Looking up, he glanced out of the window of the intercity train. Birmingham had been and gone about twenty minutes ago, next it would be Milton Keynes and then he'd be properly in the south. There'd be no getting away from it then. He shifted uncomfortably in his seat, his long legs crammed against his backpack. He'd wanted this more or less most of his life, to break out of two-bit TV work and get into film, but now that it was happening he wasn't so sure. Now he was actually doing it he longed for his old small life, his telescope and Stella. The thought of her – just her name – constricted the flow of blood to his heart for a moment, and his fingers tightened on the seat.

Pete smiled to himself as he remembered the panic of that morning when he'd realised that Stella was leaving again, the day he'd decided, for once in his life, to stop her going. After Stella had agreed to meet him at Hugo's she had dressed quietly, sweeping her long hair off her face and tying it in a loose knot, then spent a couple of moments looking through her earrings before selecting some large silver hoops. Stella said she liked the gypsy look, said it suited her nature.

'I have to go out,' she'd said. 'I've got to rearrange some things so that I can meet you tonight?' Her tone was tentative and uncertain, as if she was afraid that Pete wouldn't let her go. Except of course Pete always let her go. He always let her go and he always took her back.

'But you'll be there tonight? At eight, won't you?' he had pressed her, silently thinking he was insane to try and hold her to a time and a place that would take a sizeable miracle to arrange.

Stella had crossed the room and taken his face in her hands. For a moment Pete had been lost in the violet wheels of her eyes.

'Yes. I'll be there tonight.' She had kissed him briefly on the lips, leaving him tingling, and then she was gone. For two thunderous heartbeats Pete had stood motionless in her wake, and then crumpled on to the bed.

'How the fuck am I going to pull this off?' he'd moaned, knowing that pretty much his entire future happiness depended on him doing just that.

It was just past nine a.m. when he'd got to the restaurant, and it was firmly shut, grilles pulled down across the huge plate glass windows, and not a sign of life in the minimalist dining room. Pete peered into the gloom and he thought he could see the faintest chink of light blinking through the swing of what must be the kitchen's double doors.

'Kitchen,' he said determinedly and headed round the back. The thought had occurred to him then that turning up in his weekend jeans, the ones that hung round his hips with the hole in the knee, and his Leeds replica shirt might, on reflection, not have been the best idea. But he hadn't had much time for reflection that morning. He hadn't had time for anything much more than running around in a blind panic like a man about to face the axeman's block.

The back door of the kitchen was opened on to a small courtyard and a young lad, maybe sixteen or seventeen, was taking in a delivery of fresh vegetables. Pete paused a few feet from him and shuffled.

'All right?' he asked mildly.

The boy raised his head and nodded, turning to go in.

'Um, I was wondering, like. Any chance of getting a table here tonight? It's an emergency.'

The lad turned back and looked at Pete, a slow grin spreading across his acne-bitten face. 'This isn't McDonald's, mate!' he said with a phlegmy laugh. 'You have to book about three months ahead and you need at least two ton in your pocket to eat here. Sorry, try the Italian in the arcade, they can usually fit you in and their veal's not bad.'

Pete regarded his grey and worn trainers and wondered how it had come to this. How he, a grown man of thirty-four, had been reduced to pleading with some spotty kid for his life.

'The thing is, mate, I'm going to propose to her, my girlfriend Stella, that is. And it has to be tonight and it has to be here. Otherwise she's going to leave me.'

The kid looked at him with a mixture of horror and contempt. 'You've not heard of planning ahead, then?' he said. He propped the kitchen door open with the veg and sat down on the concrete step, pulling out a packet of fags from his apron. He offered one to Pete, who didn't really smoke but took it anyway, and sat beside him on the step. 'Look,' the kid continued, 'I've been about, me. I've got a few birds on the go and, trust me, if your lass is that demanding you don't want to be marrying her. You want to be sacking her. Pronto.' He nodded at Pete's shirt. 'So what about last season then?' he asked him.

Pete winced and shook his head. 'You tell me how we got from playing in Europe to a relegation dog fight in just two seasons.' He shook his head glumly.

'Tell me about it. I'm Si, by the way. I'm sort of dogsbody to the sous-chef, when I'm not at college. But it's all right. Training here means I can go anywhere once I'm qualified.'

Pete tried to look interested as he felt his small sliver of hope dissolve. He shook his head despondently.

'It's good you're doing what you want. Just make sure you never get stuck in a rut. I guess by now I should have learnt,' he told Si, taking a painful drag on the cigarette, 'that I can't stop Stella. If she wants to go, she'll go, and she'll leave me here waiting for her, living in the same old flat, going to the same studios every day, spending my entire life with Dougie the sodding Digger.' Pete took another drag. 'Sometimes I think if it was over, finally over for good this time, it'd even be a sort of relief, but . . .'

'Dougie the Digger?' Si's head snapped up. 'I bloody love Dougie the Digger!' He leapt up and started singing the theme tune from the children's show right there. ' "Dougie the Digger, Big and strong, He'll always be there to put right what's wrong!" Fucking ace. I fucking grew up on Dougie, man.'

Pete stared at him and felt a curious mixture of pride and horror. 'I never realised I'd been doing it for so long that actual grown-up kids had actually grown up on it . . .' he muttered.

'So then, man, what do you do, on Dougie?' Si crouched down beside him. 'Do you do the voice, do you? Hey, listen to this.' He went into a faultless impression of Dougie's rumbling Yorkshire accent. ' "Don't worry, Mr Merry, we'll have you dug out of the hole in no time. Come on, Skip!" What do you reckon? I could do your holiday cover or whatever.' Si laughed

17

and shook his head, so genuinely tickled by the idea, that Pete couldn't help grinning in return.

'I'm a model maker, the special effects bloke. I build and operate Dougie and some of the other characters as well.'

Si grinned and held out his hand. 'You wait till I tell my mates I've met Dougie the Digger. Fuck.' He paused for a minute and seemed to be mulling something over. 'Hang on there a minute, Dougie,' he said, disappearing into the kitchen before Pete could correct him about his name.

Pete waited, uncertain what he was waiting for or why. Twenty long minutes passed before Si came back. He dipped his chin and leaned in close to Pete, as if someone might overhear them.

'Right, you're in. Tonight at eight. Don't ask me how I did it, and if anyone finds out, I don't know you.' He clapped Pete on the shoulder. 'Oh, and Dougie, you're booked under the name of Mr and Mrs Everson, OK?'

Pete had spluttered a reply and thanked Si profusely before leaving. He hadn't really believed it had happened, and he'd had to double-check before he could allow himself a small celebration. For now at least there was still hope. As he had turned into the street where his building society was just opening, he had passed a bookshop with a display of Dougie books in the window.

'Cheers, mate,' he'd said, and then gone to get out two grand for an engagement ring.

He'd worried for the rest of that afternoon about whether 0.5 of a carat was enough for Stella. After ascertaining that Pete actually was a genuine buyer and not someone planning to do over the premises, the salesman had shown him a tray of rings in his price range. Pete had thought he'd get something with a bit more bling for his money, but apparently he'd need three times as much for a whole carat.

'This ring is very good sir, good clarity, good colour and an elegant brilliant cut. Plus I'll take off two fifty for cash.'

It had been over so quickly. The dream that he would one day be sure enough of Stella to buy her a ring had been in the back of his mind for so long now that he'd built up the whole scenario in detail. He'd meant to shop around to find the perfect ring that would sing out to her the moment she clapped eyes on it. He'd mentioned this to his sister once, but she'd laughed harshly and told him, 'that one claps eyes on anything she can pawn later and she'll be singing all the way to the bank!' But then Jess had never understood Stella.

Well, what anyone else thought of all this didn't matter. Pete just hoped that the ring he'd bought in less than half an hour would be good enough to keep her. After all, he hadn't even checked the size. He'd held on to it tightly, concealing it in his pocket as he headed back through Headingly trying very hard not to look like a bloke carrying two grands' worth of diamond. When he finally got in he found his favourite Stone Roses CD and put it on full blast. At once he felt all the energy, vigour and promise he'd been so certain of at eighteen. He'd have to get ready, have a bath, iron something, but right then, with the adrenalin pumping in his veins and his heart thundering in his chest, he had to dance.

And Pete remembered he had danced until his lungs were stretched to bursting and he was dizzy on the possibility of how wonderful life would be if only she would say yes.

The train had an unscheduled stop at somewhere called Berkhamsted due to signal problems. Looking out of the window Pete saw a young couple lift a buggy off the train and wheel it towards the steps. The mother was laughing at her little girl of maybe two as she tried to put on her dad's sunglasses. That was what he'd been dreaming of that afternoon he'd danced himself stupid, not Stella on the other side of the world and him off teaching in some southern backwater called St Albans, even if it did mean a shot at working on a film. As the train pulled out of the station he caught a last glimpse of the couple briefly touching hands and exchanging smiles before they carried the buggy down the station steps.

He shook his head, and as the train entered a tunnel he gave his bemused reflection a companionable shrug. It was wrong, surely, and strange that he should feel like this. That he should feel so bereft and desolate.

After all, Stella *had* said yes.

Chapter Three

'All right, Mag?' Sheila greeted Maggie with her habitual East End tendency to shorten every close friend and family member's name to one syllable, no matter what the result.

'All right, She?' Maggie returned the compliment, glad to see her.

Sheila had worked in The Fleur for almost forty years and Maggie had grown up with her. Born in Bow, she had worked there for most of her youth – a real Bow Belle she often said, with all the young men eyeing her as she whizzed down the streets on her dad's bicycle, her voluminous skirts billowing flirtatiously over the crossbar. When she was eighteen she had married the local war hero, a copper and amateur boxer ten years her senior. 'Problem was,' Sheila had told her once with her usual sanguine detachment, 'he didn't keep his fists to himself outside of the ring.' For nearly two years she'd stood it, hiding her bruises from her friends and holding her head high, still playing the part of the feisty blonde. And then he'd beat her so badly she'd lost her first baby, a girl, when she was five months pregnant. The next day still bleeding and bruised, she packed what little she had and ran away, getting as far out of London as she could afford. She'd landed in St Albans, and she'd been working in this pub even before Maggie's parents had bought it.

Sheila had never had another child, she'd never got remarried. 'Well, I never got divorced, did I?' she'd say with a laugh. 'Wasn't done in them days.'

Looking at her now, as she leaned against the bar, her hair still meticulously blonde, her thick gold chains looped around her neck and hoops in her ears, her make-up carefully applied, Maggie could see the eighteen-year-old Bow Belle still there, as clear as day. Years of smoking had kept her thin, and though her skin was etched with deep lines it was still taut and revealed good bones. She had often wondered if Sheila regretted the way her life had passed, but if she did she never mentioned it, never seemed to reflect on it.

To Maggie, Sheila was a second mum. Whenever she couldn't stand her parents' brand of hands-off parenting any longer she'd always turned to Sheila, who'd listen to her problems patiently and then tell it like it was. It was no exaggeration to say that Sheila had often saved Maggie's sanity, if not sometimes her very life. Maggie couldn't imagine life without her.

'Where you off then?' Sheila nodded at Maggie's attire. She had spent all of this morning deciding what to wear, how to look for her meeting with Christian. Eventually she'd plumped for a shortish black linen skirt that accentuated her slimness, and a dark pink shirt, one that contrasted well with her dark looks and light skin. It was a shame she wasn't getting her hair done until after the meeting, but she'd taken Sarah's advice and spent some considerable time applying her foundation and concealer until you could hardly see the shadows and soreness around her eyes.

Maggie had done all she could to remind Christian of the things he loved about her: her large brown eyes, her smooth white skin that never tanned, her slim and slender legs. Perhaps now, after this short break away from her – which felt like a hundred years – he'd see her with new eyes and realise exactly what it was he was leaving behind. He'd see how well she was coping, how well she looked, and realise he couldn't do it. Of course she hadn't mentioned any of these half-hidden hopes and dreams to anyone, least of all Sarah or Sheila, who would both laugh in her face point-blank, but somehow Maggie felt things weren't entirely over between her and Christian. They couldn't be, not after everything they'd been through together, and that tiny feeling was pretty much all that kept her breathing.

After several minutes of practising keeping her voice level she'd finally called him yesterday, just after Sarah had gone. He hadn't picked up and, wondering if he'd seen her name on his caller display, she'd left a hesitant message offering a time and place that they could meet. Today, Friday, at noon. She hadn't wanted to seem as if she had no structure to her life, as if she could just fit in with him, although all she longed to do was to just fit in with him, just as she always had done, just as she was once sure she always would do. She'd waited all of Wednesday afternoon for his call, taking her phone with her to the loo and into the shower, and then, just as she went to bed, she'd noticed an envelope flashing on her mobile. He'd sent a text agreeing to the time and suggesting that the office would be better than the flat. She'd texted back OK and switched off the light, climbed into bed and stared into the darkness, wondering and waiting.

Sheila regarded her with her smokey grey eyes, still waiting for a response.

'Oh, um, I'm off to see Christian to try and . . . finalise things. After all, we were together six years. There's a lot that needs sorting.'

Sheila snorted, blowing smoke through her nose. 'Too bloody right. You want to get half that flat for starters, and half that business. More than half of it. If it hadn't been for you keeping it going he'd have run it into the ground ages ago with his fancy ideas.'

Maggie sighed. 'That's not really fair, She. His ideas usually paid off, even if they were a bit off the wall. All I did was keep the more mundane side of things going, the weddings and the Christmas do's. And the thing is, I paid Christian rent, I was never on the deeds for the flat, and as for the business . . . well, I started out there as his employee and somehow that never changed, at least not officially. I didn't think it mattered.'

Sheila muttered something supremely offensive under her breath and shook her head.

'Anyway, that's not really what's important to me. I just want to see him, to see for myself that he really means it. I can't believe he means it . . .' Maggie's voice trailed off as she looked around the empty bar.

'Oh, he meant it, my girl,' Sheila said bluntly. 'How long did he say he was sleeping with this other tart? Couple of months, wasn't it? That weren't a mistake, love, I'm only surprised you never noticed it before.'

Maggie winced, but somehow Sheila's realism comforted her. 'Tell me about it,' she said bleakly.

'Here she is.' Maggie's mum and dad entered the bar and Maggie had to blink a couple of times to make sure she wasn't hallucinating. The old faded jeans that her dad now wore under his beer belly instead of over it had been replaced by a beige suit and brown tie, vintage eighties by the looks of it, and her mum had found a white blouse from somewhere and was wearing her knee-length 'respectable' skirt, her bare legs shining palely against the red of the material. They usually only got themselves up in this apparel for weddings and christenings, and Maggie was fairly certain no one was getting married this Friday lunchtime.

'Blimey,' Sheila said without cracking a smile. 'The whole world's all suited and booted today, makes me feel quite dowdy.' She fingered her gold chains as she spoke.

24

Marion smiled briefly at Sheila and smoothed down the skirt she clearly felt uncomfortable in before speaking to her daughter.

'The thing is, darling, we thought if you didn't have anything on you might come with us to the bank. We've got to see Mr Shah and I . . . well, I thought that with all your experience you'd be able to give us a bit of support, cut in with a bit of jargon here and there. You know me and your dad, we never really get to grips with all that.'

Maggie shook her head. 'I'm sorry. It's just that I'm on my way to see Christian. I mean . . .' She looked at her parents. She knew they hated any kind of institution, especially financial ones. They had never been happy with participating in capitalism, and if it had been up to them the whole family would have kept circumnavigating the globe for the rest of their lives, just as they had done for the first seven years of Maggie's.

As as child, Maggie had been all over Asia (barring the communist bits) by the time she was five, and had done some of South America and most of India by seven. The only places her parents never seemed to want to 'discover' were the kinds of places with basic amenities, TV and chips. But one unbearably hot morning not far from the banks of the River Ganges, seven-year-old Maggie had lain down in the dust and screamed like a banshee, shouting the same thing over and over again: 'I want to go home. I want to go home to ENGLAND!', until her throat was raw, her skin covered in an angry blotchy red rash, her eyes and nose streaming. She had had enough. Enough of mosquito nets, enough of hot spicy food, enough of temples and monks and monkeys in the street. It was the culmination of several months of pleading, screaming and howling that had always fallen on deaf ears.

Maggie had begun to feel this way after a brief trip back to England to see her grandparents. She had been entranced by the cool darkness of her native country's flat silver sky, the remarkable moist greenness of the countryside and, most of all, by her grandparents' bungalow. Restfully beige and cream throughout and relentlessly neat and clean, Maggie just ached for her own mantlepiece with her own collection of china figurines of ladies selling flowers, their porcelain faces tipped up with rosy-cheeked smiles.

Another child might have dreamt of going *to* Tibetan monasteries or Thai fish markets, but from that moment Maggie dreamed of nothing but suburbia, her childish idea of a normal, peaceful English life. She'd started crying on the plane out to India and didn't stop for three months, even recruiting her three-year-old brother into her scheme. Eventually, after the hysteria of the Ganges incident, her parents had relented, genuinely worried that they had somehow hurt their children with their plans for a free life, picking up work here and there, seriously concerned that Maggie might be in some way mentally deranged.

Within two weeks they were back home living the life of middle-class luxury at Maggie's grandparents', and six months after that they'd bought The Fleur. Neither of them could bear the thought of working in an office, and neither of them had any particular skills, so her granddad had given them the deposit and for years and years the pub – with the help of Sheila – had more or less run itself. Maggie's gran, now long gone, had even given her the little china flower-seller to put on her dressing table. She still had it in a shoebox somewhere.

Maggie focused on her parents.

'I mean, I suppose if it's really important I could try to rearrange it?' she offered, feeling a pang of guilt. But the mixed feelings of terror and relief that the thought of postponing Christian gave her showed clearly on her face, and her dad shook his head firmly, putting his arm briefly around her

26

shoulder and kissing her on the forehead.

'No, love. You stick to your plans. I know how hard it is for you as it is – you don't need us messing you around. Will you be all right on your own?'

Maggie smiled at her dad and rested her head briefly on his shoulder. Over the years, especially in the last ten or so, he had gradually turned into just a normal dad, watching the footie on the big screen on a Sunday, enjoying a pint with the locals. But her mum had never really left the sixties behind. She was still as hopeless as she had always been, wafting about with a stupid everything-will-turn-out-all-right smile.

'I'll be all right, Dad,' she reassured him, although she wasn't sure.

'You just remember Maggie, if it starts getting too much, try the mantra I gave you. You have to say it at least six times,' her mum added, before repeating. '"I am as serene and as calm as a tiny cloud in the summer sky. I am as . . ."'

'Bollocks,' Sheila said, lighting up another fag. 'You kick him where it hurts, in his wallet.' She looked at Marion. 'I haven't a single punter yet today, you know.'

Maggie didn't see her parents exchange worried looks as they all left the pub. She was too busy worrying herself.

Chapter Four

'So . . . um . . . what are your plans?' Christian asked Maggie, as yet unable to look her directly in the eye. 'Legally I mean? I'm only thinking of you. It's just that I don't think the solicitors' fees will be worth it.'

He stood up, feeling awkward about sitting behind the desk they had made love on more than once, and went to stand by the window. This was the part he'd dreaded and been tempted to delay for so long, but Lou had said it would be best to get it over and done with, and whatever her motives she was right. Dragging it on made it worse for everyone.

Having to look Maggie in the face, though, having to see her pain for himself, that was hard. Now he just wanted to be as far away from her as he could be, away from this small and airless office that they used to share.

'I thought, what if I just gave you a couple of grand, ten, say, for your share of the furniture, another month's wages and we called it quits?' He half smiled at a point just over her left shoulder, and hoped that she'd just take the money and run, that just for once she wouldn't want to talk about it. 'No, you're right. Twenty. It should be twenty grand. I'll arrange it.'

Maggie forced herself to look at him: the kind hazel eyes she'd fallen for, the strong chin. The sweet mouth that melted her with its smile and those hands she had loved to touch her.

She contracted every muscle in her body, clenched every single fibre of her being to prevent herself from flinging herself at his feet and begging him to take her back. She couldn't see them, but she knew that all five of their – Christian's – staff were hovering outside the office door right now waiting to hear her do just that.

'I don't want money,' Maggie said eventually, her voice sounding tight and strange in her own head. She felt bewildered, lost. This wasn't what break-ups should be about, was it? They should be about grief, about anguish. It should be catastrophic for them both, not a cold conversation about money. She focused on a sentence and spoke it carefully. 'I . . . I just want to know when I can pick up the rest of my stuff; my CDs and some personal things. I thought maybe we could talk then, have dinner—'

Christian interrupted her, his eyes softening for a terrible, hopeful moment.

'Mags, look. The thing is, going over it again and again . . . is not a good idea. We'll just end up tearing each other apart.' He paused, glancing down at his knotted fingers. 'I just think that it's better to make a clean break of it. And you should have some money. I'll see to it, OK?'

Christian studied her face for a moment and then looked quickly away. She was still beautiful to him. She was still there in his heart and his head, but that was just it. She was everywhere in his life, and he couldn't live like that. He couldn't lose himself in another person so completely. He needed space and his own identity. Louise was the quickest way of getting it.

'Fine,' Maggie said, picking up her bag as she stood up. And then, just as she was about to leave, something in Christian's eyes melted all of her resolve into instant desperation, and she knew that she'd do anything and say anything if there were the faintest hope that she could save their relationship, save her own

life. Maggie stood close to him, ignoring his silent pleas for space, and looked up into his eyes, just as she had in the moment before they first kissed.

'It's just . . .' she said desperately, 'it's . . . that I thought you loved me. I thought we loved each other. The two musketeers, remember? It's just, how can this be happening when only a few weeks ago we were laughing about growing old together, talking about having kids to run round after us? You were there with me, Christian. I can't believe you were putting it on, I can't believe you don't love me any more. If you didn't love me any more then I'd have seen it. I knew *something* was happening, but I can't believe that you just stopped feeling anything . . .' Maggie stared at him, at a loss for words, and Christian shook his head, searching for something, anything, to say that would help her, that would make her feel better about this.

'We can't go back, Maggie, it's impossible. I know it's all my fault, I know I've ruined it and I'm sorry. But we can't go back after this, not after I've lied to you for so long . . .'

Maggie took a step forward and clasped his hands, forcing him to look at her.

'But we could! We could go back. I don't mind. Are you certain that this is what you want? Is this really it? Six years, everything we've built up, thrown away because of her? Doesn't it all mean anything to you?'

Christian gently detached his hands from hers and settled them heavily on her shoulders.

'You know, Maggie, I'll always love you. In fact maybe that *was* it, yes – we loved each other too much.' He grasped on to the concept with both hands, grateful he'd stumbled on something to say that wasn't too cruel, too difficult for her. 'What we had *was* special, yes, but I felt like it was suffocating me, all the emotion every day. The weighted significance of everything we did together, all the things that we were meant to be, the perfect couple. It . . . it was burying me alive. Lou was a way out of that, an escape route. I'm not proud of it, Maggie. I do . . . care about Lou, but to be honest, when it began it was because I couldn't think of another way of leaving you.'

He dropped his hands to his sides and took a step back, his shoulders dropping with the relief that he had found a way to say what he had to without tearing her completely to pieces.

'Sometimes I think we found each other a little too soon,' he added softly. 'I needed to grow up first and I didn't get that chance, and now I want to try before it's too late.'

Maggie stared at him, clinging on to random words and shaking the sense from them she wanted.

'You don't really want this, do you?' she said, biting her lip. 'I mean, aren't you even a little bit sad that what we had is over?' She worked hard to keep the whine out of her voice, hoping that somehow in all the confusion he'd have one moment of clarity and realise what he was doing, that he didn't have to throw it all away.

Feeling light-headed, Christian shook his head and retreated back behind his desk, which was suddenly just a desk again, and ran his fingers through his thick hair.

'Honestly?' he said, his face suddenly open and light.

Maggie nodded, holding her breath.

'No, Maggie, I'm really sorry, but I'm not sad, only relieved that the deception is over at last. I never wanted to hurt you, but Lou has brought a . . . a lightness to my life that I had forgotten was possible. I can't be sad, Maggie. This is what I need right now, this is what I'm ready for. I'm not . . . maybe I never was ready for you. I feel alive for the first time in years. I'm sorry.'

Maggie stood frozen by the pain for a moment, and then, when she could breathe out evenly again, she turned on her heel. Keeping her eyes fixed ahead, she walked back through the main office and down the stairs, firmly ignoring the absence of conversation that followed her.

Only when she reached the cold air of the high street did she let herself cry, holding on to the one thing he'd said that she believed was true.

He'd said that he would always love her.

Chapter Five

'Yeah?' A tall man with bright pink hair shaved away at the sides greeted Pete suspiciously. For once Pete felt overdressed in his jeans and T-shirt. This man was naked from the waist up, the vulnerability of his soft pale torso belying the ferocity of his multiple piercings.

'Erm, I'm Pete Hardcastle?' Pete held out his slim hand. 'I spoke to someone called . . . Falcon about the room? Mike Cohen arranged it for me? Through the university?' Pete ran out of prompts and stuttered to a halt.

The semi-naked man regarded him for a moment before reaching out and shaking his hand firmly, breaking into a grin. 'Oh yeah, all right man. Come in. I'm Falcon.'

Pete detected a Midlands accent as he entered the musty hallway of the three-storey Victorian terrace. At least he wouldn't be the only one here from north of Watford.

'Sorry, man, you must think I'm right ignorant.' Falcon gestured that Pete should head up the stairs. 'It's cos I was drumming, and when I get in the zone it takes me a while to get out again. I'm in a punk band. We play at The Horn of Plenty up the road twice a month. We're called Fatal, you won't have heard of us. Do you play?'

Falcon had stopped outside the front bedroom and pushed open the door. Pete walked into a largish double room with an old bed fitted into the bay of the window, a desk and one of those small seventies wardrobes, the kind you only ever find in rented accommodation.

'No, no, I don't play. I wish I did, man. It'd be banging.' Pete hoiked his backpack on to the bed and looked around.

'You travel light then.' Falcon nodded at the backpack in approval.

'Oh, the rest of my stuff is coming tomorrow. Actually I've got quite a lot of . . . equipment.' Pete wasn't sure if he should mention his astrology addiction to this huge man. It might seem a bit geeky, potentially anoraky and sort of lame. In his experience it was usually a good idea to keep yourself to yourself until you knew the lie of the land. And besides, since Stella's departure he had only wanted to look at his immediate surroundings. The infinite possibilities that the night sky seemed to reflect back to him, images of what she might be doing or thinking beneath it somewhere else, terrified him. It was ridiculous, he knew, but he felt as if looking into the telescope right now might tell him more about his future than he needed or wanted to know.

'Well, that's it, then.' Falcon shrugged. 'Phone bill is itemised, leccy and gas are paid monthly and that's included in your rent. Hot water's on all the time and if you want a shower in the morning make sure you get in before Angie, otherwise you'll stand no chance until midday. Oh, and there's a telly downstairs, we've got cable. I'll leave you to it. If you fancy a pint later I'm going to my local, it's a rank old pub but at least they still sell real ale and not all this French shit. Otherwise Ange'll be in here the minute she knows you've arrived with a full guided tour and a four-course meal. She'll love you, she's a sucker for a pretty face.'

Pete laughed uncertainly. 'I'm engaged anyway,' he said, wishing he had something like a ring to prove it.

34

'Oh yeah?' Falcon asked him. 'Where's the Mrs then?'

'Away. For a year,' Pete told him, waiting for the usual stream of incredulous enquiries that followed this bit of information.

'Nice one. A year-long stag night. Laters,' Falcon said before closing the door.

Pete climbed across the bed to look out of the window. It was an overcast afternoon and all he could see was the steady stream of traffic on the Hatfield Road. He thought he might like Falcon and, although he wasn't sure about the name, it gave him hope. On his way here he'd been seriously worried about the whole escapade. He wasn't sure if he was imagining it, but the people down south seemed harder somehow, less human than he'd expected. What with that and the woman he'd almost bumped into on the high street, he'd felt really unsettled. She'd been crying, sobbing her heart out like no one could see her, and most of the other passers-by had acted as they couldn't. He'd wanted to say something to her, but she'd seemed so completely wrapped up in herself he thought he would just be intruding.

If this place made her, a local, so unhappy, God knows what it would do for Pete. He looked up into the densely clouded sky and tried to visualise the stars that would be burning brightly above it.

'So what have you got planned for me?' he asked the universe nervously, and then he started to make his bed.

Chapter Six

By the time Maggie had walked the length of the high street to meet Sarah at The Maltings, her face had cleared of blotches, even if her mascara had run slightly into her lavishly applied concealer, giving her skin an oddly greyish tint. In fact she felt positively calm, just like that little cloud her mother had described to her earlier.

She could see Sarah waiting for her outside HMV, her sunglasses on despite the overcast day and her shirt tied in a knot beneath her breasts. As always Maggie felt a slight twinge of jealousy at Sarah's curvy hips and the slight bloom of her tanned stomach over the waistband of her jeans. If she mentioned this to Sarah, however, she would scoff and laugh at her as she always did. 'You're the original model six, love! Everything you wear fits you!'

Maggie knew Sarah was right, but still, after years of hanging around her voluptuous friend it had taken a long time for her to feel that her gamine physique had any perks at all; actually it had taken up until she met Christian, who'd loved it. He'd loved her hand-span waist and her minimal bottom. Her 'subtle décolletage', as he'd once called her breasts, drove him mad with desire. 'Girls like Sarah,' he'd told her, 'they're all out front, if you know what I mean, like a market stall with everything on show. You're more mysterious, classy and delicate.

You're a new land waiting to be discovered and explored, inch by inch.'

Maggie felt the familiar swoon and flip of her heart that the memory provoked, but followed it swiftly with a brutal new censorship. She bit her lip as she approached Sarah and blinked hard. Would there be a time when it would be OK to remember the good times with Christian, or would she have to go on banishing moments like that from her mind for ever? No, Maggie resolved in that instant, because they were not going to be apart for ever. This was just a blip, she was sure of it. She *felt* it, and the fact that she felt it was pretty much the only thing pumping the blood through her veins right now.

'So? What did you get, then? Did you get the sofa?' Sarah was referring to the chocolate Italian leather one that Maggie had slept on the night before Christian told her he didn't love her any more. From the moment they'd imported it two years earlier, Sarah had coveted it for the salon. 'A touch of class, that's what I need,' she'd said. But she'd been horrified at the cost – just under four grand – and had had to make do with DFS instead. Now that the sofa was up for custody, she was hopeful again.

'I don't get anything, except my stuff back and twenty grand,' Maggie said absently as Sarah marched her into Miss Selfridge. 'Are you sure about this? Aren't I twenty years too old for this stuff?' She gingerly picked up a pair of voluminous pink silk combat trousers.

'Did you say twenty grand?' Sarah stopped two paces behind her, open mouthed.

Maggie turned round to look at her. 'Yeah, it's not much for six years, is it? Just about two-thirds of a year's wages.'

Sarah raised an eyebrow and thought 'you lucky cow', but she supposed it would be less than tactful to accuse your recently dumped best friend of being lucky. After all, Maggie, the silly mare, would rather have Christian back than his cash. Imagine wanting that overblown wanker over cold, hard, sexy cash?

'Anyway,' Maggie said, picking up a deep pink top with an asymmetrical neckline, 'it won't come to that. To the cash, I mean. I won't need it.'

Sarah propelled her friend towards the dressing room, aware of her lunch hour speeding by.

'What do you mean, you won't need it?' she said incredulously. 'Have you won the lottery? Can I have it?'

Maggie laughed and tried to work out the various bits of string and ribbon on the top that Sarah had handed her.

'I must admit,' Sarah added, 'you seem remarkably calm. I'd expected you to be a gibbering wreck and in need of a stiff whisky.'

Sarah sounded slightly regretful, Maggie noted, as she eyed herself in the mirror and then pulled off the top it had taken so much skill to put on, dropping it to the floor in a crumpled heap.

'Well, I was for a bit. I went to pieces in the street right beneath his window, but after I got that bit out of the way . . . well, you know what, Sarah? I think there was still something there. I think he still feels something for me, I really do.'

Sarah put her hand on her friend's bare arm and turned her to face her. 'Maggie, what do you mean? Did *he* say that?' Sarah shook her head in disbelief. If he had said that then he was mucking Maggie around more than Sarah could stomach.

'Not exactly, but I can just tell, I know it. He still loves me. All I need is a plan. A plan to get him back.'

Maggie's smile was so fragile, Sarah was afraid to say anything except for 'Oh.' She handed her a black halter neck, and wondered if she could allow herself to be relieved that her friend wasn't being emotionally toyed with by her ex. When the real problem was that she was being completely delusional.

★

'Do you remember Aidan?' Maggie asked, watching Sarah in the mirror as she applied colour to her hair, neatly folding strips of tin foil over each carefully sectioned piece.

Sarah paused momentarily and scrutinised her friend's face. She didn't seem to think she'd said anything stupid, so Sarah decided to give her the benefit of the doubt, on the grounds of her hopefully temporary insanity.

'Well, he is kind of hard to forget,' Sarah attempted a laugh, 'He is Becca's father!'

Maggie bit her lip. 'Oh God, sorry, I forgot. Well, I didn't forget exactly, I just didn't think for a second!'

Sarah waved her comb in a nonchalant way. 'No worries,' she said, but even now the sudden mention of his name dealt her a painful blow. She'd been out with more boys than she'd had hot school dinners back then, but Aidan . . . well, Aidan was Aidan.

Maggie gave her a wry smile in the mirror. 'Look, if you'd rather not . . .' Maggie checked Sarah's glassy expression in the mirror. 'Talk about him, I mean?'

Sarah did not look up. 'Knock yourself out,' she said, with a shrug. 'Besides, I can't wait to see how Aidan Carter and me have any relevance to Christian and you!'

If there was a slight tension in Sarah's tone Maggie did not detect it, and she went on, blithely indifferent to her tact bypass.

'He had really curly hair and he kept trying to grow it long, and he used to stick it behind his ears with soap, remember?'

Sarah couldn't help smiling as she thought of Aidan at fourteen, trying desperately to keep his naturally Kevin Keegan locks in check.

'Yeah, I remember,' she said, the sharply wistful note in her voice evaporating in the air over Maggie's head. 'It started when I sat next to him in assembly once, purely by chance. Remember we had those long wooden benches we had to sit on? and I felt his leg pressed against mine, and I had this sudden kind of physical jolt all through my body. It was the first time I'd ever felt anything like it. I thought I was going to wet myself.' The two women laughed together, unaware that by now the rest of the salon had fallen into silence, listening to them. 'I was only thirteen,' Sarah grimaced. 'All lumpy with a thick greasy fringe over my eyes and thick glasses. All the girls loved him and he never noticed me, not once.' Sarah concentrated again on the foils, surprised by the strength of emotion this impromptu reminiscing was triggering.

'Yeah, but you got him in the end, didn't you? It took you five years, but you got him.'

Sarah glanced at the ceiling, where even now Becca was religiously straightening her riot of natural curls with a furious frown of concentration. 'You can say that again,' she said wryly.

'Remember how we used to sit in my room planning ways for you to get his attention? Remember how you saved up your paper-round money for contact lenses and you kept them hidden round my house so your mum'd never know? And how you grew your fringe out and grew your hair long? And you and me went to dance-aerobics once a week for two months until you lost a stone. You must remember!'

Sarah bit her lip hard. In actual fact she'd spent most of the last fourteen years trying, and failing, to forget. But she nodded reluctantly, sensing that this wholesale trampling of her feelings was leading somewhere.

'Yeah, I remember,' she said with a shrug.

'And all the boys started to fancy you 'cos you had these enormous tits. And you went out with all of them, didn't you? Just to make him jealous and he never turned a hair.' Maggie's eyes were lit up with the memory, maybe because her own school memories faded into one seamless effort not to be singled out by anyone. 'And then one morning you said to me, "Mags,

I've got it sorted. I know how to get Aidan." And I asked you what you meant and you said, "I'm going to be his best friend. I'm going to let him get to know me so well that one morning he'll open his eyes and really look at me and he'll just see. He'll realise that he's been in love with me all along, like that story in *Jackie* last week."

'And you did. You two spent hours together hanging out. He started coming round with us whereever we went, all "just mates". And then you phoned me that night in the summer, after ten it was, and you told me he'd told you he was in love with you. Two days before your eighteenth birthday, and you'd finally got your man.'

Sarah froze for a moment, caught in the unbidden memory of the first kiss that had meant so much to her, moved her in a way she'd never dreamt was possible. She remembered Aidan's green eyes as he looked into hers and told her he loved her. For one marvellous magical evening they had lain on the grass together, under the moonlight, and she'd believed him. She'd really believed that her five years of planning had at last paid off. She finally had the man she loved, and despite all those other boy-friends, he had been her first, right there in the park under the moon. That was the last time she'd believed any man about anything.

'And then he knocked me up and scarpered to Florida with his parents, never to be seen again,' Sarah said, bludgeoning her own feelings with practised brutality. 'Your point is?'

Finally Maggie caught her friend's tone and met her eyes in the mirror.

'Oh God, Sarah, I'm being a total cow. I'm sorry, I shouldn't have dragged all that crap up. I don't know what's wrong with me.'

Sarah shook her head as if she had an annoying fly trapped inside it.

'It's years ago. Really, I don't give a toss. What's your point? I presume you did *have* a point?'

Maggie examined Sarah closely for a second and saw her discomfort, but ignored it, just as Sarah wanted her to.

'My point is, you never gave up until you got him, did you? You did whatever it took to get him, even though it took so long. You were—'

'A blithering idiotic bag of teenage hormones?' Sarah interjected. 'Who should have been concentrating on her exams?' (It was true, she reflected privately, that as far as Becca was concerned she didn't have a leg to stand on when it came to mother/daughter discussions about homework, boys or pretty much anything.

'I was going to say "single-minded",' Maggie replied. 'And that's what I need to be. I need the same kind of persistence that you showed with Aidan to get Christian back. We already know he still loves me, he said so himself, so hopefully it won't take five years.'

'And hopefully you won't be left up the duff, kicked out of home by your fanatical mother and forced into a bedsit with handouts from the State, either,' Sarah added sharply.

'You wouldn't change anything, would you?' Maggie asked her. 'I mean, OK, your mum kicked you out, but you'd have left as soon as you could anyway. And as for Becca, don't forget I was there at the birth. I was there for the first eight weeks of sleepless nights and nappies and vomit. I saw your face. Throughout all of it you were a picture of bliss. You adore her, and Sam.'

Sarah tried to imagine life without her kids and couldn't. She supposed there was a chance it'd be exactly like Maggie's but without the A-levels, the degree in business studies and the huge gaping hole in her chest where her heart used to be. No, she wouldn't change her life, at least not very much. She sat down next to Maggie and turned her chair towards her, making a few final adjustments to the foils.

'So tell me honestly,' Maggie asked her. 'Do you think I'm barking to think there's even a chance?'

Sarah returned her gaze, her hands gently gripping Maggie's forearms.

'Honestly? I don't think there's a cat in hell's chance of you getting him back. It's over, Maggie. He left you for another woman. He didn't just sleep with her and then beg and plead with you to take him back when you found out. He actually told you about her and left you for her. In my extensive experience that's not a man who's coming back.'

Maggie swallowed hard. 'But you didn't see him. You didn't hear what he said earlier. If you had, you might think differently,' she insisted, her voice low, almost a whisper. 'Please say you'll be on my side?'

Sarah shook her head and wiped away a trace of dye from Maggie's forehead.

'I'm always on your side, Mags, but at least give yourself a chance to get over him. Put all these ideas of plans and whatnot out of your head until after we've been out tonight. You might find you like the single life.'

Maggie nodded her assent and turned to stare at her foiled reflection. She looked like some kind of cyber clown.

'All I'm saying,' Sarah said, as she adjusted the dryer over Maggie's head and set the timers, 'is be careful what you wish for, OK?'

'Mmmm?' Maggie replied. She was already miles away.

Chapter Seven

'Hellooo!'

Pete jumped, dropping the shirt he'd been about to change into. The greeting had been preceded by a quick double knock and a theatrical entrance. Pete considered covering his nipples, but then thought better of it and let his hands drop to his sides, his fingers twitching uselessly, not covering anything, least of all his embarrassment. Thank God he had his kecks on, at least. The woman stopped briefly in her tracks and regarded him, raising one eyebrow just enough to make him totally paranoid.

'Oh dear!' she babbled, her accent full-blown home counties. 'I'm always walking in on people – don't usually get such a result, though!' As she laughed uproariously her silver earrings jangled. Pete mustered a smile in return and, scooping his shirt off the floor, pulled it on over his head, thankful that he'd left the majority of the buttons done up. Or rather Stella had. It was his dark green and dark blue striped Paul Smith shirt, his going-out one, which he'd been wearing on the night of the proposal. She'd pulled it off him as they were making love, just before she'd looked him in the eye and said, 'You do understand I still have to go, don't you?'

Pete blinked and realised that the woman he sincerely hoped was Angie was waiting for an answer to something.

'Um, yes?' Pete tried out of left field.

'Oh good,' Angie replied. 'And you found everything OK?' Pete looked around his room.

'Yeah, I just had a shower, I hope that was all right?' He smiled, oblivious to the instant blush that coloured Angie's cheeks.

'Of course it was. Your home too now!' She seemed delighted at the thought and hopped a little hop. 'Well, anyway, Falcon said he'd asked you up The Fleur. God knows why, it's a stinky old pub. Only Falcon, his mates and two old men drink there, so I thought if you like I could give you a little tour. I'm cooking and we could eat first, if you like?'

Pete opened and shut his mouth. Angie seemed like a nice woman, but maybe just a bit too much of a nice woman for him just at the minute. He realised she was going out of her way to be kind, and he was grateful, but he wasn't sure he had enough conversation in his head right now to manage a whole evening with her.

'Angie, right?' he said with a smile. 'That sounds good, it really does, but could we make it tomorrow? It's just that what with all the travelling and shit today, I'm knackered. I thought I'd just go out for a wander round, maybe have a jar or two and pick up a Chinese on the way home. It'd be great to have dinner with you and Falcon, but I'd like to be able to get my head in gear first, if you don't mind?'

Angie beamed at his gentle rebuttal. In fact she appeared to positively glow from the rejection.

'Of course not, of course I don't mind.' She put her hand on the door as she left. 'I can't tell you how nice it is to have a real *gentleman* living here instead of just that rough-neck so-called punk, even if I do love him!' She giggled as she shut the door gently behind her, and Pete sat down on the bed.

He caught his reflection in the small mirror fixed to the wardrobe and ran his fingers through his dark blond hair until it stood up in rough spikes. Stella liked it that way – she said it made him look a bit like David Beckham, which frankly he baulked at, but Stella had said she liked it and he'd gone with it. Funny how he'd never had a thought about what he wore or how his hair looked before Stella. In the last few years he'd picked up a few basics he knew she rated in a man: slight stubble, ruffled hair, a proper going-out shirt in the evening instead of just a T-shirt or a Leeds top. And a squirt of something he'd call perfume on a girl. He'd stuck with it even when she wasn't around, and he wasn't going to stop now. After all, she was coming back, wasn't she? To marry him? Pete gave himself a cursory glance in the mirror.

'David Beckham my arse,' he said out loud, musing as he left that he had never in his life been called a gentleman before.

'I can't actually believe you just said that!' Maggie stared at Sarah's reflection in the mirror as she examined her artificially hoisted-up breasts.

'What they never tell you about toupée tape,' Sarah said quickly, attempting to sidestep the issue, 'is that you need half a roll for each boob. You never see J-Lo or Madonna with two tons of sticky-back plastic on each tit, do you?' She glanced at Maggie's reflection and said mysteriously, 'Or do you?'

Maggie stared miserably at her chest. Considering that one of her breasts was currently an inch higher than the other one and that neither was as high as it once was, maybe letting Sarah dress her for her first officially single night out wasn't the best idea she'd ever had. Both of her boobs looked like they'd been caught in a post office sorting machine. Not even the fantastic new hairstyle Sarah had created for her, which shimmered with three or four different colours and yet still looked natural, improved the effect much.

'Can't I just wear a bra and a normal top?' Maggie pleaded.

'The black one with the V-neck? That's all right isn't it? "Deep Lunging V". It's flattering. I know because I saw it on the telly. The last time I went out on the pull it wasn't obligatory to have half your tits hanging out. And I'm fairly sure that a B cup doesn't require this much tape . . .'

She remembered Sarah's previous comment.

'Now, can we get back to what you were just saying, please?'

Cringing, Sarah attempted to distract Maggie by handing her the scarlet, glittery, plunging backless top, which Maggie, if she hadn't been told otherwise, would have called a hanky.

'Darling, it's been obligatory to get your tits out to pull a man since the beginning of time. And at least you're the right size to be able to go backless and strapless. So count yourself lucky and put on the top,' Sarah commanded, hopeful that her bossiness would steer the conversation away from her stupid, flippant comment.

She should have learnt by now, after a lifetime of friendship, that you never said anything off the cuff to Maggie, not unless you were prepared to back it up with a full theory and post-match analysis. She thought she'd made her feelings on Christian crystal clear this afternoon in the salon. But obviously, unless it was painted in six-foot-high black letters, it wasn't clear enough for Maggie, and she didn't want to risk more tears ending the night before it had even begun.

'Anyway, the last time you went out on the pull was last century. I, on the other hand, have been on the pull con-tinuously since 1989 and have fitted in bringing up two kids and running my own salon, so trust me – I'm an expert.' She tied the laces of the top. 'The aim of this evening is to get you back on the market before you pass your sell-by date, and for that we need flesh, flesh, flesh!' Sarah hollered uproariously, and liberally topped up Maggie's wine glass, hopeful that it would help her to forget.

'Get that down you. Numb the pain.'

Maggie obediently gulped down the wine and attempted a final derailment of her friend's remorseless party train.

'Look, maybe you are a come-what-may-I'll-conquer-it kind of girl, and I respect you for that, but I'm not. I'm a give-up-and-go-to-bed-at-the-first-hurdle kind of girl.' Maggie stared at her alien reflection and thought, This isn't *me* all this razzle-dazzle. I'm a simple person, neat and efficient. I pay attention to the tiny details that make up the whole picture. I'm a well-tailored suit and good shoes sort. This outfit, to me, is a fashion version of chaos theory. She looked at Sarah, who was crimping her ruby red streaks. 'When you said can we get together for a girls' night, I thought you meant staying in with pizza or something, talking things over. Not getting all razzed up and going on the piss. I'm not ready. It's only been a couple of weeks. I'll probably drink too much and cry in the bogs, or sleep with a short man with hairy shoulders by mistake.' Maggie looked at her pleadingly. 'You don't know what you're unleashing by taking me out there!'

Sarah examined her excruciatingly closely.

'This afternoon you were going on about persistence and being single-minded. Anyway, do you think,' she said, wielding a glitter stick at Maggie like a combat-standard magic wand, 'that when I've finally got a good enough excuse to have a night out away from the kids I'm going to stay in and have pizza? I haven't been out with you for eight months. I want a pint with my bestest pal!'

Sarah gave Maggie the same kind of perfunctory make-it-better hug she'd give Sam when he was crying over nothing much, and dabbed at her eyelids with the glitter stick. 'Good God, woman, you have to start somewhere, don't you? Do you want to be sitting at home all suicidal while Christian's out flinging his harlot around by the ankles? Well, do you?' Sarah demanded, thinking this was good, this was exactly the kind of pep talk Maggie needed to forget what she'd accidentally said ten minutes ago. It was tough love – bollock-hard ten-pints-a-night tough love.

Maggie returned her gimlet-eyed gaze wanly and supposed that no, she did not, and yes, even if right now the very thought of touching another man made her want to dissolve into a screaming puddle of pain, at the very least she didn't want to *look* defeated. St Albans was a small city, more of a largish town really, and in a largish town, front was very often everything, even if on this particular occasion it had been Sellotaped into an approximation of a Henry Moore sculpture. If, for example, she was to run into Christian, she wanted him to see her all dazzling with her new hair and be allured by her – or something. She wanted word to go round that she was coping well and looking good. She was only in the early stages of her plans so she wasn't sure if 'word going round' would be enough or even if it would happen, given that her local profile was a pretty low one, but it was a start, and you never knew who you might run into. And for some reason Maggie had a niggling feeling that she *was* going to run into someone tonight.

'OK, OK,' she said. 'You'd better give me some more of that wine then.'

Sarah obliged and clapped her friend lightly on the shoulder, congratulating herself on getting away with it.

'Good. Now try to remember that this is the first time in living memory that I've had one of my old mates to go out with. I'm looking upon this as a new era in our lives, Maggie. The terrible twosome reunited once again twice monthly while my nanna's still lucid enough to have the kids!'

Maggie flashed back momentarily to Sarah at eighteen, her skirts short enough to reveal the tops of her stockings, and her make-up, applied in this very room, thick enough to ice a cake.

49

She, on the other hand, had been all natural look and sensible trousers, donning a black top that fell off of one shoulder if she was feeling really risqué. She looked at herself now, hazed slightly by a flood of white wine. All she could see was two boobs at different heights bobbing despondently under a glittery hanky. She yanked the top off over her head.

'I'll wear a bra and my black top,' she said with determination, wincing as she pulled off the toupée tape.

Sarah shrugged with disappointment. 'You're *so* behind the times. Please at least make it a push-up. We're not joining a nunnery here.'

Maggie started rummaging through the suitcase she still hadn't unpacked and fished out a black Wonderbra. 'And listen,' she fixed her friend with a determined gaze. 'I want to talk about what you just said to me. What did you mean when you said that, Sarah?'

Sarah's stomach sank and she flopped on to the bed, rolling her eyes before reapplying her lip gloss and checking her roots in a handmirror.

'I meant what I said. That I never did like Christian. I thought he was a twat from the word go.' She smiled at Maggie, fluttering her lashes in an attempt to be comic, though so far Maggie had yet to see the funny side of anything concerning her one true love.

'You think he's a *twat*?' Maggie asked her in amazement.

Sarah shook her head apologetically. 'And then . . . over the years, I warmed to him. Nice manners; seemed to treat you OK. Wads of cash. I thought, you know, first impressions aren't always right. But, well, Nanna always says you *can* judge a book by his cover, and it turned out that I was right. He was always a twat, that's all I'm saying. I mean, he was shagging his new girlfriend behind your back. It's not such a newsflash, is it?'

Maggie spluttered into her wine and Sarah felt the mad urge to say what she meant grip her once again.

'I'm sorry, mate, but I said to myself the first time I met him that he was a stuck-up, ignorant wanker and that you'd be better off without him, but, you know, you seemed to like him . . .'

Maggie looked from Sarah to her bemused reflection and then back again.

'You could've said something before,' she sighed. 'Before I fell in love with him for ever and ever.'

Sarah plonked herself down beside Maggie and rested her head on her shoulder.

'Don't be so dramatic. No one falls in love for ever.' She thought briefly of Aidan Carter and dismissed the thought immediately. 'One day you'll fall in love again and it'll be better than it ever was with Christian.'

Maggie moved away from Sarah, pulling her off balance.

'What about you? When are *you* going to fall in love again?' she challenged.

'I don't do love, love,' Sarah said briskly. 'Now move your arse off that bed and let's go out!' She strode to the door and held it open.

Taking a deep breath and adjusting her bra, Maggie headed out into the real world, shaking like a nervous wreck.

Chapter Eight

'Haven't I seen you somewhere before?' Pete asked the woman at the bar. She was pretty, if not quite his type: dark, slim and small with huge brown eyes. *He* knew he wasn't hitting on her, but it occurred to him seconds after his comment that that was the last thing she'd be thinking. However, he was sure he knew her somehow.

Maggie turned to him incredulously as she tried to elbow her way to the bar and gave him her most scathing glare.

'Oh, *please*,' she said coolly, and pressed closer into the noticeably youthful crowd that thronged around the chrome bar of St Albans' trendiest nightspot, thrusting her twenty over the heads of some teenagers and shouting, 'Two vodka mules, please!'

Sarah could have gone up to the bar at least once, but no, she insisted that this was all part of Maggie's rehabilitation. More like an excuse for her to sit on her arse and play footsie with the rugby player at the next table. Maggie gave an unconscious scowl. She knew and Sarah knew that he was not the sort of bloke who'd want anything serious to do with a mother of two, but Sarah didn't seem to care. In fact she seemed to actively prefer the men who wouldn't hang around long. 'Love, my love,' Sarah often told Maggie over the years, 'just gets in the way of the game plan. You're much better off without it, you'll see.' Oh well, thought Maggie, I am seeing and I don't like it.

Maggie felt a tap on her shoulder and he was there again. Scruffy blond hair and flashy blue eyes that he probably thought got him in anywhere he wanted with anyone. Well, not with her.

'No,' Pete persisted. 'I mean, I have actually seen you before, but without all the . . . stuff on your face.'

He looked closely at her and for a moment she wondered if one of the false lashes that Sarah had remorselessly glued to each eyelid had begun to unstick and curl up like a dead caterpillar.

'I know!' Pete clicked his fingers. 'I saw you in the street this morning. You were crying.' His face softened and behind her Maggie could hear the barman ask her for some money as she carefully rearranged her face into a perfectly blank mask. 'I wondered if I should go up to you or something,' Pete blundered on, 'but you seemed like you wanted to be alone. And also, in my experience, women don't like strange men approaching them in the street.' Maggie turned away from him. 'Or in bars, for that matter . . .' Pete kicked himself, belatedly realising his clumsiness.

'I had something in my eye,' Maggie said abruptly, handing over her note to the barman and taking two bottles and some change. Disconcerted, she made her way back through the crowd. Why didn't she just say that it wasn't her? Why did she openly admit to blubbing in the street? Why was it that after having her heart pulverised into mush, her dreams ripped almost to shreds and her hopes thoroughly dashed, she was also left with a compulsive desire to jump to the front of the queue whenever a chance of public humiliation was on the horizon? She hurried over to Sarah, sensing the crowd close over the strange man as she headed back to her table.

'Christ, talk about a busman's holiday,' Maggie said to Sarah as she sat down. 'That's the trouble with working in the pub –

it makes going out seem like work. Except here there are customers. Mum and Dad don't really have customers.'

Sarah didn't answer, but instead waved a long bare arm at Maggie in agreement, which Maggie considered a privilege as her face was almost entirely submerged under the ravenous attentions of the rugby player.

'Oh God, couldn't you at least hold on until last orders?' Maggie said bleakly. She wanted Sarah to reassure her about the crying in the street thing. She wanted her to say something down-to-earth and blunt like she usually did. Instead her hand offered Maggie a 'What can I do?' apology and Maggie settled back in her chair, nursing her bottle and regarding the ravenous crowd eyeing each other with a barely concealed ferocity. It hit her then, like a sharp slap: she had nothing to do with any of these people any more. No one here, except Sarah, knew who she was, or cared.

Before Christian, before Maggie had allowed herself to believe it was safe to love him, she'd followed Sarah, hunting in bars just like this one, constantly looking, searching for that chance, for that certain blue eye, a particular kind of mouth, a sensitive nature, and she'd have dated whatever approximation presented itself. Until Christian, with his self-taught upper-class accent, his manners and his hang-ups. All these things made her love him, gradually more each day they spent together. Now here she was again, turned loose back into the field, and she couldn't stand it – couldn't stand the thought of going through it all again. She felt too tired and too in love, still, with Christian. She had to make her plan work, she had too. It was too late in her life, she was too set in her love for anything else to be an option.

For the last few years, wherever Maggie had been and whatever she'd felt, she had always known, always believed, that Christian was somewhere near because he was in love with her. Now, if she was to believe what Sarah had said to her, he was

54

gone, and she was left here stranded in a room full of people who didn't give a toss.

Maggie pushed the chair back from the table and reached for her coat, swaying slightly. She couldn't let herself believe Sarah and her newsflashes. She couldn't give up hope. She gently pinched Sarah's hand, garnering the attention of one eye.

'I'm going home, mate. I'm plastered and about to cry,' Maggie told Sarah matter-of-factly.

Sarah signalled a stop sign and forcibly pushed the rugby player away from her, her face gleaming faintly with saliva and smudged lipstick.

'Don't go!' she pleaded, her hand planted squarely in the chest of her conquest to keep him at arm's length. 'I don't have to get off with, um, Wossit here. We can go clubbing, and then I'll walk you home.' She grabbed Maggie's wrist. 'Go on, this is an occasion! I'm sure if you hold your breath and have a tequila you can stop yourself from crying.'

Maggie smiled at her, touched at her readiness to drop Wossit and shepherd her through several more hours of therapy.

'There's no point, Sarah. I'm fairly certain that gouging my eyes out wouldn't prevent me from crying at some point in the next minute, and if I have to go through it again the very least I can do is minimise the audience.'

Sarah bit her lip and nodded in understanding.

'I'd be miserable. You enjoy yourself. I'm working behind the bar tomorrow, so if you come in I'll feed you free vodkas all night. Deal?'

Sarah smiled regretfully. 'Can't, mate. Sam's presenting a fully staged version of "Beauty and the Beast" for his dad, and I promised Becca a girl's night in with all the girly videos we can find. Anyway, I'd never get another babysitter. Come by the salon tomorrow and I'll do your nails instead, make them long and red so you can scratch that tart's eyes out.'

Maggie nodded seriously and slipped on her coat.

'OK. I'll see you soon, then,' she said over her shoulder. 'That's if Wossit hasn't sucked your face off by then.'

Maggie was fine as she pushed her way through the crowds. She was OK as she opened the door and stepped out into the cool of the night air. It wasn't until she got two feet down the road that it knocked her flat. She was alone, she would always be alone, and maybe, *maybe*, Christian really did mean it was over and Sarah was right. And maybe he *wasn't* going to change his mind . . . Suddenly Maggie couldn't breathe any more. She couldn't walk, she could only cry.

She found herself doubled up, crouching on the pavement, distantly aware of how she must look: drunk, ill, mentally imbalanced. Listening to the far-off sounds of her own rasping sobs in her ears, pushing her palms against the grit and dirt of the pavement, she pressed her head into her knees and waited. And waited. It should be fatal, she thought, this kind of pain. Surely no one should have to live through this.

'Are you OK?' A faintly familiar male voice bounced off her shoulder. 'Come on, get up. Let me help you get up, please. You can't stay down there all night.'

Maggie felt an arm grip her under her forearm and gradually she found herself straightened.

'What's happened? Do you need me to call someone?'

Finally Maggie unscrewed her raw eyes, lifted her face and looked at the man – the scruffy blond from the bar again, staring at her intently.

'Do you get your kicks from following upset women around?' she snapped, finding that once the moment had passed, she was usually able to carry off the pretence of being a normal human being more or less right away.

Pete shrugged, feeling as awkward as he looked.

'I'm fine, thanks,' Maggie told him, a slight slur blurring the edge of her businesslike tone. 'Too much to drink,' she amended, and followed up with a brisk smile, allowing the stranger to guide her to a nearby bench. 'I'm all right now, just a bit pissed,' she repeated, waiting for him to go.

Pete sat down next to her and thought of Stella in the middle of one of her benders. You couldn't leave women alone in that state. They invariably did something stupid and usually with someone stupid. For some reason, after seeing her tears yesterday and again today, he felt he owed this woman something, some kind of protection at the very least.

'You can go now,' Maggie assured him with blunt impatience.

'Take deep breaths,' Pete told her, ignoring her invitation. She'll be all right when she's worked out I'm not hitting on her, he thought before saying, 'I don't think I should leave you out here alone. You were . . . sort of shrieking. At least let me call you a cab, OK? I mean, anything could happen. You could faint or collapse or . . .'

Maggie huffed out a deep breath. 'I won't faint!' she told him shakily, her voice rising as she spoke. 'I won't collapse, I won't have a seizure and die. OK? Because I'm not that drunk. I'm not even ill. I'm just chucked. I'm left. I'm abandoned. My boyfriend, who is no longer mine in any sense of the word, doesn't want me any more and I can't cope with the thought . . . with the thought that there is no point in being me any more, which is why I was crying like a baby in the street both earlier and now, OK? And several other times, which I'm assuming you didn't bear witness too. I'm perfectly well, I'm just so fucked up right now that I know no boundaries to the humiliation I'm prepared to inflict on myself, as you must surely, by now, be able to tell.'

Pete blinked at her, and his hands dropped from the sleeve of her coat as he felt a moment of panic. For a moment he wasn't sure he could cope with a woman this turbulent, but then he thought of Stella, who was turbulent even during sleep, and he steadied his nerve.

'You weren't crying like a baby,' Pete said mildly. 'More shrieking like a banshee.' He half smiled. 'I didn't mean to embarrass you before with all that stuff about you crying. Social skills are not my forte, Stella, my fiancée, always says. She always says, "Pete, it's a wonder you have any relations willing to talk to you, let alone friends or lovers, what with your lack of sensitivity." It's just that I don't know anyone in St Albans except my new flatmates and they're all a bit . . . different, to say the least. I only got here today, and socialising isn't my best thing, and I recognised you, so in I went, two bloody left feet straight in the gob.'

As he talked, Pete found himself relaxing for the first time since Stella had left for the airport. Quickly he checked himself; he was supposed to be helping her, not blathering on about his own problems.

'Oh, don't worry,' Maggie said, relieved about the reference to a fiancée. 'At least you haven't told me that I can't make you happy any more, and that actually now you come to think of it, I never did.' The man she now gathered was called Pete let her perpetual self-referencing slide silently by into the night.

'Don't worry,' Pete told her. 'I sort of know how you feel. I mean, I've not been chucked. Quite the opposite, actually. Although I must admit it's hard not to feel like I've been . . . quality controlled?'

Maggie mustered up a smile, and turned to face him, only to find him examining the skies with a faintly bemused air.

'Oh yeah?' she said sceptically, feeling her earlier anguish recede once more to breathable background levels. 'Call me jaded, but it sounds like a fancy way of saying chucked to me.'

Pete shook his head and turned his chin to look at her, the

colour and quality of his eyes hidden by the absence of natural light.

'No, I definitely haven't been dumped. Stella's gone away for a year. To Australia, the week before last. To decide things. The day after I proposed. I really miss her.' He shrugged self-consciously. 'It's like I breathe in and I miss her, I breathe out and I miss her, I blink and I miss her and—'

Maggie interrupted abruptly. 'I get the picture. You miss her so much that you think you could die, but the big difference here, my friend, is that she loves you. She's coming back to marry you in twelve months. Christian, on the other hand, doesn't care if he never sees me again, and now I've gone from Company Director to redundant barmaid in one easy step.'

Suddenly angry, Maggie felt herself letting go of The Plan, and, picking up her bag, began to rub at the dark pools of mascara that had collected under her eyes. She peeled one fake lash off her cheek and dropped it to the ground.

'I don't think we should talk any longer,' she told Pete kindly. 'Because you obviously need sympathy and I'm not the one to give it. You should make friends with someone who's still labouring under the misapprehension that happiness is more than just some flim-flam invented by God to keep us all quiet whilst he plots our excruciating demise.'

Maggie stood and shrugged in apology, but Pete only laughed, causing her to despair quietly to herself.

'It's not funny,' she told him sulkily.

'It is, sort of,' Pete replied. Despite himself he found her distress distracting, like looking at a car crash, only messier. 'And anyway, um, sorry, what's your name?'

'Maggie,' Maggie grumbled, feeling the sudden chill of sobriety creep over her skin.

'And anyway, Maggie, she's gone to Australia to decide if she really loves me, to make sure that she really wants to marry me.

59

To absolutely rule out the possibility that there might be someone better out there.'

Maggie sat back down with a bump, bemused by the expression of acceptance and, yes, even affection, in Pete's eyes. She laid a cold hand on his arm, for a split second enjoying being the harbinger of doom, instead of the harbingee.

'I don't want to have to be the one to tell you this, Pete, but I'm fairly sure you are chucked.'

Pete shook his head, running his fingers though his roughly-cut fair hair, trying to shake off a look of discomfort. He'd preferred it when they were talking about her.

'I know, I know how it sounds, but you see, it's not like that.' He tried his best to explain to this stranger what he had failed to explain to his closest friends and family. 'I'm having the courage of my convictions, is all. I love her. I know *absolutely* that she is the one for me. I know it just as I know the universe is infinite and endless, and for me that knowledge is enough. I don't need anything else, I have faith. But Stella needs . . . proof. So she's gone away for a year to make sure,' he finished with a brave smile, which slowly faded as he noticed Maggie gawping at him. 'Come to think of it, it does sound rather daft when you say it out loud.'

Pete thought of Stella laughing and smiled to himself. It was something no one could understand unless they felt her love, although when he'd told his sister that she'd laughed, and replied that she imagined that by now there were quite a few men who'd earned that distinction. Maggie's voice snapped him back to the moment in hand.

'You proposed to this Stella and she nicked off to shag her way around another continent for a year?' she said incredulously, strangely angry on this stranger's behalf.

'Well, seeing other people is part of the agreement, yes,' Pete began. 'Not that I will, I couldn't. Look, I know you think I'm a stupid idiot and a gullible fool, like most people – my mum, my mate Ian, my sister Jess – but, you see, like most people, you're all caught up with the small things in life, the minutiae, the detail. We, this planet, we are nothing, we're just a speck of dust in an endless universe, one planet amongst billions. I see the big picture, and the big picture is that I love Stella. I always will, and one Earth year won't make any difference to that. And if, when she comes back, she knows for sure she loves me too, then it will have been worth it.'

Maggie shook her head. 'Pete, sometimes it's the little details you should focus on, things like when your boyfriend's working late at the office even though you personally cleared his in-tray for him that afternoon; or like when he smiles to himself when a song that means nothing to you comes on the radio, or when he starts deleting all the text messages in his in-and-out-boxes and puts a password on his email. They are the little details that I ignored, when there was still time to have done something about it – cut my hair, bought some new knickers or something . . .' Maggie stopped suddenly, realising that once again she was making a spectacular display of self-obsession. 'What I'm trying to say is that surely, if you have enough faith in this Stella then she should have the same in you, shouldn't she?'

Pete shrugged and shook his head.

'Well, you had faith in your bloke without testing him, and look where it got you,' he said with a half smile.

'Good point,' Maggie said despondently, and then, with a tiny grin, she added, 'you're still chucked, though.' She took a deep breath and wiped her palm under her nose. 'Anyway, I have a plan. Well, at least I have the *idea* of having a plan to get him back. I'm just not sure what the plan is yet.'

Pete smiled at her. She was clearly barking, but he liked her air of optimism – and if he was so sure Stella would be walking up the aisle to meet him in twelve months, why wouldn't her 'plan' work? Her hope gave his hope foundation.

'Good for you,' he said sincerely, and Maggie nearly fell off the bench.

'Pardon?' she said, in shock.

'I mean, good for you. I hope it does work. You obviously love this bloke a lot, enough to put some effort in to keeping him. In my book that takes guts, and these days there's not many of us about. Old-fashioned romantics.' Pete laughed a little. 'Bloody hell, if my mates could hear me now they'd kick me all the way to Bolton and back. But anyway, good for you and good luck.'

They returned each other's smile for a moment in the darkness.

'And to you too,' Maggie said, heartened by meeting someone who understood. 'Oh well, I'd better get off. My parents' place is just up the road.' She nodded in the general direction of The Fleur. 'I hope you settle in all right, and maybe I'll see you around.' She stood up as she spoke and backed away a few steps.

'Yeah, maybe,' he said, and then, as he watched her go, he felt a sudden regret and kicked himself hard.

'I never asked where I could find a decent Chinese,' he murmured.

Chapter Nine

When Maggie woke up the next morning she thought she almost had a spring in her step. Not an actual spring, she mused, more like a sort of cheerful tremor, but it was a tremulously cheerful step in the right direction nonetheless. Somehow her brief encounter with the man called Pete had cheered her, given her hope and spurred her on. It didn't matter that the only person thus far not to think she was a total fool for wanting to try and get Christian back was a stranger. He'd shown faith in true love, and right now Maggie desperately needed to see that kind of faith reflected back at her. That tiny glimpse last night had been enough to give her renewed impetus. And in the early hours of this morning, she'd even had an idea about how to begin.

As she walked through the bar she found her mum sitting at one of the corner tables staring blankly at a pile of papers. Maggie reasoned that it would be plain rude not to say hello.

'Hi, Mum,' she said, sitting on the worn stool opposite her. 'I was just on my way out to see Sarah. What are you doing?'

Marion smiled at her daughter, and not for the first time Maggie wondered where she'd got her looks from. Her dad was big and pale — even in his youth he'd looked like a rotund Viking — and her mum, though slim like her, had reddish-brown hair and her eyes were periwinkle blue, intensely so, even if they were now embellished with unkempt laughter lines.

Maggie was always amazed that her mum, pushing sixty as she was, was still described as pretty by most people who met her, a description she'd always thought didn't apply beyond twenty-five. That was until she'd reached twenty-five, at which point she'd amended the limit to thirty-five, still hopeful that one day someone might think *she* was pretty. She'd been called 'attractive' and 'stylish', and Christian had called her 'beautiful' and 'sexy', but somehow she yearned for the carefree weight-lessness of being thought pretty. It wasn't that she was paranoid about her looks, it was just that in this one respect she wouldn't mind being like her mum.

During most of her childhood she had sincerely hoped that the explanation for her near pitch-black eyes and hair was that her mum had engaged in free love with a swarthy civil servant from Kensington and that he would arrive one day and whisk her away to a life of quiet (and rich) normality. As an adult it occurred to her that the former part of this scenario, at least, was entirely possible considering the policy of free love her parents' generation had indulged in, but she chose not to think about it any more, except at moments like this when she was confronted with how different she was from them both.

Her mother glanced down at the papers.

'Oh well, dear,' she sounded forlorn. 'I thought I'd have a go at sorting this out, while your dad's resting. Try and see if we could budget a bit better . . .' She paused, pressing her lips together for a moment's consideration. 'But actually our income is so low, the only thing I can think of doing is asking Sheila to retire early, and I don't know if that'll be enough.' Her mum gave her a weak smile. 'Oh Maggie, you know I'm no good at this sort of thing. I look at the numbers but all I see is pages and pages of gobbledegook. The more I try and concentrate the worse it gets. I don't know, perhaps it will all just sort itself out,' she finished hopefully.

Maggie suppressed her irritation at her mum's habitual help-lessness. Frowning at the thought of losing Sheila, she reached for the papers, bank statements, half-kept accounts and overdue invoices. It took only a brief look for her to get some idea of the situation.

'Mum!' she exclaimed, unable to keep the note of anger out of her voice. 'How did you let it get like this?' She thumbed through the back statements, seeing The Fleur's account fall further and further into the red as each month went by. 'This doesn't just happen overnight. Was this why you went to the bank yesterday?' she demanded, perhaps a little too brusquely. She saw the bright blue eyes fill perilously with tears.

'I'm sorry, love,' her mum's voice wobbled. 'I didn't want to bother you, I know you've got so much more to worry about right now. I don't really know how it happened . . . I mean, you know, we've ticked along the same way here for years and years. A few of those new bars opened up in town and things changed, but we thought it'd be a fad and that people would be glad of a traditional pub to turn to when they'd had enough of loud music and those alcopop things. I suppose times change.'

Maggie shook her head and wondered how her mum, such a crusading revolutionary in her youth, had become so stuck behind the times. For a brief moment she felt a surge of guilt; after all, if it wasn't her for they'd still be picking coffee beans in Columbia not stuck in a business they had never known how to run – or needed to until now. She reached over the table for her mum's hand, her annoyance washing away to leave only the underlying affection.

'Look, I'll need to spend some time with all this, this afternoon maybe, but at first glance this looks to me like it might be more than letting Sheila go. It might mean letting the pub go,' Maggie said more abruptly than she'd intended to and squeezed her mum's fingers. 'But let me have a look, hey?

65

Maybe there's something here we're not seeing. And anyway, you and Dad are near retirement age so maybe now's the right time to chuck it. You've got your private pension scheme, haven't you?'

Marion avoided her daughter's gaze. 'Well, not exactly,' she said.

'What do you mean "not exactly"?' Maggie asked, feeling the irritation rise on its return ebb.

'Well, it was very nice of you to set it up for us, Maggie, but it seemed like such a lot of money to pay in every month and, well, we've always preferred living in the moment.'

Maggie took a deep breath and squeezed her mum's hand just a tad more tightly than was comfortable before releasing it and drawing back.

'So if the pub goes to the bank and . . .' she gestured at the pile of papers . . . 'all these other people you owe, you and Dad will have nothing. Nothing at all,' she stated baldly, wondering if her mum was awake to the reality of the situation.

'Yes, it looks that way, but I've often said what do we need material wealth for anyway, and—'

Maggie suddenly lost it, standing so quickly that her stool shot backwards, leaving her mother open-mouthed.

'Mum! When you are fifty-nine and your husband is sixty-two you need it, trust me. You need heating and light and what if one of you got ill and you needed health care? I mean, look at me – I'm out of a job, and Jim's never had one. It's not as if we can look after you!'

Maggie stopped, realising how callous she sounded, and rubbed her fingers across her temples.

'Of course we'd try and help, but what I meant was that neither one of us is in a good position right now.' She noticed that her mum's face had blanched and that her hands were tightly clenched. Crouching down beside her, she put her arm around

66

her mother's waist. 'I'm sorry, Mum, it's just that I sometimes wish you and Dad had a bit more foresight. A few chants and lighting a couple of joss sticks won't fix this. Why isn't Dad looking at this, anyway? He usually does the paperwork,' Maggie glanced at the chaotic pile. 'After a fashion, anyhow.'

'I wanted to give him a break from all the worry,' Marion said. 'He's got a lot on his plate at the moment. The doctors told him his blood pressure is sky-high and he really needs to take some of the stress out of his life . . .'

For a moment Maggie thought Marion was going to add some other calamity to the list, but as she looked at her daughter she seemed to change her mind.

'And so have you. I'm sorry, darling, to do this to you.' Marion bent over and kissed the top of her daughter's head. 'But if you could have a look it would make me feel so much better. At least you know what you're looking at.'

Maggie stood up and collected her bag from under the table.

'Of course I will, Mum,' she said. 'Like you say, this is something I know a bit about, and it'll, you know, take my mind off things.' Maggie knew it wouldn't, but she also knew that saying it would make her mum feel a bit better about asking for help. 'When did the bank want to hear back from you?' she asked.

'A week next Friday.' Marion sighed. 'Apparently that really is our deadline.'

Maggie considered this for a moment. Almost two weeks. It would mean she'd have to put her plan to get Christian back on hold. Unless . . . the small beginnings of an idea formed in her head. Unless she made trying to save the pub and her parents part of the plan. Well, either way she'd have to have something sorted out by next Friday. But she could still manage one day clear to put phase one of the Christian plan into operation.

'Try not to worry, mum,' she said. 'Put that lot in my room and I'll go through it this afternoon, OK?'

67

As Maggie walked out from the cool, beamed interior of the pub into the blazing heat of the morning, she considered that a lick of paint wouldn't do any harm for starters.

'Good morning, The Sharp End?' Sarah had just picked up the phone as Maggie walked in and was leaning on the reception counter. Saturday was Sarah's busiest day and the salon was packed, the DFS sofa for three crammed with four anxious-looking young women no doubt worrying about what delight their Saturday night might hold if only they could get their hair straight enough.

'Sorry, madam, we're fully booked today. The next appointment I have is Monday morning at eleven?' Sarah caught Maggie's eye and, pulling her mouth down, nodded at the corner where Becca sat on one of the stylists' swivel stools spinning first clockwise then anticlockwise, her face a perfect blank of boredom.

'Did you still want that manicure?' Sarah said as she hung up. 'Only we're chocka right now, and I'm not sure how long you'll have to wait.'

Maggie shook her head. 'No worries. I thought maybe red was a bit over the top for me anyhow. What's the deal with Becca?'

Sarah rolled her eyes. 'She's pissed off because Sam's with his dad today and they're going to some miniature village somewhere. She hates me because she's never met her dad let alone gone on field trips with him. She hates her dad but as he's not available I get it in the neck for that too. And she hates her best mate Leanne for reasons that are "too personal" to discuss with her mother. Consequently she has nothing to do and no one to do it with and has decided to inflict her misery on the salon. I wouldn't mind, but Marcus offered to take her too – but apparently that would be "too sad".' Sarah looked at her daughter. 'I feel bad about it, Mags. I'd love to take her out, but what can I do? It's Saturday and I can't just jump ship. It's all this that keeps her in her trainers.'

Maggie tried to catch her god-daughter's eye but to no avail.

'I'm crap at being a mum,' Sarah sighed.

'You're brilliant at being a mum. She's just brilliant at being a teenager, and the two things never go together, as we both know,' Maggie reassured her. 'So, what about the bloke you snogged last night – seeing him again?'

Sarah shook her head vigorously and made a sour face.

'Bleugh. What about you? When you called this morning you mentioned talking to some man? Hey – hey?' Sarah waggled her brows. 'Things looking up already?'

Maggie smiled and thought briefly of Pete.

'No, it wasn't like that, and anyway he's engaged,' she said.

'Ohhhh. But still?' Sarah was relentlessly hopeful.

'Engaged and in love, like, big-time,' Maggie told her flatly.

'Well what's the point of him then?' Sarah asked.

'The point is he inspired me not to give up with Christian . . .' Sarah opened her mouth immediately but Maggie held up the palm of her hand. 'No, listen. He made me realise I have to give it a go because I still love him more than anything or anyone in my life. I have to try, and if I fail, well, then I fail, and . . .' Maggie reflected on the possibility for a second . . . 'I will die. *But*, I have to try, OK?'

Sarah regarded her coolly, and finally, perhaps more because of her waiting client's furiously tapping foot than because she really agreed, she said. 'OK. You are certifiably mad, but OK.' Sarah smiled at the waiting client. 'Two ticks, love,' she called. 'Luce, can you get Miss Bingham washed, please? Anything else?' she asked, hoping Maggie would take the hint.

'Well, to complete phase one I need you to come with me

into London tomorrow to see Louise.' Sarah looked blank. 'His other woman!' Maggie prompted.

'Are you insane?' Sarah blinked at her, stunned. 'What on earth do you think seeing her is going to achieve? It will just make you look like a stalker and drive Christian even further away, if it's possible to get further away than another woman's bed!'

Maggie shook her head, desperate to make Sarah see.

'No, listen. It's not stalking. I don't mean actually *talk* to her. I mean just go to the Fresh Talent 2 branch and get a look at her.' Maggie thought it sounded perfectly reasonable.

'That *is* stalking!' Sarah exclaimed just as the conversation in the salon lulled momentarily. 'That *is* stalking,' she repeated, lowering her voice a little. 'And I am having nothing to do with it! In any case, it's my one day with Becca and Sam and I promised to take them to the flicks. Becca even *wants* to go! Do you know what a rare event that is in this household?'

Maggie picked up Sarah's biro and tapped it urgently against the counter.

'But don't you see? I need to see her, to see what she's like, to see how she's different from me. Once I see what it was that Christian was looking for, I can change myself into that . . . .'

'And what if she's J-Lo and Gwyneth Paltrow all rolled into one?' Sarah said, thinking, even as she said it, that actually maybe that was exactly what Maggie needed to see. 'What if,' she added, verbalising her thoughts, 'you saw them together all lovey-dovey? What then, huh?' Sarah crossed her arms and waited.

'Well, I won't.' Maggie was adamant. 'Tomorrow's the Summer Organic Food Fair in Great Rissington. Christian never misses a chance to lord it around there and do a bit of wheeling and dealing. He loves it.'

'What if he's taken this Louise with him?' Sarah added. 'And you've been on a wild goose chase?'

'He won't. Fresh Talent 2 was supposed to have opened last week. They're at least two weeks behind, so even if he does . . . like her . . . he won't let her nose off the grindstone until it's open. This is Christian we're talking about: his business comes before anyone or anything. That's why he's so successful.'

Sarah rolled her eyes again. 'Are you listening to your own description of the man you can't live without?' she said, but Maggie ignored her.

'Please, Sarah, I need you to come with me. Just in case . . . you know, I go all hysterical again. Please? It'll only take an hour. You'll be back for the cinema . . .'

'Or we could *all* go.' Becca had joined them at the counter, her face suddenly bright and alert. Sarah looked from girl to woman to girl and back again, giving Maggie her best I'll-never-forgive-you-for-this stare.

'I'm not taking my children stalking. The end. OK?'

Becca tossed her hair and tutted loudly. 'Oh go on, Mum! Aunty Mags really needs us and we'd be good cover, wouldn't we, Aunty M? They'd never expect you to be stalking with a couple of kids in tow!'

Maggie started to agree but closed her mouth abruptly at Sarah's expression.

'Please, Mum, you've been promising to take me to Oxford Street for weeks! I'll be back at school soon and I'll look like a total loser in these rags.' Becca fingered her two-week-old top miserably. 'We could drop by the office and stalk this Louise on the way.'

Sarah opened and closed her mouth, taking a moment to gather her breath.

'Even if I *could* take you, your brother would hate all that shopping and I'm fairly sure he's not into stalking, unlike you, young lady.'

Becca's lower lip trembled perilously. 'Well *he* always gets

71

what *he* wants, doesn't he.' She didn't say 'including a father', but Sarah felt the implication keenly, even if only in her imagination.

'Or,' Maggie said tentatively, 'after we've, you know, had a quick peep at Louise and hit the shops we could take him to the London Transport Museum. He'd love that.' Sarah's face was implacable. 'I'll pay,' Maggie added, winking at Becca.

'Oh pleeeeeeeeeeease, Mum. I *never* do anything exciting.'

Sarah looked from her friend to her daughter and then to the client sitting in front of a mirror with a towel wrapped round her head and a furious look on her face.

'I hate you both,' she said, clearly meaning exactly the opposite. Maggie and Becca exchanged triumphant grins. 'All right. We'll all go as moral support, but neither I nor my children are taking part in any actual lurking, stalking or looking, OK?'

'Oh but . . .' Becca started.

Sarah turned on her most thunderous scowl.

'No buts. That's the deal. And then we'll go and do the shops and the museum. Take it or leave it.'

'Take it,' Maggie and Becca said together. Sarah cast them one last look before kissing her daughter on the cheek and heading towards her client.

'Shall I buy you a McDonald's?' Maggie asked Becca.

'Ugh, no, I don't want to get fat like Mum! You can buy me a salad and a smoothie though, if you like?' She was sweetly hopeful.

Maggie grinned and nodded towards the door. 'Come on, Becs. I know the high street's got nothing on the West End, but we might find something decent if we look really hard.'

As they were leaving, Maggie caught Sarah's eye and the look between them was one of simple thanks, flowing both ways.

Chapter Ten

Pete tucked his arms behind his head and stared at the ceiling. Just past the orange fringed lampshade a medium-sized spider was industriously creating a web, seemingly dipping and gliding through thin air with balletic grace. He glanced at his watch; it was almost twelve. The rest of his luggage had arrived just after eight that morning, and after signing for it and giving his telescope a cursory checking over, he'd got straight back into bed, pulled the less than fragrant duvet over his head and been lulled back to sleep by the sound of Angie singing in the bath.

It occurred to him now that in actual fact he was feeling much less depressed than he had expected to; not as homesick. Maybe it was because he'd been here for less than a day. Or, more likely, it was because usually when Stella had gone, he was left behind glued in place by his own gravity, just waiting for her to orbit over him again. This time was different, because not only did he know exactly how long she had gone for, but he knew that she was coming back, and somehow that freed him and let him loose for some exploration of his own. He hadn't been sad to say goodbye to Dougie the Digger – the ten long years of high regular wages had given him plenty to fall back on, and here he was, for the first time ever, on the brink of something exciting. Or terrifying. Or both.

'Bloody hell,' Pete said to the spider.

Mike, his old lecturer and part-time mentor, had originally called him about the job nearly three weeks before Stella had left, and first Pete had turned him down flat.

'Are you sure?' Mike had persisted; over the years he'd found various opportunities for Pete, but so far he'd never taken any. 'I know you have . . . ties up in Leeds, and I know you'd be giving up something steady for something short term, but I really think this could lead to something.'

He'd asked Pete to cover maternity leave for one of the lecturers on the University of Hertfordshire's model-making course. It was a great course, the best in the country, maybe the best in the world, and even if it was just a summer school coaching foundation students who hadn't made it to degree level the first time round, Pete knew it would look good on his so far rather predictable CV.

'And what's more,' Mike had told him, 'there's this film going into production at Magic Shop in August. All the CGI and FX are being finished there. It's a big deal, huge budget. I know the guy that runs Magic Shop. He was asking if I could recommend anyone for the team, so I recommended you. I remember how you talked about this with so much passion. I know you want it – don't pass this up because of . . .' Mike had paused and Stella's name had hung in the air for a second . . . 'for a kid's TV show,' Mike had said finally. Pete had promised to think about it, certain that while things were so good with him and Stella he wouldn't dare change a thing in case he upset their precariously balanced relationship. But then he proposed and she went to Australia, and you couldn't really upset things more than that. He'd called Mike on the way back from the airport before he had time to change his mind.

'Am I too late?' were his opening words.

'Christ, no,' Mike had laughed. 'I'm covering Sal's session myself, it's a bloody nightmare. This lot have the brains and talent of a single cell organism between them. It drains you of the will to live,' he'd said with feeling, and then added as an afterthought, 'not that it's not great fun.'

Pete had felt anxious, but was determined not to back out; one of the things Stella had said to him before she'd gone was that maybe he was too steady, too secure; maybe she needed a bit more excitement in a relationship to feel *really* happy. He knew that coaching a few failed students for a couple of weeks wasn't going to cut the mustard, but at least it was a start.

'Well, I'm coming,' he'd told Mike.

'That's fantastic, Pete. Don't you worry about anything, I'll sort it all this end and I'll see you soon.' And he had sorted it all this end, including the room in this house. The sound of Falcon practising his drums started dimly below.

'It's time I got up and sorted this lot out,' Pete said to the spider, who ignored him.

Pete looked from his telescope to his PC and decided to set up his PC first. When Stella had left she hadn't had a phone number or an actual address for him to contact her by, only her email address, *Stellashot@topmail.com*. She'd promised to mail him as soon as she got there with contact details, and as Pete quickly plugged in cables and rested the monitor on the bed, he felt his heart race a little at the thought of seeing her name in his inbox and that yellow envelope waiting to let him know where she was, how she was.

With trepidation he logged on to the Internet and waited. When the call failed he realised he'd have to phone BT and rearrange all the details on his Internet account. His heart sank. That would take hours, maybe even days, and it would be ages until he could pick Stella's message up, and she'd think he'd forgotten her, and . . .

He stopped himself and looked around the room. He'd go into town. There'd have to be some kind of Internet café

75

around. He'd log on there, update his customer profile on BT and pick up Stella's message. 'Everything is fine,' he told himself and the spider. 'Stella is wearing your ring on her finger. She loves you. She actually said it to you for the first time ever after five years! That's what makes this different. Even if you can't pick up her message today, she wouldn't just ditch you instantly, she wouldn't just forget you, not after she said that.'

He dressed quickly and, glancing at the day outside, picked up his shades. 'Everything's fine,' he told the spider as he shut the door. The spider didn't contradict him.

'So, Aunty M,' Becca said. Having picked her way through half a carrot and sweet potato salad, she was now enjoying a banana smoothie made with full cream and topped with a large dollop of ice cream.

'Mmm?' Maggie sipped her lemon tea and glanced around the café. Its two Internet terminals were in use right now, but she could come here, she supposed, to work up spreadsheets and research her business plan for The Fleur. At least until she could buy her own PC. She shifted uncomfortably in her seat; it didn't seem to matter what she wore at the moment, the heat was so intense it made her feel like slipping out of her own skin. She closed her eyes for a second and thought of low, cool, grey skies on a winter's day, but it didn't seem to help.

'Are you going to kill yourself if Uncle Christian doesn't take you back?' Becca slurped noisily on her straw. 'I don't think you should, because for starters he was ugly and looked like a pirate with that stupid goatee thing he had going, and secondly he was always very rude to me. My English teacher is divorced, so I could fix you up if you like. He's a bit of a minger, but he's all right, I suppose.'

Maggie gave herself a moment to digest Beccas's deadpan

delivery before replying, 'No thanks, Becs. Not that I don't appreciate the offer.'

She pushed her chocolate cookie over the table to Becca who took it happily, clearly believing that anything sold in a health-food cybercafé couldn't possibly be fattening.

'Haven't you ever been in love with someone, so in love with them that you just can't stop trying until you know you've done everything?' Maggie asked her, thinking not only of herself but of Sarah, at approximately Becca's age, and her passion for Aidan Carter. Becca, who loved Maggie principally because she didn't speak to her like she was a kid, nodded dreamily.

'Justin Timberlake,' she sighed, rolling her eyes up into her head. 'Don't tell anyone, Aunty M, but sometimes I just stare, like really hard, at his poster and send my love to him because I know he can feel it.'

Maggie looked seriously back at her. 'I won't tell,' she said solemnly. 'That's how I feel about Christian. I know that a lot of people don't see in him what I do, but they're forgetting I lived with him for six years. We just had this thing, a bit like you and Justin, when we didn't have to even speak to know what the other one was thinking. That means something special, something you don't just let go of.' Maggie gestured broadly with her hands. 'You understand me, don't you, Becs?'

Becca nodded. 'Ignore Mum. She's got a heart of ice,' she said mildly.

Maggie was about to contradict her when she was interrupted.

'All right? Maggie, isn't it?'

Pete had stopped at the table. He'd spotted Maggie from behind his terminal a few seconds ago and had dithered about whether or not to talk to her. Somehow he'd liked the idea of their meeting being a one-off, a sort of ships-that-passed-in-the-night thing, giving each other hope and inspiration, but when

77

he'd finally picked up his emails, his inbox had been empty except for some forms from Mike he had to fill in before Monday. All the tension, excitement and urgency of the morning had dissipated into nowhere. Disappointed he'd carefully typed Stella's address in and, feeling numbed by her absence, had struggled to find anything to write.

Dear Stella, he'd written at last. *Hope you got there OK, please let me know. I am fine, have settled in to St A well. Made a load of new friends already. I miss you and love you so much. Please let me know where you are soon.*

Have fun!

Px

Pete had looked hard at the exclamation mark. It looked sort of forced, or maybe he was imagining it. In the end he left it where it was. Shaking off any last doubts he clicked on 'send', and it was as he glanced up that he saw the woman from last night – Maggie – sitting with a kid. The kid was making her laugh and her face was lit up, her dark eyes flashing. Without all the false lashes and molten mascara, Pete mused, she was actually very pretty. His artistic instinct kicked in, and he unconsciously reinterpreted her face into a mathematical equation of planes and curves, ovals and circles, light and shade. Without even registering the thought, he noted that her face was near symmetrical, with large, faintly exotic, almond-shaped eyes, almost perfectly balanced, with an interesting nose. 'Well,' he thought. 'Might as well try and make some new friends now that I've said it.'

'Pete!' Maggie smiled up at him and Becca, her cheeks burning a furious red, stared intently into the bottom of her glass. 'Hi, nice to bump into you again. This is my god-daughter Becca. She's just been telling me her top ten best ways to get a boyfriend.' Becca squealed and Maggie guessed she might not have been quite tactful enough with her god-daughter's sensitive feelings. 'Only for my benefit though, because I'm such a sad case,' she added, hoping this would ease Becca's discomfort. Becca did raise her eyes for a moment to steal a glance at Pete before looking away again, clearly covered in confusion.

'Can I join you?' Pete asked, pulling up a chair at Maggie's nod. 'I just went to pick up my emails but there wasn't anything from Stella. It's been two weeks now. It made me feel a bit, you know . . .' He didn't know why it seemed all right to unburden, without preamble, his emotional stress on this virtual stranger, but he was just sure she'd know how he felt.

'Oh no,' Maggie said, thinking for a moment. 'But you know what? I bet she lost your email address during her journey and she's been waiting for you to send a message to her so she can reply. I bet that's it. You said she was a bit ditzy, didn't you?' He hadn't, actually, but she had somehow gathered it from the things he'd said. Maggie smiled broadly at Pete, who brightened instantly.

'Yeah,' he said. That might be it.'

The waitress brought over the coffee he'd ordered and Becca, having composed herself, straightened in her chair and flicked her hair off her shoulders.

'Are you in food then?' she asked Pete primly. He looked disconcerted.

'Um, no, I'm . . . well, I'm starting teaching tomorrow at the uni,' he told her with a small smile. Becca lost all power of speech and decided not to pursue the conversation any further.

'*I* am. In food, I mean.' Maggie seamlessly covered Becca's paralysis. 'I run, *ran*, a catering business with Christian, that's my . . . you know.' She hurried on. 'Fresh Talent we're called. We only use locally grown organic produce. We started out with weddings and christenings, but then we built up corporate contracts and we're opening an office in the City really soon. Fresh Talent 2.' Some of her brightness faded. 'Of course I'm not actually involved in it any more, at the moment, since well, you know.'

Pete nodded, feeling it was better to say nothing.

'What do you teach?' Maggie asked.

'Oh, well, nothing before. I work in film and TV special effects and model making. I used to make TV models, but I thought while Stella was away I'd make a few changes and this came up. In a couple of weeks I've got an interview to work on a film. I'm shitting myself.' Pete squirmed a little under Becca's riveted gaze and Maggie wondered if she was transmitting her love to him even now.

'Well.' Maggie gathered up her keys and purse, deciding to save Pete from any further embarrassment. 'I guess we should be going. I have a mountain of paperwork to do and Becca's got to . . .' breathe again, she nearly said, but instead she finished, 'do homework. I'm sure you'll hear from Stella again. I mean, the woman agreed to marry you!'

Pete nodded, feeling reassured. 'Well, I might see you again then,' he said, wondering if he should attempt a formal arrangement in the spirit of friendship, and then dropping the idea quickly. She'd think he was a desperate weirdo, trying to make friends with a girl he hardly knew.

'Yeah.' Maggie paused momentarily. What would he think if she suggested they meet up for a coffee sometime without the panting teenager? She dismissed the thought. Really she hardly knew him, he could be a raving lunatic in real life, and the last thing she wanted was him getting the wrong idea. Although, to be fair, he was so wrapped up in this Stella you could probably twirl batons naked in front of him and he wouldn't notice. 'Yeah, maybe, that'd be nice,' she said instead, as she escorted Becca outside.

'Oh. My. God,' Becca said, leaning against the wall of the café and fanning her face with both hands.

Maggie smiled. 'What about Justin?' she asked as she pulled Becca off the wall and linked arms with her as they headed home.

'Forget Justin.' Becca glanced back at the café. 'Pete is the dog's bollocks!'

'Don't tell your mother I let you swear,' Maggie said, shaking her head.

'I won't,' Becca promised. 'It's just that I've never been properly in love before.'

Chapter Eleven

'Wow, Mum, look at that intercity go! How fast is it going, do you think?'

Sam held on to the sleeve of his mum's jacket as the train rattled through the station at speed, and Maggie smiled as she watched Sarah offer up her best guess as an answer.

Sam was an unusual seven-year-old, to say the least, with his somewhat eccentric insistence on wearing his hair in an unruly afro, his smooth mid-brown skin set off by his light grey eyes, and his unwavering passion for musicals. He had Sarah's eyes, the only bit about him that was obviously her; the rest of him was a carbon copy of his father. He was still at that sweet stage, still into trains and JCVs (and *Cats*, the musical), still thought his mum knew everything and still, on the whole, obeyed her.

The very fact that Becca took exactly the opposite position on all of these points had been causing a fair amount of tension recently. Maybe it was because Marcus, Sam's dad, had insisted on being in his life and had tried for a long time to be in Sarah's too, that Sam seemed so unflappable and grounded. Maybe it was because Marcus and Sarah had had a good relationship that had become a great friendship. Sam had never known life without his dad. He spent every Saturday and a large amount of holiday with his father, and sometimes his extended Afro-Caribbean family. He had a very strong sense of the two cultures he came from, and he seemed to feel perfectly at home in his own world, which Maggie knew was quite some achievement on the part of both of his parents.

Becca, on the other hand, only knew life without her father, except for the bits of information she'd picked up or eaves-dropped from her mother over the years out of which she had created a shadowy, dreamlike figure. A rich American who would one day come and beg her forgiveness and sweep her off to a better life, Maggie imagined. Maggie felt for Becca. She remembered her similar hopes for the civil servant from Kensington. But at least she'd had a dad to hold on to or to push against. Becca only had Sarah and, right now at least, she clearly didn't think it was enough.

'Here, Sam,' Becca was telling her brother seriously. 'If you stand in front of this yellow line, the next time the train comes through it will suck you under its wheels and you'll get squashed to death.' Sam giggled and Sarah rolled her eyes.

'Get back from the edge, you two, our train is coming in.' Sarah looked down the line to where the city-link train was lurching towards the platform. 'I hope you're grateful about all this,' she told Maggie as she helped Sam on to the train. 'I'm expecting about a hundred years of payback. And cash.'

Maggie smiled, despite the total absence of humour in her friend's voice.

'I will be paying you back my whole life, I promise, in love and thanks and large vodkas and a free lunch today,' she told Sarah, who looked at her as if she didn't think that was nearly enough.

'Ohhh Mum, look at that crane!' Sam grabbed his mum by the arm and pointed out of the window.

Maggie glanced at Becca, who had shut her eyes and was feigning sleep. The tension, the anticipation of seeing Louise, had churned her up into all sorts of knots overnight and now she couldn't explain the way she was feeling. 'It's almost like a first date feeling,' she'd told Sarah when she'd picked her and the kids up that morning. 'I'm dreading it, but I feel sort of fluttery and excited at the same time. Don't ask me why but I just *know* that I have to do this, that it's really going to change things.'

Sarah had stopped dead in her tracks, causing Sam to stumble a little and Becca to walk into her back.

'Maggie,' she'd said, her voice low, 'I'm not really sure how I got involved in this wild goose chase, but we're going now – so fine. But listen, please. Get this into perspective. Your frankly weird insistence on getting a look at Christian's new bird is not going to change anything. You seeing her is not going to make any difference. I'm sorry, mate, but you're clearly insane and tough love is pretty much all I've got spare right now. Now let's get this over with and get to the-fun-day-out-with-the-kids bit OK?'

London Bridge station was practically empty, and as they walked out on to Tooley Street, only the few tourists who had decided that a Sunday morning was the best time to brave the London Dungeon were in the street.

'Blimey,' Becca said. 'It's like that zombie film when they have to go and hide in a shopping mall to stop getting eaten alive!'

'Becca! When did you see a zombie film!' Her mother asked her sharply.

Becca rolled her eyes. 'God, Mum, everyone watches eighteens at my age!' She looked at Maggie for affirmation, but Maggie avoided her eyes, sensing that now was not the right time to back Becca up.

'It's across the road in The Galleria: there are a few shops and a café. I thought the kids could wait there while we go and take a peek?' she asked Sarah, hoping she wouldn't make her go on her own after all. Sarah shrugged and, taking Sam's hand, crossed the empty street.

After they had installed the children in the café with two large chocolate muffins and two hot chocolates topped with whipped cream, Sarah eyed them both sternly.

'If either one of you moves an inch from here we're going straight back home. No transport museum, no clothes shopping, nothing. OK?'

Becca and Sam exchanged a look. 'OK!' they both agreed.

Sarah looked at Maggie. 'Right then. Five minutes. If we don't see her by then I'm coming back here, all right?'

Maggie took a deep breath and nodded.

As she led Sarah out of the galleria, past the Riverside Bookshop and into the narrow back streets behind it, she felt her pulse quicken and her skin begin to fizz and tingle with nerves.

'We spent ages looking for the right location,' she told Sarah. 'We wanted somewhere near to the heart of the City but with a bit of character, somewhere central but where the rent wouldn't be astronomical. I found the building; it's in a converted warehouse. A year ago it would have been out of our reach, but renting is really cheap right now. I even got them to give us a year's lease, rent free. Of course we'll have to make the business really work in that time. If we're not established within twelve months they could just boot us out. A risk, but . . .'

Maggie let her voice trail off, disconcerted by the sound of it bouncing off the high buildings and narrow cobbled streets. She stopped in her tracks and reached for Sarah's arm.

'There it is on the corner. Fresh Talent 2.'

Just as she had specified to the glazier, the large windows had been fitted with rough-finished opaque glass, within which the Fresh Talent logo was picked out in smooth clear glass. With the huge glass and steel doors set into the Victorian arched doorway, it was just as she had imagined it. Classy. Contemporary, but not bland.

'Ow!' Sarah said with emphasis, and Maggie realised she had been gripping her arm rather tightly. 'So what now? Are you going in? Do you want me too?'

Maggie stared at her. 'No! We are not going in! My God, if she realised who I was that would make me look insane!' Sarah raised an implacable eyebrow. 'No, we'll just wait here, get a glimpse of her going in or out or something.' Maggie scrutinised the window, trying to catch a glimpse of movement through the sweeps of clear glass. 'Hang on, someone's coming out!' she whispered, backing both her and Sarah against a wall.

'Oh for God's sake,' Sarah mumbled. 'We're not bloody Cagney and Lacey.'

The door swung open and some kind of workman emerged with a ladder. He propped it against the wall and shinned up it to examine the first-floor window.

'Workman on a Sunday,' Maggie said with some satisfaction. 'They must be desperate.'

Sarah looked impatiently at her watch. 'Look, she's not coming out. She's probably not even here. Let's go—' Before she could finish the doors swung open again and Louise, it had to be Louise, appeared, tipping her chin back to talk to the workman. Both Maggie and Sarah opened their mouths and gawped in silent unison. She was not what they had expected.

The first thing they noticed was her hair. A golden blonde and perfectly straight, it fell to below her shoulders and was tucked back behind one ear. Her skin was a light gold, and even from her vantage point Maggie could see that her glossed lips were full and sultry.

'Collagen,' Sarah whispered, reading her mind. 'Not sure about the tits, but silicon or not that girl is stacked!' Both women observed the curves of her breasts, which tapered into a tiny waist and a flat stomach. She was wearing hipster jeans, but it was still obvious she had a perfectly rounded bottom and strong, toned thighs. 'What was that I was saying about J-Lo?' Sarah muttered. The conversation between Louise and the workmen over, she gave him a little smile and returned inside. She'd been visible for maybe twenty seconds.

'Well.' Sarah turned to look at Maggie. 'That was a turn-up.' But the space where Maggie had been standing was empty and Sarah saw that her friend had sunk on to the curb, head in hands. She sat down next her.

'Hey, Mags?' She rested her hand on her shoulders and felt them tremble beneath her fingers. 'Come on. We knew this was going to be hard.'

Maggie raised her head and took a gulp of air. 'But she's not, she's not . . .' She gestured wildly at the space where a few moments ago Louise had stood, as if her dimensions somehow still occupied the air. 'She's nothing like me. I expected her to be . . . similar, you know? I expected her to be Christian's *type,* like I am. Like he said I was. She's all . . . She's really sexy and beautiful. Just look at her!' Once again Maggie pointed at the empty pavement outside Fresh Talent 2. Sarah sighed with exasperation as she watched the workman glance in their direction, and helped her friend to her feet.

'Come on, we're attracting attention,' she said, hooking her arm through Maggie's. Maggie glanced back over her shoulder and shook her head.

'I don't know, Sarah, I just thought that if I saw her it would be obvious what it was about her that made Christian want her, and I could change myself to be like her.'

'Well it *is* obvious why he wants her!' Sarah exclaimed angrily. 'Men are so predictable. All they want is bits and bobs to play with. '

'Yes but, but she's the opposite of me. She's . . .' Maggie

87

cupped her hands in front of her bust. 'And all . . .' She couldn't find the words, but Sarah knew she was referring to the San Tropez tan and full-lipped smile. 'I can't compete with that. All these years I thought Christian really loved *me* and wanted *me*. Stupid, skinny, flat-chested me. And all along he wanted a . . . a . . . bombshell! I've been on borrowed time since day one!'

Sarah put her arm around Maggie and brought her to a standstill.

'That's not true, Mags. Look, I know I'm not Christian's biggest fan, but I know how he looked at you when you were first together, and for most of the time you were a couple. He thought you were the bee's knees. He loved every bit of you.' She paused a moment before adding, 'You know what I think? I think this Louise is just a reaction against you. Just a really big-arsed, cowardly way of getting you out of his head. OK, so she's a stunner but that doesn't mean you aren't. You're really beautiful in an unusual way. She's just . . . well, she's just pretty in a very *obvious* way,' Sarah finished, realising that her word hadn't come out in exactly the way she'd planned. Reaching into her pocket she pulled out a tissue, which she spat on and rubbed roughly under Maggie's eyes.

'Now come on, can you pull yourself together for the kids? Let's go shopping and forget all about this until we get home tonight, and then you and me'll crack a few bottles of wine and rip the brassy tart to shreds into the small hours, OK?'

Looking at Maggie's face, Sarah instantly regretted her tough love approach of earlier. Perhaps reality smacking her friend in the face like a wet fish was the last thing she needed. Maybe it would have been safer to keep her delusional for a couple of weeks longer, just until she started to feel better about herself and had a few rebound snogs under her belt. This was too soon.

'You know, you have to stop all this crying,' Sarah said to her gently. 'It's going to give you wrinkles.'

Maggie raised a weak smile and took a deep breath as they headed back into the café.

'Mummy!' Sam jumped up and hugged his mum hard round the hips.

'At bloody last!' Becca exclaimed, eyeing Maggie closely. 'Well? Was she a total slapper?' she asked matter-of-factly.

'Total,' Sarah said on behalf of her friend. 'Now, enough of that language and let's go shopping!'

'Well.' Sarah topped up Maggie's glass and handed her another biscuit. 'It's a modern miracle, but Becca's in bed reading and Sam's fast asleep. I think we managed to shop Becca out.' She sat down next to Maggie. 'You didn't have to buy her all that stuff, you know. I mean, I know you've got that cash coming, but you're still out of a job.'

Maggie smiled wanly and sipped the wine.

'Yeah, well, Sam got a few things too and I like to buy her stuff, she deserves it. She's a good kid really, you know,' she told Sarah, who nodded silently. 'Anyway, it looks like that cash is going to be gone before I even get it.' Maggie told Sarah about The Fleur and her early investigations into its finances.

'Oh my God! That's terrible!' Sarah said as Maggie finished. 'They could be out of a home and a business and everything?'

Maggie nodded. 'Yeah, pretty much. I haven't really gone into it yet, what with one thing and another.' Maggie briskly put the image of Louise out of her mind. 'But it doesn't look hopeful. So the cash . . . well, luckily the creditors can't get their hands on my money so I guess I'll have to find us a place to live and set us up while I get a job.' Maggie gave Sarah a heavy-lidded look over the rim of her glass. 'Don't things happen in threes? Dumped for a sex bomb, made homeless twice in a row . . . What's next?'

Sarah shook her head. 'You'll be fine, Maggie. Look at

everything you've achieved in your life so far. You're young. You'll pick yourself up and get back on your feet really soon. This is a beginning for you, not an end!' she insisted, and then continued, 'Oh fuck it, let's just get pissed. Maybe when we sober up things will have got better.'

'I don't think we can stay drunk long enough,' Maggie said, holding out her empty glass. 'But I'm prepared to give it a go.'

Chapter Twelve

'I'm sorry, Mum, Dad.' Maggie looked at each of her parents in turn, feeling a little breathless. Although it was still early, the air in the bar was thick with heat. 'I spent all of Monday going over and over this again and again, but the fact of the matter is I can't see a way out of it. I think you're going to have to declare yourself bankrupt.'

Keith shook his head and looked at Marion who reached for his hand and squeezed it hard.

'I mean, look around you,' Maggie added looking around the bar. 'The place is empty except for you and me. That pretty much says it all.'

'But what are we going to do, Maggie?' Marion's voice trembled. 'Surely there must be something we can do to turn things around. Decorate, maybe? There's some paint in the cellar . . . '

Maggie shook her head grimly. 'I've been through it again and again. First of all you'd have to catch up with your loan repayments, and that's all but twenty grand.' Maggie scrutinised her parents. 'Where did that money go? It certainly wasn't into this place?'

Her parents exchanged a glance.

'Well, your brother got himself in a bit of a fix, and then . . .'

Maggie held up a hand. 'Don't tell me, I'm already in

enough trouble. I don't need a fratricide charge added to the list.'

She took a deep breath and silently cursed her free-loading brother; instead of rebelling against her parents' free-wheeling, hands-off style of parenting he'd made the most of it by manipulating and abusing them at every possible turn. What other man in his twenties would expect his parents to take out a loan to pay off his debts? She tried to get back on track.

'Then, even if we could pay that off you'd have to right things with your current suppliers just to keep the place going and to get credit with new suppliers. Say another ten grand. And then we have to make a dent in the overdraft. A big one. I did look at reopening as a really good gastro pub. I mean, the location is fantastic and premises like these are really rare these days. But even if we'd cleared all those other problems, my money would barely refit the kitchen to a good enough standard, and that would only be possible if we bought reconditioned and second-hand stuff. To *really* overhaul this place we'd be looking at two hundred and fifty thousand pounds. If we ignored the pool room and just refurbished this room to begin with, we'd still need fifty or maybe sixty grand. And that's assuming we'd already fixed things with the bank and your creditors.' Maggie sighed and glanced around her. 'I'm sorry, Mum, but there's just no way we can pull it off.'

Turning, she noticed Sheila standing in the doorway, a tray of steaming mugs in her hands.

'I'm sorry, She,' she said, crossing to take the tray, 'but you'll be retiring a bit earlier than you thought. At least I know *you* kept your pension going.'

And they all sat round the table sipping tea in silence and exchanging glances.

★

Maggie watched the warm water run in rivulets over her hand as she rinsed the mugs out. She'd had to leave the oppressive gloom of the bar, leave the sight of her parents holding each other's hands across the table, facing silently the suddenly terrifying black future. Even Sheila had remained silent for once, smoking her cigarette with diligent concentration. What Maggie couldn't understand was why it felt like her fault when she hadn't even been here? Then she realised why. If she had been here, things might have been different.

'He died two years ago, my Bill.' Sheila appeared in the kitchen doorway, making Maggie jump. Bill was Sheila's estranged husband, but why bring him up now? Maybe it was the shock, Maggie thought.

'Would you like a brandy, She?' she asked. 'I think we can still run to that.'

Sheila shook her head and sat down at the table, lighting another cigarette in one fluid movement. 'Of course we never got divorced, did we? He didn't have any family or friends. None that would go near him, anyhow, the miserable old sod.' She paused, smiling grimly. 'It was three weeks before anyone found his body, fallen down the stairs. Quite far gone by that time apparently. Caused a bit of a stink, and his yuppie neighbours went round to complain. Saw him through the letterbox.'

Maggie opened her mouth but Sheila stopped her.

'He'd been living in that house all his life – it was his parents' before his. Nothing special. Just a terrace – three bedrooms and a cellar. Little yard out the back. I prefer modern myself, like my flat. It might be small but it's got all the mod cons.'

Sheila looked at Maggie's expression of slight alarm.

'Of course, as his wife I got the lot, didn't I? It came as a bit of a shock, I can tell you. I heard he'd snuffed it, but it was a shock when I heard about the money. Two hundred and seventy-two thousand pounds.' Sheila smiled. 'The bastard paid out in the end. I bought my place with some of it, and I gave a bit away to the East End Women's Shelter. I thought that'd really rub him up the wrong way.' She smiled. 'That left over a hundred thousand, give or take.'

Sheila looked at Maggie.

'You've been like a daughter to me, Maggie. When I first came to this old pile of bricks it was all right, I got by. But when you and your family came, well, I was pretty low then, and you all gave me something to look forward to. I was part of something again, you made me feel like part of your family. I really felt that.'

Maggie smiled and put her arm around Sheila's shoulders.

'You *are* part of the family, and I know what you're going to say, She. But we can't take your money. You'll need something to fall back on, especially now.' Maggie looked at her seriously, her eyes brimming. 'Sheila, you're a wonderful woman, and the best and dearest friend to us, but there is no way we can take your money. None. I'm just relieved to know that you'll be all right.' Sheila shook her head, slamming her hand down on the table.

'But I don't need it, Mag. I own my place. I got myself a good pension. What I'm trying to say, Maggie, is that all that money . . . well, I was leaving it to you in my will.'

Maggie opened her mouth and found that nothing would come out.

Sheila nodded her head in the direction of the bar. 'I thought those two wouldn't need it because, well, let's face it, we're all going to kick the bucket around the same time, and as for Jim, well, I think giving him any cash would be another excuse for him not to do anything with his life. It had to go somewhere, so why not to you? I want you to have it.'

Sheila's eyes were suddenly bright with tears.

94

'Whenever I think of my little one, the little girl I lost, I see your face. You know I love you don't you? Silly old fool.' Sheila shook herself. 'Anyway, it turns out that despite the fags I'm in good health. Blood pressure is fine, heart's fine, lungs fine. I might be around for another thirty years yet.'

Maggie covered Sheila's hand with her own. 'I bloody hope so,' she said, her voice tight.

'Well, I'd rather see you do something with it now, while I'm still here, than have you all suffer when there's no need.' Sheila cupped Maggie's face in her hand. 'What I'm saying is, if you think it's worth investing what's coming to you in this place, then you can have the money now.'

Maggie looked at her in silence, unable to think of a single thing to say.

'Sheila, I can't. This is . . . it's too much. It's too easy. It'd be like having this Christmas fairy dropping in a few months early and . . .' Maggie stopped. 'It's an incredible gesture, but it's too much.'

Sheila stubbed out her cigarette and folded her hands.

'It's not too much,' she said grimly. 'It's not enough. It's not enough for all the times he beat me, all the times he broke me, all the times he . . . It will never be enough.' Sheila looked into Maggie's eyes. 'If I'd married someone else, if I'd been born a few years later . . . But you and your family have given me the life I thought I'd never have. If you care about me, Maggie, about everything I went through, you won't throw away a chance that I never got. Not because you think it's too *easy*, anyway. Not because of that.'

Maggie felt a tear trace its way past the corner of her mouth.

'OK,' she said, pushing back her chair. 'Let's go and have that brandy and see what Mum and Dad say.'

A few moments later, Keith and Marion were listening to Sheila's plan with open mouths.

95

'All right Mum, Dad!'

Jim greeted them heartily and slapped his sister on the back. 'All right sis?'

Maggie glared at him.

'Why the long faces, as the barman said to the horse?'

Maggie turned her back on him. 'She, you have to think this through a little more. You know how much you mean to me. Are you really sure? Whatever happens, you know we'll get by. We don't need your life savings to do it. You've been the best friend to me, so I can't just take your money lightly. Not as there's a very good chance we'll lose it all!'

Sheila pressed her lips into a thin crimson line.

'You're not taking it, I'm giving it you. I've made my mind up and I won't be shifted. You show me what you can do, my girl, you make me proud. Now talk it over while I go on my break. I'll be back before the lunchtime "rush".' Sheila bustled out, leaving silence and shadows in her wake.

'Bloody hell! Has Sheila just given us some money?' Jim looked after her. 'How much?'

Maggie turned to look at her younger brother. Tall and blond like her father and quite heavily built, she had never understood his seemingly limitless appeal to women. Maybe it was her parents' money, which he spent with a compulsive disregard for where it came from. She turned to her parents.

'I have to go after her and talk to her. I don't think she realises what she's just offered!' Maggie said, and grabbed her bag as she headed for the door, leaving her family struggling to catch up with the morning's roller coaster of events.

'Sheila! Sheila, She!' Maggie shouted, finally halting Sheila's fast-paced walk on the last shout. She stopped in her tracks and turned around, lighting a cigarette as she waited for Maggie to catch up with her. Maggie was out of breath when she arrived.

'I thought I told you to talk it through with your mum and

dad?' Sheila said as if she'd asked Maggie to choose whether or not she wanted chips for tea.

Maggie shook her head and fell in step beside Sheila.

'I'm nipping into Boots, I need some new lippy, so you'll have to keep up with me,' Sheila told her.

'How is it,' Maggie struggled to breathe, 'that you've smoked forty a day for God knows how long and are still as fit as a fiddle?'

Sheila blew smoke out of her nose as she considered the question.

'It's probably the whisky,' she said. 'It's probably pickled my lungs, and maybe the ciggies have smoked my liver. Either that or it's my genes. We're a long-living family. My Aunty May was a hundred and four when she passed.' She gave Maggie a quick once-over, the exact kind she used to give her when she was checking she had her school shirt tucked in and had taken her dangly earrings out. Marion had never known what the school dress codes were, and even if she had she wouldn't have presumed to enforce them. 'Now, why are you here and not indoors talking things over with your parents?' Sheila demanded.

Maggie shrugged. 'I never talk things over with my parents,' she said. 'Dad would say something like, "You know what's best for you, Maggie, don't worry about me even though I've got high blood pressure and the stress is nearly killing me." And Mum would say, "life is a river, and we are but leaves carried along by the current" or some such crap, and—'

Sheila cut across her as they headed into the chemist's.

'You should show your parents more respect, young lady. All right, they're not going to win business people of the year, but they are good people. They only want the best for you and Jim. Sometimes I think they're much too easy on you both. Especially Jim.'

Maggie made a face of disbelief behind Sheila's back as she examined a range of lipsticks.

'Don't you make faces behind my back,' Sheila said without turning a hair. 'I mean it. Your parents are my very good friends, and if you ever took the time to get to know them properly you'd realise what good friends they could be for you too.' She smeared a streak of orange on to the back of her hand.

'Yeah, well, surely a child shouldn't have to make the effort to get to know her parents, and anyway I do know them! I know them better than anyone!' Maggie said, a touch petulantly.

'You know them the way you did when you were a child, waiting for them to turn into some TV version of what parents should be. Now you're an adult you should try to get to know them again, as people. They love you more than anyone else ever will, you know.'

Maggie somehow doubted it. Maybe her dad did – but her mum? She supposed her mum did love her, but she loved everyone, so it didn't seem to count.

'Perhaps,' Maggie said by way of reconciliation. 'But for me to take on The Fleur? It would be a big step Sheila – a huge one. It wouldn't be a job I could just give notice on if it didn't work out.' Maggie thought of her hopes to be back with Christian again one day soon. If she took on The Fleur then they'd never work together again. 'I'd be tied to *them*,' she said, referring to her family, 'for the foreseeable future, maybe for ever. It could be kind of . . . claustrophobic . . .' Maggie trailed off as Sheila held up the back of her hand for inspection. It was covered in a rainbow of glistening lipsticks.

'I quite like that browny one,' Maggie said after a moment's consideration.

'Well, it could be a bit claustrophobic, yes, if you insist on treating your family like strangers. Or it could be a chance for

98

you to get close to them. It could also be a chance for you to do what *you* want to do for once, instead of bowing to Christian's whims all the time. For you to finally get on your own two feet and show the world what you're made of.'

Sheila selected the browny-red lipstick and handed it over the counter to the assistant.

'If you've got the guts and the gumption to do it, that is.'

She paid, and pocketed her purchase.

'Maggie, you're a bright girl. No one knows that more than me. Who was it who used to sit with you when you were doing your maths homework, pretending I was helping you when you were working it all out by yourself!'

Maggie smiled at the memory of cold afternoons, mugs of sweet tea, toast and Sheila bent earnestly over her exercise book.

'It's more than they ever did,' she said.

'"They" were trying to run a pub,' Sheila replied. 'It took a lot of adjustment. You couldn't see how hard it was for them then. Anyway, you've worked your socks off to get where you are now. I don't think you realise how much you did for Christian, how much he depended on you for Fresh Talent. I bet if you sat down and thought about it, you'd find you know a lot more about running a pub and bar than you think.'

Maggie imagined herself standing behind the newly refurbished bar of The Fleur greeting Christian with a radiant smile as he walked through the door, awestuck by the improvements and her success.

'Maybe . . . ' she said, warming to the vision, 'but Sheila, this is all a bit much to take in. It's all so fast, coming on top of Christian and me. To find out that you were leaving me all that money and that you want to just give it me now! – it's incredible. Are you sure? Are you sure you want me to have it? You might have a cousin somewhere, or perhaps you should give it all to the shelter? I bet they could use it.'

They arrived just short of The Fleur and Sheila stopped dead, causing Maggie to stumble a little as she tried to stop with her.

'I don't want no cousin I've never heard of, let alone met, getting it, and I gave some to the shelter before. Maybe that would be the noble thing to do, Mag, but it wouldn't feel right. You, your mum and dad and Jim have been a huge part of my life for the last twenty-five years. There was a long, long time before that, Mag, when I didn't have a life. I didn't have *anything* except regrets and unhappy memories. All of you mean the world to me. I don't want it to go down the pan for you all. I want you to have a chance to be successful.'

Sheila paused and looked up at the greying, flaky exterior of the pub.

'Maybe it *would* be too much for you. Maybe it's not fair asking you to commit to something like this, because you're right – you couldn't just walk out on it, even if something better came along. If you don't want the responsibility, then all right. We'll leave things as they are.' Sheila leant forward and gave Maggie a quick kiss before heading into the bar. 'You know best, Mag,' she said with half a smile. 'After all, life is a river.'

Maggie grinned as she watched her going, then, turning on her heel, she crossed the road and headed towards the park and the lakes.

She needed to think things through. If she didn't take The Fleur on, then things would be terrible. She'd have to find a place for Mum and Dad to live, and she'd have to get a job to keep things going, any job anywhere. If she did take The Fleur on, she could really try and make a go of it. Like Sheila said, it *could* be the best thing that had ever happened to her if she gave it one hundred per cent. But she wouldn't be able to just walk out on it when she felt like it. And even if Christian saw the light and asked her back, she'd never be part of Fresh Talent, they'd never be working as a team again. Maggie felt the heavy heat of the sun bearing down on her, and as she walked her head began to hurt with the infinite possibilities. There wasn't any time to wait and see what might happen; she had to make up her mind right away.

And by the time she got back to The Fleur she knew what her decision was.

'OK, Jim, in answer to your previous question,' Maggie had rejoined her family at the table, 'Sheila is *investing* in this place. I've decided I'll take her money but only on the proviso that once The Fleur is up and running I'll pay her a dividend. And I'm going to be in charge of the finances. From now on, if you want any cash you can work for it. No more allowances, no more dipping into the till. I'm your new boss and I don't carry freeloaders.'

Maggie felt a surge of power-crazed sibling rivalry and tried to contain the emotion. This wasn't about sorting out Jim; this was about making Sheila proud. And most of all it was about showing Christian exactly what she could do for herself. She'd make this place work. She'd have to, because once he saw for himself what she could do he'd take her back. He'd need her back. There was a fairly good chance she'd need breast and arse implants, a lifelong commitment to peroxide and a bulk load of fake tan, but if that's what it took then she'd do it. She'd do anything.

'Mum? What's she talking about?' Jim's ability to soft-touch his mother was almost legendary, but Marion ignored him and beamed at Maggie.

'Oh darling, I'm sure you're doing the right thing,' she said with more conviction than Maggie had heard from her about anything in a very long time. The pressure of the worry must have got even to her.

'She's telling you straight,' Keith put in, covering Marion's

101

hand with his own as he looked sternly at Jim. 'Your mother and I are handing the pub over to Maggie and Sheila is investing in it. Now, she's been good enough to offer you a job, son. I suggest you take it. We won't have anything to give you any more.' He stood up stiffly and put a hand on Maggie's shoulder. 'Maybe this will be for the best, love. I don't mind saying those late nights were starting to get to me! Sheila, Maggie, you two are . . . truly remarkable. You're giving us so much, when we've done so little for you.'

'Nonsense!' Sheila glowed as she polished one of the brass pumps.

'Well, I think we can really make it work, if we work hard,' Maggie said, looking at Jim.

'So we can leave it to you? The business plan, the bank, sorting it all out?' Marion asked Maggie.

'Yes, Mum,' she nodded. 'It's not your problem any more. I'll sort it. Why don't you and Dad go and make us all a cuppa?'

Marion sighed. 'Well I must say, that *is* a relief, a real relief.'

As they left the room, Marion leaned her head on her husband's shoulder and his arm snaked around her waist.

Still so in love after all these years, Maggie thought. It *is* possible; all you need is a bit of luck and a lot of determination. Sheila's seen to the luck part; now all I need is the determination.

'You've stitched me up good and proper!' Jim had lapsed into his mockney accent.

'Oh, grow up, Jim,' Maggie snapped. 'I'll pay you a wage as a general assistant, and for that you do what you're told when you're told. The first thing you can do is get down in that cellar, clear out any rubbish and make an inventory. I want to know exactly what furniture, fittings and stuff is down there. There might be something we can use.'

Jim hefted his bulk from one leg to the other and huffed out a breath.

'And what if I don't?' he said.

'You'll need to find yourself a job somewhere else. As long as you work here, your rent is included, but if you don't work here you owe me eighty quid a week starting from now. All right?'

Jim shook his head, looking briefly heavenward as if in prayer. 'Assistant Manager?' he quibbled resolutely.

'Assistant assistant, full stop. Although there will be opportunities to work your way up. Right. I'm taking these figures to the cybercafé to get started on a business plan. When I get in I want to see that inventory, OK?'

Jim gave a double huff. 'OK.' He sounded uncertain.

'He probably won't do it,' Maggie mused as she stuffed her papers into a bag and walked out into the sun. But it was worth a bluff.

Chapter Thirteen

Pete flopped on to his bed and looked at the ceiling. It was an unbearably hot afternoon, and the end of his first day of teaching summer school. He had been terrible, awful. Awkward and uncertain. Embarrassed at revealing his work on Dougie. Put off by the sarcastic looks of the students. After all, these kids were the bottom of the barrel, they'd all flunked at least once. If he couldn't impress them, what chance did he have at his interview? None at all, that's what.

Pulling himself off the bed he switched on his PC and waited patiently for the whizzing and buzzing Internet connection to open up his email. He held his breath as the small blue arrow in the bottom right-hand corner showed he had incoming mail. As he waited it seemed to take an age to download. It must be a long letter, he thought, maybe with photos. Pete found his heart was in his mouth and fingers crossed tightly in anticipation.

It was a circular from Tesco.com telling him about a deal on DVDs. It was a good deal, but not good enough to cheer Pete up. There was still nothing from Stella. Maybe she hadn't been able to get online? Or maybe she hadn't had the chance, or maybe his first email had failed for some reason and she still didn't know how to contact him. Pete opened up a new message and typed in Stella's address. His fingers hovered uncertainly over the keyboard.

What could he tell her? That he was useless at teaching? That he realised now he didn't stand a chance of moving into film, that he wished more than anything he was back in his old flat in Headingly, with his own DVDs and CDs, and that Stella was there with him? Soaking for hours in a bath, topping up the water till the tank ran dry. Or watching him cook in the evening, sitting on the kitchen counter with a glass of wine in her hand. Moving under him as they made love, shimmering in the moonlight. Perfectly beautiful, liquid and iridescent, like mercury.

Pete closed his email and rested his head in his hand as he waited for the physical response to the memory to subside. He couldn't write that. If he did she would never come back. He had to at least make it *look* as if he was succeeding. She'd never come back to an overbearing loser, he knew that. Stella's love was a wonderful, exhilarating mind-blowing baptism of fire. But it was not unconditional; never that.

As he turned off the PC there was a single knock on the door and Falcon's head appeared round it.

'All right, mate?' He scrutinised Pete, who, rubbing his hand across his face, wondered if his eyes might be a little damp.

'Yeah, you know, hot as a bastard and shite at my job. But all right. You?'

Falcon entered the room, revealing his glistening bare and tattooed chest, his pink hair swept back in a ponytail. He definitely had a thing for baring his chest, interesting as it wasn't exactly up to Greek god standards.

'All right. Got a creative block on, you know. Tried the drums for an hour but it's still there. I've got a deadline and everything. Fucking bourgeois fucking publisher. But what can I do? I need the money and I'm doing it for the kids.'

Pete got the impression that the tiny independent company that printed Falcon's graphic novels was anything but bourgeois, but he knew that Falcon had a problem reconciling his pretty

105

high earnings with his punk lifestyle, and if it helped him deal with it then fair enough. He had a small but very loyal following of alienated teenagers, so in some ways, Pete supposed, he *was* doing it for the kids.

'Anyway, I'm meeting the blokes up The Horn and then we might walk into town. Liquid refreshment. Are you man enough to join us?'

Pete thought of the class of blank-eyed, insolent students waiting for him to turn up hungover in the morning. Really he should just put together some pasta and go to bed early. That would be sensible.

'You're on, mate,' he said, and picked up his keys as he headed for the door.

After all, Stella never did rate the sensible option.

'You OK Maggie? You've been there almost all day and we're closing up now.'

Maggie looked up and rubbed her stiff neck. It was Declan, the cybercafé's owner. She'd met him a few times at various functions. They'd sat next to each other once at an award ceremony the year Christian had won local businessman of the year.

'Hi, Declan, hi. I didn't realise how late it had got. I think I've given myself carpal tunnel syndrome!' She laughed and rubbed her wrists. 'Can I print this stuff off here, or do I need to save it to disk?'

Declan smiled at her. He was an attractive man; small and neat with a permanent tan and greenish eyes.

'Save it on disk and I'll print it for you in my office.' He nodded to behind the food counter. 'So what's up at Fresh Talent, then? The system crash?'

Maggie stopped in her tracks and composed herself quickly before following him up the narrow stairs to his office. Double doors opened out on to a balcony and she was glad of the breeze his desk fan created in the solid wall of heat. She'd forgotten that she'd have to start explaining everything every time she met someone she knew through work now. She hadn't had time to prepare, to come up with a story. She studied Declan as he inserted her disk into his PC. He didn't look like he knew about Louise. He looked as if he hadn't heard.

'Oh, I'm not at Fresh Talent at the moment,' Maggie said after a pause. 'Christian and I are . . . having a break from things. After six years I think we needed to . . . find our feet. I'm working on my own project right now, so . . . we're going to see how things turn out?' She finished on an uncertain note despite her bright tone.

'So you're not with Christian any more then?' Declan seemed to need extra confirmation.

'Um, no. Not at present.' Maggie stumbled over the words.

'Oh, thank God, Mags.'

Maggie liked the way he made free with her name.

'I didn't like to say anything at the time, but he's so up his own arse, don't you think? Anyone would think he's the Damien Hirst of sandwiches. Jesus, and at the end of the day it's just a bit of bread and butter, right?' Declan laughed and Maggie couldn't resist returning his smile.

'Not to Christian,' she said. 'And not to me, really. Good food, made well. That's more of a passion.' She bit her lip, feeling embarrassed.

'Oh sure, but, I don't know . . . Don't you think he's a bit of a twat?'

Maggie laughed then and shook her head. 'I know he seems that way, but he had to pull himself up by his bootstraps. He never had any family to back him, no education to speak of. He's made his own way and he's worked for every single thing he has.' As she said the words she could hear Christian reciting them in her head. 'I think that toughens you up a lot. You have to be incredibly confident to pull it off and he is. Some people find that hard to take.'

Declan handed her a sheaf of papers and sat back in his chair. 'Well, he doesn't deserve a woman like you. You're incredibly cool about this "break" thing. Does it mean you can see other people?'

Maggie thought of Louise and winced.

'I suppose so,' she said eventually.

'Do you want to go for a drink, then? Annie can lock up, and if you're available a man's got to make the most of his opportunities.'

Maggie blinked, and it took a couple of seconds for her to realise she had been asked out. Sarah would be ecstatic. Better still, there was a good chance Christian might hear about it. And after all, even if Declan was only a fraction taller than she was, he was good fun and charming. One drink wouldn't hurt.

'Make it a large one and you're on!'

Maggie fluttered her lashes, sensing her flirtation was more comical than sexy, but Declan didn't seem to mind. He walked behind her as they left the café, and she couldn't be sure but she was fairly certain that he was watching her almost non-existent arse.

'Welcome to The Fleur!' Falcon bellowed as he pushed open the bar door and led Pete and his cohorts into the dark bar. It was empty except for the mature barmaid puffing on a fag, a small Asian woman in the corner nursing a bottle of Gold Label, and a large blond man leaning on the bar, covered in dust and dirt.

'Sheila, please! I've been down that bloody hell hole all day. Surely I've earned a pint or two?'

The barmaid shook her head. 'If she ain't told me you can have one, you're not getting one. Not for free anyhow.'

Jim shook his head bleakly and caught sight of Falcon at the bar.

'All right Falcon, mate? Buy us a beer. My family have turned into Nazis and they've stopped my tab.'

Falcon shook his head disapprovingly. 'Whatever he's having, Sheila.' He turned back to Jim. 'But I think you'll find the Jews of wartime Europe had a lot more to worry about than a supply of free beer.' He turned his back on him and said something to his mate.

Pete eyed Falcon's blank stare of a back and looked at the big blond man.

'Rough day, was it?' He nodded at the man's filthy clothes.

'I'll say. My sister's been dumped and she's turned into the bitch from hell. Fuck it. Women, hey?' Jim look a long draught of the pint Sheila had plonked primly in front of him.

'You're new, ain't you?' Sheila nodded at Pete, tossing her hair a little as she felt a faint echo of her eighteen-year-old beauty stir under her skin. A handsome man was a handsome man, however old you were.

'Oh, er, yeah. I've just moved in with Falcon.' Pete felt the earth shift slightly beneath him and wished he had made them stop for something to eat on the way. 'He's showing me the best pubs in town, and this is his favourite.' Pete looked around. Even for a Monday night it was as dead as a dodo.

'Won't be for much longer,' Jim interrupted. 'My sister's turning it into some godawful yuppie bar.'

Falcon turned his head and caught Sheila's eye.

'Is that true, She?' he asked her. 'Cos if it is, I'll get a protest going or something. We can't let that happen to this place. It's the only decent pub left in the city!'

Sheila shook her head and lit a new cigarette from an old one. 'No choice, love. We've been going under for years. His sister,'

109

she pointed her cigarette forcefully at Jim, 'is going to keep us all in a job. I don't think it'll be yuppies or nothing like that. She's a good girl, is Mag. She'll see us right.'

Falcon shook his head and leaned on the bar.

'Bloody travesty. Large JDs all round. Let's have a wake for the sad demise of The Fleur as we know it!'

As Sheila set the shorts up on the bar, Pete regarded his glass with alarm. He'd never been much good at whisky, let alone whisky on an empty stomach after several pints. But Falcon was impossible to refuse, and besides, there was a tiny part of him still sober enough to be clamouring for Stella. He had to drown that, at least for now, at least until he could get his head together enough to work things out.

'In one!' Falcon called out, and Pete automatically sank his shot. His stomach reeled and his head spun, but he noted as he put his empty glass back on the bar he couldn't feel any pain any more, and that had to be a good thing.

'Same again?' Falcon asked him.

'Why not?' Pete replied, and in that moment he couldn't think of a single reason.

The hand had been on her knee for maybe two minutes now, and Maggie had absolutely no idea how to get it off without making herself look ridiculous and Declan feel embarrassed. Declan had sandwiched her into a booth, and as the evening had progressed he'd sidled progressively further along the seat towards her. Maggie looked at her watch. It was ten forty-five.

'So,' Declan smiled, his fingers gently massaging her knee under the linen of her dress. 'Have I managed to take your mind off Christian?'

'Oh yes,' Maggie nodded unconvincingly. 'It's so nice to have a good *friend* to talk to at times like these. Thank you, Declan, for being such a good *friend*.' Maggie was hopeful he'd take the hint, but she should have known better. Drunk men with seduction on their mind don't really do hints. Declan's face loomed a little nearer.

'You know, you can work out of my office any time you like if you want a bit of peace and quiet. You'd improve my view tenfold.' His hand had found its way under the hem of her skirt and his fingers were gently stroking her thigh.

'Time, gentlemen, please!' the barman called out, ringing a large brass bell at the same. In one fluid movement Maggie extracted Declan's hand from beneath her skirt and reached for her bag.

'Well, Declan, thanks for the drink. I must be off. I have to cash up at The Fleur.' Declan leaned back in his chair and studied her with a crooked smile. He was quite charming, really, Maggie thought sadly.

'Surely one of your minions could do it?' he questioned her, his arm snaking around her shoulders. As Maggie laughed, she heard the note of hysteria in her voice.

'My only minion is over sixty, and actually she almost owns the place, so if you don't mind . . .' As Maggie tried to rise, Declan gently pushed her back into her seat and closed her mouth with his own in one expert manoeuvre. For a second, Maggie willed herself to enjoy the feel of his lips on hers and the sensation of his fingers on her shoulder, but she couldn't. Panic and sadness welled up inside and she pushed him away, a single tear tracking down her face.

'Declan, I'm sorry . . . I . . . It's not you. I mean really, it isn't – it's just that all that stuff I said about me and Christian being on a break – it was total bollocks. He was having an affair when we split up. He dumped me.'

Declan picked up her hand and squeezed it lightly.

'I know, Mags. Everyone knows. Everyone thinks he's a total shit. And crazy too, if that helps.'

111

Maggie blinked at him, wishing the bar floor would open up and swallow her where she sat.

'But why . . . why didn't you . . .?'

'Say anything? Because I thought you deserved to keep your dignity intact.' Declan smiled ruefully. 'And because I thought I might get lucky. You're a very attractive woman, Maggie.'

Maggie literally shrugged off the compliment and squirmed in her seat.

'It's just, I miss him, Declan, and I . . . still love him so much. I can't bear the thought of anyone else kissing me, and I hope that one day soon Christian will feel the same way. Does that make me insane?'

Declan returned his hand to her knee, but this time in a more companionable way.

'Probably, yes. But it also makes you very genuine and very true to yourself. Maybe it's not that you only want to be kissed by Christian. Maybe it's that you need to be kissed by the right man, and I'm not him, worst luck.'

Maggie held her bag over her lap like a protective shield. 'No, no,' she said firmly. 'I'm sure if I could kiss anybody else it would definitely be you,' she said, and she meant it. She just didn't believe that eventuality would ever happen.

Declan stood up and walked her on to the street.

'Well, if that day comes, you'll let me know, won't you?' he asked.

Maggie nodded. 'Straightaway,' she said.

'And if you need to come to the café, don't feel awkward now, will you?'

Maggie shook her head. 'Actually, I think I'll have enough cash to buy my own PC soon, but I wouldn't feel awkward.' There was a brief uncertain pause. 'Right, well, I'd better get back.' Maggie looked into Declan's eyes. 'Thanks, Declan, you are a really nice man,' she said, before kissing him lightly on the cheek.

112

They said their goodbyes, and as Declan watched her retreat swiftly up the street he shook his head and thrust his hands deep into his pockets.

'Too nice, that's my trouble,' he mumbled to himself as he began the long and lonely walk home.

Pete felt the dirty wooden floorboards of The Fleur creak and rock below him.

'Fucking hell, Falc,' he told his friend, 'I'm as fucked as a fucking mother fucker.' He caught Sheila eyeing him coolly. 'Sorry about the language,' he added, his voice blurred and indistinct.

Sheila took a deep drag on her cigarette and crossed her arms under her breasts.

'I've heard worse, love. You look right pie-eyed, though. What you need is some food to soak all that lot up.'

Falcon clapped him on the shoulder with a force that Pete felt might hammer him through the floor and into the cellar. His knees buckled slightly and it took him a moment to wobble himself back to a standing position.

'Nice greasy kebab, that'll see you right,' Falcon promised him and then, looking at Sheila, 'One more for the road, She?'

'On your bike. I called time ages ago,' she replied mildly. She looked at Jim, his head resting on the bar, fast asleep. 'And take him with you!' she added hopefully, but the group of men seemed to be having enough trouble arranging themselves without listening to her.

'Right then!' Falcon rallied the troops with a Buzz Lightyear-style cry. 'To the kebab shop and behind!'

Pete joined in the general cheer and as a group they lurched towards the exit.

As Maggie reached The Fleur, a group of lads spilled out on to the pavement, and as they whirled and spun around her she recognised them generically as The Fleur's only regular customers outside of a couple of old men and the Korean lady that ran the print shop down the road.

'I wonder if I could keep them coming and still attract the smart City crowd,' she mused as they lurched up the street. Just as she was about to push open the door Maggie stopped. She had the distinct impression that she had forgotten something, her keys maybe. Or rather that she had missed something she was supposed to do or someone she was supposed to meet. She paused and instinctively looked behind to the crowd of men that had just left. As she looked, the last of them turned the corner singing a very dubious version of 'Teenage Kicks' at the top of his voice. Maggie shrugged and went through the door to the now empty bar, then bolted and locked the door behind her.

'Sit down, She,' she called out over her shoulder. 'I'll cash up and make us a tea before I call you a cab, OK?'

Sheila sat down on one of the bar stools and kicked off her shoes.

'Already done it, love,' She replied. 'It didn't take long. Just Falcon, Woody and his mates in tonight. Oh, and they had some other one in tow this time. A right looker he was, even got my heart thumping!'

'Yeah?' Maggie laughed trying to imagine the kind of punk babe that could get Sheila going. 'Well, you never know your luck.' She looked at Jim sprawled on the bar and her heart sank. 'Did you . . .?'

'Nope,' Sheila pre-empted. 'He only had a pint, and then he flaked out. He's been down that cellar since you left this morning. He's just found out what it means to do a day's work and he's knackered.'

Maggie approached her brother and regarded him curiously. 'I can't actually believe he did what I asked,' she said quietly. 'Amazing. I wonder if he'll keep it up.'

114

'He seemed quite pleased with himself, all right,' Sheila said. 'I reckoned he'd worked really hard, but I never let on. Don't want him getting ahead of himself.'

Maggie smiled. Right now Jim looked about ten.

'Do you think he might pull himself together one day?' she asked.

'I'll tell you what I think,' Sheila replied. 'I think he's missed you. I think you not being here isn't good for him.'

Maggie laughed as she picked up a sheet of paper from the bar and saw that Jim had listed each item he had found in neat columns. 'See what he can do when he puts his mind to it?' She waved the sheet at Sheila. 'Right, I'll read this while I wait for the kettle to boil.'

As Maggie leant against the kitchen worktop, reading through the long list of ancient and modern artefacts her parents had stored below over the years, the strange sensation she'd felt at the door gradually seeped away until she'd forgotten she'd ever had it.

'Maggie!' Pete shouted down the street, but his voice was lost in a chorus of raucous singing. 'Here,' Pete turned to Falcon. 'That was Maggie, that really pretty girl just going in there. I need to talk to her, she's really good at listening and she totally understands about Stella. She'll know what to do . . .' Falcon swung his arm around Pete's neck, forcing him to stoop a little. 'What you need, mate,' he said firmly, 'is a *ger-reasy kebab*. That'll sort it, OK?'

Pete realised that at that moment not even superhuman strength would enable him to turn back to the pub and talk to Maggie.

'OK, a greasy kebab,' he agreed reluctantly. And that was the last thing he remembered.

Chapter Fourteen

This is how Maggie made the best and worst decision of her life.

The morning after Declan's kiss she woke up thinking about Louise. She considered this to be rather unusual, to say the least. After all, she had at least three more important things to think about. In order of importance they were: getting Christian back, saving The Fleur, which included not squandering Sheila's money, and working out why Declan's perfectly nice hand on her knee had not given her the slightest frisson of sexual excitement.

But no. As she dressed that morning she found herself searching through her rumpled collection of clothes – which still resided hopefully in her suitcase – searching for something that Louise might wear. The best she could come up with was a pair of white linen tailored trousers and a short black top with three-quarter-length sleeves and a deep V at the back to expose her shoulder blades. Even then she was fairly certain that Louise would wear both garments with a hint of disdain, wrinkling her pretty nose ever so slightly.

Then, as she went down to the pub kitchen for breakfast where her parents were already sitting, managing to eat Weetabix and hold hands at the same time, she felt herself moving as she imagined Louise would move – swinging out her hips as she leaned on the counter waiting for the kettle to boil, tipping her head ever so slightly to one side so that her phantom blonde hair grazed her pretend gold-dusted skin. She knew that under normal circumstances, if you could call her recent life normal, she'd be eyeing up the dilapidated kitchen, making a mental inventory of all the equipment they would need to overhaul or replace, and thinking of the outlets and contacts she could use most profitably. Problem-solving like this, minding the bottom line and bringing things in under budget, were practically Maggie's favourite thing to do – it was almost a treat. Christian had had all the flair and the talent, and she had had all the solid practical back-up; he'd often said so. But for some reason, this morning all she could think about was Louise, the strength of her thighs, the subtly lighter shade of her inner arm, the curve of the small of her back above her bottom . . .

'Oh fuck, I'm turning into a lesbian,' Maggie said out loud, causing her parents' respective spoons to halt abruptly mid-bite, leaving their mouths agape. Marion quickly composed herself and was about to deliver her 'whatever you do, dear, we'll still love you' speech, which she had rehearsed almost hopefully over the years, when Maggie cut her off with a sharp, pre-emptive strike. 'Oh don't be ridiculous, Mother, of course I'm not a lesbian.' Her parents exchanged confused glances and shrugs, which she thought was probably only fair as she was the one being ridiculous. In the interests of scientific exploration, however, Maggie did try to imagine her and Louise naked on a bed kissing and . . .

'Ugh!' Maggie said out loud again. Both parents remained cautiously silent, and Maggie was grateful. Nope, she was definitely not a lesbian. What was she, then? Clinically insane?

It was while she was in Mrs Kim's print shop waiting for her to colour-copy and laminate her business plan four times that a new explanation hit her right between the eyes. The eyes she was pretending were the smokey grey she thought Louise's might be.

'I've got it! She's possessed me!' she cried out loud. 'Not content with my boyfriend, the bloody gorgeous bitch has gone after my soul as well!' For at least three seconds it seemed feasible. Mrs Kim came out from her back room and looked at Maggie.

'Who are you talking to, dear?' she enquired politely, without any indication that she thought Maggie was mad.

'Oh, um well . . . myself, Mrs Kim,' Maggie said lamely. During her long acquaintance with Mrs Kim and her daily bottle of Gold Label, Maggie had never known her to be fazed by anything or anyone. So, she thought, in for a penny, in for a pound. 'I thought perhaps Christian's new girlfriend had possessed me?' Maggie gave a little defiant 'so what if I'm crazy' shrug, but Mrs Kim's smile never wavered.

'Oh yes?' she replied pleasantly. 'How's that?'

'Well, see . . .' Maggie thought she'd try choosing her words carefully for a change. 'This morning I woke up and I was dreaming about her, and since then she's been all I can think about. I'm even imagining that I *am* her, and . . .' Maggie trailed off, aware that she was possibly sounding a bit too mad even for the unflappable Mrs Kim. 'What do you think? Do I need a shrink?'

Mrs Kim chewed her lip for a moment as she studied Maggie's face.

'Have you ever considered that you might be a . . .'

'A lesbian? Yes, I did this morning. But it's the oral sex thing I can't be doing with. I think kissing and touching and all that, well, you know, I could take it or leave it. But as soon as I thought about, you know, going "downstairs", nope, it's not for me.'

Mrs Kim's serenity might have rippled just momentarily, Maggie wasn't sure.

118

'I was going to say a touch jealous,' Mrs Kim finished kindly. 'But I'm glad you've cleared that up.' As Maggie's blush radiated outwards from her blazing cheeks to the tips of her toes and the crown of her head she offered Mrs Kim her credit card, fervently praying that it would have enough credit to pay for the work.

'No need, dear.' Mrs Kim waved the card away. 'I've opened you a business account, so you can pay me at the end of the month. I've seen what you did at Fresh Talent. I know you'll make good.'

Maggie smiled at her gratefully and tucked the card back in her wallet.

'Well, that wasn't really me. But thanks Mrs Kim. I won't let you down, I swear.'

She collected her plans and hesitated for a moment. It wouldn't hurt, would it, just to ask Mrs Kim? She seemed so grounded, somehow, practically mystical. Maggie wasn't up on her eastern religions, but she thought Mrs Kim might be a Buddhist, and Buddhists usually had something pretty Zen to say on most things didn't they?

'So, um, Mrs Kim? What would you do about her? The other girlfriend, I mean?' Maggie asked her. She still thought of herself as Christian's girlfriend, even if he didn't. For once Mrs Kim's small smile broke into a big grin.

'That's easy,' she said sagely. 'I'd rip the bloody bitch to pieces!'

'She actually used those words?' Sarah asked her incredulously. She was sorting out the colour trolley while Luce was helping Becca and Sam to put rollers on a dummy head. It was training morning, but Luce had a hangover so Sarah had let her off anything harder in the hopes that when they opened for clients she wouldn't fry anyone's head under the dryer or give someone an impromptu bald spot. Again.

'Those exact words,' Maggie replied. 'And she looked like she meant every word she said. I was almost scared. I mean, you know, if Louise fell under a bus then I wouldn't be mourning, but . . . well.' Secretly Maggie felt the same way as Mrs Kim, but for once she decided to keep her more inappropriate thoughts to herself.

Sarah shrugged. 'Well, you know the world is populated by millions of people, all with their own private stories. Maybe Mr Kim did the dirty on her with a lady boy and she's got them both in the cellar. Maybe she was a ninja before settling in St As.'

Maggie frowned. 'I think you're mixing your Asian countries pretty liberally there, Sarah. But I get the general idea.' Maggie shrugged off the memory of the steely glint in Mrs Kim's eye and went back to the more important topic. 'Anyway, she made me think, and she's right. Not about killing her; about the fact that I'm insane with jealousy.'

'Well, duh. I could have told you that,' Becca interjected helpfully.

Maggie ignored her. 'What I mean is, that I need to confront my demons in order to conquer them.'

'Like Buffy the Vampire Slayer!' Sam added happily. Maggie smiled at him and Sarah worried about how he'd even heard of Buffy.

'Sort of, Sam,' Maggie said. 'What I mean is, I need to know what I'm up against so that I can be better than her. I need to see her again. And this time I need to see her in person.'

And that was how it happened that an hour or so later Maggie was standing face to face with Louise.

Chapter Fifteen

When Pete woke up that same morning, the first thing he thought of was that he was late. He leapt out of bed, walked into his tiny wardrobe, backed dizzily on to his bed again, and rubbed his hands through his hair and roughly over his face. Eventually the corners of the room stabilised and he took an experimental squint at his alarm clock. Five-forty-two a.m. Bollocks. Pete lay back on the bed and looked at the now familiar landscape of his ceiling. He knew he wouldn't be going back to sleep. For some reason, these days, whenever he woke up with a hangover it didn't matter how shite he felt, sleep always eluded him. He'd just have to kill time until he had to go and face the ungrateful fuckers that were his students, his eyes growing ever more hollow and his skin increasingly waxy. Stella would never sleep with him when he was hungover, which was a shame as shagging was about the only thing he felt up to then. A nice long, lazy, friendly shag with someone he loved. But even if Stella was here she wouldn't be up for it, he mused, so he might as well forget about the whole concept.

He couldn't remember anything after his second whisky last night. Well, he could remember bits and pieces, like fragments of a foreign-language film playing without subtitles. He remembered the unforgiving fluorescence of the kebab shop. And at some point he thought he'd put his head between his knees and

. . . no, he must have imagined this bit – but for some reason he thought he remembered Falcon holding his forehead as he chucked up over some poor sod's garden fence. Pete shook his head and smiled guiltily to himself. He'd not done stuff like that in years. Years and years, not since Stella and her taste for fancy bars and champagne cocktails.

There was something else, though. Something else tugging uncomfortably at the edges of his consciousness that gave him a deep sense of disquiet. He played back his haphazard trip home in his mind's eye, but he couldn't find anything too terrible there. Embarrassing, yes, but not terrible. He thought he remembered coming in, bumping into Angie in the hallway, and Falcon gripping her ample hips with his hands and pulling her giggling into his room. What then? Well, then he must have come up and got out of his kecks and . . .

'Oh fuck.' Pete's stomach lurched and he clapped his hand over his eyes. 'Oh fuck, fuck, fuck, fuck. Please, please let me have dreamt it. Please, *please* let me have dreamt it.' He leapt off his bed, his head banging like a drum, and raced to the PC. 'Oh fuck, it's on, it's still on. Fuck.' Pete stared at the frozen screen saver. He tried to control, alt, delete it but it was firmly stuck and he knew he'd have to reboot the whole thing. 'Maybe I left it on *before* I went out,' he said with faint hope.

With trepidation Pete logged on to his email and waited. There were no new replies, and for once he was relieved. With one eye closed he opened his sent mail and all his worst fears were confirmed. There it was, sitting there. A message to Stella sent at twelve-twenty-two a.m. He'd written to her when he was drunk. When he was absolutely mind-numbingly bladdered. When he was as fucked as a bloke with a brainectomy. As tempting as it was to just leave it, or delete it, Pete knew he had to know what he'd written. If it wasn't too bad, maybe he could try some damage limitation. Suicide maybe. After all, people are always much more forgiving of the dead.

Dear Stella, Pete read. So far so good.

Christ, I miss you so much. Why haven't you written to me? Why haven't you been in touch? How do you think it makes me feel, you on the other side of the world when we're supposed to be getting married and nothing, I've heard nothing from you. Pete closed his eyes for a moment and swallowed the urge to vomit. After the literally bitter moment had passed, he forced himself to look again.

Ha, ha! Just joking. Actually, things here are really great!! I had the interview for the film job today and got it. The bloke said I was so experienced that he gave me a better job than the one I went for, better paid even. Next month I'll be working with Bruce Willis and Julia Roberts. Pete cringed. On the one hand he was grateful that his plastered self had checked the pitiful gushing (although he had failed to delete it). On the other hand he wished with his whole being that he hadn't decided to make up a load of crap he could never live up to, just to impress Stella. He read on anxiously. *I have made a lot of friends here. Falcon, who is in a band that is about to break the States. He is also the new Damien Hirst. Angie is the blonde I live with. She's a right goer. Oh. And I met this girl called Maggie. We have a lot in common and are becoming really really good friends. I think you would like her – she's got these huge dark eyes and a sort of Audrey Hepburn thing going on. She's really funny and a good laugh too. Well, maybe you'll log on soon.*

I do miss you, baby.

Pete xxxxxxxxxxxxxxxxxxxxxxxxxxxxxxxxxxxxxxxxxxxxxxxx

Pete read the email again and again and gradually his feeling of panic subsided. OK, so, it was pretty bad, but not as bad as it might have been. Yes, he'd started out pathetic, but he'd retracted it. Yes, he'd made up a shitload of bullshit, but now he'd said it out loud to Stella, his inspiration, maybe he could really make it happen? Although he wasn't sure about the Bruce

Willis bit. And as for describing a girl he'd hardly known as his new best friend, well . . .

On the second or third time Stella had left Pete, he hadn't fully understood their relationship and, thinking she had really gone for good, he had started seeing someone else, the girl from work called Candi. Really she'd been called something like Maureen, but had changed her name to Candi at secondary school and still dotted her 'i' with a love heart. Pete liked her – she was pretty flaky, but funny. She had a slight fragility, which appealed to him, and he liked her red hair and white skin. She didn't get close to Stella and how she made him feel, but they had been good friends and happy lovers. Pete had thought that, given time, his pain over Stella might even have faded to a bearable background level.

Then Stella had come back and trampled all over it. Pete had been amazed – astounded, actually – by how she had reacted to the news that he had someone else. Until that moment, until he'd seen her eyes blazing, seen her weeping with abandon, he hadn't known that she loved him just as much as he loved her. He hadn't known he had the power to make her jealous. After a stormy and passionate argument (well, more of a one-woman tirade), they had had the most incredible sex of Pete's life. Stella had promised that she'd never leave him to fall into the clutches of another woman again. The next morning, still shaky from Stella's passion, Pete had led Candi into a spare office and told her the news. He had been embarrassed and ashamed when she'd crumpled right in front of him. He'd wanted to reach out and hold her but didn't know how to. Everything he said to her sounded trite and clichéd, but as much as he liked and respected her, there was nothing he could do to make things different. Stella was Stella and, well, everyone else was just everyone else. In the end he was relieved when she got angry with him, punched him hard in the shoulder and stormed out. She'd never

124

come back to the studio and Pete had felt bad about that, because those sorts of jobs were hard to come by in Leeds. He phoned a bloke he knew at Granada, faxed him Candi's CV and asked him to let her know directly if anything came up, making him promise not to mention his name. She'd got a job there about two weeks later so it had made him feel a bit better, but not that much, to be honest.

Even so, nothing, not even someone as sweet as Candi, held a candle to Stella's fiercely burning supernova. Pete had promised never to hurt Stella that way again, and he never had. And he never would . . . but if she thought he had a really nice female friend, someone who might just be after him even if, say, he didn't realise it? Well it just might make her come home a little sooner. Pete tapped his finger against the keyboard thoughtfully.

'But am I a total shit for fibbing to Stella and using Maggie like this behind her back when I don't even know her that well?' An idea clicked in Pete's mind as he switched off the PC. Stella had often told him the truth was there to be creative with, and since in this case he'd be doing it for him and her, it was really a romantic gesture more than lying. And if he really did make friends with Maggie, if he did get to know her, then it wouldn't be that much of a lie. After all, they were in the same boat – she was still crazy over her bloke and desperate to get him back. So he'd be telling Stella practically the truth, while hurting or betraying no one. Problem solved.

Now all he had to do was find a way to bump into Maggie again.

Chapter Sixteen

'I'm sorry, what did you say you name was?' Louise asked Maggie pleasantly, with the slightest rise of her perfectly arched brow. For a moment Maggie panicked and almost bolted for the door. For a moment she nearly blurted out, 'I'm Maggie, Maggie Johnson, Christian's girlfriend! The one he dumped for you!' but instead she breathed in and concentrated on the same slightly surreal sensation of certainty that had led her here in the first place. Noticing the Spanish ruffles on the sleeves of Louise's red silk blouse, Maggie returned her enquiry with a brisk, businesslike smile.

'I didn't actually, but it's Carmen . . . Carmen Da Vinci of, um, Renaissance Events. I'm overseeing the opening of a major new venue and I'm looking to bring in external caterers . . .?'

She took Louise's proffered hand and shook it firmly, wondering if stealing the surname of the artist displayed across the bottom of a framed print on the wall over her left shoulder was a bit obvious, but new as she was to assuming identities and working undercover she had no time to consider the consequences of her snap decision, which was probably fortunate as no doubt it would include derision, humiliation and a short stay in some mental institution. In the event, Louise released her grip first and turned on her high heel without so much as a second glance at the interloper.

'So have you come for a brochure, or do you actually have a specific event in mind?' Louise asked her, looking at the boxes of stationery still unopened at her feet.

'Oh, just a brochure at this stage.' Maggie replied.

'Well, then, follow me, Carmen. The office is not quite finished yet, but at least we can talk in there in peace and quiet without a whole load of builders ogling your arse!'

Louise's laugh was deep and throaty. Deep-throat, Maggie noted. Maybe it was her fellatio skills that had tipped the balance. She shrugged to herself and wondered if it was the hips instead. Louise had proper hips, the kind that curve out from the waist and finished in a rounded bottom. As Maggie frequently noted, her own hips were angular and flat. She had boy's hips, and very possibly a boy's bottom, although unlike Sarah she refused to spend hours analysing it over one shoulder in the mirror. Besides, Christian had always told her he liked her bottom. In fact he'd told her he loved it. Come to that, he had told her he loved her, so maybe it wasn't that at all. Perhaps it was just Louise's difference, her oppositeness, that drew him to her, because he was running away from the hugeness of their love. After all, he had said as much.

Maggie glanced around as she followed Louise picking through the boxes, cans of paint and ladders that still adorned the corridor, and smiled to herself. The official opening of Fresh Talent 2 had been scheduled for last Friday, but maybe, just maybe, the end of their relationship had created a tiny stir in Christian's life after all, a slight ripple that had delayed things just a little, and it pleased her to think it. Or then again, maybe the builders were just behind schedule again – they had been for weeks. God knows she'd spent long enough on the phone chasing them. But Maggie tried not to think about rational explanations, because that would lead her down a very tricky route, one which would inevitably culminate in her asking

127

herself exactly why she was in the office of her ex's new girl-friend pretending she was somebody else. Even as the thought crossed her mind she could hear Sarah's voice in her head demanding an answer, could see her as she had looked this morning, her arms crossed over her breasts, her lips set into a thin firm line reserved only for her children – and Maggie.

'I am not taking you back there to have another bloody look at her. Apart from the fact that I have a business to run, you've seen her once. We agreed – all tits and legs and no class! What do you need to see her again for? Just let it go, Mags, for God's sake. For your sake. I know it's early days, but all this mentalist stuff, this obsessing – it's not doing you any favours.'

Maggie had shrugged and told her friend that she was right, of course she was right. She had had the obligatory weep on Sarah's shoulder, wondered to herself how it was possible to be so bored stiff with crying and yet still need to do it all the time, and then had left the salon, turned right up the street and gone to the station to catch the first train to the City, which took twenty minutes to arrive while Maggie stared blankly into space and eavesdropped on the private lives of two old ladies.

'I said to him, Ron, I said, now stop all this silliness. I'm a married woman, my Bob's still alive, just. You can't go asking a married woman to gad about on cruises. Mary, he said, I have to have you, I don't care what it takes! Silly old fool.' Mary hadn't been able to resist a small smile to herself.

'He'd set his cap at anyone, that Ron,' her companion had said sourly, and Mary's smile had faded into the middle distance as she waited; she looked liked she'd been waiting all her life.

Twenty minutes, Maggie mused. Why am I still sitting here after twenty minutes when I could be, *should* be, going home? But her impulse to get on the train had given her the strongest sense of purpose she'd felt since Christian had told her about Louise. It was almost overwhelming, and at least, she noted,

128

since she'd made the decision she'd stopped pretending to *be* Louise. That had to be a step in the right direction.

Maggie explained to herself once again exactly why it was perfectly rational for her to want to see Louise again and why she knew it would help her. She just *knew* she had to. She had to take her in, this woman, this irresistible force that had disintegrated at a single touch the one thing she thought was immutable. She had to look at her and really *see* her, because she had to know, she *had* to know, where she'd gone wrong, where, at exactly which point, she'd lost him. It was the speculating that was driving her mad. Knowing would keep her sane.

None of it was planned, of course; at least not her new career as a double agent. She'd got off the train and found her way to the new premises. She'd stood across the street with a studied air of nonchalance, going for the persona of a lost tourist or maybe an architecture student – anything that would give her a licence to loiter. As she'd waited she'd wondered again why she had never questioned Christian's insistence that she didn't need to visit the new place until it was completely finished. That really she didn't even need to meet Louise, not until she'd settled in and found her feet. He'd said, 'You know how fantastic you are, Mags, you'll intimidate her.' Maggie sighed and wondered whether if he'd put a huge neon sign up over their bed saying 'I'M HAVING AN AFFAIR' she would have ignored that too. But then she'd trusted him, and you don't question a person you trust, do you? You expect them to tell you straight up how they're feeling. But as he'd said himself that terrible morning on the sofa, Christian couldn't bear to hurt her so she'd only got the message when one of the signs had come crashing down on her head.

Maggie had pushed her shades up her nose and watched the Victorian Gothic building, waiting for a glimpse of Louise, just like last time. Exactly as she had with Sarah. Except that Sarah had made the whole exercise vaguely sane. When Sarah had been there she hadn't felt mad or desperate or idiotic. Ripped into tiny shreds of nothingness, yes, but at least she hadn't been alone. Maggie had panicked then and nearly bolted, but just at that moment Louise had arrived.

She was dressed in a knee-length beige suede skirt and red silk shirt, her golden legs turned out beautifully in a pair of tan high heels. Maggie had almost missed her, so lost was she in her tumultuous thoughts. Louise had paused only momentarily outside the door, seemed to take a deep breath and then gone in, greeting the workmen with a practised gusto. For the second time Maggie had noted that she had grace and poise. When she and Sarah had noticed it the first time, they had passed it off as sluttish and cheap. They were wrong.

Maggie had stared at the chipped nail polish on her toes for a long moment and wondered. If she had had to sit on the train for ages, bombarded by the incessantly loud ranting of two teenage girls debating whether the best way to get a boy in class to fancy them was to let it be known that they 'did it', then the very least she could do was make the journey worthwhile. And anyway, one good look was all she needed – then she'd go back to being herself, but prepared, this time, for battle.

'Don't be an idiot, Maggie Johnson,' Maggie said under her breath, surprising herself in the quiet street. 'You're going to get on the bus, go back home, run through your presentation to the bank like you said you would, and try to cost an opening menu that doesn't involve nuggets, baskets and chips. You are a grown woman, *not* a ranting lunatic.'

But by the end of her muttered speech she had found herself standing outside the doors Louise had walked through moments before.

Cursing herself, she'd walked past the vaulted entrance as many times as she could before one of the decorators in the foyer had winked at her and waved. It was then that something happened to her that had never happened before. For the first time she'd felt light-headed and sort of cut loose, as if the whole morning had been an inexorable journey to the highest peak of a rollercoaster and now the moment had come when gravity was about to send her plummeting down to earth at speed. Before she'd had time to think about it, she'd walked through the engraved glass doors and up to the smiling decorator and tipped what little remained of her balance.

'Hello,' she'd said with a grin that was uncharacteristically flirtatious. 'I'm terribly sorry, I think I'm a bit lost. I'm looking for the Fresh Talent office and the manager, Louise? Louise Bovary, isn't it?'

At that moment Louise had risen like Venus from behind the high-topped white ash reception desk with a box of stationery in her hands, smiling benevolently.

'Oh, hi there, I'm Louise,' she'd said, setting the box down on the desk. 'Were you looking for me? Please accept my apologies for the state of the place, but it's just been one thing after another the last couple of weeks, which I probably shouldn't be telling you if you're a prospective client. My boss'd kill me!' She bit her lip on the last word and Maggie saw that she was nervous, maybe a bit harassed and worried about letting Christian down. She felt an unexpected pang of empathy and relief.

'Oh God! Don't worry. I'm sort of new to this too,' Maggie had replied as she'd returned Louise's anxious smile. She's just a person, Maggie had realised with a shock, just a rather gorgeous normal person with the same insecurities as anyone else. For a moment Maggie had felt a strange mix of guilt and joy, as she realised that it might be possible to win Christian back from her after all.

'I'm sorry,' Louise had said. 'What did you say your name was?'

★

131

'Carmen?'

Maggie stared at the brochure copy which she herself had written only weeks before, somehow unable to get the printed words to make sense on the page.

'Carmen! Are you OK?

Maggie blinked and looked up at Louise, who was now leaning across the beech radial desk that Maggie had budgeted for, her face a picture of concern.

'I'm sorry!' Maggie leaned back in the chair and fanned herself with the brochure. 'I think it's this heat. It's sent me a bit ga-ga. So, um, what were you saying?'

Louise's face relaxed and she smiled. 'Actually I was saying do you fancy getting out of this office? There's a nice place round the corner where we could have coffee. I'd offer you one here, but I haven't unpacked the machine yet.'

Maggie masked her surprise at the offer, but conceded that it was probably a good move on Louise's part. The chaotic surroundings could put a prospective client off.

'Um, why not?' she said. 'It would be nice to get some fresh air anyway.'

Louise smiled confidently at her and strode to the closed office door. 'Right, this way, madam,' she said, gripping the door handle and turning it. It came off in her hand.

'Oh shit! Oops, sorry, I mean . . .' Louise regarded the redundant piece of metal in her hand and smiled wanly at Maggie. 'I mean, oh shit!'

This is my punishment, Maggie thought. This is divine retribution for coming here in the first place. I'm going to be locked for all eternity in an airless office with a woman whose breasts take up most of the room. But then, on the upside, at least she won't be with Christian either.

Maggie looked at Louise's crestfallen face. 'Don't panic!' she said brightly. 'This sort of thing always happens at exactly the

132

wrong moment.' She crossed the cluttered office in two steps and took the handle out of Louise's hand. 'Here, let me try.' Maggie tried to reinsert the handle on to its shaft, tentatively turned it and for one moment thought she had been reprieved from her eternal doom. Then she heard the handle on the other side of the door clatter to the floor. Followed by the connecting shaft.

'Oh shit.' Maggie said, looking into the wide eyes of her boyfriend's mistress. 'Now we really are fucked.'

The two women looked at each other for a second, and then, as one, beat their palms against the door and shouted for help. After a few seconds they stopped, and Maggie felt her reddened palms tingle. Faintly, from down the corridor, they could hear the buzz of a drill.

'They can't hear us,' Louise said. She laughed unconvincingly. 'Oh God, Carmen. I'm so sorry. You're never going to use us now, are you?'

Maggie tried a consoling grin, but she was sure her newly acquired but mounting claustrophobia must be reflected in her face.

'Never mind,' she said stiffly, and then glanced at the phone on the desk. 'I know, ring them. Ring the builders and tell them to let us out!'

Louise looked apologetic. 'We're getting connected this afternoon,' she said. 'Oh, but my mobile, my mobile is . . . on the front desk. Oh fuck.' She sat back down and, pulling open the desk drawer, produced a warm can of coke. 'Look, at least we won't dehydrate,' she said bravely.

Maggie slumped back into her chair and blinked. What was she supposed to do now? Carry on being Carmen, she guessed. At least this way, in a sort of crisis, Louise might open up a little, give away a few vital clues.

'Anyway,' Louise continued, 'there's always a bright side. It'll be a nice treat for me to spend a bit of time with a girl, what

133

with all the builders around. I've only been living in London for a few months and I haven't had a chance to meet anyone much. The only friend I've got is my boyfriend!'

Maggie forced a reciprocal laugh. 'Oh no, we can't have that!' she replied heartily, hoping her brain would click into automatic pilot and do all the talking for her. Every now and then a small voice inside was screaming soundlessly 'what the hell do you think you're doing here?' but for the most part it was like some dream, some movie trailer that Maggie just happened to be floating through, and even though she knew at the back of her mind that what she was doing was ridiculous – not to mention strange – she just couldn't muster up the energy to care very much.

Louise led the conversation with an edge of mild terror, and Maggie felt for her. If Christian found out about this, the derision, not to mention the recriminations, would be endless, like when Maggie had once ordered thirty-two boxes of pak choi cabbage instead of king prawns. She'd never lived that down.

Louise fidgeted. 'Normally, I can't go thirty minutes without my caffeine fix!' she giggled.

Maggie noticed her smooth skirt first and then her hair, before adjusting the neck of her shirt. After she had performed these ritualistic movements she experienced a moment's stillness before going through the whole thing again.

'So where have you come from then?' Maggie asked her. Christian had said, but she'd not been that interested at the time. Some small place in Oxfordshire, wasn't it?

'Cheltenham. I was working at an events management company out there. When I came for this interview, to be honest I didn't think I stood a chance! I had all the wrong kinds of experience. But, well, Christian and I just clicked.' Louise giggled again. 'In more ways than one!'

134

Maggie giggled back, quietly alarmed at how easy it was for her to separate her mixed emotions into two piles, one labelled 'violent angst for later' and the other 'cool and calculating for now'.

'Oh, so your boss is your boyfriend!' Maggie laughed, grinding her teeth. 'Smart move!'

Louise dipped her chin before looking out of the window.

'Well, yeah. I don't know if it was such a smart move,' she said uncertainly. 'But Christian's just so . . . he's got this really forceful personality, you know?'

Maggie nodded vigorously. 'Yes, I know!' she said with vehement conviction. Louise looked confused. 'The type, I mean. I know the type,' Maggie amended quickly. 'My ex was *exactly* the same.'

'And, well,' Louise continued, 'he made all the moves. He came on to me, really strong and determined. And I have to tell you coming from him it was kind of sexy.'

She sipped her coke thoughtfully and offered it to Maggie.

'It was messy, though. After we'd been together for a couple of months I found out he had a girlfriend through one of our suppliers. He'd been with her for years. I wouldn't normally touch a more or less married man in a million years, but I was hooked by then. We had a huge row, but it just seemed impossible to walk away. From Christian, from my job. If it all fell through now I'd have nowhere to go back to. Well, I would, but it'd feel like failing. I feel bad about it, though, I really do.'

Maggie stifled the laugh of bitter recrimination that had blossomed on her tongue and managed instead to utter an all-purpose 'Mmm?'

'But in the end, he actually left her for me! Which is amazing, isn't it? It's never supposed to end like that for us other women.'

Louise's smile did seem genuinely surprised and delighted. Maggie struggled hard to hate her.

135

'Why should you be surprised? I mean, look at you. You're beautiful. I shouldn't imagine that many women could compete with that!' Maggie said, taking a deliberate gulp of the warm drink and feeling the bubbles burst at the back of her throat.

'Oh thank you, but I always wish I was more like . . . you. You know, all elegant and smooth instead of all these lumps and bumps. And to think some women pay thousand of pounds for the hassle of carrying these things around!' Louise patted her chest lightly. 'Anyhow, I'd be happy as a pig on clover, but . . .' she paused and lowered her voice . . . 'I shouldn't really tell you this, I mean, you're a prospective client and everything but, well, as we're locked in an office . . .'

Maggie leaned a little closer to her, mirroring her gestures.

'You can tell me, I won't tell a soul,' she whispered before sitting back in her chair. After all, if no one could hear them shouting for help, Louise could shout the details of her stolen personal life from the rooftops and no one would notice.

'Well, the thing is, this ex, Maggie her name was. He still talks about her all the time.'

Maggie sat up suddenly in her chair. 'He does?' she said, sounding far too interested. 'I mean, does he?'

'Yeah. I mean, I know that she was really involved in the planning of the new office until she decided to pack it in, but it's not just even work stuff. If we see a film he's already seen with her, he'll say something like, "Oh, I remember the time Maggie and I blah blah blah." Or if I suggest a place to go on holiday, it'll be "Oh no, I've been there before with Maggie", or "Maggie used to say . . ." Maybe not as blunt as that, but he obviously still thinks about her a lot and admires her. I feel sort of like a poor relation, you know? I'm sure I can never live up to this woman.' Louise gulped back the rest of the coke. 'In actual fact I feel like I'm living on borrowed time . . .'

Maggie curtailed her triumphant grin as she realized that Louise's eyes were filled with tears. Instinctively she squeezed her hand.

'I mean, the thing is, Carmen, I really love him, I really do. I don't know what I'll do if he leaves me. What would you do?'

Maggie froze for what seemed like an eternity, and for a moment felt the powers of the gods surging through her. Here, at last, she had a chance to shape her own destiny! Or she could just do the decent thing and um and ah and say, 'Oh, I don't really know, Louise.' She looked at Louise's open face. The problem was that she was much, much nicer than Maggie had expected. She was open and sort of innocent, with average insecurities and worries. Maggie understood what it was like to love Christian so much that you woke up every day with your heart in your mouth afraid that it had all been a dream. She had first-hand experience of how it felt to find out that it was all over. Furthermore, Louise was obviously intimidated by her vision of the distant ex, and that flattered Maggie, which made her warm to Louise just a little bit more. In a different time or place they could probably have been quite good friends.

But when it came down to it, Maggie needed Christian back. She needed him in her life to make the world keep turning, the sun keep rising, her heart keep beating. For the past couple of weeks she'd done a decent job of keeping going, she knew that. But none of it meant anything without Christian there beside her, without him there in her vision of the future. He was essential to her experience, and Louise, however nice she had turned out to be, was not.

'If I were you I'd force a confrontation,' Maggie said lightly. 'Let him see how jealous you are of this other woman and then maybe he'll see how much he's hurting you and change. You should just demand that he cuts himself off from the past entirely.' Maggie smiled sincerely. 'Put your foot down now or else he'll never change,' she finished, knowing how much Christian hated women putting their foot down.

Louise considered the proposition seriously.

'You're right, Carmen,' she said. 'I definitely will. God it's been good to talk to a girl again, it really has!'

Suddenly there was a thunderous knocking on the door, making both women jump.

'Oh, at last, the cavalry!' Louise giggled. '*We're stuck*,' she shouted.

'Right-oh.' The handle shaft reappeared in the door and a second later the door was open. 'Must be the cowboy builders,' the builder said with a wink. 'I'll sort it out for you now.'

Louise smiled at him gratefully and followed Maggie out of the office. 'I don't suppose you'll still want that quote, will you?'

Maggie shrugged. Might as well. 'Oh yes, I'd still be interested,' she said.

Louise paused at the doorway and looked suddenly shy. 'Look, I don't know if you're going to use Fresh Talent or not, but could we swap numbers, maybe meet up again for a girly drink? We sort of hit it off, don't you think? I'd love it if we could.'

Maggie imagined herself standing on a forked path where each turning led to a different type of rocky ruin.

'OK,' she said finally. 'Why ever not?'

Chapter Seventeen

On his second Friday morning as a tutor, Pete noticed that at last his latest hangover from one of Falcon's 'quick bevvies' seemed to have gone. As he dressed for college, perusing his five tops for a few moments before picking the one that was in least need of a wash, he had to admit he was relieved another week as a tutor was over. Although he knew that in two days' time he'd have to go through the whole excruciating rigmarole again, for some reason the very fact that this was Friday made him feel like he'd just been handed a reprieve from the death sentence. 'Imagine how I'd feel,' he thought, 'if I didn't have to go and teach the fuckers at all.'

Pete bundled his dirty laundry under one arm and carried it down to the kitchen with him, hopeful that Angie would lend him some washing powder. If he was really honest about the whole teaching debacle, he was disappointed in himself. He'd imagined enthusing a bunch of bright young things, imparting his knowledge to them in the time-honoured tradition. Like Yoda to Luke Skywalker. He'd imagined them thanking him effusively for giving them the skill and insight they really needed to succeed, maybe mentioning him in an Oscar's speech or something.

Maybe he hadn't tried hard enough. Maybe he was taking the whole experience for granted, counting down the days to his interview at Magic Shop which was now only four days away. Today, he decided, he was going to try harder. He was going to get all Robin Williams on their arses and be inspirational. Make them stand on their desks and shout *carpe diem* or something along those lines.

Pete felt his stomach tighten when he imagined this, so he dismissed the thought and instead concentrated on Stella. He still hadn't heard from her. His seriously flawed plan to impress her with tales of a potential love rival, which had seemed so sane when he was drunk, grew ever more ridiculous as his multiple hangovers gradually receded. Did he think he was in some stupid bloody romantic comedy? The kind that Sandra Bullock was always in, the sort that was all dialogue and no decent effects. Plans like his only worked in the movies, and besides, he wasn't any good at being devious.

As it turned out, he hadn't even needed to engineer a meeting with Maggie. He'd bumped into her again on Tuesday, purely coincidentally, in Marks & Spencer. He'd been trying to buy a blouse for his mum's birthday in his lunch hour (hours, actually – the college job wasn't all that taxing). He'd cornered an assistant but, for some reason, the more he'd tried to explain what he was after the more she'd turned red and started to sort of, well . . . tremble.

'She's sort of this big.' Pete gestured vaguely in front of him, wondering if she was having trouble with his accent. 'And she likes flowery stuff. Stuff with flowers on.' He waited for the girl to speak. 'Have you got any flowery stuff?' he reiterated, but she just stared at him like a rabbit trapped in headlights. He was just about to give up and go and buy some chocolates when Maggie appeared at his shoulder.

'Hi? Pete?' She glanced curiously at the tremulous assistant. 'What *are* you doing?'

Pete sighed with relief. 'I'm *trying* to buy a blouse for my mum, for her birthday. I thought I'd make a special effort as I won't be there this year. But I don't know her size and this young lady seems to be unable to help me.' Pete caught Maggie repressing a smile. 'What? Am I being an idiot?'

Maggie shook her head. 'Only a bit.'

She smiled at the girl, who was edging away, hopeful that she would regain the power of speech when she was out of sight of the most gorgeous bloke she had seen in ages. She just had to tell Maxine, and maybe both of them could have a peak at him through knitwear and casual cotton-mix.

Pete watched her bolt towards a Staff Only exit and cursed himself.

'She thought I was a flipping trannie, didn't she?' he asked Maggie with horror.

Maggie snorted a very unladylike and quite charming laugh.

'Well, you did look a bit suspicious. What's she like?' Maggie asked, thumbing through the racks of clothing. 'Is she bigger than me, say?'

Pete looked at the top of Maggie's head.

'Much,' he said thinking of his mum's broad bust and solidly cushioned hips. 'Like, really much.'

Maggie stopped and smiled up at him, shaking her head.

'You can't really guess women's clothes sizes, Pete. It's a minefield. If what you give her is too small, she'll be embarrassed and feel fat, and if what you give is too big, she'll be mortified that you think she's that big and feel fat. See what I mean?'

Pete shook his head and then nodded. 'I don't think my mum cares either way, but I get your point. I'll bear it in mind for the future. I'd better buy her some chocolates.'

Maggie laughed at him again, in a friendly sort of way, but he was offended.

'No, chocolate will melt in the post! Buy her some vouchers.

141

Basically, all a woman ever wants for presents is expensive jewellery and vouchers to her favourite shop. It's a simple but somehow elusive concept for most men.'

Pete grinned at her.

'Actually, with Stella it's just the jewellery.'

And they'd chatted while they stood in the unfeasibly long queue full of old ladies. It must have been pension day. Pete had said something along the lines that this town clearly wasn't big enough for the both of them as they kept running into each other, and Maggie had said that sometimes this town didn't feel big enough to swing a cat in. She told Pete that if he stayed here he'd soon find that out. He asked her why she stayed then, and she said because she'd been everywhere else and she wasn't that fussed. They laughed and chatted and exchanged 'my mum's as batty as a fruit cake' stories. That was until he realised she was holding a five-pack of black thongs in her hands. After that it was she who chatted, while he tried not to look at them. When it was time for them to part, she'd hesitated before saying, 'Got time for a coffee?'

Pete was unexpectedly pleased at the invitation, and anyway he had another hour before his afternoon lecture, so he'd agreed. Now, as he got ready for work, he smiled at the memory. It had been a laugh, that cup of coffee that had turned into a pint with Maggie. They had talked about Stella and her bloke – Christian, was it? She seemed to know what he was going through, and she'd made him smile and even laugh. Actually, really, really laugh like a demented fool. She was a funny girl, and a nice one. He didn't think it would be fair to use her to make Stella jealous. At least not now in the sober, more or less reasonable, light of day.

In any case, now he was worrying for a whole new set of reasons. What if Stella had read that last email and thought he didn't want her any more? What if his attempt to sound happy and successful had made her think he didn't need her any more, that he wasn't waiting for her? What if – Pete swallowed hard – he had been wrong to let her go? What if she had found someone over there already? Someone better than him. Pete had always known that you couldn't keep Stella if she wanted to go, but this time, especially after all the things they'd said to each other, after all the promises they'd made, his raised expectations made her absence harder to bear. He missed her so much that the pain seemed to grate at his edges, making him tender and sore all over, bruising him the instant he touched the hard possibility that she might never come back. Pete shook his head firmly. No, she had his ring. She was coming back. She'd promised.

As he turned into the kitchen, he stopped dead in his tracks, opened and closed his mouth a couple of times and then shuffled and coughed. But it seemed that neither Angie, who was sitting on Falcon's lap and kissing him deeply, nor Falcon, who had his hand thrust very far up her nightshirt, revealing a large expanse of wide white thigh, noticed Pete's attempts to make his presence felt. Pete stood frozen by uncertainty for a couple of seconds until Falcon's hand finally released Angie's breast, and then headed purposefully between her thighs. Pete had been wondering about the exact nature of their relationship. At least that was cleared up.

'Coffee anyone?' Pete said brightly, making both parties jump apart.

Angie pulled her nightshirt belatedly over her knees and giggled. Falcon wiped his hand across his damp mouth.

'Oh dear, we've been caught out!' Angie said smoothing Falcon's pink hair back from his face. Falcon caught Pete's eyes over her shoulder and winked. 'You must wonder what on earth's going on, Pete,' Angie said.

Pete shook his head. 'It was fairly obvious, actually,' he said, spooning instant coffee into three mugs.

143

Angie looked at Falcon. 'I said we couldn't keep it a secret for very long with Pete in the house, didn't I?' Falcon gave her an uneasy shrug. 'Well, Malcolm and I . . .'

Pete turned to look at the couple, a small smile beginning in the corners of his mouth.

'Malcolm?' he said, looking at Falcon, the smile spreading into a grin.

'Well, yes, Falcon is just a pen name, isn't it, darling? Didn't you know?' Falcon glowered at Angie, who wound her plump arm a little tighter round his neck and planted a kiss squarely on his forehead.

'We've had a bit of an on–off thing going for, oh, a couple of years now. Sort of a friendship with added extras now and then. Perfect arrangement, really. Anyway, I hope we don't disturb your sleep!'

Angie giggled and hopped off Falcon's lap, picking up her steaming coffee mug as she went.

'I'm going for a shower. See you later, lover!' She practically skipped out of the kitchen and thundered up the stairs.

Pete looked at Falcon.

'We're mates. Sometimes we fuck. There's no emotional shit and everyone's happy. It's all good.'

Pete considered whether such an arrangement was really possible, and then supposed it must be. Falcon had found nirvana. He raised a bloke's eyebrow, one that said, 'I don't care if you don't want to elaborate.'

Falcon returned the gesture with a bloke's 'shit happens' shrug, and the subject was cleanly, quietly and quickly closed.

'Sometimes,' Pete thought, 'it's great being a man.'

The companionable silence continued as Pete shoved his washing into the ancient machine and nicked some of Angie's soap powder.

'Right, I'm off,' he said as he headed towards the door. 'Have a good day, Malcolm.'

Falcon replied with a bloke's grunt. It was a grunt that said, 'Call me that again and I'll lamp you.'

Pete smiled to himself as he glanced up at the faultlessly blue sky. It was going to be another very hot day. He steeled himself and headed towards the college.

'*Carpe diem*,' he mumbled to himself.

He was depressed to note that he didn't sound that convinced.

Maggie eyed herself in her wardrobe mirror and held her hand out forcefully, trying to ignore the Jason Donovan sticker that still reposed in the top right-hand corner, seemingly winking at her.

'Mr Shah, hi. Great to see you again. I think you'll find the plans we've got for The Fleur are really exciting . . .'

She trailed off and took a step closer to the mirror. She studied her eyes – still a little shadowed but not so red-rimmed, with the hint of a sparkle just waiting to be ignited. She turned her face from side to side and stretched her skin a little over her cheek-bones. Still reasonably elastic, she thought. The unremitting sun had coloured even her fair skin a little and brought out a flowering of light freckles across her nose. Christian had always liked her freckles. He said they were natural and sweet.

She tucked her hair behind her ear and smoothed down her smart meetings-at-the-bank shift dress and smiled at herself, then laughed and pirouetted around and around on the spot, her fingers outstretched until the room span faster than she did and she had to collapse on to the bed and wait for the world to slow back down. When the corners of the room reinstated themselves in their rightful order, she sat up gingerly, took a deep breath and began to pack her briefcase, carefully putting

145

the four copies of her business plan on the top, along with her pen, calculator and phone. She wanted everything in easy reach. Whatever the rest of the day might bring, would bring, she had to make sure she did the best job she could today at the bank. The best job for her parents, for Sheila and – she considered with a smile – for herself. An independent woman running her own business.

Maggie stopped stock-still and closed her eyes. She felt her stomach bubble up with happiness and her fingertips fuzz with magical anticipation. She felt powerful and beautiful and really much more like running naked through a field of waist-high wild flowers than sitting in a bank meeting. Because this part of her life, this chapter of misery, was almost, *almost* over. Her plan had worked much better than she had ever imagined, and tonight she was going to see Christian. Tonight her life was going to start again.

At first she'd thought that going to see Louise was the worst mistake she had ever made. On her way back from the meeting she'd felt sort of high and giggly, as if she had the most wonderful secret power that no one else knew about. As soon as she got off the train she headed straight over to Sarah's to tell her all about it. Then, as she rehearsed the conversation in her head, she realised that Sarah would go ballistic and that, what's more, she'd look at her in that way she had recently, as if she might be a little bit unbalanced, a little bit more than was normal, at least. She'd realised that the last thing she wanted to do was tell Sarah that she'd met Louise, posed as a client and thrown a hefty spanner in the workings of hers and Christian's relationship. She stopped dead in her tracks and turned round.

As she headed back to The Fleur, she realised she didn't want to tell anyone what she'd done to Louise, which meant that not only was she aware of how insane it might seem to anyone in the world who was not in love with Christian, but she also felt bad about it. Which, on the bright side, meant that she wasn't the heartless sociopath Sarah seemed to think she was. But on the downside, she'd done something really, really terrible that even she was finding a little tough to justify. She tried to console herself with the fact that Louise had stolen Christian from her in the first place, with her cleavage and her bum and her 'Oh, aren't I sweet' demeanour. But then she remembered Louise telling her that she hadn't known about Christian's girlfriend, that he'd come on to her from the outset. And worse still, Maggie knew it was impossible to resist Christian when he was on a full-on charm offensive. She didn't really blame Louise. In fact a large part of her had wanted to fess up almost straightaway and settle down to a good girly session of comparing notes.

Maggie had never been a conniving, manipulative bitch before, and she was surprised by how awful it made her feel. She just hoped that she was so bad at it that it wouldn't count in the scheme of things, not really.

For a week she waited for the fall-out from her despicable actions with literally bated breath. She accompanied Sheila on trips to her solicitor and then to her bank. She helped her mum and dad go through piles and piles of endless papers, trying to organise a filing system that hadn't been touched in maybe ten years, until at last she found all the documents they needed to transfer the business into her name. In the end they decided that the deeds to the actual building should remain in her parents' names. Maggie would lease it from them at a discounted rate, but still enough to give them an income.

'That way,' Keith said, looking at each of his children in turn, 'when your mum and I are gone you'll have half of this place coming to you each. That could be a lot of money.'

'That is, if Maggie doesn't get it repossessed in the meantime,' Jim said.

'I won't if you pull your bloody finger out and try earning

your half,' Maggie retorted. She shook her head and wondered what had happened to their relationship over the years. For a long time they had been cohorts, each other's protector and friend, and then when she'd left for university they'd started to drift apart until they hardly talked, and when they did it was the kind of angry childish exchange they had never had as children.

She tried her best to concentrate purely on her meeting with Mr Shah at the bank and block everything else out of her head, but it seemed almost impossible. All the planning, all the work that needed to be done seemed like an irritating distraction from her real business, the business of getting Christian back. She constantly had to remind herself how important it was that she got everything right.

Then she realised it had been a week since she'd visited Louise and nothing had happened. There she was, trembling with fear over her deeply suspicious actions, and it had all come to nothing. She felt secretly embarrassed, relieved and distraught in turn. It might have been a terrible plan, but at that point it had been her only one. If Christian gave in to Louise's demands, then it meant he really had left Maggie behind; it meant she was out of his heart permanently.

To take her mind of it, and realising she had less than a week until her meeting with Mr Shah, she finally gave her business plan for The Fleur her full attention. Gradually, as she went over and over the figures and her presentation in her head, she began to realise she could make it work. She could make The Fleur into something exciting, new and, what's more, profitable. She'd started to feel a sense of purpose and control that she hadn't felt since . . . Maggie couldn't remember when. It was only a small beginning, but it was like a sort of anaesthetic, a way to numb the pain that had been unrelenting until that moment.

On Wednesday morning she realised, as she rifled through her suitcase, that she'd run out of clean underwear. She'd put a load on the day before but she'd forgotten to collect it and drape it over her windowsill to dry in the sun. She contemplated the prospect of clammy knickers and, after a morning in her pyjamas, set out commando-style to M&S to buy some more. A girl can never have too many knickers. She drifted through the rails of clothing, wondering if Louise had taken her advice at all and, if she had, wondering how Christian had reacted. She was picturing him sheltering Louise against his chest and stroking her hair, murmuring something along the lines of, 'Of course that wizened old hag means nothing to me! I shall never speak her name again!', and was just about to torture herself with the thought of them kissing when she caught sight of Pete, and just in time too. He'd been reducing the teenage assistant to a pool of liquid hormones.

'What *are* you doing?' she said to him. They had quite a laugh in M&S and, reluctant to go back to the dense heat of the pub and work, Maggie had thrown caution to the wind and asked him for a coffee. They were talking so much they walked right past two cafés and, rather than turn round, plumped for a drink in The Blacksmith's Arms instead.

'Still no news from Stella?' Maggie asked Pete as he sat next to her. She wanted him to be happy but was sort of glad that there was one other person in the universe as unjustly miserable as her.

Pete's shoulders dropped and his smile disappeared.

'Nope. And it's been ages now since she went. I mean, we're supposed to be getting married – you'd have thought she would have called or found time to email or something.' Pete frowned hard at the polished surface of the table. 'What does it mean, Maggie? Does it mean that everyone else is right and I'm a twat?' he looked up at her. 'I don't want to be a twat.'

Maggie gave him a sympathetic look.

'You're not a twat Pete. You're just in love. Stella's probably finding her feet, getting settled in. I'm sure she'll be in touch.'

Honestly, Maggie thought that she probably wouldn't be, but she liked Pete and she didn't want to add to the chorus of 'I told you so's' that everyone else in his life seemed to have contributed to. He commiserated with her about Christian, although she was too embarrassed to tell him about her meeting with Louise. There had been a moment when things had looked perilously maudlin, and then Maggie had told Pete a joke about a bloke and a panda in a pub. It wasn't a very good joke, but for some reason – maybe it was the way she blurted out the punchline first, maybe it was her terrible attempt at an accent and panda-style voice, or maybe it was because they were drinking in the middle of the day – but they hadn't been able to stop laughing. For at least five minutes they had both giggled like idiots, calming down just enough to catch each other's eyes and start off all over again. When they parted without either one suggesting that they meet again, they were both smiling. It had been a kind of a tonic.

By Thursday, Maggie was starting to feel a bit better. Still pathetic and incredibly needy, but better. More in control. She was sure the whole sorry Louise incident would just slip into the shadows, never to be thought of again except in those small dark hours of the night when she'd remember what she did and wince in shame. Really it was nothing more than a grander, supersized version of those dreadful chucked letters you sent to your ex that were three pages long and stained with tears. Embarrassing, but not actually fatal. So apart from that – oh, and the fact that Christian was never coming back and she'd never be happy again – everything was fine. But then, just as she felt she might be making some kind of slow progress out of a long nightmare, Louise called her mobile. It was Thursday evening.

'Carmen? Hi, it's me, Louise. Look, I hope you don't mind me calling you like this. It's not about work, but . . . Oh God, we've just had the hugest row and I couldn't think of anyone else to talk to!'

Louise didn't pause for breath and Maggie guessed it was because she knew if she stopped talking she'd start crying.

'I spent a whole week trying to pluck up the courage to talk to him about it and, well, he hadn't said a word about her for ages and I thought maybe I wouldn't have to. Then this afternoon he came into the office and started going on at me about this order I'd forgotten to chase up, and he just shouted right at me "Maggie would never have forgotten that". I couldn't stand it! I tried to explain to him how I felt about this Maggie, and how I couldn't stand him flinging her in my face all the time, you know, like you said to, and he just went off on one. He said I was clingy and too pushy. That I wanted too much too soon and that he was sick of women trying to pull pieces out of him. He just walked out on me, and, and . . .'

Louise stopped talking and started crying, and Maggie, her hidden agenda all but forgotten, wanted to reach out and hug her. She had the strangest sensation of déjà vu. That she was talking to herself, counselling herself on how to deal with Christian's mood swings, and then she realised that that was what she often did do. Almost every day that they were together she'd have to take herself off and give herself a good talking-to about how to say certain things or be a certain way, the certain way that would keep him happy, tender and loving. She was the official expert on how to handle him. She practically had letters after her name.

'OK, it's OK, babe. Calm down. Listen, he'll calm down, and when he does you can talk things through again. He hates people pushing him into corners so you'll need to let him have his space for a while. Let him come to you. Let him talk himself into thinking that he's in control. That way he doesn't feel bullied,' Maggie stopped herself from adding 'like he was at school' just in time. She snapped sharply back into her own head and tried to shake off the sensation that she'd just had an out-of-body experience.

There was a wet sniff and then a pause. 'How do you know all that stuff?' Louise asked inevitably.

Maggie stalled momentarily, and in that second fought her own private battle with good and evil. On a much smaller scale than, say, *Lord of the Rings*, but in its own way just as epic. Good triumphed, and she decided not to manipulate Louise any more. Nothing she could say and do now would make a difference anyway. She should have realised sooner. Christian would only do what he wanted to do. No one had ever made him do otherwise, not since the moment he'd left home; it was a promise he'd made to himself.

'Oh, because he's a man,' she said to Louise. 'All men are the same, aren't they? And anyway, like I said before, I had an ex just like him. Once.'

If Louise could detect the note of resignation in Maggie's voice she didn't mention it, and why would she? She didn't know that Maggie had more or less handed her one true love to her on a plate.

'Look, it would be great to have someone to talk to face to face – do you want to go out tomorrow night for a drink? Christian's got a business dinner, and if I could say I was doing something else it might make him feel I was a bit less dependent on him? Also it'd be really nice to have a good old girly chat. I really miss my friends. It's so hard to meet people in this city. All the men just want to shag you, and all the women ignore you.'

Maggie felt a pang of empathy for Louise and wondered about it for a second, but she knew she couldn't, that she had to pull herself out of the whole sorry mess as quickly as possible and try to put it behind her. Somehow the prospect of the several years of misery it would take to get over Christian was strangely liberating. She'd have The Fleur, she thought, and even if she was alone and childless for ever she'd have Becca and Sam. She could mother them when Sarah was busy at the salon and babysit their kids. In the moment that she gave up all hope, she found a comforting sort of vacuum instead. It was really a relief.

'I can't, Louise, I'm sorry. I'm leaving the country for a while to go to, er . . . Australia. Urgent business. I'll call you, though, when I get back, I promise,' Maggie lied, and said her goodbyes, adding on a silent apology.

She looked at her dormant phone and decided to call Sarah to tell her that she'd stopped being insane and decided to try and get on with her life instead. When the phone suddenly jumped into life in her hand, Maggie dropped it, answering it before she could look at the caller display.

'Mags?' it was Christian, his voice suddenly right there nestling in her ear. Although it had only been a week since she had last seen him, the whole world seemed like an entirely different place. To hear his voice again was an incredibly welcome rush of familiarity.

'Christian? Hello.' She tried to neutralise all nuance of meaning out of her voice. Her whole body was once again as taut as a string on a bow.

'You've been on the phone for bloody ages. Gossiping to Sarah, were you?'

Maggie sat down on her bed and took a deep breath. He sounded normal, he sounded as if he'd just called her on his way home from the office. He sounded like he was still her Christian.

'You know me,' she said, her voice holding an uncertain smile. 'Can't stop talking once I start.' This wasn't actually true, but Christian had always teased her about it and for some reason she'd never got round to correcting him. There were some sounds on the other end of the phone. Maggie thought she heard traffic, maybe, and the sound of other people walking by. Louise had said he'd stormed out. Maybe he was coming here! Maggie leapt up from her bed and went to the window, her heart thundering in her chest. The street below was empty, at least of Christian.

'Mags, listen,' Christian said, making her jump. 'Are you free tomorrow night? I know it's a bit of a cheek, but . . . I really need to see you, darling.'

Maggie clasped her phone with both hands, pressing it into the side of her face. Was this it? This couldn't be it, she wasn't ready, she hadn't prepared. Her chest tightened and she bit her lip hard until she could taste blood. After all of her dreaming and hoping and planning, now that the moment had come she found she was losing her nerve. 'Come on,' she told herself sternly. 'Don't blow this now. The rest of your life depends on you getting this right.'

She lay back on the bed and clasped the phone to her cheek as if it was a lover's hand, hoping to sound seductive and offhand all at once.

'Well, I did have something on, but they've just cancelled. So, yes,' she said simply. 'I'm free.' She heard Christian breathe out what might have been a sigh of relief.

'Good. Good. I'll meet you, OK, by the abbey at eight o'clock?'

'OK.' Maggie said. It was all she could say.

After he'd gone, Maggie lay on her bed and dreamt of being in his arms again, sure that by the end of Friday night she would be. And to think that she had been on the verge of giving up on it all. Everything was going to be fine now, everything was going to be all right. Christian was coming back to her.

Chapter Eighteen

Pete shut the front door behind him with a satisfying thud.

'*Carpe* bloody *diem* my arse,' he told the dust-laden plaster cherubs that garlanded each side of the hallway arch.

He'd tried his best today, he really had. He'd stood up there and talked about the day he knew he wanted to go into special effects more than anything in the world, more even than being a striker for Leeds FC. It was the day he was watching *Forty Million Years BC* on the telly; he was about eight. 'You'd laugh your socks off now,' he'd told them, 'if you saw it, but back then – well, it was revolutionary. And as a young bloke I couldn't imagine anything more exciting than making creatures I'd only ever seen in books come suddenly, amazingly to life. It seemed like . . . magic.'

He'd neglected to mention that actually Raquel Welch in a fur bikini had run a very close second to the T-Rex and populated his dreams fairly constantly for very many years afterwards.

'We're all about CGI and 3D animation now, but what will we be doing in twenty years' time, or thirty? That's what excites *me* and inspires *me*! I want to be part of that revolution. I want to create it, and you should too, otherwise you're just wasting your time here!'

As Pete stood in front of the students, his hands on his hips,

155

he'd scanned each one of their faces for something – anything – that he might be able to take a spark of hope from. But it had looked to him as if they were all a bit hungover, and one of them very possibly had the plague, or at least a very messy case of flu.

'So, er, Pete.' Charlie, maybe the only halfway decent one there, had piped up. 'How do you think you contributed to the revolution on Dougie the Digger then?' The rest of the class had sniggered. Pete's hands fell to his sides and his shoulders slumped; then he thought for a moment. In ten years on Dougie, actually, he *had* seen a lot of changes. He'd even implemented a few. Maybe it wasn't all Final Flipping Fantasy and Keanu Reeves in a catsuit or whatever, but it was still revolutionary in its way.

'I'm glad you asked me that, Charlie,' Pete had begun, and he hadn't stopped for another two hours and forty-two minutes. He was fairly sure that none of them were very inspired by his lecture, and by the end some of them were even catatonic, but at least he'd got through the afternoon in one piece, and at the very least it had clarified his own feelings. He had to get this job at Magic Shop, he *had* to. It was his life's dream and it *did* excite him – just the thought of it invigorated him in the same way a clear night sky and the Milky Way did, or Stella's slender finger unbuttoning her jeans. Although a very small, nearly silent part of him was quietly glad that Stella wasn't there to distract him this time. He felt he had an almost clear head at last.

'Does anybody fancy a pint?' Pete called out to the house at large.

He waited for any kind of reply and decided that Ange and Falc must both be out. Then a small noise, like a strangulated whine, rose unmistakably from Angie's room. 'Oh fuck, they're shagging.' Pete looked resentfully at the door. He was an easygoing bloke; he didn't care who shagged who or when as a rule, but for some reason on this summer evening he'd really rather that the rest of world were as celibate as he was. He had a flash of memory – Stella's breasts crushed against him, her nails on his back, her teeth pulling at the skin on his neck – and felt desire surge though him like an electrical current. Pete began walking rather stiffly up the stairs.

'Pete, is that you?' It was Angie. Her voice seemed muffled and damp. He stopped on the third stair and looked back at her bedroom door. She knew it was him, so he couldn't really sneak away upstairs and do what he'd been planning to do. He tucked his hand inside his waistband and adjusted himself into a marginally less obscene position before replying.

'Yeah, it's me. You all right?' Pete said, knowing already what the reply would be. Girls in the middle of passionate sex didn't stop to enquire on the obvious identity of house mates. Girls crying their eyes out did, though. The door opened and Angie emerged, her round face further swollen and red with tears.

'Oh, Pete.' Angie held out her arms to him in an alarmingly disarming plea to be hugged. 'I just don't know what I'm going to do. What am I going to do?'

Pete took Angie in his arms and held her as she sobbed noisily against his chest for several minutes, until at last she was able to lead him back into her room. He tried not to notice the damp patch that had formed just below his right shoulder, and fortunately at the sight of Angie in tears his hard-on had dwindled almost instantly. She sat on the bed and looked at him miserably. After a moment's consideration Pete sat next to her, caught somewhere between being genuinely worried for her and feeling like a condemned man.

'Can't you tell me what it is?' he said eventually, handing Angie some bog roll he found lying by the side of the bed. She took it gratefully and blew her nose loudly, balling up the damp tissue in her fists.

'It's Falcon. Or rather, it's me.' She shook her head,

157

genuinely bemused. 'When we're together we have such a good time, a really great time. The sex is . . . incredible, and I don't think it's just great for me. And most of the time I'm OK with the way things are. It's not as if I see myself marrying him or anything, it's just that sometimes I want more. I don't even know if I want more with him. It's just sometimes I wish I had that kind of intimacy you must have with Stella, that kind of trust.'

Pete didn't tell her that he wished he had that kind of relationship with Stella too.

'And then I start feeling miserable,' Angie continued, 'and I start crying and I just wish I didn't care, like I'm supposed to. Like Falcon thinks I don't.' She looked up at Pete. 'I don't even know why I'm crying. I'm fairly sure I don't love him.' Her expression changed. 'You're in love, you must know all about it. What's wrong with me?'

And in that moment Pete considered death row an appealing alternative to the hot seat he was in right then. He thought for a moment and then decided just to start talking and hope something reasonable would eventually come out.

'Maybe, if you're not enjoying it, you should just stop?' he suggested half-heartedly. But he knew better than anyone that stopping something you didn't enjoy but seemed to need was easier said than done.

'Well, yes,' Angie nodded, 'yes, I did think of that, but then I wouldn't have anyone or anything, would I? And I think Falcon cares about me, otherwise why would he sleep with me?'

Pete avoided her eyes and looked at his hands. He couldn't tell Angie the truth that blokes like sex more than most things – OK, anything – and that getting it was usually preferable to not, particularly if there was supposedly a guaranteed absence of emotional aftermath. Even Pete, who would never cheat on Stella, had struggled recently with all the women in their strappy tops and short skirts. With their tanned legs and cleavages. Pete had found his thoughts straying from Stella. In his heart of hearts he knew that part of her final quest to make sure that he was the man she should marry would involve her sleeping with someone else, maybe more than one person. But he couldn't reciprocate. To him the thought of having a meaningless shag while he was marking time waiting for her return would demean everything he felt for her. Well, maybe not the *thought* of a meaningless shag, but he definitely wouldn't actually *do* it. After Candi there had been no one else, not even during their many relationship breaks, and he accepted the double standards that applied to them. He couldn't risk making Stella that angry again. He might lose her for ever.

'Angie.' Pete put his arm around her and patted her bare shoulder awkwardly. 'I'm sure Falcon cares about you. In fact, I know he does. But you're not happy with this "arrangement", are you?' He squeezed her shoulder. 'So perhaps you should just tell Falcon "mates only" and get on with your life, find someone who deserves you.'

He felt slightly hypocritical, but you couldn't compare him and Stella to Angie and Falcon. For starters, with him and Stella it was more than just a one-sided fling. Theirs was a grand passion, it was his destiny. And secondly he *had* won her over in the end, despite what everyone else had said. She *had* told him that she loved him, even if it was just before she left. They had a commitment between them now, and he had faith in it, even though sometimes it was difficult. Angie, on the other hand, was wasting her time treading water, too scared to move on from the familiar even if it didn't make her happy. Any fool could see that.

'Listen, Ange, Falcon's a mate of mine. He's a good bloke and that, and I don't think he really thinks about what he's doing to you. If you like, I'll have a chat to him about it. But look, you're

159

a lovely woman. A good-looking, funny and, um, sexy woman and there are loads of blokes out there who'd die to get close to you. You just have to open your eyes and see them.' Angie wiped the back of her hand roughly across her nose, leaving a faintly glistening trail along the top lip. Pete hoped she wouldn't want to kiss him.

'You're such a lovely man, Pete,' she said, laying her head on his shoulder instead. 'Your fiancée is so lucky to have you. If I was her I just wouldn't be able to leave you for a whole year! She must be very dedicated to her career.' Pete saw no point in correcting Angie and telling her that actually Stella had never had a proper job, let alone a career. Instead he took the opportunity to get up off the bed.

'Listen, how about you fix yourself up a bit and you and me go out for a meal? We could get a curry down the road and then walk into town have a couple of pints? What do you say?'

Angie's smile broadened. 'You don't have to spend your Friday night with me, you know,' she said coyly.

Pete shrugged and smiled, because on the one hand the only other people he knew were Maggie and Falcon. Falcon was already out, and he realised with surprise that he had no idea how to get hold of Maggie, which was strange because it felt like they were properly friends by now. On the other hand, he realised that he actually really did like Angie's company. She was flaky and sometimes a bit overly bouncy, but she was a good laugh.

'Don't be mad,' he told her. 'I'll go upstairs and check my emails while you get ready, all right?'

Angie nodded gratefully and began picking up scattered items of make-up from her bedroom floor. 'Oh, Pete?' she said just as Pete got to the door. 'Can we go to The Fleur after? For a drink?'

Pete stopped and looked at her.

'We can, but you know Falcon will probably be there.'

Angie shrugged and looked apologetic. 'I know,' she said, 'and I know you're right about the moving on thing. I'm just not ready yet.'

And Pete couldn't argue with that.

As he reached his bedroom, Pete looked at his PC sitting there innocently in the corner. He switched it on and waited for his Internet connection without much hope; it was more a formality than anything. So when he saw her name in his in-box he had to check it twice and blink hard to make sure it wasn't his imagination. He looked at the email heading. 'Hi!' it said brightly, nonchalantly, like he hadn't been waiting every second since he'd last seen her for this moment. He opened it up and scanned the brief paragraph quickly before taking in the details. For starters it wasn't just addressed to him. There were maybe eight other recipients – Stella's long-suffering mum, a few of her friends and some names he didn't recognise. He tried to stop his heart from sinking. At least she'd included him on the list, third after her mum and best friend Sunil. That was practically top.

Dear All

    Sorry it's taken me so long to get in touch. Well, I am finally settled in Melbourne and it's been a crazy non-stop party. It's a great city, much more chic and cosmopolitan than I expected. Very trendy. I have a job in a French café and I am living over the top of it with a couple of really fun guys which is great because I've met a lot of people but better than that I've got the chance of some extra work coming up! I've met some great people and I love it out here. Will be in touch again soon.

    Miss you all,

    Sx

Pete reread her generic gesture of affection again and again. There was nothing there, no special message for him, no PS. She would have had the opportunity to write another email to him when she sent this, even two lines. But she hadn't. He closed the mail and then opened it again and double-clicked on her name. The address that came up was one he'd been sending his messages to. So she definitely did have his emails. He closed her letter again and disconnected from the Internet. After a while his PC screen saver came on, the endless wheeling field of stars speeding him recklessly into cyberspace. On the bright side, she hadn't mentioned anyone in particular, not even her mum. She hadn't specified whether 'guys' was just Aussie slang for 'mates' guys or actual men–type guys. 'She said she misses us all, which means that she misses me. She does miss me,' Pete told his telescope as he switched off his PC. The telescope had remained shrouded since the moment he'd moved in here. For some reason he hadn't been able to look at the stars, knowing that somewhere far away Stella was under them too, maybe looking up at them while someone else kissed her neck.

'Who does?' Angie stood in the doorway, her hair brushed, her face made up and her mirror-sequinned bag tucked under her arm. 'Are you ready?'

Pete glanced back at the now blank PC, which still crackled faintly with static.

'I've been ready for ages,' he said.

162

Chapter Nineteen

Christian was late, but it didn't matter. It was a perfect evening, the perfect end to a perfect day. The heat of the unremitting sun was still strong enough to warm Maggie's bare arms, and it dappled the wood of the ancient abbey door, casting and recasting it in molten amber. Maggie felt a moment of pure and perfect contentment.

Everything had gone well at the bank today – better, even, than she had thought it could.

Mr Shah had explained to her that he was doing them a special favour sorting things out at branch level, because they'd all known each other for so long. Apparently, as a young man he'd even spent a weekend with them at some rock festival back in 1970. Maggie suppressed a smile at the thought of the suited and slick Mr Shah in hippy gear, dropping out and tuning in or whatever it was they did in those days.

'These days it's all head office and call centres,' he told them. 'The last thing you need is some eighteen-year-old stranger sorting out your finances. We go back a long way, and I wanted to help you all that I could.'

Maggie smiled her gratitude, and, handing out the copies of her plans, launched the presentation. It had taken maybe half an hour for her to go through her ideas, her cash flow plans, her graphs and her charts. At the end Mr Shah leaned back in his chair and laced his long fingers behind his head.

'Well, Miss Johnson, what can I say? You propose to clear your debts with the bank and most of your creditors in one fell swoop. And you want to use your own capital to invest in the pub; I can't argue with that. As far as this bank is concerned, you are well and truly off the hook.'

Maggie nodded and bit her lip. 'I know, Mr Shah, but even this money won't fully refurb the pub, and it will be a good while, years maybe, until we make a return on that. I'm showing you this now so you can see how serious we are and how prepared we are. If phase one goes according to plan, then in due course I will need help in funding phase two and eventually phase three. If the terms are right, I could be giving you that business, Mr Shah.' Maggie had been practising that particular line all the way to the bank. She thought she'd pulled it off pretty well.

Mr Shah glanced down at her presentation again. 'Well, Maggie, come back to me in a year and we'll talk – I'm sure we'll do everything we can to keep your business here. In the meantime, I must say you have impressed me very much.' He looked at Keith. 'You're a credit to your father,' he said.

The moment they got out of the bank, Maggie and her parents hugged each other tightly.

'Maggie,' Marion said, 'I didn't know you could talk like that, that you knew all that stuff. You were fantastic!'

Maggie looked at her mum and realised that her mother hardly ever praised her directly. She flushed with pleasure and felt an unexpected rush of affection for her.

'Really? You thought so?' she asked. Her mum nodded and hooked her arm through Keith's.

'Well, darling,' she said, looking up at him. 'We've officially retired. Now all we have to do is make sure we keep your blood pressure down and enjoy the rest of our lives. What do you want to do?'

164

Maggie looked at her dad's face. The relief that the burden of The Fleur was no longer his was clearly visible, which made her feel kind of good about her selflessness.

'I want to be with you every hour of every day for the rest of my life,' he told Marion, and he kissed her right there, tongues and everything, in the middle of the road. Maggie studied the pavement with fascination for the best part of a minute. Finally she couldn't stand it any longer.

'Mum! Dad! Remember the blood pressure!' Her parents broke apart and giggled like a couple of kids. 'Sorry, Maggie,' Marion said. 'Let's go back and tell Sheila the good news, and we can open a bottle of champagne – what do you think?'

'Have we go a bottle of champagne?' Keith asked her.

Maggie looked at her watch. It was just after three. She handed her dad twenty-five quid.

'Go and buy one, but, um, I have to go out right now, over to Sarah's, and then I have this meeting tonight . . . with a prospective supplier. I really have to go. You lot celebrate without me, OK though? I'll see you later.'

Maggie kissed her parents and walked away quickly, hoping to avoid any further questions. She didn't know why she hadn't told them about Christian. Maybe because she didn't want to worry them, or maybe because she didn't want them prying. Or probably because she wanted to keep the secret of their meeting to herself for a few delicious moments longer.

The thrill of anticipation she felt whenever she thought about seeing Christian again face to face was more exciting than anything she had felt before. Better than any first date feeling she'd ever had, and better even than her first kiss with Christian. Because this time all the excitement and newness was mixed up with how perfect she knew they were together. How tender, romantic and passionate Christian could be, or at least had been

165

back in the early days before things all got a bit 'routine'. There'd be no bumping of noses or the uncertain exploration of clumsy fingers. Each one of them knew the other's body perfectly, and that, combined with the intense emotional experience of being back with him again, would be the most incredible thing Maggie had ever felt. Maybe this whole interlude really was for the best. Maybe it was just what they had needed to kick-start a relationship that might have been becoming ever so slightly stale. It was like having the best of both worlds after enduring the very worst.

Maggie was glowing as she walked into the Sharp End. She waltzed up to Sarah, whose head was bent over her appointments book.

'Ms Johnson for her three-thirty appointment,' Maggie said primly.

Sarah looked up and eyed her. 'It's all sorted at the bank? You're in charge of The Fleur?'

Maggie nodded and the friends squealed with delight as they hugged each other over the counter.

'Oh God.' Becca emerged from the flat door and looked at her mum and godmother. 'I wish you two would stop trying to be young. It's *so* embarrassing. I'm going to Leanne's, Mum. Don't forget I'm staying over.' She waltzed to the door, waving her fingers over her shoulders as a farewell.

'I'm phoning Leanne's mum to check!' Sarah called after her, her anxiety manifesting as suspicion.

'What*ever*.' Becca slammed the door shut, leaving the shop bell jangling in her wake. Sarah gave a little sigh and returned her attention to Maggie.

'So is this what the trim and blow-dry is in aid of? You want to look all sleek for your first night as manager?' Sarah's eyes sparkled. 'Hey, Sam's at his dad's, you know. They're off at some ungodly hour of the morning to Alton Towers for the day. We could really celebrate tonight, push the boat out! What do you say? A few bars, a couple of clubs?'

Maggie looked at her friend. 'I can't, Sarah.' She paused for a heartbeat. 'I'm seeing Christian tonight. He phoned yesterday and said he absolutely has to see me.' Maggie give a shiver of delight. 'He wants me back, Sarah, I know he does. I heard it in his voice as clear as day.'

Sarah's expression didn't change, exactly, it just froze into a grim parody of her delighted grin.

'How do you know that?' she asked carefully. 'Maybe he just wants to talk about your settlement, or something to do with the business.'

Maggie shook her head. 'I *know*. He's had an argument with Louise, over me! And as soon as he walked out on her, he phoned me! He misses me! Sarah, he's beginning to realise that he needs me.'

Sarah banged shut her appointment book with a sharp snap and came out from behind the counter, pointing Maggie towards her chair.

'And he told you all this, Christian did? In those words?'

Maggie was about to say 'no' when she realised that she didn't really want to tell Sarah about the whole Louise debacle, even if it had paid off in the end.

'Yes, he did. He told me that,' she said instead, avoiding Sarah's eye in the mirror. Sarah separated out two strands on Maggie's hair on either side of her centre parting and smoothed them down against her jawline.

'You don't really need a cut, it's only just been done. When Luce has finished with Mrs Ellis I'll get her to wash it and then dry it lovely and straight, OK? I've got an army of Friday-nighters due in soon, all hoping six tons of hairspray is going to get them their man.'

Maggie nodded her assent, and Sarah examined her closely.

167

'Well, if he said that then yeah, it sounds like he does want you back,' she conceded. 'But Mags, are you sure you want *him* back?'

Maggie looked up at her crazy friend. 'Are you kidding? Of *course* I want him back, I love him!' A momentary hush fell over the salon, and Jackie, Luce, Mrs Ellis and Karen, the part-time manicurist all looked in their direction. 'I love him,' Maggie repeated, lowering her voice. 'This is what I've been waiting for, working for.'

Sarah leaned a little lower over Maggie's shoulder.

'But Mags are you sure? I mean, you're on the brink of getting your own business off the ground, and it's more or less been handed to you on a plate.' Sarah thought of her long and debt-ridden struggle to get The Sharp End open and the seemingly endless battle to keep it open. 'What if he wants you to go back and run Fresh Talent for him? He must realise how good you were at your job?'

Maggie shook her head. 'No, I've already thought about that. I think it was the working together thing that hurt us in the first place. He needs to see me as a separate entity. An independent person who can succeed without him. I was talking it over with Pete —'

'Pete? The engaged man from the other night?' Sarah interrupted her, wondering how he'd cropped up again.

Maggie nodded impatiently.

'Yes, I met him buying a blouse in M&S and we went for a drink. He's a nice bloke, that woman doesn't deserve him, but *anyway* we worked out that I was too clingy and needy before, which was funny, because Pete said he wished Stella would show that she needed him sometimes. So anyhow, this time I have to show him I can make it on my own if I want to hold on to him for ever and make sure he never leaves my side again.'

Sarah's brows furrowed deeply.

'I know I was in labour for the English A level exam, but isn't that a, you know, an oxy-thingy, that thing that means the opposite of what you're saying?' She shook her head irritably. 'Isn't that total bollocks? Don't forget you're talking about a man who seduced his new girlfriend right under your nose. How *could* you trust him again, let alone want to?'

Maggie thought for a moment.

'Because, well, the first time around, trusting him was the biggest mistake I made. I let myself grow complacent. I made the assumption he'd never look elsewhere. This time, though, I'll be on my toes. I'll know how to keep him interested.'

Sarah shook her head again and threw in some eye rolling for good measure.

'Mate, you sound like you're signing up for a lifetime of hard labour! What with being a hard-headed glamorous business-woman, not to mention having to monitor your boyfriend's interest in your relationship full-time, you'll be a burnt-out wreck inside a year. That doesn't sound like blissed-out love to me.'

Sarah put her hands on Maggie's shoulders.

'I know I don't know much about long-term relationships, but I do know they should be all about being able to trust someone. Being sure and certain of how they feel for you. Not walking a constant high wire of emotional terror. Sarah grinned. 'I should sack hairdressing and take up hosting daytime chat shows – I'm good at this.'

Ignoring her, Maggie stretched out her fingers and examined her bare nails.

'Could Karen do me a French manicure, do you think?' she asked, suddenly picturing her fingers raking down Christian's back. She blinked the thought away and suppressed a lustful smile.

Sarah, glancing over at Karen, nodded. 'I expect so,' she said.

She was worried about Karen. She liked the girl, and she thought the three days a week she came in for were good for the salon – for starters it meant she could call it a salon and not just a hairdressers – but her books where hardly weighed down with clients, and Sarah wasn't sure if she could really afford her.

'Let me just see him, Sarah.' Maggie broke her train of thought. 'Maybe after tonight it will be like you said. Maybe when I've seen him I won't want to see him any more.' Maggie thought of touching Christian's skin again, and her heart took a double loop around her ribcage. 'But relationships take work, and I'm prepared to work at this one. It's hard to just wipe away six years of my life in one clean sweep. All that time together wasted, and for what? Because I couldn't be fussed to try a bit harder? I love him, Sarah, and that's all there is to it. And he loves me, I know he does.'

Maggie looked at her own reflection, a picture of absolute certainty.

'I'll never love anyone else.'

Sarah had been exchanging 'God, I knows!' with Leanne's mum when Luce had finished her hair, and wanting to avoid any more 'advice,' Maggie had slipped out of the shop, leaving her cash on the counter. Sarah always insisted that her friend never pay, and Maggie always did; after all, the first rule of small business was never give freebies to friends and family. If only her parents had abided by that one.

She had two hours to kill – two hours of trying not to get all hot and sweaty, not to mess up her hair or rub her eyes. She walked towards the abbey slowly, carefully, across the small city taking its narrow back streets and high-terraced pavements, hoping to avoid meeting anyone she knew. Although St Albans Abbey had earned the town its city status, it was a remarkably insular place, and Maggie knew far more people than most. But if she talked to anyone now she risked wearing off her lipstick. And she wanted some time to prepare – to think and be quiet.

As she trailed down the gently sloping, curved streets of the old town, she looked in through the small-paned windows of the cottages that crowded the pavement. Two hundred, maybe three hundred years old some of them, especially here, clustered around the abbey. Maggie caught glimpses of dark polished tables, a bowl of fatly overblown roses scattering their petals on a windowsill cluttered with antiques. She heard people's dogs barking and children shouting down stairs.

It was all these small, ancient slices of English life that she had longed for as a little girl, that she had dreamt of. Her life back here hadn't been exactly what she had imagined it would be, but it had been better than it was, at least. Her mum hadn't had her hair bobbed and joined the WI, but at least Maggie knew where she was most of the time. Nor had her dad bought two suits and gone to work every morning on the train, but at least he had created some order and routine in their lives, even if it did always revolve around last orders and no one ever sent her or her brother to bed.

Her childhood had still been fairly chaotic: Jim and her packed off to school with unironed shirts and a pound note each instead of a lunch box. When they got in, it'd be either her mum or Sheila waiting for them in the kitchen with two sandwiches on a plate and a can of fizzy pop bursting with E numbers. Gradually she'd found herself hoping it would be Sheila, with her tales of a wartime childhood and her no-nonsense take on life. Her mum would ask them about their day, but while Jim chattered on about painting or PE, somehow, for some reason, Maggie would clam up into a tightly balled little fist of silent fury. Her mother made her furious. She never really knew why, except that she just wished her mum was less of a person, all kooky and original, and more of just, well a mum.

171

When Christian had first kissed her on her third week of working for him, part of her, the only part that wasn't singing with joy, thought, 'Well, about bloody time. Finally I've got someone in my life who can take me out of this disjointed craziness, who can make me normal, who can make me happy.'

During her three years at university, before Christian, she had found the space to create a little order for herself and to shape the person she wanted to be out of still raw material. She'd discovered that she loved organising, arranging and creating success out of nothing. She was a meticulous planner and seemed to be able to generate ideas amongst her fellow students; she felt in control and fulfilled. But after she'd graduated she'd had no choice but to return to The Fleur, for a while at least. And she'd found she resented its freestyle oppression even more. Her relationship with her mother had disintegrated into Marion's passing flurries of attention and Maggie's steadfast rebuttals. She got her own studio flat as soon as she could, and worked her way through a variety of jobs, none of them offering the challenge and opportunities she wanted.

Then Christian gave her a position and her whole world opened up into a beautiful vista full of possibilities. She'd moved into his flat at his first invitation, eagerly, almost greedily. She thought that after a year or two they might find a cottage with wisteria climbing over its windows. There might be children. She might give up Fresh Talent then and stay home with them. She might bake. Six years later she had still been waiting; they had still been talking about it as some distant future they would one day amble into together, and Maggie had always been certain that it would come one day. Now she had the pub, the cottage and the children and the wisteria were further away from her than ever, but she could still have the promise of a future, she could still have her heart intact if she only had

172

Christian. He was really all that she needed – all her other dreams could just melt away.

Maggie glanced at her watch: she still had half an hour to wait. She wondered what Christian was doing right now, if he was shaving or picking out a shirt. If he was making excuses to Louise or practising what he was going to say to Maggie. She walked into the abbey grounds, and although it was getting on for eight the light was still bright and the heat still strong enough to penetrate the cloth of her dress and prickle her skin as she walked up the abbey steps. The cool dark interior of the immense building was very welcome. Inside the choir was singing and there was a service going on. A small collection of people had congregated and were singing, almost silently, in unison with the choir.

Maggie walked quietly along the right-hand aisle and past the main service to the Lady chapel at the back of the abbey. One other woman sat on the last row of wooden chairs, her head bent, her closed fingers pressed to her forehead, her lips moving silently. Maggie sat gingerly on the end of a row and looked up at the high, vaulted ceiling, and let the coloured light dazzle her.

She had been confirmed here, in the mid–eighties, in a boxy white suit with black plastic buttons from Etam. She had told her mum she wanted to be confirmed like Sarah, and her mum had told her it was up to her how she wanted to connect with her inner spirit, but that she'd probably need to get christened first, because she was fairly sure it was a prerequisite. Maggie had been mortified and ashamed. It had never occurred to her that she hadn't been christened. Everyone was christened, surely? Sarah's mum even had a picture of Sarah's christening framed on the wall in her hallway.

Sarah and at least three others in her class were starting the confirmation classes that term, and Maggie really wanted to be the same as them. Sarah, who couldn't stand the thought of it,

173

had earnestly begged Maggie to wag it with her in the park instead, but as Maggie had pointed out, her mum was bound to find out if they did. And if she found out, Sarah would be dead. Besides, Maggie had wanted to be confirmed. She wasn't sure it was because she believed in God; in actual fact the idea had terrified her. But she liked the idea of being confirmed in its most literal sense. She wanted someone important and good resting his hands on her head and telling everyone, even God, if he existed, that she was *really* there. That she was *real* and that she *mattered*. In the end she'd arranged her christening herself, and it took place quietly at the end of the regular Sunday service, with just her parents. Sheila and Sarah there to watch her.

When finally the day of the confirmation had arrived, in those few brief moments kneeling alongside Sarah Maggie had felt special, had felt at home and at peace. Twenty years later, and still the abbey was somewhere she could go, somewhere she felt at home. She closed her eyes and dropped her head a little and listened to the sounds of the choir echo in the vaulted ceiling. She closed her eyes and waited.

Christian was late. But it didn't matter.

Chapter Twenty

'Maggie.'

His voice rich beside her made her jump out of her reverie. Ten minutes before, she had re-emerged on to the abbey steps and had become gradually lost in her thoughts and her day-dreams. Now he was here in the flesh and for real, Maggie found she could not look him in the eye. 'God, you look fantastic!' he told her, and she dipped her head instinctively as he bent to kiss her cheek, forcing his mouth to graze her hair. As if sensing her discomfort, he took both her hands in his and turned her to face him.

'Look at me, Mags,' he commanded softly.

Gradually Maggie allowed herself to look into his face once more, her breath catching and her heart pounding.

'Oh, Maggie,' Christian breathed, his eyes roaming the length of her body before returning to meet her eyes. 'It's *so* good to see you. I've missed you, you know. So much.'

Maggie smiled. 'Me too,' she managed to say.

Christian's smile broke into a grin and, dropping one of her hands, he began to lead her briskly through the back of the abbey grounds and out into the centre of the town.

'Come on, I've booked us into Luigi's. I called him earlier, he's going to cook for us off menu. He's got in new season asparagus and some French truffles – it's going to be fantastic.'

Maggie followed him, her hand securely slotted into his familiar grip. For a moment the world around swam with dizzying lights and she felt as if Christian were leading her into thin air. She took a deep breath and followed him anyway. After all, this was what she wanted more than anything – whatever it took.

Maggie's head swam with Pinot Grigio, and as another mouthful of dark chocolate torte melted in her mouth, she felt that all the anguish of her separation from Christian had been worth it for this perfect moment of bliss. He was so attentive, so sweet, so kind. He made her feel like she was completely precious to him, priceless. His hand covered hers and she smiled back at him.

'I always did love the fact that you ate what you wanted and didn't stress out about a bit of cake or chocolate – it's so sexy,' he grinned, leaning in a little closer. 'Lou is always at the gym and *always* stressing out about calories. Apparently fat runs in her family. I mean, she looks fantastic, but it can wear you down after a while.'

He smiled as he spoke about Louise for the first time that evening, and Maggie squirmed uncomfortably in her chair, unsure if it was her betrayal of her fake friend or Christian's obvious fondness for her that made her feel uncomfortable. She'd almost forgotten all about Louise, sitting at home on her own, with no friends nearby and about to have no boyfriend. Maggie took another draught of wine and put Louise out of her mind.

'So, are you seeing anyone?' Christian asked her. His eyes crinkled a little around the edges as if he thought the idea of Maggie seeing someone was faintly amusing.

'Well,' Maggie said, determined to prove him wrong. 'Declan Brady asked me out a few times, but I, well, I didn't really want to see anyone else but you.' At the last minute her resolve crumbled away. She smiled weakly, the distress of the last few weeks reflected clearly in the sheer black of her eyes.

'Oh Maggie.' Christian squeezed her hand. 'I'm sorry for what I've put us through. I really am.' He paused and withdrew his hand from hers. 'I like Louise, you know, she's a great girl. Lots of fun and very warm, but she's . . . well, she's not you, Maggie. She hasn't got your class, and sometimes I wonder if she's not a bit too frail for the world.' Christian grimaced.

Maggie wanted to be pleased, but actually she felt that he was being a little too tough on Louise. She'd seemed like the epitome of class to Maggie, and as together as anyone was in these days when falling apart was practically obligatory.

'It's funny,' Christian continued, 'but when we were together I felt like our relationship was suffocating me. Now, when I look back on what we had, I realise exactly how much you meant to me and to Fresh Talent. It was you who allowed me to breathe and to grow. I miss that, and it's been hard adjusting to life without you.'

Maggie opened her mouth to speak just as Christian reached into his top pocket. He pulled out a long cream envelope. Maggie closed her mouth again, feeling an unbidden sense of foreboding.

'Anyway, here's your cheque. There's a rumour going around that you're going to take on The Fleur. Good luck! You'll need it!'

He laughed as he slid the envelope across the table to Maggie. Her finger withdrew from it as if it was red hot, and she stared at it, a cold horror creeping up her spine.

'But surely now that we're . . . I mean, this was when we were splitting up. I mean, it would come in handy, sure, but you don't need to give this to me now, not now that —'

Christian cut across her. 'Luigi, the bill please, maestro!' he called out with his usual theatrical embellishment. He turned to Maggie, his tone gentle but firm.

'Now look, no one is more pleased than I am that we can sit across a table from one another and talk like old times. I think the thing I've missed about you most, Maggie, is your friendship. To have that back is really precious to me, really special. Lou's got a lot going for her, but conversation isn't really one of them, if you know what I mean.'

His grin was less than subtle and Maggie felt every muscle and tendon in her body freeze with fear, her mind racing to catch up with the words that Christian was saying. Suddenly the whole world had been turned on its head, and this was all wrong, like a scene from *Alice in Wonderland*. Her world was shrinking all around her into a single point of nothing. She had followed Christian off the precipice and he had failed to catch her.

'If I could get you back on board at Fresh Talent I would, but I don't really think it's fair on Lou – she's already so intimidated by you. And besides, it's about time you had a crack at your own business. God knows I trained you long enough! And even if we are friends now, Mags, even if we can put all of that stuff behind us, you still deserve the money. You put a lot into that business over the years. The best employee I've ever had by far.'

Luigi arrived, and Christian tucked his credit card into the bill with a wink. 'This one's on me,' he finished.

Maggie forced herself to move, forced her brain to fire up her muscles and nerve endings and her lungs to breathe again. Even as every part of her rational self screamed that she should keep her mouth shut, her heart got her tongue working, with only partial success.

'But I thought all this was . . . I mean, when you wanted to see me. I thought it was because . . . you said you missed me?'

Christian looked at her. 'I do, I do miss you. Louise drives me up the bloody wall sometimes with her incessant chattering,

178

she's so jealous of you – it's like she can't accept that you and I are in the past! I do miss you, Maggie, but . . .'

He stopped mid-sentence, a look of horror washing the colour out of his face.

'Oh Christ, you thought that I wanted to . . . that we were going to . . . Oh fuck. Oh Maggie. I'm sorry, I'm so sorry. I never meant you to think that! God, I'm so crass. I'm an idiot. I was just so pleased to see you, so pleased we were getting past the split and you were going to be OK. And . . . Oh Maggie, I'm sorry. I don't want us to get back together.'

Maggie pushed back her chair and rose from the table.

'I know,' she said stiffly. 'Of course I know. Now if you'll excuse me . . . Thank you for the meal.'

Leaving the cheque on the table, she stumbled towards the door, the deliciously drunk feeling she had felt only minutes earlier now a painful hindrance to her exit.

'Baby!' she heard Christian call out after her. She ignored him, and after weaving her way though the closely-packed curious diners, she finally made her way out on to the street. Christian was at her side almost immediately, his eyes blazing with some kind of emotion that Maggie could only guess at. He caught her by the shoulder and stared down at her.

'Maggie, please . . . Don't be like this, please,' he said. 'If you only knew how hard it is for me to sit across a table from you and not be able to . . .'

Maggie took a confrontational step closer to him, her mouth set in an angry line.

'And not be able to what? Humiliate and embarrass and hurt me any more?'

The anger that she realised had been waiting to ignite ever since the morning he had first told her bubbled up in her chest like red-hot lava.

'When will it be enough for you, Christian? When will you

179

have finished hurting me? You can't have both. You can't have me as your "little friend", looking on benignly as you rebuild your life, our life, without me. It doesn't work that way!'

Maggie was breathing hard, her finger pointing sharply at the centre of Christian's chest. This wasn't how it was supposed to be. She was supposed to be easygoing and charming, not some bitter harridan out for her pound of flesh. She shook her head and took a step back.

'Oh God . . . I'm sorry,' she said, but as she turned away from him he grabbed her arm hard and pulled her close into his chest. Maggie shook her head.

'Maggie, it's me that's sorry. I never meant to make this worse for you, I was trying to make it better. If you only knew how much I wanted to kiss you all through that meal . . . but . . .'

Maggie pulled away from him, trying to resist the urge to collapse right there in his arms and weep. 'Please, I just need to go,' she said, but she couldn't move.

Christian shook his head. 'Maybe I'm crazy, I don't know. I look at you, Maggie, and I want you, I still want you so much, and I think about you all the time . . . but I just don't think we can work together any more, I don't think that we can. I don't think I'm good for you – you deserve more than me, but . . .'

Without warning, he crushed his lips against hers and kissed her hard, and her body gradually melted under his touching, melding into his hard, metallic passion. Aeons might have passed in those few seconds, and for the first time since he'd left her, Maggie felt at home. When they parted at last, Maggie felt as if all the air had been sucked out of her, and she was numb, spinning gratefully in a vacuum.

'To be honest, Maggie,' his voice was hoarse, 'I just don't know what I think. I don't know, and because I don't know . . . I need some time. To think about all of this and the way you make me feel, and how I feel about Lou. Is that terrible? To treat you like this? I don't mean to, you know. I really don't. It's just that whenever I think I'm in control I look at you and . . .'

Christian shook his head, and Maggie detached herself from his embrace by sheer force of will. As she stepped back he handed her the cheque, and this time she took it. There was something here, a chance – a faint hope glimmering in the dark confusion of her mind. Whatever happened she mustn't blow it, because she was certain she would not get another. She composed herself and measured each word before she spoke it.

'Obviously,' she said carefully, 'there's a lot of chemistry between us still. But I think you're right Christian – for now at least we need to keep it just friends. We need space to discover what our real feelings are.'

Of course in her head she was replacing 'our' and 'we' with 'you' and 'your', but it was important she put some small doubt in Christian's mind about how she felt about him. Right now she was just too damn easy. She needed him to see there was a real chance of losing her.

'Let's be friends, OK? Like you said. Have dinner every couple of weeks and keep kisses like *that*,' she smiled with flirtatious fragility, 'off the menu. I think that's best, don't you?'

Christian nodded. 'You're an incredible woman, Maggie, you really are.'

Maggie smiled, and, kissing him lightly on the cheek, she began to walk away.

'I'll call you,' she said, keeping her voice and her gait steady until she was sure he could not see her any more. She stepped off the high street into the loading alley that ran alongside Woolworths and slid down the side of the wall, feeling the brickwork scrape her skin through her dress. Then she let herself cry, soft, rasping sobs, regardless of who might see or hear her.

★

181

Pete looked over at the bar and then back at Angie, whose eyes were fixed on Falcon. He'd been talking to this woman, a curvy tall brunette, for the last twenty minutes, more or less ever since Pete and Angie had walked in through the door. The woman was leaning with her back against the bar, both elbows propped behind her, making the best of her impressive breasts, and Falcon was mesmerised. But despite her come-on body language, her face was another story and she regarded him through heavy-lidded eyes with only a take-it-or-leave it level of interest. Both Pete and Angie watched six-foot-something pink-haired Falcon jump through hoops to get a smile out of the woman. Pete cursed him as he sipped his pint. He should never have let Angie come here, not to see Falcon try and pull another woman right in front of her. Surely a casual relationship doesn't have to be *that* casual?

'We could go if you like,' he said, putting his arm on her forearm to get her attention. She glanced at him quickly and then back at the woman.

'No, it's all right.' She smiled without conviction. 'I'm fine, really!' She turned to Pete and he was alarmed by the mildly delusional look in her eye.

'I'll get the drinks in. Same again?'

Pete glanced at his near full pint and then at Angie's, which she had finished in under ten minutes.

'Um, well . . .' he began, but she was gone before he could say anything.

The door creaked open and Maggie walked in, her head down, her hair shrouding her face. Pete had to double-take before he recognised her. He was about to call out her name when the woman Falcon had been attempting to impress broke away from him mid-sentence and rushed up to Maggie.

'Darling, what is it? What's happened?' Sarah asked her, wrapping her arms around her.

Falcon looked like he'd been slapped in the face, a demeanour that was not improved when he realised Angie was standing right behind him.

Maggie and her friend headed speedily into the ladies. The older barmaid, Sheila, gave the middle-aged couple at the end of the bar a concerned look and they all stared at the ladies' door in confusion. The woman, Pete realised, as he studied her profile, must be Maggie's mother. Which meant that this must be Maggie's parents' pub. Pete congratulated himself on his powers of deduction and, noticing that Angie had now engaged Falcon in a close and intense discussion, commiserated himself on the loss of his next pint, which even now stood despondently on the bar.

Pete had wanted to take his mind off Stella tonight, to try and clear his head of all the guessing and second-guessing that her absence was forcing him to do, but somehow, with people crying and fighting and generally spreading their emotional pain around like it was manure, it seemed impossible. He wondered again about Maggie's bent head as she'd hurried into the ladies with her friend. He'd have liked to have had a chat with her about Stella again, get her perspective on things. He'd really enjoyed his 'coffee' with her the other day. He liked the way she talked to him and the way she listened. He was surprised by the realisation that not many people did listen to him all that closely. Not Stella, not his students, and obviously not Angie, Pete observed with some distress, otherwise she'd be at home right now with a cocoa.

In any case, it looked as if Maggie had enough problems of her own tonight – that idiot bloke who'd chucked her, more than likely.

Falcon said something to Angie, who simply shrugged and made her exit without even a glance of farewell to Pete. Pete wondered if Falcon regretted hurting her, or sleeping with her, or both. He knew that at some point he should probably try and point out to Falcon that if he really wanted Angie to be just a friend, he should stop sleeping with her. The only trouble was, he didn't think he could do it in bloke semaphore, with just a grunt of a look. He was sure he'd probably have to actually talk to him, which he knew would make both of them awkward and embarrassed. Perhaps he could just buy him a pint instead, a really meaningful one.

As Pete glanced once again at the black silhouette of the lady in the A-line shirt who guarded the female toilet door, he concluded that all the signs indicated that tonight was not a good night to try and find out the truth about true love. With that in mind, he tugged himself out of his seat to go and collect his next pint.

'Say that again, but more slowly.' Sarah handed Maggie another Wet One; she always had a pack in her handbag even now the children had grown out of them. Maggie roughly removed what was left of her make-up, wrinkling her nose against the acrid scent of the wipe.

'He said he didn't want us to get back together. That he just wanted us to be friends . . .' Maggie paused and looked at her reflection. Her hair was tangled and her eyes were red and swollen. Her lips still tingled with Christian's taste, though. 'And then he kissed me and said he didn't know, he just didn't know, and he needed time to think . . .'

'Fucking bastard.'

Sarah reached for another wipe but then realised the packet was empty. She pulled a tissue out of her back pocket, spat on it and wiped away the last traces of Maggie's mascara.

'Bloody fucking coward. Wants to have his cake and eat it, as usual, to have that slapper at home and you on the go. You know what he wants, don't you?' She took out her hairbrush and, turning Maggie away from her, quickly restyled her hair into a semblance of order. 'He wants you to be his other woman now. I hope you told him where to go, young lady?'

Maggie turned and looked at her friend. She could tell Sarah was in no mood to hear the truth from her, and that if she mentioned even an approximation of it she would be sent to her room and grounded for a month. No wonder Becca had become an habitual fibber.

'Of course I did,' she said quietly. 'I mean, I wouldn't let him mess me around *that* much.' Maggie heard the words bounce off the ancient, cracked tiles of the loo and half wished they were true. In reality, of course, she'd let him mess her around as much as he wanted, as long as he took her back one day.

'And that other girl, that Louise. I feel sorry for her, poor cow. She's got no idea what she's let herself in for, has she? I almost feel like telling her,' Sarah said grimly.

Maggie thought of Louise and her mind spun – she felt bad for her too. After all, she was just as caught up in this whole mess as Maggie was, and she didn't even know that she was. And she didn't have any proper friends to talk about it to. For all she knew, she had just found Mr Right and her life was about to begin.

Maggie looked at her friend and hugged her hard.

'God, Sarah, I'm so glad you were here. God knows what would have happened if I didn't have you! I can't let Mum and Dad know about this. Not even Sheila. I'll just have to say it's the stress or my period or something.'

Sarah nodded and squeezed her tightly before releasing her.

'OK, listen, mate. You're handling this really well, you know? Now you're past all the false hope and stuff you can really start to move on, all right?'

Maggie gave her a faintly guilty smile and hoped Sarah wouldn't see through her.

185

'There's a bloke out there with pink hair who wants to shag me,' Sarah added. 'He's not really all that, but he's got nice shoulders, you know? I might snog him and see how it goes.'

Maggie laughed. 'That's Falcon. He drinks in here all the time. Haven't you noticed him before?'

Sarah shrugged. 'I haven't noticed him notice me before,' she said. 'Come on, once more unto the breach . . .'

As they walked out into the bar, Sarah stopped dead, her hand barring Maggie's progress.

'Who the fuck is that!'

Sarah was staring at the bar, her mouth agog, and when Maggie looked, Pete was standing there exchanging a tenner with a particularly coquettish Sheila.

'Oh!' Maggie smiled with relief. Someone who would understand and who she could really talk to. 'It's Pete!' she looked at Sarah. 'That's the Pete with the fiancée, the one Becca has a crush on – oops, I wasn't supposed to mention that. Never mind. Hi, Pete!' She waved at him and moved quickly to his side.

Sarah looked after her and shook her head. 'That girl,' she mumbled to herself, supposing that the tall blond was off-limits on two counts now, 'wouldn't know *real* talent if it tap-danced on her arse.'

Sarah eyed Falcon in a new light, as if she was being forced to buy budget when prime was right there. She gave a little shrug and crossed over to him, giving him her best smile. After all, the kids were away all night and she had nothing else on.

'Are you all right, love?' Marion asked her daughter as soon as she joined them at the bar.

Maggie smiled at her. 'Course I am. Um, it was just, you know,' she glanced at Pete and whispered, '*girl things*. The, er, supplier I met was a bit of a hard bargainer, but I think we can do business. So did you open the champagne?'

186

Marion shook her head. 'We were waiting for you, dear.'

Sheila reached behind her into the fridge and handed the bottle to Keith, who opened it completely incorrectly with a large pop and a sudden gush of froth. Sheila shoved six miscellaneously-sized glasses underneath it until each one was filled and then grabbed the largest.

'Pete.' Maggie handed him a glass. 'Join us. We're toasting the new era of The Fleur, which officially started today!'

Pete took the glass and eyed it. If he drank this then he'd be officially drunk, again. He'd been almost permanently pie-eyed since he'd arrived in this town, and he knew he couldn't blame it exclusively on Falcon. It was because it was negative Stella time. During positive Stella time he stayed meticulously sober in case she sprang any new surprises on him or tried to get into a fight or clinch with someone. He became her po-faced minder. Negative Stella time consisted of many more physical head-aches, it was true, but much, much less demanding ones.

'Sarah!' Maggie called out to her friend, but when she looked Sarah was engaged in kissing the face off Falcon, her fingers entwined firmly in his ponytail. Maggie set her glass aside and turned back to her family.

'Well, then, to our chief investor,' she nodded at Sheila. 'And to The Fleur! Long may she sail!' she giggled and sipped her champagne. 'Where's Jim?' she asked her dad. Technically, she supposed, he should be included in the celebrations.

'He left you another inventory behind the bar to look at. He's found all those old books down there, you know, the ones we bought years ago just after we got the place.' Keith turned to Pete. 'You used to go to these huge warehouses full of old bits of furniture, mirrors, signs and that and buy stuff for dressing the pub, you know. You could buy books by the yard – never even thought of looking to see what they were. Anyway, we took them down maybe fifteen yeas ago. Must be a hundred of them.

187

Jim thinks a few of them might be worth something. He's worked hard, and it is Friday, so I gave him fifty to have a night out.'

Maggie looked at her dad and pursed her lips. At some point she'd have to sit down with her parents and explain to them that her taking over the pub wouldn't work if they insisted on dipping in and out of the business when they saw fit. But that could wait for tonight, at least.

'Maggie.' Pete interrupted her train of thought. 'So are you OK, then? When you came in you looked like you were —' He stopped abruptly, remembering just in time that Maggie had seemed pretty sick of him always catching her crying.

'Yes, I was. Crying, I mean. *Again*.' She glanced around the largely empty bar, rolling her eyes. 'Perhaps I'll get a listing in the *Guinness Book of Records*, like that person who hiccupped for seven years.' Maggie extended her hand as if picturing a headline. "Girl who blubbed most over break-up!" Why don't we go and grab a seat? My feet are killing me.'

Pete was happy to and they made their way to the other side of the pub. Glancing at Sarah and Falcon, Maggie remembered she had briefly seen the blonde girl she thought was Falcon's girlfriend when she'd stumbled into the pub earlier.

'What happened to your flatmate?' she asked, hoping that Sarah wasn't getting into someone else's trouble again.

'Oh, Angie? She left. Abruptly.' He nodded at Falcon and confirmed Maggie's fears. 'Long story.'

Maggie sighed heavily. 'God, there's a lot of it around, isn't there? I saw Christian tonight.' Maggie began her story without feeling the need for any preamble. Somehow she sensed that Pete wouldn't mind. She lowered her voice and glanced furtively at her family, indicating that this was just between her and Pete.

'I thought – I was being monumentally stupid, but anyway I *thought* – that he wanted us to get back together. I've been a bit

188

mental recently, and I *thought* I'd found something out when I don't think I actually did, if you know what I mean?'

Pete did not know what she meant, but he kept his trap shut.

She smiled sheepisly. 'I thought I was being all Alexis Carrington.' Pete laughed, largely to cover his confusion. 'But he was really all over me, Pete, touching me, complimenting me, and so I think I was entitled to be a *bit* drawn in by it all. Anyway, then I go and tell him how I feel, and he tells me I've got it wrong, and I run out of the restaurant and he chases me, and then he . . .' Maggie looked up at Pete with a new intensity in her eyes that Pete found rather stirring. 'He kissed me, really passionately, full-on sexy. Much better than he's kissed me in ages, actually. Like he really meant it.'

Pete felt himself blush inexplicably as he pictured the image. Maggie was actually very sexy, if he let himself dwell on it. He really *had* to do something about his libido as soon as he got home, release the build up of pressure, so to speak. He crossed his legs and tried to look nonchalant.

'And he said he still wanted me, but he didn't know if we could be together again. He said he needed time to think.' Maggie leaned forward on to the table. 'What do you think?'

'What do I think?' Pete mused. 'Well, for starters I think he's insane. When you've obviously got all that chemistry going for you, he's mad to walk away from it. I wouldn't.' Pete grinned at her a little shyly, clearly unused to making obvious compliments.

'That's what *I* think,' Maggie agreed heartily, deciding he was sweet for trying to cheer her up.

Sheila clanged the bell for last orders, making Sarah jump and slide off Falcon's knee. He began to laugh until she silenced him with one look. Maggie smiled. Her friend was so hard; nothing ever got to her.

'But the question is, what can I do about it? Do you want another drink?'

Pete thought that another drink would cloud his head completely and he declined.

'I know, let's go for a walk!' he said suddenly. 'It's such a clear night, we might get a look at the stars if the light pollution isn't too bad.'

Maggie sat down again. 'Um . . .' she said uncertainly. Pete laughed. 'Oh Maggie, you know I'm not going to try anything. It's a warm night and we need to clear our heads and form a plan of attack. Walking is the best way of thinking, I've always found. We can go to the lakes by the abbey. What do you reckon?'

Maggie wasn't sure she was ready to go back to the abbey so soon after tonight's near humiliation, but she suddenly found the thought of strolling in the moonlight with Pete the pleasantest she had had since . . . well, OK, since Christian's hand had briefly but firmly gripped her crotch about two hours ago. But even so it seemed like a cool and calm antidote to that heady and frustrating memory.

'OK,' she agreed. 'Why not?'

She returned to the bar. 'I'm just going out with Pete for a bit, OK? Would you mind locking up, Dad? Don't put the bolts on, though, cos I'll need to get back in again in half an hour or so.'

Sheila raised a pencilled brow and crossed her arms. Maggie ignored her obvious implication and headed out of the pub and on to the high street. The air was still warm and it was a busy night: gangs of girls and groups of lads crossing and clashing, mingling and mixing as they made their way home or on to the next place, hoping that some kind of entanglement would hold and last for that night at least.

Pete took Maggie's hand and led her across the street and down the cobbled alley that went behind the abbey and to the large park.

'Anyone sees us,' Maggie said, laughing and secretly charmed

190

by the unconscious way in which he'd taken her hand, 'they're bound to think we're up to no good.'

Pete smiled at her. 'Well, it doesn't matter what people think, does it?'

They walked along by the lakes, the gravel crunching under their feet, and up on to the ridge of the slope where a small section of Roman ruins still stood. Finally, when they'd reached the highest point of the incline, Pete stopped and tipped back his head.

'There,' he said, nodding at the expanse of glitterng sky. 'That's what it's really all about, Maggie, out there. That's the real mystery. And we are all made of stars, you know.'

He released Maggie's hand and sat down, lying back on the dry grass and stretching his long legs out. He patted the grass beside him. 'Come on,' he smiled, and Maggie shrugged and joined him. Somehow the incline of the slope and the dazzle of the cloudless sky made her feel a little dizzy. She held on to earth by entwining her fingers in the rough grass.

'It is beautiful,' she said, amazed at how little she ever bothered to stop and look up at the sky. 'Incredible, really.' She turned a little to look at Pete's profile. He was smiling broadly, and he looked very young at that moment – boyish almost.

'So which constellations can you pick out then?' he said, glancing at her quickly.

She looked back at the sky. 'Um . . . none. It's rubbish, I know, but unless they're in the back of a magazine with the little lines joining up the dots, and a little name attached to them, I can't tell the difference.'

Pete laughed and took her wrist in one hand and formed her fingers into a pointer with the other. He slid over the grass a little until his body was flush against hers. Maggie found herself holding her breath; if she had been uncertain about Christian's intentions earlier, she really had no idea what was on Pete's mind now. Maybe he'd given up on Stella? After all, he hadn't mentioned her. Maybe all this midnight walks and star-gazing was a way to get her on her own . . . She panicked and stiffened, but just as she was about to pull away, Pete began to talk, and she realised that her body next to his was absolutely the last thing on his mind. She felt, but barely registered, an unexpected regret at the departure of tension that the thought of him trying to kiss her had created.

'Up there, to the right,' Pete directed her hand. 'Cassiopeia. You can trace it with your finger. And everyone knows the Big Dipper, don't they?' He traced her pointed finger along the lines of the constellation.

'Oh yeah!' Maggie entirely forgot the previous moment of anxiety. 'It looks like a big saucepan!'

Pete threw her a look but said nothing. He concentrated his gaze back on the view.

'That really bright star there' – he picked out a star that shone more intensely than the others – 'that's actually a planet. That's Mars. It's closer to the earth now than it has been for sixty-five thousand years. The last people to see it like this were the cavemen.'

He put down Maggie's wrist and withdrew his hand.

'Don't you think it's incredible? Just a few miles of atmosphere and a bit of gravity keeping us from being out there. And we are able to see another *planet* with the naked eye. Can you imagine, Maggie, the millions and millions of planets there must be out there? And maybe, somewhere, people not so different from you or me are doing the exact same thing that we are. Doesn't that blow you away?'

Maggie stopped looking at the stars and looked at Pete instead.

'It puts things into perspective a little,' she agreed as something of an understatement.

192

Pete turned on to his side, shifting his body a little so that there was a gap of a couple of inches of grass between them.

'Exactly. That's what I tell myself when I think about Stella.' He mentioned her name for the first time that evening. 'She sent me a general email. I was on it, but so were the rest of the world and his wife.' He sighed and shook his head. 'I don't know, Maggie. I'm beginning to think that that's it. After all those years of fighting to keep her, she's out of my reach now. She's gone.' He nodded at the sky. 'She might as well be on Mars.'

Maggie studied his shadowed face.

'You can't say that for sure, Pete,' she said.

She wanted to reach out across the small expanse of grass and touch him, but the fear and potential embarrassment that he might think she was making a move on him prevented her.

'I mean, if I'm right it sounds like that email was the first communication she'd had with anyone, not just you, so it's not as if she's left you out. She's probably just finding her feet and testing her feelings . . . it's *exactly* like with Christian,' she added quickly. 'He needs to be sure, Stella needs to be sure. The thing is – and you can't do this, really – that I managed to get Christian to keep seeing me "as a friend" while he makes his mind up. I'm going to show him how independent I am now, and how I can stand on my own two feet without him. I thought I might even make up a sort of boyfriend to really get him going —'

Maggie stopped herself. Not only was she sounding mental again, she was completely trampling all over Pete's own worries with her own.

'Sorry,' she concluded. 'If only you could make Stella see how you were without her. I think if she realised that she didn't have this cataclysmic effect on your life she might want to be with you more.' Maggie thought for a moment. 'Actually, that's a bit sick, isn't it?'

Pete grinned ruefully and dipped his head.

'That's human nature. It is sick,' he said, pausing thoughtfully. 'As it goes, I *had* thought of writing to her about seeing someone, I mean, not exactly seeing someone but getting close to another person.' He paused and then looked up into her eyes. 'I'd thought about writing to her about you.'

Maggie opened her mouth and then closed it again.

'I'm sorry, I know it sounds really weird, but you're really the only person I know here except Angie, and, well, I can't seem to think of her in that way, and I'm no good at making things up like that, so . . .'

Maggie tried desperately to sort out the sense from what Pete was saying instead of just focusing on the fact that he had mentioned he could see her 'that way'.

'I just thought that if I could write about my friendship with a really smart, sexy girl like you it'd make her think twice, a bit like your plan with Christian? Oh God, I've said too much, haven't I?'

Maggie sat up and drew her knees under her chin, wondering if Pete realised how much he'd just complimented her. She felt ridiculously grateful. Just to know that someone else, even someone who was in love with another woman, thought she was smart and sexy gave her cause for hope.

'No,' she said, 'No, really. Actually, I've thought of a way we can help each other.'

Pete sat up and mirrored her position.

'Well,' Maggie said slowly, 'We like each other, right? We have a lot in common, so . . . let's hang out more.' She lifted her palm skywards as if the suggestion was obvious. 'You can write to Stella about it and it won't be a lie, and since this is a very small city, word is bound to get round to Christian that I'm being seen with some blond hunk.' Maggie grinned at the prospect. 'That's bound to make his mind up for him.'

Pete blinked and looked a little uneasy. 'A blond hunk?' he said uncertainly.

Maggie clapped her hand over her mouth and giggled.

'Oh! Oops. Becca, my god-daughter, calls you that. She thinks you're "lush" – I think that was the word she used. That's the second person I've accidentally told today, and given that the first one was her mum, if she ever finds out she'll kill me.'

Pete shrugged. 'I'll try not to blow it for you,' he said, and then, 'Don't you think it sounds a bit like one of Tucker Jenkins' plans for an early episode of *Grange Hill*?'

Maggie laughed and clambered to her feet.

'Well, maybe, but simple plans are often the most effective. I mean, how do you feel when you think about Stella with some Aussie bloke?'

Pete said nothing as he stood up, but even the absence of daylight could not disguise his thunderous expression.

'Exactly, and that's how I feel about Christian with Louise, except I met Louise and I quite liked her and that's confused things. That was a real never-to-be-repeated mistake!'

Pete caught up with her in two easy strides as she began to walk back down the hill.

'You met her? How?' he asked.

'It's a long story!' Maggie said, wondering if she should confide in him. 'Oh, what the hell?' she thought, and began to tell him.

'Bloody hell,' Pete said as they drew to a stop outside The Fleur's doors. 'Don't take this the wrong way, but you are well out of my league with your conniving!'

Maggie was surprisingly flattered. 'Well, yes, but it all back-fired on me, because it made *me* feel like a cow instead of her, the one that nicked him in the first place!' She glanced over her shoulder at the door. 'So do you want to come in for a drink?'

Pete shook his head. His walk with Maggie had done nothing to calm down his rebellious libido, and he really needed to work some of it off. Not to put too fine a point on it, he was worried that if he hung around her any longer and drunk any more he'd pull a Falcon, lose sight of what really mattered and make a stupid pass at her. That would just ruin everything.

'No, no offence, but I've got this email I want to write about some star-gazing I did tonight.'

Maggie smiled up at him. 'Well, I hope it works. When you think about it, it's lucky that we met, isn't it?'

Pete shook his head and nodded towards the moon.

'Luck's got nothing to do with it. It's all down to fate,' he said seriously. 'But it's down to chance whether or not the person we feel for feels the same way.' He looked momentarily very sad. 'It's just a lottery.'

Maggie looked at him sternly before she turned to put the key in the lock. 'No, it's not,' she reminded him. 'It's *fate*. And fate is on our side, or we would never have met each other.'

Pete and the ceiling above his bed exchanged equally blank looks. The night had finally begun to cool off and a breeze raised goosebumps over Pete's bare skin. He sat and looked at his clock. 2.55 a.m. He resisted the urge that had come at last to fall instantly asleep and instead sat naked at his PC.

Dear Stella, he wrote, and then sat there staring at the two words for several seconds.

It was great to hear from you. Life here has been really hectic recently. Pete remembered he'd told her he'd already got the studio job. *Work is fantastic, getting better every day. I've met loads of really cool* . . . He deleted the word *cool* and replaced it with *hip. I've met loads of really hip people. I have been hanging around with the owner of the local pub (I know what you're thinking, typical!) She is a really cool girl, though, her name is Maggie. I think I might have mentioned her before. Earlier this evening I took her out to show her the stars and I wondered what you were doing right then? Probably having your lunch!*

Pete sat back, pleased with himself. He'd managed to drop in his midnight walk with Maggie and still show that he was thinking of Stella. Genius.

I miss you, Stella, and I love you. Write soon, Pete xx

Pete wondered if *write soon* sounded too needy. He tried a few other alternatives but settled finally on simply *Love Pete* and three large capital *X*'s. He sent the email, feeling a sudden frisson of excitement. He didn't quite know why, but he really felt that this was the beginning of something new for him and Stella.

He clambered back into bed, grateful to be finally turning the light out, but dismayed to find his head was still buzzing with thoughts he shouldn't be having. When he'd got in earlier, he'd undressed and lay on the bed, taking his time to think about Stella, savouring her memory. He remembered the last night they'd spent together and how she'd looked as he moved above her, eyes half closed like two silvered half moons, her hands flung above her head in pure abandon. The diamond he had bought her sparkled in the dark, glitterng just like Venus. He recalled the moment they had come in unison again and again until his thighs trembled and his heart felt sore. But towards the end something strange had happened. Mixed in with the jumble of images of him with Stella, Pete found flashes of Maggie crossing his mind like sheet lightning. Maggie in a way he'd never seen her, and certainly shouldn't be thinking of her. Naked and hot for it, frankly.

'Well,' Pete reasoned out loud, 'she's a pretty girl and I'm a bloke – it's only natural, it doesn't mean anything.' But as he shut his eyes Pete saw Maggie's face as it had looked earlier this evening, bathed in starlight.

'Steady there, tiger,' he mumbled, already half asleep.

197

Chapter Twenty-one

The bar was quiet. Morning sun steamed in through the dirt-streaked windows highlighting the shafts of dust motes that seemed to raise the scent of beer, ash and polish from every surface. Maggie set out her papers into piles in order of priority and began a list. She would pay Christian's cheque into her own account on Monday so she'd have ready cash when she needed it. The rest of the funding would be in place in The Fleur's account by the end of the week, and the new cheque books and cards that needed only her signature would arrive soon after that. She'd need an accountant eventually, although she could do the basic stuff herself, and she made a note to call Christian's.

First on her list of priorities was planning and costing the refurbishment of the kitchen and the main bar. Until she consulted fitters and maybe even builders, she couldn't really say how long she would have to close The Fleur for, but she wanted it to be for as short a time as possible. She had to have every detail, every contingency plan in place before one stroke of work was done. And, she mused, she needed a chef. A really good, really cheap chef. 'Catering college?' she wrote in the margin of her notes. It was a long shot, but maybe she'd find a budding Nigella fresh out of NVQ III. There was much more to think about, but whenever Maggie felt like she was finally getting into it, her gaze would slip off the horizon of her coffee cup and focus on the middle distance. She still couldn't work out exactly what had happened last night and what it all meant.

Of course there had been her tumultuous meeting with Christian, his rebuttal and then the kiss. Maggie had relived that feeling over and over again as she drifted off to sleep at last, hoping that her dreams would bring it to its rightful conclusion. She had not been disappointed.

But then there was Pete and the way the starlight and the champagne and, yes, even Christian's kiss had seemed to transform them from mere passing acquaintances into a mutual alliance before her very eyes. He'd told her about getting the idea to use her to get Stella jealous before he even knew her very well. She had told him about how she'd met Louise and how it had all backfired. They'd instinctively trusted one another to tell each other things that anyone else would think were at best ludicrous and at worst highly questionable. What's more, neither one of them thought the other was particularly barking.

Maggie smiled unconsciously; it was a relief to have someone she could be properly ridiculous with. Sarah was fantastic, but she seemed to think it was her mission to get Maggie back 'on track'. She didn't seem to realise that Maggie *wanted* to be careering headlong down her own personal mountain into chaos. She was sure it was only by taking risks that she'd secure Christian once more and for good this time. Pete agreed with her.

She realised she was really looking forward to seeing Pete again later that evening. On the walk home, they'd agreed they'd go to a bar up in town that Christian's best friend managed. OK, he wasn't so much a best friend as a business associate Christian also played golf with, but there was a good chance he'd be there, and if he was word would definitely get back to Christian.

But even that walk home had not been the end of the

strangeness, Maggie recalled. As soon as she had walked into the shadowy bar she had realised that something was not right. She'd stood stock-still listening to the dark as the tiny hairs on the back of her neck stood up. She'd walked quietly over to the bar and checked the till – the drawer was left open as it should be, empty, to show any thieves that what little cash there was was safely locked away.

Suddenly she heard a muffled thump and possibly a groan behind her. She span round and waited for her eyes to adjust to the half-light. Then she realised what was wrong – the light in the ladies was still on, glowing faintly through a crack in the door. She heard the noise again and then the unmistakable clatter of breaking glass. Someone was in there. Despite her better instincts, Maggie crept towards the door – after all, it might just be her mum or Sheila in there, or maybe one of Jim's conquests. If she could just push the door open a crack more . . .

Sarah walked right into her, screamed, and then dissolved into a fit of giggles. She was very, very drunk and in her right hand she was swinging an empty bottle of house red.

'Sarah!' Maggie said. 'What are you doing here?'

'Oops!' Sarah held out both of her upturned wrists. 'It's a fair cop, guvner,' she slurred. A large shadow loomed behind her and Maggie realised it was Falcon still buttoning the fly of his jeans. To give him credit he looked mortified to be caught red-handed.

'Oh, er, all right? I'll give you the cash for the wine. Sarah said you wouldn't mind?'

Maggie looked from one to the other and then stumbled back two quick steps as her friend flung her arms, with most of her weight behind them, around Maggie's neck.

'I love you, Maggie,' she said blurrily. 'I mean, you're flaky most of the time, but I still love you. I want you to know that. You do know that, don't you?'

She burped loudly and rested her head on Maggie's neck, seeming to drop off for a second before jerking her head up and staring around her. 'Whooo! Steady as she goes!' she giggled as Maggie guided her haphazardly to a chair, with the help of Falcon. She realised that he was relatively sober.

'Did you get her drunk?' she challenged him, relieved that he looked stricken at the very idea. They plonked Sarah into a chair, where she promptly leaned her forehead on the table and began to snore.

'No!' Falcon insisted. 'No, honest, it was her idea, the wine and the . . . ladies. I don't even drink wine, but she was mad for it! All of it.' He paused and looked at Maggie. 'I just went along with her, she's a pretty hard lady to turn down!' he said, his expression a mixture of wonderment and alarm. Sarah sat up suddenly as if no time had elapsed since her last garbled comment.

'OK, so you can be a bit spoilt and don't know a good thing when it's staring you in the tits! Ha! Tits, get it? But you've always been there for me and you always pay for your mani —' The word morphed into a Richter-scale snore, and Sarah's forehead hit the table again with a not inconsiderable thud. Wincing, Maggie held out her hand to Falcon.

'Give me twenty pence,' she demanded, and he coughed up speedily. She stuck it in the payphone on the bar and waited for the owner of the local cab firm to answer.

'Tariq? Hi there, it's Maggie from The Fleur. Yeah, I'm at The Fleur now. Yeah. Anyway, listen, I've got Sarah here, a bit worse for wear. Are there any of you lot brave enough to take her home?' Maggie laughed. 'Excellent, I'll see you in ten minutes then.' She hung up and looked at Falcon, who was now crouching down by her friend.

'There's no need,' he said. 'I can walk her home. I don't mind, least I can do.'

Maggie shook her head. 'Mate, does it look like she can walk?' she said, and Falcon had to agree. 'Besides, even if you are a nice bloke, what kind of friend would I be if I let her go off into the night with a man she's just met when she's in that state?'

Falcon had to agree again. 'I see your point,' he conceded, and brushed a strand of hair from Sarah's sweaty face. 'Sarah? Sarah?' he said. Sarah opened one unfocused eye. 'Cheers then, for . . . er . . . everything. You're a really great bird.'

Sarah furrowed her brows, as if she was giving the matter some serious thought. Then, out of the pit of her stomach, a large growl began steadily to build. Before it could reach its crescendo, however, two large retches forced Sarah to sit upright in her chair, and she vented a stream of dark vomit that filled the room with the stench of acrid house red. Falcon was covered in the splatter. Sarah was snoring peacefully once more, her brow now smooth and carefree.

'Oh fuck!' Maggie clapped a hand over her mouth, stifling her laughter. After all, the big pink-haired man with piercings might not think it was so funny. 'She'll be mortified when she remembers this,' she told him, suspecting it was a lie.

'No worries.' Falcon said, but his face was wrought with dismay. He headed off to the gents to sponge himself down, and realising that Sarah wasn't going anywhere yet, Maggie cancelled her cab.

'You're so going to regret this in the morning,' she'd told Sarah as Falcon carried her upstairs to the sitting room. Maggie had put a bowl, two panadol and a pint of water within easy reach of the sofa, and set her own alarm clock to make sure that Sarah got home, showered and conscious, possibly in that order, in time to open the salon and greet Becca after her pyjama party. Something she'd eventually achieved by the skin of both of their teeth.

She'd been impressed that, despite the vomit incident, Falcon had stayed to help her clear up not only the mess in the bar but a broken glass in the ladies. As she let him out, he'd stopped and shaken his head.

'She'll be all right, will she? Sarah, I mean. About tonight?' He'd shifted from one foot to the other. 'I like her and everything, but I don't really want a girlfriend, you see . . .'

Maggie's laughter had shocked Falcon. 'Don't worry, mate,' she'd told him. 'Sarah's got the original heart of ice. Better men than you have failed to thaw it.'

Falcon had looked at her for a moment, clearly trying to decide whether or not to be offended. 'Nice one,' he'd said eventually, and Maggie had bolted the door behind him.

Maybe in the end, she thought as she sipped the last of her coffee, the whole damn thing was just an endless series of merry-go-rounds.

Her phone jumped into life and began to vibrate across the polished surface, dislodging a pile of papers, including her list, enough so that they scattered on to the floor.

'Oh fuck!' Maggie swore earnestly as she tried to grab the papers and answer the phone at the same time.

'Carmen?'

Maggie froze, her arm outstretched towards the floor as she bent over in her chair. She took a breath and straightened up, unconsciously flicking her hair out of her face as she composed herself.

'Louise! Hi!' She tried to sound pleased to hear from the girl as she scrambled to remember exactly what she had told her the last time they'd talked. She closed her eyes. It was only two days ago but it felt like a lifetime.

'Gosh,' Louise's brightness sounded brittle. 'I didn't know mobiles could get a signal halfway across the world these days. That's amazing!' She laughed a high, hollow laugh. 'I was just going to leave you a message to call me when you got back. I put together some quotes for your for the opening on the new bar . . .'

Maggie was confused. 'Got back?' she said, just as she remembered her Australia lie.

'Oh, you mean from Australia!' Both women spoke at the same time.

'I didn't go,' Maggie said simply. 'There was, er . . . a crisis at work, and it all got cancelled at the last minute. It's been busy, busy, busy or I would have called! But thanks for that, the quotes, I mean.' Maggie felt guilty. Here was Louise, doing her best to get much needed new business that would never materialise. 'How are *you*?' she rushed on, hoping to distract Louise from any more business talk. Fortunately – or maybe not – Louise had something else on her mind.

'Terrible,' she said, trying to laugh, but it turned into a sob and a rush of jumbled words instead. 'Oh God, I'm sorry, I don't know why I'm calling you, I mean, I didn't even think you'd be here! It's just that I told everyone at home that things were going so well for me here, bragged a bit about Christian, you know? It's just that telling them how awful I feel, even Mum, would be so . . . so . . . I just can't, not now. Not until I know there's no hope. The thought of going back to Cheltenham with my tail between my legs would be awful. I made such a big fuss about going off to London . . .'

Louise took a much needed breath.

'. . . And you just seemed to know exactly how I felt. Do you mind me calling you? I'm so glad you haven't gone. I know we don't really know each other that well, but you're the first woman who's been kind to me since I got here.'

Maggie waited for any further additions to Louise's monologue before allowing herself a moment to ingest all that Louise had just said. For the first time since she had engineered her meeting with Louise she was beginning to get the sense that there was more to her than just pretty packaging. She was quite a bit younger than Maggie, and, despite her beauty, vulnerable and easily bruised. She was scared stiff of losing the one thing that Maggie wanted more than anything, and she was panicking. It was the kind of panic that would turn Christian right off her, Maggie knew. She also knew that as much as she wanted Christian, she didn't want to deliberately hurt Louise any more, not now that she knew she was human, a real person, and not some pneumatic automaton. An idea, straight out of Maggie's recent school of ideas based on folly and impulse, sprang into her head. Maybe she could persuade her to leave Christian of her own accord. That would be much better. Better for Louise, better for Maggie, and much, much better for Carmen, whose nerves were in serious tatters.

'It's OK,' Maggie said, cautiously optimistic about Plan B. 'Of course we're friends. Calm down and tell me what's happened.' Maggie made an attempt at nonchalance. 'Has Christian said something?' She heard Louise blow her nose on the other end of the phone.

'Not exactly,' she began. 'You know he was due to go out on this business meeting last night? Well, he told me he'd come back to my place in Southwark, you know, near the office. We never go back to "their" flat in St Albans, I've never even seen it. I told him he didn't have to, I knew he was going back to St Albans for the meeting and he might as well stay as his place, but no, he said he'd come back to mine, said he'd be here before midnight and that I should "wait up" for him, if you know what I mean? I was so pleased, I felt that if he wanted to see me that badly he must really like me, you know?'

Maggie chewed her lip anxiously.

'And?' she prompted.

'And midnight came and went and then one and two and

205

three, and at four I gave up ringing his mobile and just fell asleep on the sofa. The first thing I saw when I opened my eyes this morning was him sitting in the armchair opposite me, still in the same clothes, a five o'clock shadow on his face.'

Maggie gripped her chair, feeling an uneasy, tilting sense of déjà vu. Apart from anything else she had parted from Christian at no later than nine o'clock. Where *had* he been all night?

'Inconsiderate bastard. What did he say?' Maggie asked, appalled for more than one reason.

'He said he'd been for a walk and a think.'

Maggie's heart skipped a beat. A walk? And a think? A walk and a think where? Had he seen her and Pete lying in the grass holding hands? She didn't know how to feel about the prospect, because although she wanted Christian to think she might have someone, she didn't want him to give up on her.

'A walk where!' she found herself demanding petulantly, in exactly the kind of tone that would drive Christian bonkers. She couldn't help it.

'He didn't say. Just a walk. To think. I asked what about, but he said that he couldn't talk about it with me yet because he hadn't finished thinking. And of course, Carmen, well, I thought he was with her, with Maggie. I mean, what do you think? He had to be, didn't he? I played it really cool, though, because he totally went off on one before when I tried to get him to talk. So I didn't say anything. I just said, "OK, if you want to talk about it I'm here." I thought, well, even if he was with her, he came back to me, right? That has to mean something, right? I'm not giving him up with out a fight. Right?'

For a briefly liberating and instantly forgotten moment, Maggie wondered what two fantastic young women like Louise and herself were doing fussing over a man like Christian who didn't know a good thing when he'd got it, and had to go on "walks" to "think" when it should have been patently obvious to him what he needed? And then she remembered that she loved him and that she didn't have a choice in the matter. Neither, by the sound of it, did Louise.

'Um, right,' Maggie said, her brain on serious overload.

'Oh Carmen,' Louise's sigh was heartbreaking. 'Are you around tonight, this afternoon? Christian's gone out – more thinking, I gather – but he said he'd take me out later to talk. I'd love to see you, you know. You can help me form a strategy. Which part of London do you live in? Perhaps I can come to you? Carmen?'

Maggie realised she'd not been listening.

'Oh. Er, no, I live miles away from you. How about I meet you in Soho for a coffee?'

She quickly rearranged her day. She'd have to put back her planning work until tomorrow, and call Pete and tell him she'd meet him at the café she'd arranged to meet Louise at instead of at the station. She was careful to give herself at least half an hour's clear space between Louise departing and Pete arriving – she'd need time to adjust her persona – it was hard being a double-double agent, if that's what you called it.

'Oh, I'd love that, thank you! Thank you!'

Maggie glossed over how grateful Louise seemed and arranged to meet her at a café she knew and hung up the call. She had a feeling she would never need to fly to Australia, as pretty soon she would have dug herself a hole big enough to get there by foot. That would cheer Pete up, at least.

What was she up to? she asked herself silently.

'What you up to, then?'

Maggie jumped out of her skin, knocking her cup on to the floor. She looked on in dismay as the dregs of her coffee were soaked up by her list of suppliers. Sheila stood over her as she retrieved the soggy bits of paper, her arms crossed beneath her breasts and her mouth set in a thin, lipsticked line. Maggie began to clear her work away, avoiding Sheila's eye.

'I'm just trying to get started on sorting this place out, She! But if it's not one thing it's . . . another.' She looked meaningfully at her phone and then hopefully at Sheila. She had not fooled her.

'You don't fool me, lady,' Sheila confirmed briskly. 'Who was that on the phone? You're up to something. I've always known when you're up to something, like that time when you stole entire boxes of crisps out of the cellar to flog to the other kids at school . . .'

'That was Jim!' Maggie protested, but Sheila went on regardless.

'Listen, I know it's something to do with Christian and I just want to say this.' She paused and took a breath. 'I am showing a lot of faith in you, giving you the money to sort this place out. Now I'm not doing it because I want to see you beholden to me, so don't think that I am. I'm doing it to give you a chance to make the most of your abilities. I know you're a grown woman and you'll do what you will as far as your "love" life is concerned. But I'm asking you, for my sake, not to throw this chance away. Because it's the chance that I never got, that I never got to give to my baby. And I want you to make it more than anything, OK? It'll mean that *something* good came out of that marriage, at any rate. It'll mean that I've achieved *something*.'

Maggie dumped her papers in one pile and hugged Sheila's unrelenting body.

'I'm sorry, Sheila,' she said. 'I promise you I will get this right, whatever happens with Christian.' She fished out her soggy To Do list and showed it to Sheila. 'Look, I'm going out to all these industry suppliers on Monday to do costing for the kitchen, and I've got a friend who works in interiors coming in for a chat on

Tuesday to get some ideas going. I'm engaging an accountant, and once the finance is in place I'll settle the outstanding invoices. See?' Maggie took Sheila's hand. 'I won't let you down, I promise. Nobody's ever shown the kind of faith in me that you have. And anyway, you *have* achieved something in this life – you've always been here for *me*. Maybe you don't think that's very much, but I do, and I love you for it.'

Sheila squeezed her fingers tightly and blinked. 'Here, this came this morning.' She produced an official-looking letter from her trouser pocket. 'It says the money'll be transferred by the end of the next week. And I love you and all.'

She threw Maggie one last chastising look for good measure as she prepared to set up the bar.

'It's not me I'm worried about you letting down, Mag, it never has been. It's you letting down yourself I'm worried about.'

Chapter Twenty-two

On her way into town, Maggie stopped by The Sharp End to see if Sarah was still alive. By the look of her – her skin waxen and greasy, her eyes still the colour of claret and her lips drained of all colour – the answer was yes, but barely. The salon door was open and several fans buzzed around the clients. The place was jam-packed and extremely hot. Maggie caught Sarah's eye and waited as she excused herself from her client.

'Can't stop,' she said, rolling her eyes. 'Can't move, speak or breath without wanting to throw up, either. At least the kids are still out. Leanne's mum's taken Becca to the flicks, thank God. I couldn't stand her sermonising on top of all this.' She gestured at the salon. 'Thanks, by the way, for looking out for me last night.'

'That's what friends do, and it's nice to have a turn for a change, anyway.' Maggie gave her a sympathetic smile. 'Still, you had a good night, though?'

Sarah wrinkled her nose. 'Did I?' she asked hesitantly. 'I remember you coming in and saying you'd binned Christian once and for all, thank God. I remember you slinking off with the fit bloke, you dark horse – must pin you down about that later. I remember snogging Falcon and I remember . . . no, I don't. That's it.'

'Well, you and Falcon were . . . you know.' Maggie paused, aware of the attentive ears of some waiting customers.

'Did we . . . you know?' Sarah asked her.

'Yeah!' Maggie was shocked but surprised that her friend could not remember having sex with Falcon. After all, it wasn't the first time.

'Oh Christ, I'll have to go to the chemist. Better not leave it to chance this time, hey?'

Sarah laughed nervously, and Maggie knew she was referring to Sam's conception after a particularly rowdy night with Marcus, his father. A night which had also started in The Fleur, Maggie remembered, back when it used to have customers, and when Marcus and the rest of White Watch used to come in for a drink after a shift at the fire station. Sarah had been smitten with his pumped-up muscles and jet-black eyes. She hadn't expected him to be sweet and sensitive along with it. His romantic side had shocked her considerably, and his constant attempts to be more than just a fling finished them off in the end. When he'd found out about Sam he'd been thrilled to be a father, but gutted that Sarah wouldn't keep seeing him, let alone marry him. Maggie had always been sad about that. He was a great dad, Becca got on with him and it was clear he wished that Sarah had given him a chance to stay in all of their lives on a more permanent basis. But she wouldn't have any of it. Just as she would never have had an abortion, she would never have a husband. It was some kind of mad logic that made sense only to her, and which, despite Maggie's numerous attempts to get her to talk, she would never explain.

'You should be all right – Maggie dropped a voice to a whisper – 'I found a used condom in the sink.'

Sarah shook her head and closed her eyes to try and shut out the excruciating embarrassment. Maggie went on in her normal voice, 'Falcon was worried you'd fall in love with him,' she smiled.

Sarah clapped her hands over her face and then regarded

Maggie through a gap in her fingers. 'I don't think I'll be going *there* again!' she said, as if the notion was preposterous.

Maggie laughed. 'That's what I said, sort of.'

'Thanks, mate. Listen, I'm chocka all day. You couldn't pop into Boots and get me a . . .' She lowered her voice to a whisper. '. . . a morning-after job, could you? Best to be double-sure.'

Maggie thought of the day's plans. 'I could, but I'm going up to London. I won't be back until late. Will that matter?' Maggie had never needed to take the morning-after pill.

'Yeah, I think you can take it within seventy-two hours,' Sarah said. 'I mean it's probably fine, but I don't want a brummie baby with pink hair in nine months' time! Two's more than enough! Right, I'd better get back. Thanks, mate.'

Maggie caught her friend's arm just as she was about to turn away. 'Are you OK?' she asked, looking into her eyes.

'Me? Yeah. I mean, hungover but yeah,' Sarah said making a considerable effort to sound bright and breezy.

'OK.' Maggie paused. 'Let's do something tomorrow, you, me, Becca and Sam. A picnic or something?' she called out as Sarah retreated into the salon.

'Yeah, the kids'll love that.'

Sarah turned back to her client. Maggie stood for a moment longer and examined Sarah's profile as she bent over the woman in front of her. She was always so tough – hard as nails, Sheila would say. The kind of woman never to let anything get to her. But Maggie thought she'd seen a tiny tear in her tissue-paper armour, a tiny glimpse of something else – something lonely, frightened. Maybe it was just the hangover and the thought of having unprotected sex – that would scare Maggie rigid. But maybe it was something else, something that was always there to be found if Maggie would only look hard enough.

'I'll ask her tomorrow,' Maggie resolved, and as she walked back up the road towards the station she began practising being

Carmen Da Vinci, events organiser, girl about town and international spy.

'Carmen, hi!' Maggie blinked behind her shades as Louise bent to kiss her on each cheek. 'Sorry I'm late – I got a bit delayed on the tube.' She sat opposite Maggie and looked around at the busy street, full of café tables and Soho's Saturday crowd all glammed up to the nines, poised for an eventful Saturday night.

Maggie's heart sank. Louise looked incredible, really beautiful. Her skin glowed and glittered in the sunshine and her curves filled out her white V-neck vest and pink Capri pants in exactly the right places. Even the gay men were checking her out, although probably for make-up tips.

'Have you been here long?'

Maggie shook her head and pushed her shades up her nose. She had in fact been sitting in the full glare of the midday sun for twenty minutes, long enough for her skin to become slippery with sweat.

'You look like you must love the sun, anyway. What is your background? Spanish? Italian? Anyway, you look great!'

Louise sat opposite her, and as she stretched her arm above her head to attract the attention of the waiter, Maggie, along with most of the rest of the café clientele, assessed the rise and fall of her breasts during this manoeuvre, trying to guess if they were real or fake. Maggie had to concede that they *were* probably real, just as Louise had said. This impressed her, but whether Christian cared one way or the other she had no way of knowing. He'd always told her he wasn't into big tits and arses. Had he been lying? Let's face it, he had set a precedent for dishonesty.

'What are you having? I'll have an iced tea, I think,' Louise told the entranced waiter. Her teeth sparkled as she talked, just like the diamond pendant that hung around her neck.

Maggie eyed it suspiciously, and before she could stop herself she found herself asking. 'Did Christian buy you that? I mean, it's so lovely!' She had not managed to cover her defensive tone, and she hoped that Louise would interpret it as just plain envy. Christian had never bought her anything very much – aside from the sofa, and he still had that.

Louise's fingers sprang to her neck and she gave a little girl's laugh.

'This? Yes, I feel so lucky. I mean, he takes me out to dinner and he pays for the rent on the flat . . .'

Maggie tried to clamp her lips into a tightly fashioned smile, but it was no good. 'He pays your rent?' she all but growled.

'Oh yeah. When he first offered me the job, I told him I was worried about how much it cost to rent in London. After all, I'd always lived at home in Cheltenham. And he just got out his chequebook and wrote me a cheque for a thousand pounds right then and there. He said I should use it as a deposit and that I could consider accommodation a perk of the job. He said he'd need a London stopover anyway when Fresh Talent was fully operational. Of course I didn't realise then that he intended us to be sharing a room!' Louise giggled again and closed her eyes as if remembering something Maggie didn't want to guess at. 'It wasn't long after that that he made his intentions perfectly clear, though!'

Maggie swallowed the last of her coffee in one hot gulp. If Louise was telling the truth – and she had no reason to suspect otherwise – then Christian had set her up in her own flat before he'd even made a move on her. That made it all premeditated, as if infidelity – any infidelity – had always been on his mind, not just some hopeless attraction he couldn't walk away from. No wonder he'd had to tell her so quickly. He wasn't being noble and thoughtful; he must have known she'd spot it in the accounts eventually. Why? What had she done

214

that was so wrong that it would drive him away like that?

'Yes, the necklace was from him.'

Maggie returned her attention to Louise, her last words still stinging painfully in her ears, and realised she was still fingering the pendant tenderly.

'It was his first gift to me. It's not a bad one, is it? He said when he saw it he knew it would suit me perfectly. You know, Carmen,' Louise continued with a small secret smile, 'I've had quite a lot of boyfriends. But there's something about Christian that's much more special than all the attention and the presents he gives me.'

Maggie swallowed hard — she knew what was coming.

'It's that he makes me feel that it's really *me* that he loves. Not just the packaging, but really me. The inside me. That means a lot.' Louise gave Maggie a direct, solemn look. 'And that's why, Carmen, I can't lose him. To anyone.'

Maggie nodded and sat back in her chair. Apparently Louise did need Christian as much she did. Maybe even more.

'So what do you think?' Louise made it clear she wanted to change the subject. 'Do you think Christian was with Maggie last night?'

Maggie flinched as Louise spat her own name at her. She leaned forward a little and met Louise's eye.

'No,' she said with palpable certainty. 'I know he wasn't with Maggie all of last night.' She wanted Louise to believe her, for what it was worth.

'Really?' Louise bit her lip. 'How come you're so sure?'

Maggie thought for a moment.

'Because if he was lying to you he'd have come up with a better excuse. Something like the meeting went on longer than he expected and he got too drunk to travel, or he missed the last train home. Something like that.' Maggie recalled two of the excuses that Christian had given her during the beginning of his

215

affair with Louise as she had made him his morning coffee and toast, being all sympathetic about his late nights. 'He wouldn't have said "I went for a walk and a think". I mean, even a man knows that saying something like that is bound to make you crazy and start you asking questions. You did absolutely the right thing to be so cool about it. He won't have been expecting that.'

Maggie noticed Louise visibly relax, the tension seeping out of her face and limbs. She warmed to her subject.

'No, he was just being a typical dumb-arsed man and "walking" and "thinking" like he doesn't already know what's right for him, like it's not staring him in the face!' she exclaimed, making Louise laugh and nod her head vigorously.

'Exactly!' Louise said. 'Sometimes I just want to go up to him and shake him by the shoulders and shout "Why don't you know what's right for you?"'

Maggie laughed, letting her guard slip ever so slightly. OK, completely.

'Yeah, I know I just want to get right in his face and tell him straight. It's me. I'm the one who's right for you, you idiot!'

Maggie's laugh faltered to a stop as she saw Louise's expression freeze.

'*You* want to say?' Louise questioned her, looking justifiably confused.

Stifling the urge to say the first thing that came into her head, Maggie struggled to string together her story before the end of the sentence and settle on an approximation of the truth. Any more out-and-out lies and she was bound to blow it.

'Oh yeah, but not to Christian, duh! I don't even know him!' She wondered if the hint of Becca had possibly been a bit over the top. 'Nooo. Actually, I haven't mentioned him before, but there's this bloke I'm seeing. Pete, his name is. And well the thing *is*,' Maggie said. 'The thing *is* that he's engaged, but his

216

fiancée upped and went to the other side of the world *for a year* the day after he proposed to her . . .'

'No!' Louise was open-mouthed.

'I know! It's obvious she's just stringing him along, but he can't see it. He *loves* her, apparently.' Maggie rolled her eyes for dramatic effect. 'We're supposed to be having this no-strings-attached sex thing, but I know I could make him twenty-five times happier than her. He just can't see what's right for him, do you see?' Maggie finished.

'Oh, I do see,' Louise said. 'Christian and I were supposed to be having a no-strings-attached sex thing and then we just went right ahead and fell in love anyway. Couldn't help it. How come you never mentioned him before?'

Maggie wondered what her chances of getting off for the double homicide of Louise and Christian would be if she cited temporary insanity. Slim to nil, she guessed regretfully.

'Um, because, well, I'm older than you and I can handle it and besides we came here to talk about you, not me.' Maggie smiled warmly and was caught off guard as Louise reached for her hand and squeezed it before letting it go.

'You know what?' she said. 'I am so lucky to have met someone like you. Someone older and wiser and so kind. It's not often you meet someone and you just know you can trust them, sort of instantly, don't you think? Mind you, they say calamity – like getting trapped in an office – can bring people together.' Louise giggled. 'I wish I could get you and Christian together, then maybe you could talk some sense into him. You're such an insightful person, I bet he'd listen to you.'

With murder out of the question, Maggie wondered what would happen if she had a heart attack right then. She'd probably die; it'd be a nightmare getting an ambulance across the centre of London on a Saturday. Still, anything was preferable to this stupid bloody ridiculous mess she'd got herself into.

217

Unable to take the pressure any longer, Maggie was about to confess when something unexpected happened. As if delivered direct from heaven, Pete dropped into the chair next to her with a cheery 'All right? I didn't think you'd be here for ages yet. It's cool, though, because there's only so long you can window shop in *Agent Provocateur* without looking like a perve!' Pete was completely unaware of the open-mouthed awe he was attracting from every member of every sex in the immediate vicinity as he leaned back in his chair and stretched his arms over his head. He did look particularly fine, Maggie supposed, in his tight pale blue T-shirt with his skin all brown and warm and firm. She pulled herself abruptly out of *that* runaway train of thought and back to the problem in hand.

What was Pete doing here so early? She wasn't supposed to meet him for an hour yet, and Louise was supposed to be well gone! Besides, even if she had been about to confess to Louise, at least that would have been her own (admittedly ridiculous) idea. The last thing she wanted was the humiliation of Pete accidentally blowing her cover for her.

'You're early!' She sounded slightly accusatory, and Pete looked slightly taken aback.

'Well, I thought as I was meeting you up here I'd come a bit early and check out the studios where I've got my interview on Tuesday.' He nodded towards Wardour Street. 'They're just up the road. I thought it'd be a good idea to scope it out, try and beat the nerves and all that.' He directed a quick smile at an entranced Louise, and then, as he did a double-take, Maggie witnessed him unleash the full force of his smile on the girl. His blue-eyed gaze almost burned a trail, Superman style, across the table top cluttered with purses and coffee cups, over Louise's torso and directly into her come-to-bed eyes.

Maggie was surprised and more than a little disappointed that Louise didn't spontaneously combust. She rolled her eyes churlishly and sighed. For the first time in her life she understood what people meant when they banged on about levels of attractiveness. Here were two people from the very top level displaying open admiration for each other. And the worst thing, or maybe the best thing, was that Pete had absolutely no idea that he was doing it, she was certain, because he just wasn't the type to have a pulling look or a chat-up line. It must be some deep primaeval impulse within him to get hold of the nearest woman who looked the most likely to be able to breastfeed fifteen children, Stella or no Stella.

'This is *Pete*.' Maggie said flatly, emphasising his name as he reached out and took Louise's hand. She found she wanted her to know that as far as she was concerned, Pete was spoken for.

Louise shot Maggie a quick 'what-a-hottie' glance, and Maggie remembered what mortal danger all of her plans were in.

'Pete,' she said quickly, 'this is *Louise*, remember, who I was telling you about last night?' She tried to weave a secret message into the sentence but ended up sounding as if she were talking to a slightly retarded four-year-old.

'Oh yeah,' Pete said brightly, and then he remembered what they had talked about. 'Oh! *Yeah*.' He nodded in a none-too-subtle way at Maggie. 'Hi!' he said again to Louise, as if she was now an entirely different person. Maggie wondered if she should have tested his undercover skills a bit more thoroughly before embarking on the night's planned expedition, but she couldn't think about that now, she had to think about the situation in hand.

'Well, Carmen!' Louise said, helpfully reminding Pete of Maggie's pseudonym. She didn't seem to think any further comment was required, and Maggie understood her implicit admiration for Pete. Maggie smiled wearily and noticed that now a full one hundred per cent of the café's occupants were checking out her table in one way or another. And none of them were looking at her, she'd lay money on it.

'So, Pete.' Louise leaned towards Pete a little and Maggie noticed she used the tops of her arms to squeeze her ample bust together just a little to emphasise her already deep cleavage. 'What do you do for a living?'

Maggie was gratified to see Pete's eyes widen slightly with alarm as Louise focused on him. As for Louise, in love with Christian or not, it seemed that just being near an attractive man started her flirt ignition. It was hard to work her out. One minute she was poor, lovelorn, grief-stricken child, and the next she was a full-on nuclear reactor of sexual power. Pete, she noted with a sort of off-key pride, seemed to be more intent on explaining to her the intricate workings of something called Avid that he did on admiring her charms, and, while her smile remained attentive, Maggie noticed Louise's eyes had begun to glaze over.

'Anyway.' Pete finished talking and disarmed Maggie in a single manoeuvre by dropping his hand on to her knee and squeezing it. 'Do you want to get going? I know it's only early, but I thought we could have cocktails at the bar while it's still quiet and then go on for dinner. Seafood, maybe?'

Maggie stared at him and then at his hand on her knee. It didn't feel as strange as Declan's hand, which had been on exactly the same knee only a short time ago. In fact it felt sort of nice and tingly. She was beginning to wonder exactly how Pete saw her when she realised that . . . Pete from Leeds drinking cocktails and going out for seafood? He was far too much of a lager and curry man for all that nonsense.

Pete caught Maggie's eye and raised an anxious eyebrow, confirming her suspicion that he was looking for the quickest way to get away from Louise's unrelenting magnetism. He was actually scared of her. Typical, Maggie thought. No one is ever scared of me. He just wanted her to help him lose Louise.

'Ooooh, where are you two going? Anywhere fancy?' Louise asked Pete, clearly fishing for an invite and excluding Maggie from the question. She jumped a little in her chair as she said it and her breasts made the return journey a split second after the rest of her body. Even Pete couldn't help noticing that little ploy.

Maggie almost growled out loud. The little minx had already got her claws into one man in her life. She certainly wasn't going to get Pete too.

Of course, if Maggie had been thinking straight she'd have thought that Louise's obvious attraction to Pete was a way for her to distract her from Christian and get her to take her eye of the ball, whilst Maggie made her move on Christian and got him back for good. But Maggie wasn't thinking straight. She was barely thinking at all.

'Oh,' Pete said cheerily. 'We're going to this bar up the road. I've never been before, but . . . Carmen says it's really cool. It's called The Drinking Den? Do you know it?'

Louise nodded enthusiastically. 'Yeah! One of Christian's mates runs it!' she said.

'You should come too,' Pete said, clearly realising what he'd said only after it had left his mouth. He shot Maggie an apologetic look. She ignored him carefully, afraid of what her eyes might give away. She couldn't tell if he was being deliberately stupid or just idiotically friendly, but right at that moment she could have killed him with her bare hands. Apart from the fact that he was supposed to be seeing *her* behind his fiancée's back she had no way of knowing if Paul, the bar manager, had ever met Louise. If he had, and he saw Louise, Maggie, who was also known as Carmen, and Pete all together at the same time in the same place, everything would hit the fan all at once, and it wouldn't be pretty. Maggie's cover would be blown in two seconds flat and she'd have to retire to a nunnery. In Austria. No, she couldn't let that happen.

'Ah! But,' Maggie jumped in quickly, 'you said Christian is taking you out tonight, you know, for the big talk? You don't want to miss that, do you? Or to let him down now when he might be wavering?'

Maggie couldn't believe she was actually pushing her rival into the arms of her lover, but events seemed to be overtaking her and she was having trouble thinking on the spot, let alone keeping the one step ahead that she needed to.

Louise paused and gazed at Pete, making him squirm once again under her naked admiration. A hint of colour grazed the tops of his cheeks, and Maggie forgave him. He wasn't trying to be a sex god, it was just being thrust upon him, so to speak.

'You're right, I suppose,' Louise said reluctantly as she rose from the table. 'You two have a good time.' She directed the comment at Pete, the hint of suggestion lingering in her voice.

Pete smiled back at her, and without any warning he removed his hand from Maggie's knee and put his arm around her shoulders. He drew her close against him and dropped a quick, soft, intimate kiss on her neck, just below her ear. Louise must have really rattled him.

'We always do,' he said, smiling at Maggie.

Louise gave a little shrug and a wave, and headed off into the thickening crowd, shouting, 'Call me!' over her shoulder. It wasn't clear who she was talking to.

'Ha! I won!' Maggie thought to herself as Pete headed inside to pay the bill. For a golden moment she bathed in the glory of her triumph.

And then she remembered. It wasn't Pete she was supposed to be fighting over.

Chapter Twenty-three

What neither Pete nor Maggie knew just at that moment was that things were about to get a whole lot more complicated than they already were.

Maggie seethed, Pete noticed, for all of the short walk from the café to the subterranean bar. In fact, periodically she actually hopped with fury as she recounted her conversation with Louise. Pete had never seen anyone literally hopping mad before, and he had to admit, it was quite charming in a peculiar sort of way.

Maggie huffed out a loud sigh of anxiety as they descended the steps into the bar. It had opened a year ago with celebrity backing under one of Soho's most exclusive restaurants. Deliberately shady, with only soft, ambient lighting, it had a carefully constructed air of designer seediness which gave credence to its name, The Drinking Den. Paul's opening press release had said he wanted his customers to feel as if drinking there was ever so slightly dangerous. He hadn't done a bad job, Maggie supposed as she looked around the bar. Except that later on, when the now near-empty room was filled to the rafters with designer totty gabbling on about whatever it was the very rich and beautiful do gabble on about, it would somehow take the edge off the atmosphere. It would make it look a bit more like the centre pages of *OK!* magazine than somewhere the Krays might have frequented.

Maggie huffed again. Louise, with all her contradictions and red herrings, had completely thrown her off kilter and she wasn't nearly as calm and collected as she needed to be. The whole purpose of this trip was for Paul to see her with Pete and report back to Christian, and that was it. She had to remember that and not get carried away with the confusion of new and unfamiliar feelings Louise had stirred up in her. She was blurring the edges of her feelings for Christian and Pete, and that would get no one nowhere, and fast.

'I mean,' she said out loud as Pete lent over the dark veneered bar and nodded at the barman, 'did you see her? She was all over you and you were supposed to be *my* illicit love-doomed affair, not hers,' Maggie spluttered. 'I don't know, when I first met her I thought she was all sweet and misunderstood, and all –' Maggie put on a high-pitched voice – ' "Oooh, I'm just a country girl, please be kind to me." I really thought it was Christian who had seduced her, and she was giving it all that again today until you turned up and she became some sort of bionic Marilyn Monroe. I mean, before you showed up she was all misty-eyed over the love of her life – who is *my* boyfriend, by the way!' Maggie slapped her palm on the bar indignantly, making the waiting barman look a little nervous.

'Um, ah,' Pete said, not quite sure how to reply, and giving the barman an apologetic look. 'Anyway, what do you want to drink?'

Maggie studied the row upon row of jewel-like alcopops that lined the clear-fronted fridges behind the bar.

'It's stomach-churning,' Maggie told Pete. 'Apparently Christian is the only one who's ever loved her for herself. Which begs the question, if she's so bothered about her inner beauty, then what's with all the cleavage, huh? Oh, I don't know. I don't want anything too alcoholic. I'll just have a tequila.'

224

Pete suppressed a smile.

'Better make that two tequila slammers, mate,' he told the barman before turning back to Maggie. She had climbed up on to a bar stool and he joined her. 'That's quite something though, isn't it?' he said. 'If Christian makes her feel like that, he must really mean a lot to her.'

Maggie picked up her shot glass and downed the tequila with neither the salt nor the lemon nor the slam. In the interests of equality, Pete followed suit and indicated to the barman to set up two more.

'That's what *I* thought.' Maggie's voice rose with indignation. 'In fact, you actually saved my life. I was about to give up on the whole bloody shambles and let her have him. And then you turned up and she was practically clambering over the table to get to you. She's obviously psychotic or something. What do you think? Do you think she's got that borderline personality whatsit?' Maggie asked Pete seriously.

Pete couldn't help laughing.

'Let's pause for a moment,' he said, 'and consider which one of you made up a pretend name to infiltrate the other one's life in the hopes of getting her to chuck your ex-boyfriend? Let's face it, Maggie, if there was a national bunny boiling contest, you'd win it. Hands down.'

Maggie gave him her best fiery, black-eyed look as she sank the second tequila, and Pete found his heart rate increase unexpectedly. He took a deep breath and gripped the side of the bar. Sometimes, he'd discovered over the last week, something Maggie would do, some tiny gesture, would seem to sort of pull at him. It was last night that had really done it. He shouldn't have let her into his fantasy. He had to get a grip and just put the whole thing down to experience. And tequila.

'Look,' he said, making himself look directly into Maggie's dark eyes. 'Why don't we make these our last tequilas for a

225

while and just have a nice sensible, alcoholic beer, OK? Otherwise we'll both be ratted in about five seconds and forget what we're supposed to be doing here.' Pete realised he wished they *could* forget what they were doing there and just get drunk and have a laugh instead. Just for once, he'd like Stella to be surgically removed from his head and his heart so that he could go two heartbeats without feeling her absence, see what the world might be like if he didn't love her. But somehow the hopelessly needy never get a night off.

Maggie agreed reluctantly and took the bottle of Hoegarden that the barman produced as if by magic. She gazed at the label despondently.

'Do you think I should serve this at The Fleur?' she asked Pete, taking a sip.

'Probably. Falcon wouldn't be pleased, mind.'

Maggie brightened as she thought of The Fleur.

'Ah yes, I know, but I've had an idea what to do about Falcon and his crew and Mrs Kim. There's a pool room past the ladies, with its own bar. We haven't had it open in years – never any point, not enough customers. It's got its own street entrance and everything. I thought I could keep that open while the refurb is going on, keeping a little bit of cash trickling in, and then maybe I could keep it going as a sort of niche bar. You know, an authentic pub bar, with the real ale and the strong bitters and the smelly carpets. And then the main area would be a lighter, grown-up sort of bar with good food served from twelve till ten. What do you think?' Maggie's eyes had begun to glitter as she talked. 'What do you think?'

'I think it sounds fantastic. I don't know much about running bars and all that, but I think it could work, and I think it's good of you to think of the existing clientele, all three of them.'

Maggie smiled warmly at him, it felt good to have someone's approval for her plans, she realised. In fact, Pete was the first person she had discussed them with, and it was a relief to have them met by enthusiasm, even if it was uneducated. Had she been talking to Christian, she would have been holding her breath with apprehension, waiting for him to come back with a whole ream of 'constructive criticism', comments and his own suggestions, until all of her ideas had transformed magically into his.

Maggie felt a moment of panic and loss. What if she did get it wrong? What if her ideas really weren't any good? After all, Christian had never taken her too seriously whenever she'd made suggestions for Fresh Talent, at least not at the time, although sometimes she'd see them being put to use somewhere down the line. Whatever people thought about Christian, he was damn good at what he did. Maggie wished desperately that he was there with her now, that the whole of the last few weeks had been some terrible dream. She had to remain focused on what she needed, and she needed Christian. All the other ups and downs of the last few days were nothing but the emotional fallout from his absence in her life. When she had him back, everything else would settle down again into the nice peaceful English tranquillity she so treasured. Not this heated wild-goose chase involving coffees with a blonde sex bomb and beers with a . . . well, a blond sex bomb. Maggie had her faults, she knew that, but sustaining any kind of deception was not one of them, and the pressure was starting to get to her.

'You do realise,' she said sternly, 'that we're going to have to wait here until Paul shows up and sees us in person. I mean, he might have clocked us on the CCTV, but I really need to make sure that he actually sees us – *together*.'

Pete nodded, and directed a pointed look at the listening barman in the hopes that Maggie would be a little more discreet.

'Anyway,' he said, smiling so that the blue of his eyes seemed to glow, 'I can think of worse ways to spend my evening.'

227

A little fazed by his billboard attractiveness, Maggie took a deep and determined swig from her bottle of beer with practised aplomb.

Pete suffered a sudden flashback to his rampantly inappropriate thoughts about her in the early hours of this morning. The sensation of lust jolted through him at speed, freezing his smile on his face as he desperately tried to cover up his reaction to the split-second parade of images. He turned on his stool to face the bar and glanced in the mirror that ran along behind the bottles of spirits. He didn't look too guilty, he noticed, and thanked Christ it was so gloomy in the bar. He took a moment to get a grip on things. OK, so he'd been celibate for a few weeks now, and OK, so Stella was far away, but this sudden onslaught of attraction for Maggie was completely out of place and out of character. What's more, it had to be based on nothing more than his bottled-up libido struggling to be free; any other explanation would be crazy. There had hardly ever been other women – not even one-night stands – between bouts of Stella. The only person who had come close to meaning anything to him had been Cindi, and that was more or less because she had been so persistent and nice that he'd given into her more with affection than passion. Even she had been swept away in one gesture by Stella.

If he'd handled these separations from Stella before, why was he experiencing these kinds of *physical* feelings now? Maybe because somehow, this time, when his separation from Stella should have felt temporary, it felt more permanent than ever, Pete realised. Maybe because somehow these new feelings made him wish it *was* permanent. Pete finished his beer and ordered two more. He couldn't let Maggie see the impulses she was stirring up in him. For one thing she would run six thousand miles in the opposite direction, and for another, even if she didn't run, he liked and respected her too much to cross that line. In the short time he'd known her, he found he liked being in the company of a woman who wasn't constantly poised to break his heart. He couldn't put her deliberately into the crossfire there would be when Stella came back. If Stella came back.

'Are you OK?' Maggie asked him. 'You seem a bit rattled. If it's all this crap . . .' she gestured at the empty bar, but Pete knew she meant their own complicated lives . . . 'you know, we could just go home. You don't have to hang around being kind to me, really. In fact, maybe we —'

Pete shook his head firmly and turned back to face Maggie.

'No,' he said categorically. 'No, it's not you. I just had a moment, you know. A Stella moment.'

Maggie nodded sympathetically. 'I know. I had a Christian moment a while back. God, we're pathetic, aren't we?' she smiled weakly. 'So tell me about your housemates? Any good gossip?'

Pete grinned. 'Well, Angie's avoiding Falcon. Falcon's avoiding solid foods and suffering from the mother of all hangovers. And I've been lying on my bed and . . .' Another unbidden image of Maggie flickered in his mind's eye. 'Missing Stella like crazy,' he said quickly. It felt strange saying those words and realising that, for the first time ever since Stella had first crash-landed into his heart, they were actually untrue. It had to be some kind of Star Trek-style anomaly, some blip he'd get over anytime soon. Pete forced a laugh. 'It's a good job Angie says she's not in love with Falcon, otherwise the Sarah thing'd really cut her up. I know what it's like to see the person you love with someone else in front of your eyes.'

Maggie tipped her head a little to one side. 'Do you?' she asked him.

'Oh yeah.' Pete gave her a wry smile. 'A couple of years back Stella took a fancy to this bloke I worked with on Dougie. She

229

sat me down one night and told me that she had to explore her impulses and give in to her attraction to him, otherwise she'd grow resentful and it would weaken our relationship . . .'

Maggie's jaw dropped. 'She expected you to sit back and let her shag some other bloke under your nose? Someone you knew, when you knew about it?' Maggie couldn't decide if Stella was pure evil or a manipulative genius. Or maybe a manipulative evil genius. 'You didn't agree did you?' she asked him, scandalised. Even she, willing as she was to be walked all over in the cause of standing by her man, thought that was going a little too far.

'No!' Pete said with gusto. 'I got on my high horse and said it's him or me. She picked him. For two weeks they were all over each other, and I mean, not just round his place or hers but everywhere I looked. My local, the bus stop outside the offices, in the studio. They never gave it a rest. It was a nightmare. I nearly packed it all in then.' Pete remembered the night he'd more or less decided to leave Leeds for good and try something new somewhere new, but Stella had had other plans for him. 'Then one morning she came into work and found me. She said she needed to talk, and pulled me into this empty editing suite. She shut the door behind her and locked it, and as she described every detail of her sexual encounters with him she . . . stripped.' Pete looked at Maggie's shocked face. 'Oh God, sorry, is this a bit too much information?'

Maggie shook her head, mute with astonishment. For reasons she didn't want to speculate on too closely she was feeling rather jealous of Stella.

'Well, we, er,' Pete coughed. 'Right there on the floor on the editing suite. Anyway, halfway through we realised that there was someone banging on the door tying to get in – it was so funny. We were laughing, but like really turned on at the same time, trying not to, you know, make any noise . . .'

230

Pete checked himself elaborating any further, not quite believing that he'd just told Maggie all that stuff. Somehow, telling it to her made it seem a whole lot less exciting and erotic than it did when he went over it in his head.

'So anyway, when we'd finished she got up and got her clothes on, all in her own good time, like. She opens the door and there's this bloke she's been seeing standing there open-mouthed. Stella hates to be cornered or pushed into anything. She just looks at him, gives him this little shrug and goes, "Look, I'm sorry and everything, we're finished, OK? I'm back with Pete." And she walks out, leaving me and him staring at each other, like either one of us is remotely hard! In the end he walked off, slamming the door shut in my face. When I got home that night she was waiting for me as if nothing had happened.'

Pete smiled at the recollection.

'It sounds mad, but I loved her then more than I ever had, even though in the end she got what she'd wanted all along. She had her fun with him, and I was there waiting for her when it was all over. God, do I sound like an idiot?'

'I'll say!' Maggie couldn't contain herself, despite their tacit agreement. 'Jesus, are you *sure* you love her, Pete? I know I'm not the one to be throwing stones or whatever, but good God, the woman sounds like a, like a . . .'

Maggie couldn't think of anything bad enough.

'Pete,' she said finally, 'have you ever thought that maybe, just maybe, Stella might be stringing you along until she finds someone better or richer or just new? I mean, I know you blokes love all that sexy slutty stuff, but –' her gaze swept up and down the length of him – 'look at you. She could go round the world fifteen times and never find anyone nicer or sweeter or let's face it, better looking than you!'

Maggie flushed, realising she had maybe said a little too much with a little too much conviction.

231

'I don't know about that.' Pete blushed, touched by her concern. 'Yes, I do think that she might be a lot of those things, but most of that's bravado – it's just show. She needs me, she needs someone to rely on. And until very recently, being in love with her has always seemed to eclipse that. And she can be so sweet, Maggie, so loving. It's like some kind of amnesia, it makes you forget all the pain.'

Maggie shrugged. 'I do know how you feel, although until Louise, Christian was pretty much a model boyfriend. More of a husband, really. But I'm serious here. Do you really not notice the string of women that fall in your wake? You could have anyone, and by the law of averages, at least one of them would have to be a nice person who deserved you!' Maggie clamped her mouth shut and opened it straightaway. 'I'm sorry, no sooner have we made a pact to help get each other's lovers back than I'm telling you to give her the heave-ho. What do I know, eh?'

'More than me by the sounds of it. Anyway, I've never understood what makes men attractive to women. With blokes, right, it's simple. Big tits, nice round arse, long legs or something like that.' Maggie wilted imperceptibly; none of her attributes had made it on to the list. 'With girls, though, it's all forearms, or hands, or ear lobes or side partings. Totally arbitrary. So when you realise that, it doesn't really matter what you're like – if you don't have the right kind of ear lobes you don't stand a chance. You sort of give in before you've started. It's terrifying let me tell you. Much better to let a girl make all the moves, and Stella is certainly very good at that.'

Maggie wanted to tell him that, in some cases, with some men, like movie stars, for example, or models and, oh, let's say slightly geeky special effects guys who liked astronomy, that rule didn't apply. OK, so with the average guy you had to focus on the one tiny part of them you could be crazy about. But with Pete, the whole package, Maggie realised, was fairly spectacular. Come to

232

think of it, even Christian, who had more than his fare share of parts to be crazy about, didn't compare to Pete's one-hundred-per-cent-satisfaction-guaranteed-or-your-money-back handsomeness. As Maggie finished her second beer and ordered another round, a little light bulb came on in her head. She looked at Pete as if for the first time, and finally realised what all the fuss was about. Why Becca never stopped mooning about him, why Sarah had lusted after him, and why, most importantly, Stella kept coming back for him. But Maggie didn't tell him any of that.

'Well,' she said instead, suddenly finding it difficult to look him in the eye, 'I think Stella's sort of given you a false image of yourself. I think you're . . . great. Actually.' She shrugged awkwardly and glowered at the barman as she caught him smirking at her. He turned abruptly and began to slice a lemon.

'Well, if I am,' Pete said, feeling secretly pleased with himself, 'then you are too. Christian is mad to let you go. I mean, look at you – you've got brains and you're funny and you're really pretty . . .'

'Pretty?' Maggie said, sounding a touch needy she thought belatedly.

'Yeah, why not? Is that not PC down here or something?' Pete said.

'No, it's just, Christian said I was "classy" and "attractive" but never "pretty".'

Pete rolled his eyes.

'Well, call me simplistic, but in my book – and it's a very short one with lots of pictures – a girl is either pretty or not. And you are. Very. Pretty and sexy. It's not rocket science.'

They held each other's gaze for a long moment, each following the same dangerous train of thought, imagining themselves in a bar in a parallel universe where Stella and Christian didn't exist. Maggie tried to shake the memory of the warm touch of Pete's lips on her neck, and he struggled not to notice the gentle curve of her beasts under the fine material of her top. They both took a long drink.

'I mean, look at The Fleur,' Pete said suddenly, perhaps a touch too loudly. 'You took that on without a second thought. That shows guts. I've always admired guts in a woman. Very admirable, guts are. I've always thought so.'

Maggie stepped back into the reality of the moment with some difficulty.

'Oh well, I mean, that was an amazing chance,' she said. 'You don't turn down chances like that, not with everyone relying on you. Besides, I think it will really work. That's when I'm not thinking it will sink without trace and I'll lose all Sheila's money and make the family homeless, that is!' She smiled at Pete.

'What about you?' he said, changing tack again. 'I mean, you're lecturing me on Stella, but what about Christian? What if you decided not to go after him tonight and we just turned this into a few innocent beers in a bar instead? Maybe in a couple of months, when you'd stopped rebounding like a ping pong ball on speed, you'd feel ready to find a decent bloke. The sort of bloke who'd appreciate you and respect your independence. Who'd take care of you when you needed it and be proud of you.'

Pete held his breath before he said any more. It occurred to him that the line he had been so determined not to cross only minutes before was now right beneath his feet. It was sort of like when you have a sexy dream about someone you work with or sort of know. The next day you just can't look at them, and you feel all funny when you see them even if up until then they've always repulsed you. Except his dream about Maggie had been a conscious fantasy that had got out of hand, and it was about two million times worse because he found all he wanted to do was to reach out and make it a reality.

'Mmm,' Maggie said, contemplating a future without Christian. 'I wish I could imagine it, you know? But I can't see past the fact that he's not there.' She sighed. 'What would you do if you decided tonight not to try with Stella any longer? What would you do a couple of months down the line when you'd stopped rebounding?'

Pete wondered what he would do if Stella suddenly disappeared from his life. He'd take a chance and go to Hollywood probably. Really try and turn his career from a dream into a reality. He felt a rush of blood to his head and his mouth ran dry. Oh, and there was one other thing.

'I'd join the queue of blokes waiting to take you out,' he said, realising as he completed the sentence that he'd spoken out loud.

It was the wrong time and the wrong circumstances, but never since Stella had Pete felt something so strongly for someone who *wasn't* Stella. Looking at Maggie was like looking at what the future might be like if only he could pull himself out of his current trajectory – a crash course set for his latest and last reunion with Stella. It was all academic, though. You don't spend over five years being in love with someone just to throw it away on a short, inexplicably heated acquaintance. After all, he was bound to run into someone else he was attracted to sooner or later – like Maggie said, it was the law of averages – and with Stella so far away her light was much less blinding.

'I'm sorry,' he said, looking at Maggie at last. 'I shouldn't have said that.'

It took Maggie several moments to digest what he had said. He was probably trying to be kind, trying to give her some kind of hope about her future which was rapidly speeding out of control. But he shouldn't have said it, and he shouldn't have kissed her neck. It had muddied the waters and now everything was unclear.

235

'Well,' she said robustly, 'it's not down to us, is it? It's down to fate, remember? We couldn't be free of this even if we wanted to be.'

Pete's eyes glinted and he reached into his pocket.

'I know,' he said, fishing out a tenpence piece. 'Let's test the fate theory, shall we? Let's be a little reckless and flip a coin.'

He held Maggie's gaze.

'Heads and I forget about Stella, you forget about Christian and we party hard all night, free as birds. Tomorrow we go off for a couple of months and we rebound all over the shop and then when that's over and done with we go out together again. On a date. Or we go out on a date tomorrow and sod the whole rebound lark.'

Maggie wondered if Pete was completely serious and felt herself lean a little closer to him, drawn by the magnetism of his recklessness.

'Tails,' Pete finished, 'and we go back to Plan A and try to get back the two people who we have so far maintained are the loves of our lives. Fate decides – agreed?'

Maggie laughed, trying to show him she realised it was just a game, but still shivers of anticipation ran down her spine.

'Agreed!' she said.

The barman poured them each a shot of tequila unprompted, pretty certain that they were going to need it one way or another.

Pete balanced the coin on his thumb and flipped it expertly into the air. For a few moments it glittered and shone, caught in the beam of the spotlights that ran above the bar. For a few moments time stood still and the future stretched out before them, empty and clean. Pete caught the coin on the back of his hand and covered it with the other one. Maggie held his gaze, and they both held their breath as Pete uncovered the coin.

They looked down.

'Tails,' Pete said, and he felt a shocking sense of disappointment. They were both silent for a moment and then Maggie picked up the shot glass and raised it in a silent toast to Pete before downing it.

'It just goes to show,' she said desperately, 'that we were right all along . . .'

Pete kept his eyes down as she talked, staring at the coin. Maggie glanced over his shoulder just as Paul walked into the room.

'Oh look, there's . . .' But she never got to finish her sentence. Before she realised what was happening, Pete's hand was on her waist pulling her into a standing position and then towards him. He placed his palm on her face and tipped her mouth towards him and kissed her. And kissed her. And kissed her some more.

Maggie swooned into the kiss in an instant, feeling the heat of his lips, the touch of his fingertips cupping her face and the firm grip of his hand on her waist, feeling each sensation minutely and separately, falling into the dark chasm of his embrace completely. His hands didn't move or try to touch her anywhere else. He just kissed her deeply, sweetly, thoroughly. It was a kiss that knocked seven balls out of Christian's drunken grope last night.

It was a kiss, Maggie would realise much later, that she had been waiting for all her life.

'Maggie?'

The pair broke apart at the interruption, torn between being unable to look at each other and not wanting to stop looking.

'Paul! Hi!' Maggie flushed from head to foot. 'How are you?' she said, feeling the absence of Pete's touch keenly as he withdrew his hands.

'Not as well as you, evidently!' Paul said, nodding at Pete knowingly. 'Brad, get these two another drink on me, will you?'

Brad nodded eagerly and set up two more tequilas. Tequila

seemed to make these two more than a little crazy, but it certainly passed the time. He was quite sorry that the bar had slowly begun to fill and that soon the evening shift would come on, crowding him out of the action.

'Oh, er, this is Pete,' Maggie told Paul uncertainly. 'My, um, friend . . . Pete, meet Paul.'

The two men nodded at each other.

'I heard about the split from Christian. He was pretty cut up about it, really worried he'd ruined your life and all that. I said to him he was a fool for letting you go. Anyway, I'll let him know there's no worries on that front, shall I?'

Maggie laughed sharply. 'Yeah!' she said, for want of anything better to say. Very possibly permanently.

'OK, well take care, now, my public awaits me!' Paul said, winking at Maggie as he drifted into the gradually increasing crowd.

Maggie and Pete looked at each other. Actually they both looked at the spot just above the right eyebrow of each other.

'Bloody hell,' Maggie said.

'I know,' Pete said. 'Look, I'm sorry, I think the sun and the tequila and the role-playing and all that has gone to my head. I just wanted to see . . . I just wanted to know what it would be like if the coin had come up heads, that's all.'

He looked at her, wanting to give her an out from the whole mess and wanting her to just laugh and say who gives a fuck about the flip of a coin and kiss him right back, right now. Instead she looked paralysed with fear.

Maggie's heart sank. Here she was, only seconds after the most thrilling event of her life, and he was already telling her it was a drunken mistake. The lightning bolt of emotion and passion that had just riveted her to the spot must have been in her head only. For one stupid, splendid moment she had really thought Pete was changing both their lives for ever with his

238

bold move. But in actual fact it seemed like he was just being a tourist, and now he was going home.

'Oh,' she said, finally, brightly. 'Not to worry. I mean, it's been a funny day and, well, you couldn't have timed it better! It's bound to get back to Christian.' As Maggie said each word she heard them echo all around her, as if she had been emptied of anything living or real.

Brad looked from the crazy woman to the crazy man. Maybe, he thought, I should just bang their heads together and tell them to stop being so fucking stupid and just get it on. But people never listen to barmen, do they? Especially not Australian ones.

There was a long and painful lull in the conversation until eventually Pete stood up and, reaching into his pocket, emptied all of his cash on to the bar in a clatter of coins and notes.

'Shall we go home then?' he said at last.

Maggie nodded, and, taking a twenty from her wallet, added to Pete's pile of cash. She had no idea how much was there – probably more than they needed – but the barman deserved a tip after the floor show they'd put on.

'Might as well,' Maggie said.

As what seemed like the rest of the world piled out of Leicester Square underground station and on to the street ready for Saturday night, Maggie and Pete descended into the suffocating heat of the tube. Neither one of them looked at or spoke to the other. Not as they made their way to the train station, not on the short journey back to St Albans. Out of the heat of the capital, at least Maggie felt like she could begin to breathe again. They walked out of the station in silence and stopped, not quite facing each other, uncertain of how to say goodbye. From here they would be going in separate directions.

'Maggie, look . . .' Pete started.

'You don't have to say anything.' Maggie said.

'No, I do, because I feel like I've messed you around and I feel bad about that.'

Pete paused. What he should say now was that she'd shaken his whole belief system to pieces and he needed time to work out how he felt about everything – about Stella, about her. But he couldn't risk doing that to her, not when the thing might just have been that anomaly he'd been thinking about. She had her life and her own problems to sort out, problems that didn't include him.

'I like you, Maggie,' he said with forced understatement. 'I think you're a good person. You deserve better than getting caught up between me and Stella.' Pete felt his stomach lurch as he spoke. 'I don't know what came over me to think I could just sweep away all the years I've been with Stella and all the feeling I have for her. To think that those could just disappear in the space of twenty-four hours. I wanted them to disappear, but . . .' Pete searched Maggie's face for any sign that she might have wanted that too, but she seemed reluctant even to look at him. 'But it's impossible, just like it's impossible for you. I thought our stupid plan might work, but it was a bit of a catastrophe really, wasn't it?' Pete winced as everything he tried to say came out slightly warped.

Maggie stared at the chain-link fence behind Pete's head, hoping she could stall the confusion of tears she could feel gathering there.

'Yeah,' she said. 'You're right. A bit of summer madness . . .' She paused, determined not to be the victim again. 'But maybe it was what we needed – you know, because it helped us realise how we really feel about Christian and Stella. You're a nice kisser, Pete, but, well . . . I love Christian.' Maggie hadn't expected him to look so crestfallen at her words. After all, they'd hardly sounded real or heartfelt even to her.

Pete struggled to adjust to the new slant on their rollercoaster friendship. Even if Maggie had just more or less mirrored his own thoughts, he found it was difficult to think of just 'knowing' her, without the kind of intimacy they had touched on with that kiss.

'We're still mates though, aren't we?' Pete said, 'And I don't mean that in a false way, the way people do when they don't want to see each other again. I'd miss you,' he finished simply.

'Of course!' Maggie said awkwardly. 'Of course we are. You must let me know how you get on. At your interview, and, I mean, over the next few weeks I'll be very busy with The Fleur, but I'll see you around, I'm sure!' She sounded harder than she meant to, angry almost. She just didn't want him to see her cry again, not when she didn't know why she wanted to cry any more. For so long she'd wanted to cry over Christian, but now she realised that even if he walked round the corner and into her arms right now, she would still want to cry.

'OK,' Pete said, and kissed her awkwardly on the cheek. 'So I'll see you around then?'

Maggie nodded. 'Yep,' she said. 'See you.'

They turned away from each other and began walking home.

Pete bent his head and shoved his hands as far as he could into his pockets as he walked. Today had made him realise the very last thing he had expected. As soon as he got home he logged on to the Internet and began an email to Stella. He had to bring this whole mess to a head once and for all. He had to get his own life in control again and find out where he stood. The trouble was he wasn't sure where to begin.

Chapter Twenty-four

Maggie opened her eyes and gazed at the sun-bleached face of Jason Orange. He had always been her favourite.

'Will I still be waking up here in the *Blue Peter* time capsule in another five years, Jason?' she asked him bleakly. 'I mean, The Fleur might have made it into *The Good Pub Guide* and got an AA rating, and I could still be here in this ten-by-six hellhole looking into your eyes and wondering, after all these years – why did you get a Mohican? You were in a boy band, for Christ's sake!'

'Love?' Maggie heard her mum's anxious voice on the other side of the door. She looked at the clock. It was only just gone eight. What had she done to deserve this honour?

'It's all right, Mum, I'm up – come in.' Maggie sat up and pushed her hair out of her eyes as her mum opened the door, a mug of tea in her hand.

'I thought you might like this,' Marion said, extending the cup out to her daughter and sitting on the edge of the bed.

There was a long pause as Maggie sipped the hot tea.

'Well, we haven't done this in years, have we?' Marion said as Maggie eyed her over the rim of the steaming mug.

'We haven't done this ever, have we?' Maggie said, perhaps a little abruptly.

Marion didn't reply. She looked around the room and smiled

to herself as if remembering something Maggie had long forgotten. She patted Maggie's legs under the duvet.

'I'm worried about you, love. I'm worried that all this is too much for you right now. To have the pressure of this place on your shoulders so soon after you and Christian have broken up . . . You always convince the world you're so strong, but we'd all understand, you know, if you wanted a break. After all, the pressure's off with the bank, and if you wanted to travel for a few weeks maybe—'

Maggie cut across her mum. 'I think I've travelled enough, don't you?' she said, sounding petulant and accusing. Maggie regretted her words instantly. 'I'm sorry, Mum. It's just that travelling is the last thing I need to do. I need to be here, focusing on this place. It's all that's keeping me going!' Maggie tried to make it sound like a joke, but she knew her mother must have heard the same desperate edge in her voice that she had.

'Maggie . . .' Marion paused, trying to collect her thoughts. 'I know that I've made you angry a lot of the time. I know you think I haven't been there for you, haven't been the right kind of mum for you.'

Maggie shifted uncomfortably and looked longingly at the door.

'You have!' she said, hopeful that the conversation might end right there.

'No, no, I haven't,' Marion persisted, and Maggie sighed inwardly. 'My own mum, your nanna, was the old-fashioned kind of mum. She created this world of order and rules for me and I – well, I hated every minute of it. As soon as I was old enough I wanted to get out there, get out of endless rows of identical houses filled with identical families. I couldn't wait to get out of school and explore the world.'

Marion smiled wistfully. 'It seemed like it was a different

243

place then, Maggie, it seemed new and full of optimism. We really believed, your father and I, that we could change things, make the world a better place. That we stood a fighting chance. I gave you and Jim the childhood I wanted for myself. I thought if you two had the freedom to find your own path you'd both be better people for it, I thought you'd be happier than I was as a child. I know how much you hated it when we travelled, and I know how disappointed you were with The Fleur when we first arrived. I should have tried to talk to you then, but I thought you'd find your own way to happiness.'

Maggie rolled her eyes and, seeing her, Marion flinched.

'You felt,' she continued, 'that I should have been there for you more as a child and maybe I should have been, because . . . because then maybe you'd talk to me now when you're so very unhappy. Maybe we'd be friends now instead of just . . . relations. I got it wrong, Maggie. I'm sorry.' Marion picked up Maggie's hand. 'I'm so sorry that I let you down, but I've always loved you, every moment – please remember that.'

Maggie withdrew her fingers, set the mug of tea on the floor and got out of bed.

'Mum!' she said awkwardly, trying to contain the sudden fury her mother had inspired, 'I'm fine, really fine! Honestly, what's brought all this on?' She opened the lid of her suitcase and looked for something to wear, secretly wishing she could climb into it and zip it shut behind her.

'I heard you crying when you came in last night. We all did. You were crying for a long time, Maggie. Sobbing. You don't seem fine . . .' Marion's face was a picture of dismay. 'I wish you'd talk to me, sweetheart. I wish you'd let me help you.'

Maggie shut her suitcase lid with a bang, and hastily pulled on her jeans and a vest top.

'Look, I'm fine, OK, I'm fine. I've never needed you to help me before, and I don't need it now. I'm very grateful that you had me back here and I'm really glad to be able to help with The Fleur. Really glad. But let's not pretend we're best friends, OK? Just because I'm here now, Mum, I don't expect anything more from you than usual. You don't owe me anything, least of all your pity.'

Maggie picked up her bag and keys and headed down the dusty corridor, down the dark stairs, and through the empty bar. Only when she was out on the street did she pause for breath and wonder where her anger had come from. And who, really, she was angry with. Pushing her disquiet to the back of her mind, she started walking.

If she had stayed a moment longer she would have seen Marion's periwinkle-blue eyes fill with tears.

Sarah was not best pleased.

'This is not a picnic,' she said again, despondently.

'Yes it is!' Sam said excitedly. 'It is!'

'No, darling, a multipack of Hula-hoops and four cans of coke is not a picnic. You just think it is because Aunty M has given you a can of hyperactivity for breakfast. I know, why don't you go and work some of it off on the climbing frame?'

Sam whooped with simple joy and raced at speed over to the children's play area. Sarah looked at Maggie over the top of her sunglasses. 'Please tell me again why we are having our picnic at nine-thirty in the morning? Without a blanket, or a basket, or any proper refreshment? Without so much as a pic or a nic?'

Becca giggled and rolled her eyes. 'Because Aunty M is bonkers, Mum, and for some reason you always seem to go along with her.' She fitted her set of headphones over her ears and went through the small selection of CDs she'd brought with her.

'Out of the mouth of girls with "babe! written on their T-shirts . . .' Sarah said pointedly. 'One minute I'm in bed thanking the Lord God for my one day of rest and that Sam is still sleeping, and the next you're banging my door down, shouting like a demented banshee and demanding we go out straightaway. Not in an hour, not in ten minutes, not after we've been to the shops, but now. It's not really what I had in mind, mate.'

Maggie looked apologetic. 'I'm sorry,' she said. 'I had a huge argument with my mum. Well, I argued and she just sat there looking all pathetic. She just drives me crazy, trying to be all caring and sharing *now*, thirty years too late! And last night – well, last night I went out for a drink with Pete and he accidentally kissed me and it me made me go all strange and now I don't know . . .'

'What?' Becca ripped the headphones off her ears and stared at Maggie. 'You kissed Pete? *You* did?' She looked appalled and Maggie winced. She'd forgotten that Becca was in love with Pete, and she'd rather hoped that Becca had forgotten too. She also didn't like the look of utter disbelief on Becca's face that it was possible that Pete should stoop so low as to kiss frumpy old her.

'I thought you were listening to Christina Aguilera!' Maggie looked at Sarah. 'It's a long story, but basically we were talking about what life might be like if we didn't still love Stella and Christian, and he flipped a coin and it came up tails but then he kissed me anyway and it's made me go all crazy.'

Sarah looked at her. 'Well, you told me you were over Christian, so what's the problem? The guy's so-called fiancée doesn't appreciate him or she'd be here, not thousands of miles away. Go for it. I would in a heartbeat!'

Becca howled.

'Mum! That is *so* disgusting!' she protested. 'Pete doesn't want to snog either of you two old bags. He wants a younger woman, someone like me.'

'Not if he doesn't want to get arrested, he doesn't,' Sarah said sternly. 'Now shush. Go and help Sam on the climbing frame or something.' All three of them looked over at Sam, who had hooked up with another boy from school and turned the slide into an Alton Towers ride. He was having a sugar-fuelled whale of a time, and the last thing he needed was Becca cramping his style. 'Or listen to your music, *very loudly*. Maggie and I are talking.'

Becca huffed and pouted as she put her headphones back on and made a point of showing her mum she was turning up the volume.

'Any other mother would take an interest in their daughter, not encourage her to rupture her eardrums,' she grumbled as she picked up Sarah's copy of *Company* and, distancing herself a few feet from the adults, lay on her back and began searching the problem pages, holding the magazine above her to shade her from the sun.

Sarah waited for a few moments and then said. 'Oooh, look, there's Justin Timberlake! Naked!' Becca didn't so much as flinch.

'Right, now we can talk, she's off in la-la land. So like I said, you are over Christian, he is over you, and you like this Pete bloke and he seems to like you. He's fit, you're not bad for your age. Why not go for it?'

Maggie drew her knees up under her chin and drew a figure of eight in the grass. It was only a little further up the park that she and Pete had sat on the ridge of the hill and gazed at the stars. The evening had seemed so innocent at the time; now the memory throbbed with resonance.

'I lied, sort of,' she said.

Sarah let her head drop to the ground with an audible thud.

'I knew it! Lied about which part?' she asked, looking up at the sky.

'Well, when I saw you on Friday I hadn't given up on Christian. I hoped that when he'd thought about it he'd realise he wanted me and not Louise, so I lied about that. And then Pete and I went for the walk and we seemed to understand each other. We seemed to know *perfectly* how each of us felt. We sort of decided to help each other out . . .' Skipping the part about Louise, Maggie told Sarah, through gritted teeth and half-closed eyes, about their plan to go to The Drinking Den, ending with the kiss and its confusing aftermath. 'It seemed like a good idea at the time,' she finished.

Sarah remained stock-still and silent, her eyes hidden behind her shades.

'Are you still awake?' Maggie asked eventually.

'Yes, but I'm just tying to think of something to say to you that won't wreck our friendship for ever,' Sarah said mildly. 'Give me a moment, OK?'

Maggie rocked on her heels and watched Sam and his friend swoop in and out of the swings, their arms outstretched like wings. Becca had dropped her magazine over her face completely. Her chest rose and fell evenly: she was probably asleep.

Sarah sat up.

'OK,' she said in an even tone, removing her sunglasses. 'Maggie, I love you. God knows why I do, but I do. I don't want to see you hurt and I don't want to hurt you, but Maggie, you've let things go too far, much too far. I don't know, maybe it was all those years playing prim housewife and secretary to that arsehole you're supposed to love but in any case now you've gone to the other extreme and it's *because* I love you that I'm telling you this.

'One: When are you going to get over yourself about your mum? Jesus Christ, don't you know how lucky you are to have a mum that cared for you so much she turned her whole life upside down to try and make you happy? She stood by, smiling on as you did your own sweet thing, and she was always there for you. Wasn't it your mum who found the cash when you got into debt at university? Wasn't it your parents who stood there with tears of pride in their eyes when you graduated? Wasn't it them that took you back in without a second's thought when, after years of more of less ignoring them, you needed their help? Think about it – you knew they'd take you back in; you didn't even have to ask them. I'm serious, Maggie. I'd do anything to have a mum that cared for me like yours does. You've got to stop being so selfish and start seeing everything you've got!'

Maggie opened her mouth and closed it again; she could see Sarah hadn't finished, not by a long way.

'Do you know how much I'd have loved to have gone to university? To have had all the years you've had to find out about yourself, to find what you really want from life? I didn't have the choice. I scrimped and saved and I built up my business from scratch. I'm proud of it and I'm proud of my kids, but you, you get your business dropped into your lap and you treat it like it's a consolation prize—'

'Now that's not fair—' Maggie tried to stop Sarah in full flow.

'Shut up, I'm talking. Right, Two. You and Christian. Maggie, you never loved him, I could have told you that from day one. Actually I did tell you that, but you didn't listen to me then, and you haven't listened to me now. You liked his security, you liked his rules, you liked him ordering you about and telling you what to think. You *wanted* him to turn you into the automaton that he did, and then when he got bored of your simpering servitude and upped and left you you were surprised! I've tried to be there for you, Maggie, I've tried to support your stupid plans one after the other. "It's just a phase," I thought. "She'll get over it – the stalking, the whining, the out-and-out

249

idiocy." ' Sarah looked disgusted. 'I really thought you were moving on, and then – and *then* – you tell me that you and Pete, who must be as stupid as he's good-looking, cook up some ridiculous plan to make Christian jealous! I mean, let's look at the facts, shall we? You are lying on the grass under the stars with the best-looking bloke within a fifty-mile radius, and you're talking about getting Christian back! Christian who, at that moment, was probably shagging his new bird—'

'Actually he—'

'Shut up. Maggie, Christian doesn't love you. You don't love Christian. If you've got even a ghost of chance to make it with someone else, then you should at least try. You shouldn't throw all your chances of happiness away on some hopeless dream that will never come true. Trust me.'

Maggie laughed, and Sarah looked as if she'd been slapped in the face.

'I can't believe that *you*, ice queen Sarah Mortimer, have just come out with all that crap! What do you know about being in love? You haven't been in love since we were at school, and that was probably just a crush that got out of hand. You don't even know what it feels like to really feel for a person, to *really* care. I'm sorry, Sarah, I've been a fool, I know I have – but you! You can't talk to me about *love*! When was the last time you were *in* love?'

Sarah's jaw tightened and Maggie was shocked to see tears standing in her eyes.

'I've been in love,' she said, her voice tightly strung. 'Of course I have. I was so *in* love with Aidan—' Sarah glanced over at Becca's prone form and lowered her voice to a hoarse and angry whisper, 'I gave him everything I had, all that love I was never able to show my parents, all of that and all of me. Every day, every week, every year for years after he left, all I thought about was him. At first I waited, and then I wished, and then I knew. I knew he was never coming back for me. I practically killed myself trying to make that pain stop. And whenever I start feeling like that again, I remember what it felt like to be left by him. I still think about him, Maggie, I still feel the pain of it all. That's why I've never got close to anyone in all these years, because they all walk out on you in the end, and I'm never, *never* going through that again. I know *exactly* what love is about. Aidan wasn't playing some game like you and your idiotic friend. He's not popped off on holiday or experimenting with someone else. He went – for good. And he'll never come back, and I'm left behind in this . . . this empty, useless bloody shell for the rest of my life. Because he's gone.'

Maggie shook her head in disbelief. 'That's not true,' she said. 'How can that be true? If it was I'd have known about it, I'd have seen it.'

Sarah lowered her eyes. 'You might have if you'd looked. Maybe if you hadn't been off at university or wrapped up in Christian and the business. Or chasing around on one of your ridiculous episodes. If you'd asked me I'd have told you. But you never did.'

'Oh Sarah.' Maggie reached out to touch her friend's bare arm. Even in the heat of the morning her skin was ice cold. 'I . . . I just don't know what to say to you. You always seem so in control, and I just . . . thought you were happy, that's all. I thought you wanted to be on your own. Oh Sarah.'

Maggie put her arms around Sarah's stiff shoulders and tried to hug her.

'If that's how you feel, we could find him,' Maggie told her. 'I'm sure we could. He might be on Friends Reunited or some other kind of website – it's amazing what you can do these days. It's a risk, I know, but you hear about these people getting back together after years apart, don't you?'

Sarah shook her head and removed Maggie's arms. She

looked at Becca, who had rolled on to her side with her back to them.

'I don't want to find him. It's not him I miss any more, it's the optimism and trust that went with him. Anyway, I don't need to find him,' she said, her voice still a whisper. 'I know where he is. He's in Boston. He's working for some export company in the legal department. He's got a wife and two kids. He saw Stephen Mills from our class on the plane back home one time. He asked him about me and Stephen told him, about the salon and about Becca and Sam. I suppose he got home and did the maths and wondered about Becca. He wrote to me. About two years ago now. Well, actually he wrote to my mum first of all, but she just wrote "not known at this address" on it and sent it back. Then he wrote to my nanna, and she gave me the letter. He told me he'd written before, all those years ago, and that I never replied. I suppose my mum didn't bother returning those letters. He asked me if Becca was his daughter. He said if she was, he was sorry that he'd left me to go through it alone and that he would have come back, he would have tried to be there for me. He said he thought I didn't want to know him any more. He said if she was, he'd really like to meet her to get to know her. He'd really like to be a father to her.'

Maggie looked at Becca's sleeping back. At some point her redundant headphones had fallen on to the grass beside her.

'But if you knew, why didn't you tell her?' she whispered, nodding at Becca.

Sarah dropped her head into her hands and ran her fingers through her hair. 'Because . . . because I couldn't bear it, Maggie. I couldn't bear the thought of him wanting her and not me, and I was so scared that she'd leave me for good. I know I was wrong, but . . .'

'You bitch.' Becca was sitting bolt upright, staring at her mum with the kind of fury that no child should know. 'You

252

stupid, selfish, fucking *bitch*. How *could* you. HOW COULD YOU?'

Across the field, Sam stopped dead in his game and looked over at his mum and sister. Without a second thought he began running towards them.

'You were right!' Becca screamed through her tears. 'You were right, because I *am* going to find him, *right now*. I'm going to look him up on the Internet or something, *anything*. I'm going to find him, and when I do, I'm going. I'm getting as far away from you as I can, and I'm *never* coming back. Not *ever*. How *could* you? What gives you the right? No wonder he didn't want you, you stupid, fat, selfish bitch. But he wants *me*, and that's more than you do, because if you did, if you cared about me at *all*, you'd have let me see him. You'd at least have let me know that he cared!'

As Becca turned on her heel and began running across the field, Sam slid into her mother's arms. He wound his arms around her neck and began sobbing.

'Mummy, where's she going, where's she going?' he pleaded. Sarah rocked him gently, kissing the top of his head.

'It's OK,' she whispered, looking desperately at Maggie. 'It'll be OK, Sammy baby.'

'I'll go and find her,' Maggie said. 'I'll calm her down and try and explain things to her. I'll bring her home. But . . .' She paused, glancing over her shoulder at Becca's rapidly retreating figure. 'Sarah, everything you said about me today was true. I know that, and I promise you not one of those things matters now, not until we've sorted this out. OK?'

Sarah nodded, rocking her son close against her.

'I'm sorry, Maggie . . .' Sarah began.

'Don't be sorry. You were right about me. I'll go and find her. Don't worry, OK?' Maggie knew the request was point-less. As she began to follow Becca into the town, the sky

253

darkened and rumbled and the first few heavy drops of rain began to fall.

Maggie felt like the summer was over for ever.

She lost Becca as she disappeared around the back of the abbey, half running, half walking, her head down, her hands over her face. But Maggie thought she knew where she would find her, and she was right. The cybercafé could only have opened minutes ago, but Becca was there, sitting at one of its two terminals staring blankly at the screen with tears streaming down her face. She looked completely lost, Maggie thought. Completely desperate and lost.

'Maggie, hi! Good to see you!' Declan appeared by her side. 'You're quite the early bird, aren't you? Come in to get out of the rain? I'd almost forgotten what it looked like, it's been such a dry summer. I haven't seen you in a while. Everything's OK, is it, between us?'

Becca's head snapped in Maggie's direction when she heard Declan say her name, and she began to scramble her stuff together in preparation for a quick exit. Maggie kept her eyes on her as she talked to Declan.

'Yes, Declan, of course it is, but look –' she nodded at Becca – 'I have to speak to my god-daughter, OK?'

Declan took one look at Becca's blotched face and made a hasty retreat behind the counter, mouthing 'talk later' at Maggie as she went. Maggie heard the clatter and bubbling of the cappuccino machine crank into action.

'Becca.' She grabbed her arm as she tried to rush past.

'Let me go,' Becca said, shaking her arm vigorously. 'I don't want to talk to you! You're just the same as her. Both of you, you think what I feel, what I think, doesn't matter. Like, just because I'm not grown-up yet I don't have any feelings.' She yanked her arm hard. 'Let me *go!*'

Maggie let go of her arm, relieved that she didn't immediately run out of the door.

'I'm not the same as your mum,' she said, desperate to get Becca to stay. 'I didn't know about it, did I? The letter and all that? I assume that you were listening to everything we said, and not by accident, so you know. I didn't know about it, did I?'

Becca shook her head slowly. Maggie brushed her damp hair back from her face.

'Oh Becs, why were you eavesdropping anyway?' Maggie asked, pulling her into a hug.

'Because I thought you were going to be talking about sex. And because I thought you were going to be talking about Pete, and I wanted to know if you were going to go out with him. I didn't think you'd be talking about . . . Not, not . . .' Becca began sobbing again, her slight frame shaking against Maggie's body. Maggie guided her to a chair in the corner, grateful that the café was still empty. Becca would be mortified if she thought any of her friends had seen her like this.

'Here you go.' Declan appeared at the table and set down two steaming mugs topped with whipped cream and marshmallows. 'Hot chocolate. I thought the rain storm merited it.' He smiled at Maggie and went back behind the counter. For those two moments of silence that followed his gesture, Maggie thought he was the nicest, kindest man in all the world.

'She's just a lying, conniving bitch, that's all,' Becca said with brutal frankness. 'She doesn't want anyone else to be happy because she isn't. She doesn't even want you to be happy, Aunty M. She wants to split you and Christian up because she's so bitter and twisted and . . .'

'Shhhh.' Maggie took Becca's hand. 'That's not true, Becca, it isn't.'

'Yes it is,' Becca said. 'Why can't she just be a normal mum, like Leanne's mum or the other mums at school? Why does she

255

have to sleep around with any bloke? She thinks I don't know, but I do, I can see it – and soon Sam will. Why can she never have a proper boyfriend, like Marcus? All she does is work and go out. She's hardly ever there for me and Sam. If she loved us she'd be a proper mum. You don't know what it's like. I feel like I'm having to grow myself up. That's how I feel. At least if I had a dad to talk to that would be one person in the whole world who'd stand up for me.'

Maggie dropped her head and thought for a moment. Everything that Becca had just said could have been her words at fourteen, or at twenty-four. Her words earlier that morning. But Maggie knew that Sarah loved Becca. She knew Sarah would die fighting for her children's happiness and do anything to make them happy. Would her mum do the same, Maggie wondered? Had she ever given her a chance to?

'Listen. Your mum, Becca, loves you so much. So much. It was a shock for her when you were born, admittedly. She was hardly much older than you are now when it happened. She was only your age when she fell in love with your dad. I suppose what you said is true – no one then thought they could *really* feel anything for each other. Everyone – even me – assumed that it was over as soon as your dad's family left the country. I thought that she'd been unlucky and got caught out. I never realised how much his going hurt her, not really. Your mum's always put a brave face on things, always been determined to show that she can cope on her own. She's had to because her mum didn't want her any more. Can you imagine that? Out in the world on her own with a baby on the way at just eighteen?'

Maggie thought back to the Sarah she had known then, defiant and hard-faced on the outside, but, Maggie then and now thought, a terrified, lonely little girl on the inside.

'It was hard for her, Becca, harder than I think I understood at the time. For most of it, her pregnancy, when she moved into the hostel, I wasn't even there, I was at college. But I was there when you were born. I stayed with you both for a while, and I can tell you, your mum used to hold you in her arms and just look at you for hours and hours, and she'd say to me that looking at you was like looking at a tiny rose bud. A tightly closed rose bud. And that each day you opened up just a little bit more and grew just a little bit more beautiful. She told me she wanted to spend the rest of her life watching you blossom. That your happiness was the only thing that mattered to her.'

Becca's tears had stopped and she wound both her hands around the warm mug in front of her and held it close to her chest.

'I think maybe over the years she's been so busy trying to give you security and a home, trying to make sure you and Sam had everything you needed, that she's forgotten, sometimes, just to be there for you,' Maggie bit her lip. 'And sometimes, Becca . . . Well, sometimes you've made it pretty clear you don't really want her there.'

Becca took a noisy sip of her chocolate and gazed out of the rain-sheeted window.

'I've only got sandals on,' she said eventually.

'I know,' Maggie smiled cautiously. 'Me too. Flip-flops, actually. I'm going to get soaked.'

Becca shrugged and looked at her.

'She was wrong, though, wasn't she?' She seemed to be testing Maggie. 'She was wrong not to write to Dad and tell him about me. Not to let us have a chance to know each other. That was wrong, really wrong, wasn't it? Now he might have moved, or anything, and I might never find him. He might think that it's because I don't want to know him and that . . .'

Maggie intervened before Becca could work herself up again.

'Yes, Becca. Yes. She was wrong. She was even wrong for the wrong reasons.' Maggie paused, searching for a way to explain

257

things clearly. 'It's like you said earlier about grown-ups thinking that kids don't really feel things. Well, I think some-times you forget that your mum really feels things. Sometimes you think she should just be this sort of big cosy cushion for you to come to and hug when you want her. In some ways maybe she should be. But she's also a real person and she makes real mistakes. She made the wrong choice over that letter, it's true, but it's one wrong choice out of hundreds and thousands of right ones, all of them made for you and Sam. Whatever she did, Becca, whatever the reasons, she loves you so much, *so much*. And I think that if someone loves you that much, you owe it them to give them as many chances they need to get it right, don't you?'

Becca said nothing as she drained her cup, leaving traces of chocolate around her mouth. For a moment she looked like that little rose-bud baby girl again.

'I don't really want to leave home,' she said finally.

'I know,' Maggie said. 'Why don't we finish these and see if we can borrow an umbrella. We can go back and talk —'

'I'm not going back there unless you promise to stick up for me!' Becca said. 'I want to see my dad. I want her to promise to call him for me and arrange things. And if he's not there any more, I want her to look for him and not stop looking until she finds him.'

Maggie nodded. She knew it would be difficult for Sarah to do all of these things, but she also knew that Sarah would do all of them. That Becca deserved no less.

'OK, Becca, I'm sure your mum will agree to that. But you do understand, don't you, that your dad has another life now. He won't just come over here for ever. He's married to someone else. There won't be any fairy-tale endings for him and your mum. You might not even like him,' Maggie said, stopping short of saying "he might not even like you". It was

258

harsh, she knew, but it was a possibility, and she wanted to be the one to say it to Becca. She wanted to spare Sarah that at least.

'I know that,' Becca replied tentatively. 'But I can't go through life not knowing, can I? I can't just go on wondering what it might have been like.'

Maggie sat on the floor of Sam's room whilst he performed *South Pacific* for her with his toys. Right now his Action Man was getting it on with one of Becca's discarded and headless Barbies as he crooned 'Some enchanted evening' over the top of the makeshift scenery.

Becca and Sarah had been in the living room for over an hour now. There had been shouting, at which point Sam had stopped mid-song and turned to look at the door. Then there had been a loud thump, followed by a crash and then silence. Maggie had quickly got things going again by starting to sing 'Happy talk', which annoyed Sam intensely as she got the words wrong and it wasn't even in the right place. Finally, as she'd listened over the top of Sam's singing, there had been silence from the rest of the flat. She clapped as Action Man, headless Barbie and a couple of teddies took a bow.

'Shall we go and see how Mummy and Becca are now?' she asked Sam, supposing it was probably safe.

'But I was going to do you *Chitty Chitty Bang Bang* next!' he cried, holding up his model of Dougie the Digger. Maggie stared at it and felt inexplicably sad. She pulled herself together with a smile.

'I know, darling, maybe later, OK?' He nodded, and with her hands on his shoulders Maggie guided him into the living room. The worst case scenario, she supposed, was that they could have knocked each other out. She didn't think either one of them would go for out-and-out murder.

She pushed open the door. Sarah was on the phone, holding

a tatty-looking piece of paper in her hand. Becca was standing beside her, staring at her intensely.

'Oh, hello?' Sarah said. Her voice was shaking. 'Is that you, Aidan? Hi! It's, um, Sarah, Sarah Mortimer, here. Hi! Yes, it is a bit out of the blue, isn't it?' She looked at Becca and nodded. 'Um, Aidan, I'm sorry to call you so early, but have you got a minute to talk? It really *is* important.'

Maggie guided Sam back out into the hallway.

'So, big fella, what were you saying about *Chitty Chitty Bang Bang* then?'

'Hooray!' Sam shouted as Maggie followed him back into his room and shut the door behind them.

Chapter Twenty-five

Pete had spent his Sunday writing and deleting at least twenty half-baked versions of the things he wanted to say to Stella. He'd get so far each time, work his way through a lengthy preamble to prepare her for what he had to say, and then he'd stall. *The thing is, Stella,* he'd begin, and then he'd stare at the liquid blue-white of the screen and sit back on his rickety chair borrowed from the kitchen and he'd wonder what exactly was the thing?

It wasn't that he didn't love her any more. He was fairly certain that he did still love her, he thought, after the third attempt, at which point he went for a walk and kept walking, even though a sudden shower of hot rain soaked him through to the skin. Sheltering under a tree for a moment he closed his eyes and thought of her, testing his response to her image. He saw her standing in front of him, that special half smile of hers the tiniest implication that she might, just might, be his after all. A promise which had been enough to keep him in love with her for over five years. But it was more than that wasn't it? It had to be.

Pete opened his eyes and felt the sting of a heavy droplet of water, which temporarily blinded him. Shaking himself like a dog, he stepped out into the rainstorm and kept walking – he was saturated anyway; it was pointless to try and resist it. The real reason he'd loved her for so long, the reason his friends and family couldn't see, was that Stella had something else buried deep in the middle of her, under layers and layers of artifice and theatre. Deep inside all the magic and light, Pete had found a very ordinary person, just a girl who had first-hand experience of the hard edges of the world. A girl who was petrified of making the wrong choices.

After all, her mum had got married at sixteen, when she was three months pregnant with Stella. Her father, barely eighteen himself, had left them within three days of her birth. Left because of her, Stella always said, as if her presence alone had wrecked what otherwise would have been a perfect romance. Stella and her mother had never seen him again, and she remembered a childhood of endless shifting from hostels to council B&Bs and finally a flat on the thirty-second floor of a high-rise on the outskirts of Leeds. Stella had told him that she used to pretend she was Rapunzel letting down her long hair, waiting for a prince to carry her away. Stella explained to him that her mum had made all the wrong choices too quickly without ever stopping to think what might happen, as if life was just something you could leave up to fate, and that both their lives had been blighted because of it. She told him she was terrified of doing the same, terrified of ruining everything because of the wrong choice. She had to make absolutely sure she was making the best possible choice for herself, giving herself the best possible chance in the future.

Once he'd known this, Pete thought she'd given him the key, the vital clue to, understanding her and keeping her. Pete had asked her often if the fact that he loved her and would stand by her and be with her whatever happened wasn't enough. Stella would look at him sadly and tell him that no, it wasn't enough. She needed more. God knows he'd stayed long enough in that well paid, dead-end job trying to make enough to make her feel as if she had enough. It seemed he'd never manage it, though.

262

There was always the chance that someone, sooner or later, might be able to give her more.

Pete felt the rain trickle down the back of his T-shirt, which clung ever closer to his skin. He could understand, he supposed, her need to surround herself with material proof of her happiness. He'd grown up in a literally solid family in the posh bit of Oldham, an ex-*Coronation Street* actress had lived at the bottom of his road. He'd never thought of his family as rich, but he knew they were nothing like poor. He'd never really worried about cash, never really had to. Maybe if he had, he reasoned as he turned on to the high street, he'd feel the same as Stella did. She kept a dog-eared copy of *Breakfast at Tiffany's* which she'd stolen from a library as a teenager that she took with her everywhere, and although Pete had never found time to read the book, he'd watched the film one Stella-less Sunday afternoon on TMC. He imagined that Stella thought she was Holly Golightly, using her charms to find herself the security she craved. But in the end, George Peppard had prevailed and Holly had realised that love, even dirt poor love, *could* be enough to make life worth living. That was two years ago, and Pete had been certain that in the end Stella would one day stop in her tracks in the same kind of pouring rain he was standing in now and come to the same conclusion. She'd realise that Pete loving her would be enough. But that day hadn't come yet, and Pete realised, as he mounted the steps to his front door, that it might never come.

He opened the door and listened to the house, the sound of him dripping on to the tiles magnified by the quiet. There was no noise coming from Angie's ground-floor bedroom and nothing else resonating on the two floors above him.

'Hello!' He called out to be certain, uncertain why he wanted to be so absolutely alone. He supposed he wanted to be sure he wouldn't be interrupted. Just to talk to anyone right now, he knew, would break his train of thought. He couldn't risk the thin, frail, brightly shining thread that was leading him through his maze of emotions. The house was silent in reply and Pete breathed a sigh of relief. He mounted the stairs, and once he had shut the door of his bedroom he peeled his wet clothes off layer by saturated layer. A warm wind billowed through the net curtains that hung at the open window, raising goosebumps on his skin.

And then there was Maggie. That was the other part of the equation. He didn't know what to think about her, what to say. He couldn't say he'd fallen in love with her, not after two weeks' acquaintance, he knew that much. He could say that she moved him, inspired in him the need to be close to her somehow. He liked her very much, she made him laugh. And he wanted her, he let himself confess. He felt a jolting, jangling attraction to her that he hadn't experienced since the first time he'd seen Stella, and maybe even then it hadn't been as intense. He thought of her dark flashing eyes and the pale curve of her long neck. He found himself imagining his lips on her breasts, his hands moving as lightly over her skin as the damp breeze was moving over his. Pete stopped himself from thinking and pulled out whatever clothes lay piled under his bed before the thought of Maggie eclipsed what he was trying to do entirely.

Was it just lust, then, with Maggie? If he could have her, in some alternate universe where she would even consider the idea, then would he still love Stella afterwards? Or would he be sacrificing that love just to know what it felt like to be with Maggie?

Pete sat on the edge of his bed. He knew that if he made love to Maggie it would mean that he didn't love Stella any more. He hadn't ever believed in the 'it didn't mean anything' excuse, for himself, anyway because he knew that it did mean something. It meant everything.

Before Stella he'd had his fair share of one-night stands, of promising to call and leaving half-stranger's beds at dawn with half-baked excuses. At the time he thought he'd wanted all of that, the thrill and rush of pleasure with no consequences. But then came Stella, and the first time Pete lay down with her he knew that it meant something to take another person to bed. It meant everything. If Maggie wasn't so firmly out of bounds, if last night she had reached for him and kissed him back and taken him in her arms, Pete knew that he wouldn't have held back, he wouldn't have stopped her and said 'No, what about Stella?' He knew that all thoughts of Stella would have been flooded out of his head by the touch and sensation of Maggie.

That was the thing, he concluded as he turned back to his PC at last. It wasn't that he didn't still love Stella. It was that Maggie had shown him a future where loving Stella wasn't inevitable any more. When he looked at Maggie he saw a bright horizon, a future where everything he'd thought was laid out wasn't inevitable.

After the twentieth attempt, Pete gave up trying to express what he was feeling in words. Instead he simply wrote. *Stella, something's changed. I've met someone. I don't know how to feel any more. I need to talk to you. I need to hear your voice. And then I'll know. Please call me, you can reverse the charges.*

He typed in his phone number at the flat and pressed send. Only after the email had gone, fizzing and buzzing its way into the ether, did Pete realise what he'd done. He'd given her an ultimatum.

Chapter Twenty-six

Maggie stretched on Sarah's sofa and contemplated getting off it and making her way to the bathroom. She knew she should because apart from the fact that she'd heard Sam complaining outside the closed door a while back that he was missing his cartoons, she had thousands of things to do today, having a pee being the most pressing right now.

Somehow, though, every part of her body felt coated in lead and all she wanted to do was turn and face the back of the sofa and curl up and stay there, staring at minute row upon minute row of sage green chenille. This hadn't happened to her in a long time, in a very long time. Even when Christian had left her she had managed to get out of bed in the morning, fired up with the prospect of getting him back. But now, finally, on this Monday morning when everything should have been beginning, it had hit her – the same lurching disability that had used to waylay her whenever she was faced with having to do something that seemed almost impossible. Total, wanton, deadly apathy. She forced herself into a sitting position, her head hanging over to one side.

It must just be everything that had happened recently. She must be experiencing some kind of delayed shock, a fear of how terrible things would be if she messed it all up even more than she already had done, which was fairly spectacularly, even for her. Only it wasn't fear, it was apathy – she didn't care any more. Suddenly, she just didn't care about what happened to The Fleur or her parents or Christian or Pete. Maggie huffed out a breath with some effort. The last time she'd been like this was just before the finals of her degree.

'But you've done all the work!' her friends had told her as she lay in her bed, her duvet pulled over her head. 'You're the star pupil, and anyway the degree's marked on continuous assessment – you've probably already passed!'

'I don't care!' Maggie had managed to tell them. 'I don't care if I pass or not. Go away.'

They'd had to drag her into a standing position, force her into her clothes and frogmarch her into the hall. She'd sat the exams, of course, and once they'd begun she'd forgotten all about the apathy. But now it was here again, and she felt paralysed by it. The enormity of everything she had to do to straighten out her life and the lives around her overwhelmed her. She couldn't begin to see how she could ever release herself from the deadlock, and she just wanted to go to sleep instead.

Sarah's living room door opened a crack and Sam's afro made a tentative entrance two inches before one of his light grey eyes did.

'Are you awake now?' he demanded loudly, ensuring that she would be.

'Yes, Sam, come in, darling.' Maggie told him, and he ran in, skidding on his knees to the TV set which he switched on to his favourite channel. Maggie watched whichever cartoon it was with him for a minute or two before the pressing need of her bladder forced her to her feet.

'Hi,' Sarah called out to her from the small galley kitchen as she padded down the hall. 'How are you? You didn't have to stay last night, you know. It was kind of you, though, to stay up

267

to God knows when listening to me going on about . . .' Sarah glanced at Becca's shut door . . . 'everything.'

Maggie shrugged without pausing and pointed herself towards the bathroom.

'I'll make you a coffee then?' Sarah called after, taking her silence as assent.

Maggie looked at herself bleakly in Sarah's bathroom mirror. For a moment, when Pete had kissed her, she'd felt incredible, beautiful and powerful. She baulked at using the phrase, but then, with a what-the-hell shrug, told herself she'd felt . . . sexual. It wasn't that her sex life with Christian hadn't been satisfactory, it had been more than. But somehow that *almost* chaste kiss, the static passion of it, had swept through her like a forest fire. If Maggie was a character in a romantic novel, she'd say it had awakened her to the possibilities of sexual love.

She filled Sarah's sink to the brim with ice-cold water and shoved her head into it, emerging a few seconds later to see her bedraggled self staring back at her, resembling nothing more than a drowned rat.

'This is what I'm *really* like,' she told herself in a hoarse whisper. 'Scrawny and thin and . . .' she examined the darkly black recesses of her eyes . . . 'and dark.' She didn't know what Stella looked like, so in her mind's eye she melded her into one being with Louise. A sort of uber-nemeses, light to her dark, full curves to her wasted emptiness. She grabbed Becca's wide-toothed comb from the sink and combed her hair back off her face. Of course she knew she was being overdramatic, but she didn't care; it was one up, at least, on the apathy. Stripping off Sarah's nightshirt she began to dress in yesterday's crumpled clothes.

With everything that had happened she'd forgotten to worry about Christian and his date with Louise, proposed especially, Louise had said, to 'talk things over'. She thought about it now and found that even this she didn't have the energy to care about. Perhaps Christian had left Louise, and perhaps he was sitting on her doorstep right now with a dozen roses, waiting for her return. Maggie pictured the image and tried to feel something about it, but she couldn't. She tried picturing Christian and Louise in each other's arms having worked everything out, and found at last a small sensation of disquiet. Disquiet not at the thought of them being together, she realised, but that – as it turned out this morning, at least – she wasn't really all that fussed. Maggie tapped her forehead hard with the heel of her palm.

'Come on!' she told herself angrily. 'Get going, you idiot!' She didn't just mean out of the flat and back to work, she meant literally, emotionally, physically. She felt as if she had spluttered to a haltering stop. Stalled.

'Maggie?' Sarah said from the other side of the door. 'Your coffee's here?'

Maggie opened the door and took it gratefully, tanking at least half of it in one gulp, regardless of its heat. She looked at Sarah, who beckoned her into the bedroom.

'Are you OK?' Sarah asked her.

Maggie noticed her friend's skin bruised with shadows, her eyes still swollen and red.

'Are *you* OK?' she replied.

Sarah shrugged. 'I'll be OK when I think that Becca and I are really OK. I know she doesn't understand why I did it. *I* hardly understand it. I just wanted to cling on to everything that I've got, everything I've fought for despite him. And I was afraid of seeing him again. I still am, actually. Petrified.'

Maggie nodded, remembering Sarah's retelling of the phone call last night after Becca had finally gone to bed. He'd been shocked to hear from Sarah for a start, and then, Sarah had felt, had been really delighted to talk to her again. When she told

269

him about Becca, he'd been stunned into silence and for a while, as she'd talked, she wasn't sure if he was still on the other end of the line. She'd tried her best to explain, in that oddly disconnected way, things that should only be explained face to face. She'd told him the way things were and why it had been so hard for her to admit to him that he was Becca's, leaving out as much about her personal feelings about him and what he had meant to her as she could. It was tragic, Maggie realised, almost Shakespearean. If Sarah's mum had passed on the letters that Aidan had sent her and hadn't thrown them away, they might have worked things out differently. Unlikely given their ages at the time, but they'd have had a chance, and Becca would have known her dad from the start. Fourteen years later and it wouldn't be possible for a mere letter to wreck a long-distance romance, not with email and international phone calls being so cheap. Just a few short years would have made the world of difference to them. But in that time, in that place, they were not meant to be. Anyway, after a halting conversation Sarah had finally handed the phone to her daughter and left the room to join Maggie and Sam.

'Is he coming?' Maggie had asked her.

'Yes, as soon as he can,' Sarah had told her, her face perfectly still as she pictured eighteen-year-old Aidan the last time she had seen him. 'He's even got an American accent, imagine that.'

They hadn't talked about it again until Becca had finally come down off the ceiling and gone to bed, exhausted by triumph and elation. She'd have to be here, Maggie realised, at Sarah's shoulder through all of the things that were to come: Sarah would need her. Maggie breathed a sigh of relief as she felt how much she cared about Sarah and her small family. It wasn't the whole world, then, that she didn't give a fig for, just her small part of it.

'You were talking to yourself in the bathroom.' Sarah interrupted her thoughts. 'Not out of character, I know, but anyway, *are* you OK?'

Maggie sighed and plonked down on Sarah's bed in one fell motion. Sarah looked at her alarm clock and looked fairly alarmed herself. She had to open up in ten minutes.

'I've got the apathy,' Maggie said. 'I don't care about my life any more. I've tried and tried and tried, and where's it got me? . . .'

She was about to finish 'nowhere', but Sarah stepped in.

'Um, a business, family, friends who love you? Two men fighting over you?'

Maggie sat up, remembering Sarah's previous lecture before the whole Aidan thing had blown up.

'They're not fighting. No one is fighting. Everyone is decidedly not fighting,' Maggie said, at least finding the impetus to string a sentence together. 'Oh, I don't know, Sarah, this whole kiss thing. It's, well, it's like this. Pete kissed me and it was all . . . wooooo.' Maggie realised her powers of description were lamentable, but Pete's kiss had tended to make her speechless whenever she thought about it, which had been approximately every two point four seconds since the moment it had happened, even, to her shame, during yesterday's dramas.

'The kiss was "all woo". Right,' Sarah replied matter-of-factly, as if Maggie had handed her a two-thousand-word essay on the subject. 'So go to him, tell him. Make it happen, woman!'

Maggie shook her head despondently.

'I can't. Because of Christian. Because he's the one I'm meant to be with. We've got this whole life that's waiting for us to get back to it, and I can't just abandon that on a whim.'

Sarah rolled her eyes but kept her mouth shut.

'And anyway, because Pete's got this other girl, and he told

271

me that one kiss doesn't change how much he loves her . . .
which I understand, because of Christian . . .'

Maggie trailed off and Sarah looked at her watch pointedly.

'So forget it, then, if you're not going to do anything about
it. Just forget it.'

Maggie took the hint and stood up, gathering her belongings
with an effort of energy.

'No, it's not that. I mean, it's not *just* that.' She chewed her
lip. 'The kiss was all "woo" and blew me away, but it's not the
kiss by itself, it's Pete. He's just . . . I really like him, Sarah. It's
like I feel I've always known him. If the kiss and the other
woman mean I can't know him any more, then I'm going to be
sad about it. Really properly sad. It'll take me a long time not to
be sad, I think. Stupid, isn't it? A couple of weeks ago and I
didn't even know him.'

Sarah looked at her. It occurred to her to say all the obvious
things, like for God's sake, woman, you are clearly in love with
this man, forget about Christian, who has probably forgotten
about you, and just go and get Pete. But her tactic of stating the
obvious had never worked so far with Maggie; not once, in
actual fact. If anything it always seemed to drive her in the
opposite direction.

'So if you mean that,' she said instead, 'go to him and tell him
that. Make sure you stay friends.' That way Sarah thought, at
least they'd be in the same room together and nature might take
its course.

'Do you think so?' Maggie said.

Sarah nodded.

'OK, I will. I'll do that. He's got an interview tomorrow, so
I could go round after that to see how it went and everything,
and talk to him about it, clear it all up, and we can be real friends
again!' Her face had suddenly animated into a smile at the
thought of having a sensible reason to see Pete again. 'I have to

do the whole supplier thing today,' she said, 'I've made appointments. Jim is taking me in his Capri, so I might be dead by tomorrow, but if not I'll definitely go and see him. That's a good idea. Thanks, Sarah. I'd better get going!'

Maggie kissed her friend and descended the stairs into the salon two steps at a time. The apathy had gone the moment she'd thought of seeing Pete again. Of course, Maggie didn't make that connection. She'd forgotten all about her morning sense of doom by the time she hit the street.

There was someone waiting for her outside The Fleur as she hurried back, but it wasn't Christian or Pete, it was just Jim, leaning against the side of his double-parked Capri, resplendent in its matt silver bodywork, red passenger door and blue driver's door and hood. Jim loved his car with a passion she had never seen him reserve for anything human. For years he'd worked on it in his considerable spare time, turning the whole of the customer's car park into a garage and spending a fortune of mostly his parents' money. He said it was a classic car. Maggie thought it was a pile of junk, but right now it was the closest thing they had to a company car. She wondered if she could reasonably ask Jim to park it out of sight of the places they were going so she could walk the last few feet without embarrassment. She decided that she probably could.

'You're late,' Jim said, looking at the part of his wrist where a watch would be if he owned one.

'Yeah, well, you're on time,' Maggie scoffed out of habit. 'Which, frankly, is nearly as shocking as that tie you're wearing.' She gestured to a paisley effort that he must have lifted from her father's wardrobe. 'What were you thinking?'

Jim sighed. 'I was making an effort. I put on a tie and got ready on time, which is more than I can say for you.'

Maggie looked down at herself: her trousers were crumpled

273

and her top was not so lightly fragranced with Sarah's cigarettes and red wine.

'I'd better nip in and have a shower . . .' she said, making for the door.

'Oh no you don't!' Jim grabbed her arm. 'We'll be late for Brownly's. I spoke to him yesterday, he said he's got this almost complete kitchen out of a hotel, only ten years old, in really good nick. The hotel got bought out and got a refit for good measure. He said it'll be gone by the end of today.'

Maggie stared at him, wondering if he actually cared about second-hand professional kitchens or if he just wanted to see her walk into the reclamation centre looking like the littlest hobo. Either way, he did have a point.

'OK,' she conceded. 'Maybe if I keep the windows down it'll blow away the smell.'

She looked up at the sky as she climbed into the car. There had been no sign of the sun since the rainstorm had broken on Sunday morning. Now the air that had burned so brightly for the last two months was humid and damp and the clouds sat low and heavy in the sky. Jim climbed into the driver's seat and reached into his pocket.

'Before we go —' he began.

'Jim!' Maggie interrupted him. 'We're going to be late. Whatever it is, the answer is no. You can't have, do or say it. All right?'

Jim pressed his lips together and, instead of speaking, took a folded brown envelope out of his pocket and threw it in Maggie's lap. She picked it up and, scowling at him, looked inside, expecting to see some kind of final demand.

'It's money!' she said, looking at the wad of notes. 'Quite a lot of it by the looks of things.'

Jim nodded with satisfaction. 'It's four hundred and eighty pounds,' he told her. 'From the books I found in the cellar. The ones Dad bought by the yard all those years ago. I thought some of them might be worth something, so I took a few to a dealer's in Bloomsbury on Saturday. That's what he gave me for them, although to be honest, sis, I think if I'd have really known what I was talking about I could have got more. But still. It's not much, I know, but it might help buy a hot plate or something?'

Maggie thumbed through the money and looked back at Jim. Secretly she couldn't believe he'd given it to her at all. She'd had no idea the books were worth anything. He could have kept it and she would have been none the wiser.

'I'm not *that* cheap,' Jim said resentfully.

'What do you mean?' Maggie said guiltily.

'I mean that you were just wondering why I didn't pocket the cash, and that I'm not *that* cheap,' Jim repeated, looking away from her.

'Thanks, Jim, it will come in handy,' she said, and then despite herself, 'but what's brought all this on? You have to admit it's a bit of a sudden transformation!' Jim sighed and started the ignition of the car. The engine rattled loudly as he pulled out into the street and began to negotiate the busy one-way system out of the city.

'Do you remember when we were kids?' He had to speak loudly over the engine, and Maggie leaned towards him a little. 'When we used to build a "castle" out of sheets and chairs and stuff in the upstairs living room?'

Maggie nodded with a half-smile.

'And you used to be the princess and I was your knight and Sheila was the dragon?'

Maggie couldn't help but chuckle. They had never bothered to tell Sheila when they cast her in this particular role, so whenever she came in to check on them, finding Maggie squealing underneath a sheet and Jim charging at her with a

275

wooden spoon, the look of mild alarm on her face used to crack them both up.

'What's that got to do with this?' Maggie said, still holding the envelope.

'We used to be friends. Not just then, when we were kids, but before you left home, we used to be friends and have a laugh. Then when you left you seemed to leave that behind too. I missed you, Maggie. I got used to the idea that you didn't miss me.'

Maggie looked out of the window.

'I did! I just got angry with you, Jim. Angry with the way you drifted in and out of college, let Mum and Dad take care of you when you were perfectly capable of doing it yourself. I know everyone lives at home until they're eighty-two these days, including me, by the looks of things, but I just wanted you to make the most of your life. You're letting it slip away. I mean, if you'd have helped Mum and Dad out they might not have gotten into this mess.'

Jim shrugged. They'd left the town behind now, its wide road quickly turning into fast, narrow country roads.

'Maybe,' he said, 'but maybe it's hard to do anything living in your shadow. And sometimes it seems like everyone at home annoys you because they're not like you. And us not being like you makes you hold back for some reason, and you resent us for it. Even Mum and Dad – especially Mum and Dad . . . You're pretty harsh on them, you know. Too harsh sometimes. It can be sort of . . . debilitating. And maybe it's just me, but . . . oh, I don't now, Maggie. But now you're back, and we've got this new start. It feels like a new start to me, doesn't it to you?'

Maggie felt a sudden surge of anger. 'Of course I do! Don't you think I'm not grateful? But don't go blaming me for the fact you've never done anything with your life. I can't help that.'

Jim pulled into the car park of Brownly's Professional and

Architectural Reclamation Centre, a large square industrial warehouse. He switched off the engine of the Capri, which came to a juddering halt.

'I'm not blaming you for anything that has or hasn't happened in my life,' he said stiffly. 'I know that's down to me. What I'm trying to say is that if you weren't so angry with us all of the time – angry with me – maybe I could have talked to you about things. Maybe you could have helped me get it together.'

Maggie opened her mouth and shut it again.

'Am I always angry?' she said uncertainly.

'Mostly,' Jim told her. 'At home at least. Angry and sad. And sometimes loopy since you came back,' he added as an afterthought.

Maggie thought about her last conversation with her mum on Sunday morning. He could be right; partially right, at least.

'But I'm saving The Fleur,' she said a little bit petulantly.

'Yes, I know, but that doesn't make you queen, does it?'

Maggie smoothed her hair in the wing mirror and tried not to pout like a six-year-old.

'And just because you're busy all the time, you don't have to march around the place like the rest of us are getting in your way. I mean, Mum and Dad have run the place for twenty-five years, more! They do know stuff, Maggie. You should ask them for advice sometimes, even if you don't need it. It would make them feel better about all of this – make them feel part of it still. You could try and be a bit . . . kinder and a bit less . . . martyrish?'

Maggie looked at her brother as if he were insane. 'I'm not a martyr! And anyway . . . they've retired!' She raised her voice. 'That's the whole point!'

'They've retired from the pub Maggie, not from the family,' Jim said, opening the car door. 'Come on, let's get inside.'

Maggie got out of the car and smoothed the cotton of her

277

trousers against her legs. She caught up with Jim as he headed into the centre.

'Are you telling me that all of a sudden you're just going to get all superefficient and wise and start making money out of mouldy books?' she said defensively. 'Because that's pretty rich.'

Jim shook his head. 'No,' he said. 'I'm saying that I'll try and be good at this. For Mum and Dad's sake, because I owe them. And I'm saying that I miss you, Maggie. The old you that used to be my friend, that used to need my protection from dragons. Can't we try and get a bit of that back, even just a little bit?'

Maggie stopped, smiled and waved at Bob Brownly who had spotted them from a balcony walkway. He began to make his way down to them like a sales-seeking missile.

'I do the talking,' Maggie told Jim. 'You look hard.' She tucked her arm through his and glanced up at him. 'I know I can be . . . prickly, Jim. A lot has happened recently. Things that have knocked me for six. But I'll try. I'll try and you try and we can both try with Mum and Dad and see how it goes, OK?'

Jim nodded. 'OK,' he said with a smile.

'Well you can wipe that smile off your face for starters!' Maggie nudged him. 'I thought I told you to look hard!' But they were both still laughing when Bob Brownly arrived at their sides.

Chapter Twenty-seven

Pete looked from Angie to Falcon and then down at his plate. Maybe this house celebration dinner hadn't been the best idea he'd ever had. It was just that he felt he had to mark the occasion *somehow*. His so-called fiancée was on the other side of the world not ringing him, and – as he was still getting flash backs from kissing her – he'd decided it was best not to see Maggie, at least until he'd spoken to Stella. If he ever spoke to her. He was giving her until the end of the week to make the call, and then he was letting her go: he'd made up his mind. Or at least he'd made up his mind until midnight on Friday. Then he'd probably review the situation, because he knew that whatever the future held for him and Stella, he couldn't let them end with a whimper, with a silent non-goodbye. If he had to, he'd fly out there himself and resolve the relationship; he'd have to. Otherwise five years of his life really would have been wasted and he couldn't bear the thought of that.

He filled Falcon's and Angie's glasses again. So far they had both drunk a lot more than they'd eaten, and he got the feeling their 'friendship' was at breaking point.

'So we'll drink a toast, shall we? To my new job!' He lifted his glass, forcing both of them to reciprocate.

'To Pete's new job and exciting new future,' Angie said with a decidedly sharp edge to her voice. 'I am pleased for you, Pete, really I am. I know how much you wanted this. It's just . . . look, I'm sorry. I feel so tired all of a sudden. I think I'll go to bed, OK?' And she pushed her chair back and hurried down the hallway into her room, slamming the door behind her.

Pete looked at Falcon. 'Well, that worked out well, then,' he said, pushing his half-empty plate away. 'Maybe I put too much chilli in the con carne.'

Falcon grimaced. 'I'm sorry, mate. I think I've really gone and done it this time.' He nodded in the general direction of Angie's room. 'She keeps changing the rules. One minute we're seeing other people, and the next I'm getting the cold shoulder.'

Pete despaired quietly to himself. This wasn't what he'd had in mind when he'd invited both of his housemates to dinner via their mobiles. He'd assumed that they'd assume that the other one was also coming, but it seemed that he'd made the wrong assumption. When Falcon had walked in on Angie sitting at the kitchen table, his face had fallen, and witnessing it, Angie's had frozen. Pete wasn't sure how they expected to go on living together without seeing each other ever again, but in any case they'd been giving it a good go until he'd invited them both to dinner. He'd pictured a nice boozy chilli followed by a few beers out. Not *Kramer versus Kramer* in the kitchen.

After all he did have something to be cheerful about. Magic Shop had given him a six-month contract to work on the digital effects of a real film, a real Hollywood blockbuster. Yes, he'd be stuck in a studio mostly, and no, he wouldn't get anywhere near anyone famous, but his name would be on the credits, somewhere near the end, in really small print that you could hardly see, but it would be there. Pete had literally whooped for joy as he'd emerged back on to Wardour Street. People had looked at him and smiled knowingly as if that sort of thing happened every day around there, but Pete didn't care, because this was his day. His beginning – not a new beginning, but a *first* beginning. The beginning of everything he'd dreamed of since he'd been a little kid with a picture of Raquel Welch taped over his headboard.

And it had been so easy; almost too easy. After all those weeks of worrying and fretting and all those *years* of dreaming and hoping, all he'd had to do was turn up and talk about himself. He'd gone into the interview and within five minutes found himself engrossed in a chat about the thing he loved most in the whole world. He found himself reminiscing about dinosaurs made out of modelling clay and dreaming about what the future of FX might hold and how he might contribute to that. Most surprisingly he found that he had a reputation – just a small one, but even so people knew his name and associated him with good work. Just as he was leaving, wondering if he'd been a bit overexcited, they'd stopped him at the lift and told him he had the contract if he wanted it.

Pete's elation had lasted all the way round the supermarket as he gathered the ingredients for his meal, until in the queue for the checkout two things hit him. That he should have done this years ago, shouldn't have let Stella push everything else out of his life until she had become his only ambition, and that he found he wanted to tell Maggie more than anything; he wanted to see how her eyes filled with midnight lightning when he told her. But he couldn't tell her yet because he'd promised himself he wasn't going to see or speak to her again until he'd spoken to Stella and given her a chance to make his love for her live and breathe again. Then he'd know how to feel about Maggie. He'd know what he needed to say to her and how he needed to say it.

Right now, he thought, all he had was a half-empty bottle of wine and a grumpy-looking punk to deal with.

'Mate,' he said, 'why do you do it? Why do you sleep with her when you know it's going nowhere?'

Falcon raised a bloke's eyebrow and Pete sat back in his chair and crossed his arms in reply. Falcon leaned over the table and dropped his head in resignation.

'Because I like her, and I fancy her, and she's good in bed and she's got really nice . . .' Falcon stopped himself. 'And because I want to – I want to sleep with her. I just don't want to have to be her boyfriend. I mean, we're both adult, right? She knows how I feel, but she still lets me shag her. We agreed that was how it would be.'

Pete shook his head. 'Falc, we're not kids any more. We know better, and if you truly like Angie and care about her, you shouldn't treat her like this. She's all messed up and it's confusing her. She's not as tough as you think she is. I don't think you really knew what you were doing with the "friends that shag" lark. Those things never work. Why don't you go in there now and explain and make sure you never cross that line again, because . . . I like you, mate, but I like Angie, too, a lot. She deserves better, and what's more, you know that.'

Pete looked at the piles of plates laden with food. 'I'll wash up,' he said grimly.

'OK, I'll help you,' Falcon said as if Pete had just made his speech to the table.

'Falc, mate!' Pete was exasperated. 'You have to live here with Angie, and I have to live with both of you. I like you. I don't want to move out. Look, you've known each other for years. Don't just bin all of that because you're not man enough to talk to her. Girls need words. They don't seem to understand anything else!' Pete said seriously.

Falcon stood up and took a swig directly out of the bottle.

'All right, I'm going in,' he said with the face of a condemned man. 'I may be some time.'

Pete watched him go and then picked up what was left of the wine. Somehow it didn't seem so appealing any more, so he tipped it down the sink.

He didn't expect the knock at the door and it made him jump. He turned to face the kitchen door and leaned his back against the sink, finding himself suddenly uncertain what to do. It must be Maggie.

They'd said something about getting together after the interview, but he'd thought, after everything that had happened, that it had just been talk, a polite way of saying goodbye. But she'd actually come, and now he'd have to see her and he didn't know how that would make him feel or how, if faced with her in the same room, he could wait to speak to Stella without doing something stupid, without wanting to reach out and touch her again.

But Pete knew with sudden certainty that he did want to see Maggie again – he wanted to see her right now and find out what would happen to his heart when he did.

Galvanised into action, he headed for the door as the knock was repeated more loudly and insistently this time – somehow unlike Maggie, he thought. Before he could reach the door, though, Angie emerged, rubbing her eyes, from her bedroom and opened it first, obscuring his view.

'Sorry, Angie,' he said as she stepped aside. 'Maggie I—' Pete stopped, quite literally. His speech stopped, his mind stopped and for a moment his heart stopped. When everything started again the world was an entirely different place.

'Stella,' he said, looking into the silver-gilded eyes of his fiancée. 'You're back.'

'Pete!' Stella squealed, and wrapped her arms around him, spinning him in her embrace. 'Oh my God I've missed you!' She kissed his face, his lips, his cheeks, his closed eyes in a frenzy of joy until finally she leaned back a little, her arms secured around his neck like an anchor.

'I got your email and I thought, if Pete says he needs to *talk*

283

to me, then he means that he needs to *see* me. He needs to know how much I love him!' She lowered her lashes for a moment. 'Oh Pete, all I did in Melbourne was miss you and realise how wrong I was to leave you at all, let alone for a whole year! How could I ever think I would survive that long without you? Well, I'm back now, for good, I promise you.'

Pete gazed down at her. Despite arriving in Australia during their winter, her face was bronzed and glowing, throwing her extraordinary eyes into brilliant relief. Her hair had been bleached even lighter and it looped over her shoulders in loose curls. He felt her small hard body in his and the weight of her arms around his neck. All of these things he felt and saw, and he waited for everything else to catch up with the moment. He waited to love her again. Because she was back now, and he'd made her a promise that he'd be here for her when she came back, no matter what. And that he'd never let her down the way she feared he might. She was back, and he belonged to her, so he had to love her again just as he had for the past five years. He had to. But somehow, the moment she had walked back into his life, the last of his love for her had left.

'Kiss me,' Stella said, tipping her chin back and closing her eyes, and Pete did kiss her. He felt the crush of her breasts as her body arched into his and his own response to that sensation harden and grow. But that was all, only that physical, mechanical insistence. It was the shock, he told himself, it was the surprise of having everything he'd ever wanted all in one day. He needed time to readjust to having her here in this new place, in his new life that had just begun without hope of her. It was just because he wasn't prepared to see her here – not here, not now.

Pete realised that both Angie and Falcon were standing in the door frame of Angie's bedroom looking on with undisguised curiosity. He stepped away from her.

'Oh, er, Stella, this is Falcon and Angie – my housemates.' He looked back at Stella as if to make sure that she was still really there. 'And this,' he said, more to himself than anyone else, 'is Stella, my fiancée.'

There were greetings and kisses, and Stella performed her usual trick of making both Falcon and Angie love her instantly. After a while Pete realised they couldn't go on standing in the hall for ever, so he picked up Stella's backpack.

'You must be shattered,' he said. 'I'll show you my room.'

Stella giggled. 'I thought you'd never ask!' she said, winking at Angie, her hand resting lightly on his arse as she followed him up the stairs.

Pete led her into his room and, unable to quite look at her, leaned her backpack against the wardrobe.

'I never expected you to actually come here!' he said, half laughing, at a loss for anything else to say.

Stella's hands snaked around his waist and she turned him to face her, resting her head against his chest.

'Well, you know I never like to do what people expect.' She looked up at him. 'I'm sorry I didn't write sooner. I meant to, I really did, but I just got swept away by everything. It was all so new and for a while . . . well, for a while there was someone, hardly anything, really, but just someone who distracted me . . . I think I was testing myself to see what happened. And then, well, I was up in the middle of the night because I suddenly realised how much I missed you and needed you, and I was just about to finally write to you when there it was, your email. Saying you weren't sure how to feel? Saying that there might be someone else?'

Stella's voice took on a reproachful edge. 'I couldn't believe it. I couldn't believe that I had been so stupid as to nearly lose you – *you*, Pete. The only one that has ever mattered. And I knew I had to come back. I knew a phone call wouldn't do, I had to come back and be with you, Pete. To tell you face to face that I want to be with you always, always and always from now on. So I took my ticket to the airport and got it transferred on to the first flight back and I came straight here. You don't have to worry about how to feel any more, because I'm here to make sure you'll always know. I know we'll have to talk about it later and make things right again, but right now you don't have to do anything but be pleased to see me. You don't have to do anything now but make love to me.'

Stella took a step back from him and pulled her T-shirt over her head. She wasn't wearing anything underneath. Pete felt his jaw tighten and muscles tense. It would be now, he told himself – any moment now, while he was in her arms, his skin against hers, he would start to feel for her again and everything would become clear and right again. He pulled her on to the bed and, as he started kissing her, he closed his eyes.

Maggie knocked on Pete's front door again and waited, bouncing impatiently on her toes. What with one thing and another she hadn't been able to make it round until after nine, but she knew that someone was in. The front room lights were on and the first-floor bedroom, Pete's room, was also lit, but so far there had been no reply. At last she saw movement behind the frosted glass of the door and smiled as Falcon opened it.

'Oh!' He looked surprised and then glanced up at the ceiling. 'All right? How's Sarah?'

Maggie blinked at him. 'Fine. Um, is Pete in? I wanted to find out how he got on with his interview?'

Falcon nodded and shifted from one foot to the other and looked at the steel toe-caps of his boots.

'Oh, he got it, he got the job,' he said, looking up at her as if she should go away now. Maggie felt pleased and disappointed all at once. She'd wanted Pete to tell her so she could have an excuse to throw her arms round his neck and hug him, purely out of courtesy, of course.

'Oh great,' she said, starting to sound slightly irritable at Falcon's self-assumed guardianship of the entrance. 'Well? Can I see him then? He *is* in, isn't he?'

Falcon looked at her blankly, completely at a loss for what to say.

'I don't think that's a good idea,' Angie said, appearing at his side, a small, tight smile on her lips. 'Not right now. You see, Stella came back an hour or two ago and they're still upstairs . . . reuniting. I don't think Pete would thank us if we interrupted him.'

Maggie felt her chest tighten around her ribcage, forcing out a rush of air that resulted in an involuntary 'Oh!' She stood on the doorstep not sure exactly how she was going to leave it in one piece. She settled on neutral cheerfulness. 'Oh. Well, that's great! Really great for Pete. Right, well, tell him . . . oh, don't worry, just tell him well done, and – OK! Thanks, then, goodbye.'

Maggie turned on her heels and stumbled down the steps back on to the street.

'You could have been a bit more tactful,' Falcon said to Angie as he closed the door. 'I think she had a bit of a thing for Pete.'

Angie shrugged, pausing in the door frame of her room.

'Yeah, well, it's better to have the truth, even if it is brutal, isn't it?' She slammed the door shut and Falcon guessed that their little chat was over. Surprisingly, he realised he actually felt better for getting it all out in the open. Pete had been right about birds and talking. Angie was inexplicably furious with him, and hurt, but at least when she'd started looking psychotic and vengeful she'd stopped looking needy and hopeful. He thought it would probably work out for the best for her in the

287

long run, and he was glad of that because he did like her, he really did. Just not enough to do what would make her happy.

Maggie walked fast and steadily back up the Hatfield Road towards the high street. The last vestiges of the day were sinking behind the silhouetted skyline, drawing down with them the remains of the dull silvered light. And Maggie was glad of the darkness. It covered the confusion that had engulfed her the moment she'd realised what had happened to her when she wasn't looking.

'It's OK,' she told herself. 'It's OK. Stella's back now and that's OK. I don't have to think about it any more because it's all decided, it's all fine. I just have to get on with things and . . .'

Maggie stopped as she turned into the high street and looked down the length of it as it lit itself up for the evening, fairy lights strung out along the trees, twinkling and sparkling, shop signs luminescing and humming, car headlights blinking, converging and separating in a steady rhythmic stream. She felt the turn of the season in the slight chill of the evening and smelt it in the heavy scent of the exhaust. Everyone, everything else was moving on now, and would keep on going without her if she didn't force herself to go on too, regardless of what had happened.

'That's it,' she told herself as she started walking again. 'If Pete is back with Stella, then that's it, it's settled. Nothing else matters any more except getting on with things and getting The Fleur on its feet and getting on with my life. So that's it.'

There was no point in pretending any more. It was just a shame that she'd had to go and fall for him.

Chapter Twenty-eight

Maggie sat on her time-capsule bed and looked around her in bewilderment.

Up until this moment it had been fine for her to pretend that the reason she was sad about having possibly compromised her friendship with Pete was because she liked him. Up until now they had just been two people getting to know each other, under unusual circumstances maybe, and possibly a little too quickly when it came to the whole kiss debacle; but they had just been two people for whom, given some time and a bit of peace and quiet something really special might have happened. Or at least Maggie thought that it might have, secretly, quietly to herself. Stella's meteoric crash-landing had thrown all of that up into nothing more than a cloud of meaningless dust and detritus. There was no possibility of anything any more with Pete, and therefore, Maggie supposed, no point in pretending, to herself at least. She had to face up to the facts.

She wasn't exactly sure when she had fallen for him – it hadn't been clear cut. She hadn't suddenly thought, 'Oh, I really like Pete, and guess what, I don't mind at all about Christian any more'. It had been sort of gradual and stealthy, until yesterday morning on Sarah's sofa when she'd realised she really, *really* didn't mind about Christian and Louise. She'd put that down to simple, and probably temporary, resignation, something she had felt before and which would no doubt give way to frenzied angst once again. But now Stella was back, Maggie somehow doubted that. Strangely, she felt that she still loved Christian but in an entirely different way – in a sort of past tense.

Maggie couldn't help smiling as she looked at her knees. All that insanity over Christian, all her plans and counterplans had been rendered pointless in one single sweep, and not by her getting together with Pete but by her realising that she was never going to get together with Pete. It made an illogical kind of sense.

She should have listened to Sarah, of course. Deep down she'd known that all along. She should have waited – just as Sarah had said – for the shock and grief to subside before she went wading into the breach after Christian and everything that he represented. Now, in the cool, still, calm of the eye of her personal storm, Maggie could see it wasn't him that she'd been desperate to cling on to, it had been the shape and order of her life that she'd been terrified of losing. She had always been terrified of change, and life without Christian had seemed like a change too great to bear.

He had been right all along, too. When he'd told her he was leaving her it was because he'd seen that there was nothing magical between them any more. They had a deep, occasionally passionate affection for each other, but it was passion kindled by memories of what had once been. Because they had stopped dead maybe a year, maybe two years before the morning Christian told her he was leaving, and the relationship had been quietly decaying for all that time. Maggie couldn't put it down to an incident or any particular event; there was just an implicit sensation of things falling apart. They had stopped being lovers and started being friends who sometimes had sex, and who often weren't friends. Given time, she would have come to realise it herself, but the sharp slap of realisation that she could feel something so strong for someone who was not Christian had accelerated the process.

Any chance of friendship she might have had with Christian, Maggie realised sadly, had probably been squandered along with everything else she had trampled over in her confusion. Besides, she couldn't quite see herself inviting Christian and Louise to dinner and revealing her double identity as she invited them in.

Maggie smiled to herself again as she pictured the scene. She was glad, at least, that she had been so incompetent at being devious that she hadn't managed to meddle her way back into a relationship with Christian. That would have been too terrible – to have woken up next to him one morning feeling the way she felt now. Thankfully, given his and Louise's silence, it was certain that Christian had made the right choice, and Maggie half wished she could call him and congratulate him and tell him what a terrible idiot she had been. Louise was a bit intense and sort of unpredictable, but she was basically a nice girl, and maybe the right kind of girl for Christian.

'So I don't want Christian,' she said softly to herself, 'and I can't have Pete.'

She felt amazingly calm, she realised. Almost kind of liberated. It was as if wanting someone she absolutely could not have had freed her from all the pain of anxiety and hope. She was free now just to carry around the small warm glow of her feelings without feeling obliged to risk the consequences of acting on them or worrying about them coming to some cataclysmic end. Knowing how she felt about Pete would light her up from within just enough to help her get through the next few weeks until she had left Christian behind for ever and found her future on her own. After that she'd just have to wait for the feelings to fade. A small nagging voice, Sarah's voice, was telling her that if she had any kind of sense she'd put up some kind of a fight and make a bid to win Pete from Stella, but Maggie was tired of fighting beautiful women for men who were looking the other way, and she was tired of hurting. She just wanted some peace and quiet in her life, and simply knowing that there was someone in the world who could make her feel so much gave her a peculiar kind of joy.

She just hoped that Stella would come through for Pete and make him happy at last.

'Anyway,' Maggie told Morten Harket, 'I've still got a lot. I've got The Fleur, Sheila. Sarah and the kids. They're going to need me more than ever right now.'

Maggie thought about her conversation with Jim that morning.

'And I've got a family who love me and are there for me. If I let them.'

She stood and went over to inspect her A-Ha poster. It was faded with age and torn at the edges, and the Blu-tack that attached it to the wall was hardened and shiny. It hardly seemed like any time at all since Maggie had carefully extracted this poster from the centrefold of *Smash Hits* magazine and pressed it carefully against her bedroom wall, smoothing down the corners with loving strokes. Between that moment and this, Maggie had been making the same outwardbound journey as far away from her family as she could get. After all her travelling, though, all her trials and tribulations, she'd ended up in the same place, looking at the same four walls, standing on the same dirty pink carpet. How was it possible then, she wondered, that she still felt so far away from them?

Maggie pushed her thumb under the knob of hardened Blu-tack and it pinged easily off the wall. She took the poster by the loosened corner and then pulled it down quickly, ripping the poster in half. 'Sorry, Morten,' she said, looking at half of the erstwhile star's chiselled jaw as it lay on the floor. The second half of the poster followed, and then poster after poster, poster under poster, old bits of receipt and a telephone number a boy had once given her – the first ever, she thought. She screwed them all up into satisfying balls and threw them on to the growing pile of debris that had begun to cover the floor.

Hung over her bed was a noticeboard where she'd used to pin everything she thought would mean something to her for ever, like the crumbling red rose, her first ever valentine's gift, given to her at the age of twelve by the softly rounded ginger-haired boy that sat at the back of the class. Maggie hadn't known whether to be flattered to get anything at all, or mortified that the least popular boy in class thought he had a chance with her, so she had kept it and pretended it was from Jon Bon Jovi. There were three round-cornered photos of various school trips featuring laughing, pointing, two-finger-waving groups of kids whose names she could no longer remember and had mostly never associated with since the day she'd left school. A dried leaf crumbled to dust in her hand as she took it down, and she couldn't for the life of her remember why that had meant so much to her.

As she peeled away the last of the meaningless mementos, Maggie felt like she was taking down her personal battlements stone by heavy stone. She was dismantling everything she had carefully constructed to separate her from her family and what she had always thought of as her constricting life in the pub, turning the time capsule that had once been her refuge, and which had seemed like her prison since she had returned to The Fleur, into a blank canvas. It wasn't her parents who had imprisoned her here in this room with her expectations, Maggie realised; it had been her own desire to live in a small, neat, ordered space, knowing what each day would bring and then each day after that. Her parents had tried to give her the world, quite literally, and she hadn't wanted it. Somehow she had carried her understandable childish need for comfort and familiarity into her adult life, until trying to keep it in place had nearly smothered her. It was time to let it go. What she had to do now, Maggie told herself, was broaden her horizons – reach out there into the unknown and just see what happened. OK, so she wasn't exactly going to go to Tibet to discover herself; she wasn't going to go anywhere soon. Far more courageous, she was going to make this place work, and her life without Christian work – without all her usual securities and insecurities holding her together like hard, shiny Blu-tack. Maggie was scared, sad. But exhilarated, too.

'All I need to do,' she said, her voice echoing off the bare walls, 'is take that first step.'

When Maggie had rubbed every last scrap of Blu-tack off the wallpaper, she headed down into the kitchen to find some binbags. It was late, almost midnight, she realised as she looked at the wall clock. Sheila must have called time and cashed up without bothering to call her.

She walked into the quiet dark of the empty bar and stood there for a moment listening to the rhythmic hum of the fridges. She and Jim had bought most of a good kitchen yesterday and today she'd sat down with a builder and costed gutting and renovating this room, which had hardly changed since the day she'd walked in as a child. In just under a week this part of her life was to be ripped out and broken up for kindling or sold on for scrap. Maggie pressed her hand against a table top and leaned against it. She knew it had to be done, she knew that without these changes The Fleur would sink into the depths of the past without leaving a trace, but for the first time she felt a sense of regret and she understood how her parents and even Jim must feel – as if they were losing a close and trusted friend. Maggie thought of losing Christian's sup- port, and then, with a sharp pang, she thought of Pete. If anyone could understand what losing something important felt like, she thought, it was her.

As she walked upstairs to the flat, she paused by the living room door. Her dad was slumped in his armchair, his head lolled back, snoring in front of the TV. A now cold cup of tea was balanced precariously on his robust stomach, falling and rising with each breath. Maggie smiled to herself and, walking over to him, gently extracted it from his pliant fingers.

'Wha . . . what?' her dad mumbled as she disturbed him.

'You're asleep in the chair, Dad,' Maggie said. 'Go to bed or else you'll get a frozen neck.' Her dad mumbled something in reply, but by the time Maggie had reached the door he was snoring loudly again.

As she left, Maggie noticed that the light was on in the 'spare' room across the hall. Long and narrow, without a window, it had always been used for storage, but Maggie had thought it would make a good galley kitchen which, if sufficiently equipped, would mean that for home cooking they wouldn't have to keep using the pub kitchen downstairs, which would be essential once they were serving quality food again. Pushing open the door, Maggie found her mum sitting on the floor surrounded by boxes, piles of papers and old photos. Marion looked up and smiled.

'I just thought I'd make a start on clearing this lot out.' She gestured at the piles around her. 'This lot's for the bin, this lot needs to get filed, and these . . .' she patted a haphazard pile of photos . . . 'need to go in an album. I've been meaning to do it for years and years, but now we're retiring I'm sure I'll get it done.'

'It must be a day for clearing out,' Maggie said, holding up the binbags she had retrieved from the kitchen. 'I've just been doing the same thing in my room.'

Marion smiled up at her and held out a photo.

'Look, that's me and your dad, just before we found out I was pregnant with you.'

Marion took the photo and stared at it. Her parents were standing in a field somewhere, apparently by a tepee, with their arms wrapped around each other, and next to them, with his arm flung over them both, was a dark young man in an orange embroidered shirt. He had long, thick, black hair that fell past his shoulders and long, fuzzy sideburns that were almost a beard. He looked very familiar, somehow, and Maggie felt the beginnings of an old uneasiness stir in her stomach.

'Mum, is that Mr Shah?' Maggie asked, squinting at the photo.

'Oh yes! That's him. Isn't it funny how he's changed? He was so handsome then. Any of the girls we knew would have died to get together with him . . .' Her mother drifted off mid-sentence with a dreamy look on her face.

Maggie looked from the image of Mr Shah to her mother's rapt expression and back again. Before she could stop herself she blurted out, 'Mum, is Mr Shah my real dad?'

Marion blinked and looked at her daughter. A look of uncertainty and worry flashed across her face and Maggie prepared herself for the worst. Then Marion laughed. She laughed so hard that she had to press the heels of her palms against her eyes to stem the tears. Maggie hadn't seen her so amused since . . . she couldn't actually remember.

'Oh Maggie, you are funny!' Marion said, shaking her head. 'No, Mr Shah is *not* your father. Your father is your father. I don't know. I can't tell when you're joking these days . . . Imagine me and Ravi Shah! Oh dear, I haven't laughed so much since . . .' Marion glanced back up at her daughter, whose face was stone cold sober.

'You weren't joking, were you?' Marion said slowly.

Maggie shook her head, feeling suddenly ridiculous. Feeling ridiculous had almost become her default setting.

'Well it's just that I don't look like Dad, do I? And I don't look that much like you, and Jim is almost Dad's exact carbon copy, and so . . . well, I just sometimes wondered, what with the free love and all . . .'

Unfortunately, despite her experience in making a fool of herself, Maggie still felt excruciatingly embarrassed and realised it wasn't so much the question that had disarmed her but the display of insecurity which she had become used to hiding from her mum.

'And, you know . . . because my hair and eyes are so dark and you are all so fair. Where did it come from, then? Not you or Dad.'

Marion cleared a space beside her on the floor and, indicating that Maggie should fill it, began sifting through the photographs until she pulled out a white card scalloped round the edges and yellowed with age. On the front it had an embossed design of roses and a gilded date – 1938. Marion opened out the card to reveal a wedding photo.

'Well, you've got your father's brown eyes, although a shade darker, and the rest of it did come from me, in a way, via this lady – your great-grandma Constantina.'

Marion handed Maggie the photo.

'My grandma. You never met her, of course – she was long gone before you arrived on the scene. She was Argentinian, came to this country in the thirties. She always said she was running from something, but we never did discover what. She'd never talk about it, just press a finger to her lips and give us one of those black-eyed looks that you do so well. She didn't have a penny in her pocket or a hope in her heart, but she had bucketloads of determination and she loved to dance.

'That's how she met my granddad. He was a farm worker, but

it was a bad time, lots of unemployment. No one had much money, but when they could they'd let off a bit of steam and there used to be a local dance on in the town, and him and his mates all went down there one night hoping to catch a kiss from a pretty girl. He wasn't a big man, not much taller than me, really, but he had this sort of spark, Maggie. Right up until the end he had eyes that burned so brightly with the passion of just being alive.

'Grandma Connie always used to say that until she met him she'd wondered daily what on earth it was that brought her to this wet, cold, miserable country when everyone else she knew had stayed at home or gone to America. Until the night that she danced with my granddad. And then she said she knew – God had brought her there to meet the love of her life. I wish you could have seen them dancing together – it was so beautiful, almost like a ballet the way they moved together. And they were so in love, Maggie, right up until the end. They even died within two weeks of each other. I don't think Connie could see the point of anything after he'd gone.

'When I was a girl I promised myself that when I fell in love it would be with that kind of intensity and passion, not the sort of friendly politeness that my parents had. When I met your father I found that, and I still feel that way about him even now, with his big belly and his bald patch. So no, Mr Shah is not your father. I don't know . . . when *I* look at you, I see your dad reflected in some way in every one of your movements and looks. I don't see why you don't see it.'

Maggie looked down at the photo. The dark young woman was wearing a drop-waisted wedding dress which showed her ankles neatly turned out in button-through shoes with a granny heel. Her meticulously waved hair was crowned by a garland of flowers and a veil. Her nose was a little longer than Maggie's, and her chin a little more square, but other than those small differences, Maggie realised, it could have been a photo of her. She looked at her great-grandfather, fair and slight. She could see a faint echo of Marion's smile reflected in his stiff formality, a certain restless look.

'Why didn't I know about her?' Maggie asked her mum.

'Well, you never knew her, I suppose. And we only got these photos after Mum died and I don't think I've looked at them until now. Whenever we talked about her it was always Grandma Connie – not very exotic sounding, I know! And you never said anything. If you'd told me you were worried so long ago I'd have explained. It's just, well, you're my baby – part of this family. I'd never have guessed you felt like this!'

Marion reached out and rubbed Maggie's shoulder.

'I'm glad you asked me, though. Look, you can keep that photo if you like. As proof.'

Maggie shook her head and a large tear hit the cardboard edge of the photo. Maggie wiped it quickly away with her thumb.

'I'd like to keep it,' she said, 'but not as proof, Mum. I don't need proof that I belong to this family. It was just that I sometimes wondered, that's all . . . And I know that this is a hard time for you and Dad as well. I know I've been wrapped up in my own problems recently, and maybe a bit . . . distant.'

Maggie looked down at Connie's photo and suddenly felt at a loss for anything else to say. Marion put a cautious arm around her daughter's shoulder and pulled her a little closer.

'What's wrong, love? Is it too much, looking after us all and splitting up with Christian? You know that the last thing your father and I want is for you to feel obliged—'

Maggie stopped her quickly. 'No, Mum. No, I don't feel obliged, that's the last thing I feel. If anything it's The Fleur that's kept me going. And you and Dad being here for me. I haven't thanked you, but I am grateful. It's just . . . oh, I don't know, I thought I'd worked it all out in my room just now and

299

that I could handle everything, but I guess maybe it's the shock or something . . . Everything's got into such a huge mess . . .' Maggie faltered and stumbled to a halt.

'Maggie,' Marion said, pulling herself to her feet and then holding a hand out to her daughter. 'Come downstairs and I'll make us some hot chocolate. If you like you can tell me about your huge mess. Maybe I might be able to help you. At least I could listen?'

Maggie reached out and took her mother's hand, letting her help her to her feet. As they padded into the kitchen Marion took a desk lamp out of the larder, unplugged the toaster and switched it on.

'I've been coming down here a lot recently in the middle of the night. It seemed more sensible to have some soft lighting,' she told Maggie as she filled the kettle and waited for it to boil.

'Have you, Mum?' Maggie asked her. 'I didn't know . . .'

Marion spooned chocolate powder into two mugs and filled them to the brim with boiling water.

'When I was your age,' she said, sitting down, 'I'd already met your dad and had my kids. Yes, it was the tail end of the sixties when your dad and I met, and it was supposed to be a revolution, but in some ways at least we were much more sheltered than you are today. I met your dad and married him not so long after. He's been my only lover . . .'

'Mum!' Maggie opened her eyes wide. '*You* weren't much of a wild child, were you?'

'Well it wasn't the sleeping around I believed in, love, it was love and peace and freedom. I still do believe in those things, but it's hard to keep believing in a world that doesn't seem to want or understand them.' Marion paused. 'Anyway, what I'm trying to say is that although I haven't gone through what you're going through with Christian, that doesn't mean I can't help you, and if you wanted to tell me . . . well, if you wanted to, I'd listen. I figure that when you've been alive for a certain number of years you're bound to have picked up at least some good advice.'

Maggie thought about everything that had happened with Christian and Louise and Pete and looked at her mum.

'I've been pretty flaky,' she said cautiously – it was something of an understatement.

'I'm not about to start telling you off now, am I?' Marion said with a faint smile. 'Unless you want me to, that is. No, I'll leave that up to Sheila and Sarah.'

Maggie shook her head, returning the smile.

'OK,' she said simply, already feeling a little lighter. 'I'll tell you.'

And it was almost two in the morning by the time she'd finished telling her mum everything that had happened to her since the moment Christian had told her about Louise.

Chapter Twenty-nine

Pete sat hunched over the edge of his bed, rubbing his hands back and forth through his short hair. There had been times, more than a few during his relationship with Stella, when he'd hated himself. Hated his inability to please her, his failure to keep her, and his weakness for her that made it impossible to stay away. But never had he loathed himself as much as he did now. After everything he'd said to Falcon yesterday about sleeping with Angie just for the sake of it, what he'd done last night had been just as bad, maybe worse.

He'd had sex with Stella because he wanted to have her when he wasn't so beguiled by her. He wanted to know what it felt like to have power over her for once. It had been a brief, explosive experience, one without tenderness or a trace of love, which made Pete wonder if it had been his love for her and his love only that had fuelled all their previous encounters with such meaning. Stella hadn't seemed to notice or mind the difference; in fact she'd seemed incapable of noticing anything, and Pete had wondered in that moment of cold detachment if what she really wanted was men who didn't really want her. Maybe it was his loving her that had kept them from ever finally resolving their relationship. The thought of it kept on tying knots in his head, and when he climaxed it was painful and raw, sending a wave of radiation burn through his body. Afterwards

Pete rolled off Stella and turned his face away from her, looking at the wall.

'Well, someone was a bit pent-up, weren't they?' Stella had said, lightly positioning her cheek against his chest and stroking his stomach with her fingertips. 'How about we try for an encore?'

Pete had closed his eyes and concentrated on keeping his breathing steady, feigning sleep. After a while he sensed Stella prop herself up and look at his face.

'Pete? Pete?' she whispered. Pete kept resolutely still. She lay back down and for a while she tossed and turned, sighing and huffing as she fought off the confusion of jet lag and Pete's mixed reception. Then at last she was still, and after a few moments more she slept. Pete had turned to look at her in the half light. She looked the same as she always had, still beautiful and fragile, gilded with all kinds of shimmering tones and lights. Once the sight of her sleeping like that would have filled his chest with such emotion that it threatened to burst out of him at any second, but last night and now, this morning, he couldn't fathom what he was feeling for her. He simply didn't know. Except that it was nothing like it had used to be.

'Baby?' Stella's slender arms snaked around his neck and she rested her chin on his shoulder. 'Come back to bed.' She pulled him back on to the bed and clambered on top of him, murmuring, 'We've still got a lot of catching up to do.'

Pete shook his head and attempted a smile. 'I can't, Stella, I've a class to go to . . .' he began.

Stella looked at his alarm clock. 'But it's only seven-thirty. And a class? Don't you mean the film job?'

Pete winced, remembering one of the things he'd told her. 'That job is, um, suspended for a couple of weeks. Some production hitch. I'm teaching until it starts. Again,' he said, trying to extract himself from under her slight but insistent weight.

303

She pressed down on to his groin with her pelvis and began to lightly kiss his chest. 'Oh, but you don't have to go just yet, do you?' she said. 'You've got time for Stella to make you feel all nice, haven't you?' she whispered as she began to trace her way down the length of his torso.

In one swift movement Pete extracted himself from beneath her and got out of bed.

'Pete!' Stella sat amid the tangle of sheets looking bewildered. She had never been turned down for oral sex by anyone ever before. It was unprecedented.

'I'm sorry,' Pete said. 'I . . . just don't feel like it.' They looked at each other, neither one of them pointing out that Pete had considerable physical evidence to the contrary on display right at that moment.

Stella drew her knees up under her chin and watched Pete as he hurriedly pulled on his boxers, turning his back on her. She felt a small cold fear begin to grow in her stomach. She couldn't lose Pete, she needed Pete. He was her rock, her safety net, and she had decided, she really had decided this time, that she was going to stay with him. This new distance he was showing to her, the way they'd made love last night, made things worse, it made them more complicated. Stella realised she wanted him more as he seemed to want her less. She cursed herself and tightened the grip around her knees. She knew what she had to do: she had to play it cool. She had to be calm and not ask any questions, least of all about this Maggie he had mentioned.

Stella had let Pete's emails collect in her in box, unopened since the moment she had arrived in Melbourne. At first they had seemed like the links of a chain stretching halfway around the world to restrict and restrain her. She was angry with Pete for not understanding that she needed this time to be completely free of him to see if she could stand up on her own two feet without him. And then there had been this man, AJ, who came into the bar she worked in more or less every day. He was the kind of guy who lit up a room, the sort of man who attracted attention the second he entered the atmosphere – sort of a local celebrity, a local radio DJ with a small TV profile. The moment Stella saw him she wanted him.

It wasn't that he was better looking than Pete, but rather that he had the kind of confidence and self-assurance that Stella had often wished for in Pete. God knows, Pete could have broken more hearts than most if he'd had a little sharper edge.

Girls just flocked around AJ like moths drawn to a flame. Every night it would be another one, and they didn't seem to care that he didn't seem to care about any of them. Stella had been fascinated by the whole charade, witnessing it all unravel before her very eyes in a three-act play. The seduction, the consummation, the rejection. The gratuitous torture of one helpless little girl after another. But Stella had felt confident, too, more than confident. She'd felt certain that she could have him, but not in the same way as the ever growing line of simpering women that sulked in corners and glowered at him as he got it on with someone new. Stella knew how to work a man. She had got her plane ticket, her job in Melbourne and, yes, the ring on her finger by doing just that. She had her own wake of lovers ebbing behind her for thousands of miles. She was certain that AJ would not be immune to her charms and that he would be as beguiled by her. There was even some part of her that thought maybe this man was her equal – her other half and her mirror image. As she watched him operate, she allowed herself to daydream, allowed herself to believe that she could be the one, perhaps the only one able to tame him. So Pete's emails were left unread, packed away in the chaotic miasma of cyberspace, waiting to take shape under her gaze.

After two weeks of planning and plotting her seduction, AJ

305

asked Stella back to his place. It wasn't like she'd imagined it would be, the two of them melded in a union of equals – it was all show, and all about him. Every one of his laborious tricks and techniques to turn her on, even, was more about his prowess as a lover than consideration for her. And yet Stella still wanted him. When he turned his back on her and fell straight to sleep, Stella had missed Pete more than she ever had, but she still *wanted* AJ; she wanted him to look at her and actually see her, for some spark of emotion to disrupt that perfect face. But Stella knew that if there was some woman out there capable of creating that effect in him, it wasn't her – which made the whole experience even more humiliating. Stella thought she'd be equal to him, but she wasn't. The next day he was charming but remote. The day after that he blanked her.

Stella had found herself crying in the stock room, rocking on her heels, feeling the sting of humiliation more keenly than she ever had. Her flatmate and fellow barman André had found her and held her shoulders as she cried.

'Darling, I thought you had more sense,' he'd told her. 'I thought you had a bit more class than to go *there*!' He tossed his head slightly and Stella got the fleeting impression that he might have been *there* and suffered exactly the same fate that she and countless others had. 'Anyway,' André said, picking up her ring finger and holding her hand inches in front of her face. 'What about *him*?' Stella had begun to cry in earnest then and André had sent her home, where she'd watched TV and drunk beer into the small hours. It was sometime around three that she finally plucked Pete's emails out of the air and read them for the first time, from the most recent bombshell back to the first one. She got on the next plane home.

Stella knew Pete: she knew he wouldn't back out on her unless he really had to. She was pretty sure she could keep him if she played her cards right. If she could show him how much she needed him, he wouldn't leave her. He just wouldn't; he'd promised he never would.

Pete paused as he buttoned up his shirt and glanced at Stella. Each time he looked at her she seemed slightly diminished, as if she were somehow fading. His chest constricted and he felt a wave of his old empathy for her, his perpetual desire to save her. He sat down on the bed cautiously and looked at her. Perhaps if he gave it a chance, everything would come back gradually. There was no point in hurting Stella if he didn't have to.

'It's just . . .' he said. 'It's just that it's a lot to take in . . .'

'I'll say!' Stella giggled coquettishly, and then kicked herself for trying to be flirty when he was trying to be serious. 'I'm sorry,' she said, showing rare candour. 'I'm nervous, Pete. You're making me feel as if I have to be nervous . . .' She picked up his hand. 'I've never felt like that with you before. Do I? Do I have to feel nervous?'

'No! I mean . . .' Pete paused. 'I just need to get used to the idea that you're here, that's all. That you really are here . . .' he said lamely.

Stella fell back on to the bed and stretched her arms above her head in a carefully arranged display of her breasts. Pete looked at her, his eyes travelling the length of her body. She was beautiful and sexy – he could still see that, still feel it in the pit of his groin. But his desire for her had somehow disentangled itself from the intensity of his emotion and reformed itself into something new and . . . cold. If he got back into bed with her now it would be like last night all over again but worse, because last night he'd had every reason to believe that being near her would be enough to make things better.

Now he knew he had to give them both a little time. He had to give the jangle of feelings that had shaken him up and pulled him in all directions time to subside. In a week or so, maybe the memory of kissing Maggie would dissipate. Maybe the desire to have something that strong and that simple would wane. Perhaps when he'd got used to Stella and her tightly-packed neurosis again, things would start to get back to the way they were.

At that thought, Pete felt a small cold stone form in the pit of his belly. There was one thing he did know – he didn't want to go back to standing still, caught in suspended animation. If Stella was staying, she'd have to stay on his terms. Finding a way to not sleep with her, not talk to her and not tell her anything while he tried to sort his head out was the problem. Pete smiled to himself and thought of his talk to Falcon last night. He'd just have to bite the bullet. Girls needed words, and Stella probably needed more than most. He was nearly cacking himself with fear, but he'd have to talk to her, get his cards on the table. It was the only way.

He picked up her jeans and T-shirt and tossed them on the bed.

'Come on,' he said. 'Get dressed. I've got a bit of time. Let's get some breakfast.'

Stella looked at him reproachfully and then pulled her T-shirt on over her head.

'I just hope,' Pete thought to himself, 'that I've worked out what my cards are by the time we get there.'

Despite the possibility of seeing Maggie in Declan's café, and maybe because of it, Pete walked Stella past two perfectly good places before turning her into the now familiar coffee shop. The place was near empty, with just a few business people on the way to work staring blankly at folded papers or with pens poised above lined notepads until the caffeine kicked in. Pete nodded at Declan and ordered two coffees and a giant chocolate muffin for Stella on the grounds that it seemed to be a universal panacea for most Women's Ills, and at the very least it'd give him a chance to get his words out when Stella realised what he was trying to tell her, which would be sometime after Pete had worked it out himself.

'Mmmmm,' Stella said as he set the muffin down in front of her. 'This place is all right, quite chic, although I was thinking as you're working up in London, we could get a place up there. Notting Hill. Or Ladbroke Grove?'

'I don't think we'd afford that kind of rent, and anyway—' Pete began.

'But you've got some in the bank, haven't you, and I bet you'd earn more really quickly, and I could . . . help. It's very important to have the right address in the movie business, Pete.'

Pete looked at Stella and wondered when she had become the expert.

'Only when your name's listed above the opening credits,' he said. 'And anyway, I like the house. I like Falcon and Angie. It's nice having flatmates again. And it's cheap. I don't want to move.' Pete averted his eyes as he sipped his coffee expecting Stella to go all . . . well, Stella.

'Oh,' she said, watching him over the rim of her own cup. 'Oh, well, OK then. Sharing could be fun.'

Pete looked at her hard as she took another bite of her muffin. She was being uncharacteristically deferential and demure. He steeled himself. Now was as good a time as any.

'Stella, about that email I sent you,' Pete began.

Stella waved her hand dismissively and talked through a mouthful of muffin.

'Oh, forget about it,' she said, or at least that's what Pete thought she said.

He pressed on, as tempting as the suggestion was. 'No, no, I can't just forget about it. We have to talk about it, talk about how I felt when I wrote it. I mean, that's why you came back, isn't it? Because of that email.'

Stella washed down the muffin with a swig of coffee and thought of AJ.

'Partly,' she said, her mind racing. Stella hadn't expected this. She hadn't expected a head-on confrontation with Pete – it wasn't his style. He liked to leave things unsaid until they didn't need saying any more, or at least until both of them could pretend that they didn't. 'It helped clarify my mind,' she said, smiling warmly at him. 'But that's all I needed . . . Look, Pete, if you were with someone else, then don't tell me. I don't want to know. I understand why you did it and it hurts, but . . . well, all I want to know is if we are going to be all right – that's all that matters now. I know that *I'm* ready now, to be with you and marry you and settle. Settle down, I mean. I'm ready. The question is, Pete,' Stella raised her chin a little defensively, 'are *you?*'

Pete didn't speak for a moment. Those seconds of silence hit Stella's bravado hard and shook her to the core. This was going to be harder than she'd thought.

'We've been together now for a long time, haven't we?' Pete began, feeling his way along the sentence like a man on a cliff edge. 'And it's been a rollercoaster, hasn't it? You've been like the centre of my universe for all of that time. I've jumped through hoops for you, Stella, walked on broken glass. Done the whole mountain high, river deep number to try and get you to see that I was the one who could make you happy. I was the one who could save you . . .'

Stella nodded vigorously. 'Yes, I know! And you've done it, and I see that now—'

Pete interrupted her. 'No, you don't understand. While you were away, when you *still* went away after I said the one thing that I really thought would make you stay, things changed. I started getting altitude sickness from climbing all those sodding mountains and it felt like I didn't have the energy to swim another bloody river. *I* wanted to be swept along, Stella. I didn't know it or believe it until it happened, but I did. And I met someone, who . . . well, she wants to be with someone else and so nothing happened, not really. But she made me feel *differently*. She made me think that maybe it doesn't have to be a constant battle to be with someone, not if it's the *right* someone. If you're right together, you should just both want it and let it be. And I'm not sure that we both want it, Stella. I'm not sure that we'd ever have that.'

Pete stopped speaking and waited, forcing himself to look at her.

'I . . .' she began.

'Pete! Hi! What are you doing in this godawful town this time of the morning?'

Louise was standing beside their table, her smile as bright and as hard-edged as the diamond at her throat. Pete stared at Louise and blinked.

'Um, I, er, well, I live here,' he said finally.

Louise pulled up a chair and sat down, setting her own coffee between him and Stella as if she were laying down a gauntlet.

'Hello,' she said to Stella. 'I'm Louise. Maybe you've heard of me?'

Stella looked uncertainly at Pete, dumbstruck, and Pete could see her wondering if this was the other person he'd been talking about.

Louise rattled on without waiting for further introductions. 'It's just that when I saw you in London with *Carmen* I got the impression you lived in town. *Carmen* does, doesn't she?'

Pete shifted slightly under Louise's inexplicably close scrutiny; he had no idea where Maggie had told her she lived.

'Um, yeah. In, um, Notting Hill,' he said, pulling the place name out of the air.

Louise pressed her lips together and smiled at Stella with more

311

than a hint of pity. 'So you must be the erstwhile fiancée,' she said, and then, turning back to Pete, 'Oh God, I hope I haven't dropped you in it!' She giggled, but the laugh was brittle and high.

Pete shook his head, feeling confused and embattled. It was like Louise thought she was having an entirely different conversation from the one that was coming out of her mouth.

'Are you OK, Louise?' he said, hoping to deflect her unsettling attention from himself and to calm her down a bit. 'You seem a bit . . . hyper? I mean, what are you doing in St Albans anyway?'

Louise's shoulders sunk a little and she spooned four large heaps of sugar into the froth of her cappuccino, watching it sink beneath the surface.

'Good question, Pete.' She huffed out a breath and took a moment. 'Christian and I went away. Italy, the Amalfi coast. He said we needed to get away from everything here, we needed to get far away from the past. Clear the air – give ourselves a chance to be together without all the "pressure" and "confusion". There we were sitting at dinner, you know, Pete, that night I saw you and Carmen, and I was expecting the whole "I'm sorry it's not going to work out" speech, and he produces these tickets! I couldn't believe it. I mean I said to him, "What about Fresh Talent 2?" It's opening on Friday, you know. But no, he said we'd be back in time for that, most of the work was done and one of his managers here could tie up the loose ends. He said that *we* were more important. Can you imagine that? Christian, who has never put anything before work before, putting *me* first! I thought, this is it. This really means he loves *me*. I've won.'

Pete noticed that Louise was talking exclusively to Stella now, as if his very maleness excluded him from the conversation. That and the fact that she seemed to be somehow angry with him, which, he was fairly sure, was why she was sitting here in the first place. Stella's reply was a blank façade thinly covering whatever her reaction to everything he'd just said was. Pete wished he could make Louise go away but he didn't know how. Stella would know how, but she seemed unable to speak.

'And it was perfect, Stella, I really thought it was perfect. Perfect hotel, perfect view over the bay, we made love every bloody hour of the day. Jesus, what more could I do? So we get back this morning, early hours, and he brings me back to his flat because it's closer. The first time ever and I thought, that proves it, he's going to ask me to move in with him. I slept like a baby.'

Louise paused as every muscle in her face tightened by one degree.

'And then I wake up this morning and he's sitting on the end of the bed crying. *Crying*! I ask him, what's wrong? And do you know what he does? He holds out this photo of *Maggie* and he tells me that he's sorry, he loves me, he really does, but he thinks he has to give it another go with Maggie. He says that he still loves her too and that he thought he'd be able to let her go once and for all but he just can't, he says that it's not fair on me to be in a relationship that he's not sure about! That he can't throw away what he and Maggie had over . . . me! Even if apparently I make him happier than he's ever been. And that she, *she*, deserves better!'

Pete opened and closed his mouth, at a loss what to say. It was a pretty tough break-up, after all, but in the back of his mind he knew there was something, some small detail, that was really, really important, but he couldn't seem to focus on it. There were too many other whopping great big things to get round first. Things like his suspended conversation with Stella and the fact that Christian was definitely going back to Maggie. Pete felt a small flame of hope – that he hadn't even known was there until this moment – blow out in his heart.

'I mean, you tell me, Stella,' Louise's voice had risen and the few people in the café were watching her, 'would you rather have someone because they loved you, or because they felt a sense of duty towards you? Because that's what it is. It doesn't make sense to me. How can it be that I make him happy, and he still wants her, the woman who practically bored him to death?' Louise looked sharply at Pete. 'Or maybe you could answer that question?'

Pete shook his head. This was all getting too much. He was sorry for Louise, but he was about to leave his own life crashing against the rocks. He couldn't take time out to counsel her.

'Louise, I don't know what to say. Sometimes people make the wrong choices,' he said, mentally urging her to leave.

'Exactly,' Louise said, pushing her chair back so hard it toppled over. 'Well, it isn't over yet. I'll show them, I'll show them both. Now, if you'll excuse me, I think I'd better go. Nice knowing you, Pete.'

Louise picked up her bag and made her way out of the café, clearly irritated that the door was too heavily weighted to slam behind her.

Pete looked at Stella, whose head was bowed.

'God, I'm sorry about that. She's sort of an acquaintance, a very angry one.' Pete reached for Stella's hand. 'Are you OK?'

Stella gave a small laugh and looked at him.

'Was that the one? Was *that* her?'

Pete shook his head. 'No, it wasn't her. But that's not important now. You said it wasn't . . . Look, I'm not saying we're over, Stella,' he said, feeling like a coward. 'I'm just telling you how I feel. You have a right to know how I feel.' Stella withdrew her hand from under his. 'I feel exhausted.'

'If we're not over then what are we?' she said. 'How can we be together if you say you're tired of being in love with me?'

Pete shook his head. 'I'm tired of trying to make you love me, that's what I meant.'

'So you still love me, you still want me?'

Pete stared at her, uncertain of what to say, so he tried honesty. 'I don't know, Stella. It's pathetic, I know, but I think I began to realise that love can be different from how I thought it had to be. I thought it was like a kind of quest, that after I'd passed all the tests you set me you'd be mine. Now I don't feel that. Now I think we just need to be happy to be with each other. We need to make each other happy. I don't know if we are capable of that kind of relationship . . .'

Stella leaned across the table towards him. 'But I do love you, Pete, I do. You have made me love you, I realise it now, please . . .' Stella's eyes filled with tears and Pete felt his chest tighten as he looked at her. 'Please,' she said again.

Pete swallowed hard and asked her the one thing he really needed to know.

'Do you, Stella? Do you love me, or are you still feeling hurt and bruised from someone or something in Australia? Do you just want to be with me because I'm the safe and secure one? Just until I bore you again and you feel good about yourself? If you can say that it's none of those things, that you want me because being with me makes you complete, then I'm willing to give it another try. If, after all these years, you've finally started to really feel like that then I won't walk out on you, I'll stay.'

Pete felt ashamed. He pretended to himself that the whole purpose of this talk had always been to try and work things out, but he knew that he didn't want to work things out. He wanted to be with Maggie, or on his own. Stella's light had suddenly blinked out of his vision. But he couldn't just say that; he couldn't tell it like it was. He had to walk all around the issue waiting for her to see it. Waiting for her to say it. Waiting for her to end it. He felt his body tense and a surge of sudden panic at losing something he had become accustomed to wanting for so long.

Pete was sure he knew what Stella would say.

Stella's head was bowed as she thought for a moment, twisting her engagement ring around and round on her finger. She looked up at him.

'But I do love you, Pete. You do mean the world to me. I do want to marry you.'

They stared at each other for a long moment, a moment filled with dark double meanings and implicit revelations.

'So you'll stay with me, won't you? Like you said?'

Pete nodded his head and attempted a smile as he took her hand.

'Of course I will,' he said.

They both knew that Stella was lying. They both knew that one day she'd take off again and leave Pete behind. But Stella needed him now, and after everything they'd been through he was unable to let her down. She knew as well as he did that neither one of them would talk openly about the agreement; they'd both go on just as they had before. Except that this time, for the first time, Pete really understood what that meant.

Chapter Thirty

'But I thought he said next week!' Maggie exclaimed as she watched a builder begin to white out The Fleur's windows.

'It *is* next week!' Sarah told her impatiently.

'But I thought he meant next *week*, *next* week – it's Wednesday. You only spoke to him on Sunday! And the refurbishment team have arrived and the kitchen's getting ripped out!' Maggie returned anxiously, feeling as if someone had decided to start spinning the world twice as fast without telling her.

'I know! But he didn't, he meant this week, he meant today. He phoned me last night to tell us! Aidan is coming in on the eleven-thirty flight today, and I have to take Becca to meet him. What am I going to do, Maggie? What am I going to say, what am I going to wear?'

Maggie looked at the chaos that was gradually beginning to form all around her. It was OK, it was all right, she just had to get a grip and put her faith in gravity.

'Hang on,' she said before pressing her hand over the mouthpiece. 'Jim! JIM!' Maggie shouted to the pub at large. After a few seconds Jim lurched through the flat door and looked around him.

'Fuck me, it's Armageddon,' he said helpfully.

'Not yet, but it's going to be. Look, Sheila's going to be in at

317

nine, you need to help her get all the stock into crates and into the pool room bar. You need to make sure the bar's spotless and that all the pumps are washed through and hooked up. You need to move the pool table down to the cellar and set up some tables and chairs – I want it open for business tonight. You need a business as usual sign with an arrow pointing to the new entrance and you need to make sure that what's staying in here stays and what's going goes. OK?'

Jim blinked twice. 'And what will you be doing?' he said.

'I'll be going out. It's an emergency.' Maggie gave him a hopeful smile. 'Come on, just pretend you're slaying a few dragons and I promise you can have the whole of tomorrow off. And a sub on your wages.'

Jim half smiled. 'A sub? Really?' he asked.

'Yeah, well, it's a perk of the job,' Maggie winked at him. 'Assistant Manager's job, that is. You've been promoted.'

Jim smiled broadly. 'I've got the feeling that somehow you're still the winner here, but thanks anyway, sis, it means a lot.' He looked around him, his hands on his hips. 'Go on, go off for your "emergency". I'll see you later.'

Maggie grinned at him and spoke to Sarah. 'Are you still there?' she asked.

'Yes, but don't worry, I've been waiting so long the boredom's taken over the panic and stress.'

Maggie laughed. 'I'll be there in ten minutes then, OK?' she said.

'Oh, thank God,' Sarah said and hung up.

Sarah watched Becca swirl around in front of her in her tenth outfit so far that morning, which had been a long one, hot on the heels of a very short night. Becca had been up since six. First she'd spent half an hour laboriously straightening her hair and then, after Sarah had finally rooted out an ancient photo of

Aidan and casually remarked that Becca got her curls from her father, she'd run back into the bathroom and washed again, madly scrunch-drying it with half a can of mousse.

'I want him to think I look like him,' she'd said when she emerged a second time. 'I want him to see I'm really his. I don't look too much like you, do I, Mum?'

Sarah had swallowed the pain and shook her head. 'No, you look a lot like him, but darling, it won't matter what you look like. He's not going to worry about that.'

Becca had shaken her head. 'It does matter. It matters to me,' she'd said, and gone off to find the first of many outfits. This one, Sarah calculated, admittedly with a sleep-deprived brain, was the tenth.

'Lovely,' she told her daughter, wishing to God that Maggie would get here fast.

'You always say that,' Becca sighed, smoothing down her top as she looked in the mirror.

'That's because they are all lovely. You look lovely in whatever you wear,' Sarah told her. She winced as Becca whirled to face her.

'No I don't. You don't even care. If you did you wouldn't lie like that! You don't care what I look like. You want me to look terrible so that he won't want me, don't you, don't you? You don't want this to work at all, do you? You must really hate me!'

Sarah took a deep breath and gave a small prayer of thanks that Marcus had the day off and had been able to pick Sam up this morning before he'd even been properly awake. The last thing she wanted was for him to hear all of this.

'Darling, I thought we'd talked about this. That's not true, and you know it,' she said, holding out her arms to her daughter, who stayed resolutely on the other side of the room. After a few seconds Sarah let her arms return to her side, feeling the most excruciating sense of rejection she had ever felt since

Aidan had gone almost without warning all those years ago. She dropped her chin in defeat.

'I'm sorry, Becca. I never seem to say the right thing. This is hard for me too. I'm nervous about seeing him. I'm worried that it won't work out the way you want it to . . .'

'See!' Becca started.

'No, wait.' Sarah raised her hand. 'Just wait. I hope that it will, I think that it will. More than anything I want you to be happy. But Becca, you are so precious to me, I'd do anything to protect you. I know you're all grown up now, but you're still my little rose bud. I just want to keep you close and safe, even when . . . even when I know I can't.' Sarah didn't know which part of what she'd said got through but before she knew it Becca had crossed the room and put her arms around her neck. Sarah held her there, held her slim body against her own for a long moment, closing her eyes as she remembered the first time she'd ever held her daughter, feeling just the same – so in love, and so terrified of getting it wrong.

'I'm not a kid any more,' Becca said after a while, leaning back to look at Sarah. 'Well, I'm not a *little* kid, anyway, not like Sam. I know what might happen. Look at Leanne's dad – she hasn't seen him in two years. I know that it's not automatic for dads and kids to like each other or love each other. I just want the chance, and I want the best possible chance, and you might think I'm silly but—'

'I don't, I don't think that,' Sarah said.

'But Mum, I still need you. I will for ages and ages. I won't leave you or anything if that's what you're worried about.'

Sarah looked at her daughter and bit her lip hard.

'Thank you,' she said. 'For saying that. And you do look lovely in that outfit, you do look lovely in all of them. Any father would be proud to call you his daughter.'

Maggie opened the flat door and called out hello.

'Luce told me just to come up. Hi, Becs, you look lovely!' she said, and stood waiting patiently for her friend and her god-daughter to explain to her what it was they were laughing about.

'Are you OK?' Maggie asked Sarah as they waited for Becca to emerge from her third trip to the ladies since they'd arrived.

Sarah stood looking at the arrivals gate and chewing her lip.

'I'm OK. I'm just worried that when I see him again, all those emotions I spent so long getting rid of will just flood right back and I'll go to pieces. I'm worried I won't be able to be the person Becca wants me to be. And that I'll forget that this whole thing isn't about me, it's about her and what she wants – what I think and feel doesn't matter.'

Maggie hooked her arm through Sarah's.

'It does matter, it matters to me. But anyway it's a long time, fourteen years. He probably won't be sexy any more. Actually, to be honest with you, I never thought he was sexy – too tall and gangly and, let's face it, too spotty for me.'

Sarah attempted a smile, but the muscles of her face seemed to be frozen.

'Well, I fancied him,' she said instead. 'And anyway, he might be even sexier now he's aged a bit. Look at us – I'm a bombshell and frankly, for you aged eighteen, the only way was up.'

Maggie bit back her retort and let Sarah's comment slide, seeing as it was more or less true.

'We're still sexy, aren't we?' Sarah said, and then, 'Oh God, I think I have to pee now.'

Becca bounded up between them, throwing an arm round each of them as she arrived. Besides the rather obvious symptom of repetitive trips to the loo, she seemed more excited than worried.

'It's in, the flight is in! I heard it over the speaker thingy in the loo. Didn't you hear it? Come on!' She leaned forward, attempting to drag both of the women with her.

Maggie ducked out from under her arm lock and exchanged glances with Sarah over her head. Sarah disengaged herself from Becca's grip and took her gently by the shoulders, looking her in the eye.

'Are *you* ready?' she asked Becca. 'Are *you* OK?'

Becca jiggled on her toes as if she needed another trip to the ladies.

'I'm fine, Mum, *come on*! He's going to be waiting for us.' Becca started walking ahead of them to the arrivals area.

'It'll be ages yet, Becs,' Maggie called out. 'There's luggage to pick up and passport control, it'll be ages!' But Becca was weaving off ahead of them, forcing the two women to break into a trot to catch up with her.

Eventually the first few passengers began to file through the arrivals gates, there were a few quiet whoops of joy and several hugs, followed by more than one business traveller catching sight of his or her name scrawled on to a piece of dirty cardboard.

Sarah watched the crowd, feeling the racing of her heart pulsing in every nerve. As she scanned the sea of bobbing faces, she tried to picture Aidan as she had last seen him under the half light of a streetlamp as they'd said goodbye for what she had thought was the last time. His green eyes were cast in shadow, the curl of his hair resisting whatever gel or style products he tried to tame it with. He *had* been tall and gangly and spotty and all of the things Maggie had said, but Sarah had *loved* him. And the sight of him then, and the memory of him ever since, had filled her with such a longing that for years her chest would still tighten and her skin would still tingle. Just as it was now.

Gradually the crowd began to thin out, until all that remained were the last few stragglers: a woman trying to manoeuvre two huge wheelie suitcases at once, a large man in jeans and baseball cap lumbering in their direction and finally a nun, hurrying past them all with some secret purpose.

'Where is he?' Becca asked, looking down at the photo she'd brought with her. 'Is he still coming?'

Sarah glanced at Maggie, feeling her heart plummeting into the pit of her stomach. What did she say to Becca now? How did she explain this?

'I expect he's been delayed, or—' Sarah stopped mid-sentence, aware that the large man in the baseball cap had stopped directly in front of her and Becca and was staring at them both.

'Sarah? My God, you haven't changed a bit,' he said with a Boston accent. Sarah blinked at him, and for a split second wondered who it was that Aidan had sent in his place to greet his first-born daughter. And then she realised this man *was* Aidan, still tall, yes, but now carrying a huge bulk that seemed to gather mainly around his middle, tapering down to a neat pair of feet and up towards a perfectly bald head. Every last one of the wayward curls he'd hated so much had gone, revealing a smooth pink surface that reflected the fluorescent lighting in its slight shimmer of sweat. The only thing left of the eighteen-year-old Aidan was in his eyes, still warm and green and sparkling behind the folds of flesh that had grown around them. Sarah looked into those, and for a moment she was back lying on the grass under the moon with Aidan in her arms. But it was only for a moment, and she laughed with relief.

'Aidan! It's so great to see you!'

She felt able to smile at him, safe in the knowledge that she wasn't going to fall in love with him all over again. It wasn't his weight or his hair loss or his appalling taste in T-shirts that had done it. Although they had helped. The instant Sarah saw him she remembered something she'd forgotten for all those years in the shock of his abrupt departure. That even on the grass under the moon, she'd known that although he was her first love he wouldn't be her last, and she wouldn't love him for ever. It took seeing him again to remind her of that, and to wipe away the mythological status his absence had given him. If only he'd managed to write to her, if only they'd had a chance to drift apart naturally, perhaps then she wouldn't have spent all these years trying to avoid getting hurt by another man again.

'Aidan, my God, you look so . . . well!' She put her arm around Becca's shoulder and brought her forward a couple of steps.

'Here's Becca. Becca, meet your dad.'

Becca and Aidan looked at each other, their mouths set in exactly the same line, each trying to smile and each frozen with nerves.

'You're tall,' Aidan said finally. 'Like me and my girls, my other girls, that is. They're both tall, but luckily, like you they've got their mother's figure.'

He grinned and Becca smiled tentatively back. Sarah saw her lip wobbling slightly and wished to God that she could read her mind, find out how she was coping.

Aidan picked up Becca's hand. 'And you've the family curls. I hope you don't hate them as much as I did. If you're anything like Gracie and Faith, you will. You've got your mother's eyes, though, and her mouth.' Aidan smiled at her and paused. 'Becca . . . I know that I only found out about you a few days ago, and I know that it's strange . . . We've got a lot of getting to know each other to do – but I think we'll do just fine, don't you?'

Becca nodded uncertainly and glanced at her mother, then back at her father.

'I thought that when I saw you I'd want to hug you or something, but I, um . . . well, I feel a bit weird about it, so I won't at the moment if you don't mind?'

Aidan laughed and put his arm around her shoulder. 'I don't mind. Let's find a place to eat, shall we, and then work out how we're going to spend the next few days. Is that all right, Sarah?'

Sarah nodded. 'Sure, the car's outside. I thought we could eat at your hotel, maybe. You must be tired . . .'

Aidan shook his head and looked at Becca. 'I'm fine. Come on, kiddo, let's go.'

Maggie was quietly trailing behind them, wondering if they'd all fit in Sarah's mini, when Aidan finally spotted her.

'Maggie! Maggie Johnson, is that really you?'

Maggie stopped and glanced down at herself. 'Um, yes? Hi, Aidan,' she said, a little nonplussed by his reaction.

'Maggie Johnson, you look incredible. Who'd have thought it?'

Maggie laughed. 'Thanks, I think . . . And, um, so do you look . . .'

'Fat and bald, a regular sex god – yeah, I know,' Aidan said, and laughed the kind of laugh that set them all off until eventually people started to look at them and raise their eyebrows.

Chapter Thirty-one

Maggie noticed that it was already dark and that the air held the slight edge of the damp chill as she headed back to The Fleur just after eight that evening. It had been a strange day, to say the least, but she thought probably a good one. Or at least the beginning of something good for Becca, and maybe even for Sarah with a fair wind and some good luck.

Of course it had been awkward at first, the four of them crammed into Sarah's tiny and at the best of times rickety mini. Once the nervous laughter had subsided, Sarah had asked Aidan all sorts of polite questions about his home, his family and his job, and he in turn had asked after her family and congratulated her on running her own business, which she had accepted with self-deprecation. Becca and Maggie had sat together on the back seat, knees touching and exchanging glances when Becca wasn't staring studiously out of the window.

Maggie wondered if Becca was somehow disappointed with the reunion, if she had expected something more dramatic or even romantic, in the traditional sense of the word. She wondered if Becca had thought there could be no long silences between a reunited father and daughter, or if she had allowed for the fact that, after all, the two of them were strangers with a lot of ground to make up. It was hard for Maggie to really understand what it meant, or to appreciate how difficult a journey it would be. She reached for Becca's hand and held it, relieved and touched when Becca did not take it away.

'So, Becca,' Aidan said over the starter at lunch. 'What do you want to do while I'm here? We've got a week this visit. We could catch a film? Or maybe I could take you bowling. Gracie loves bowling, though Lord knows she's so little she practically shoots off down the alley after the ball! What do you like doing?'

Becca looked at him across the table and then at her mum. She opened her mouth, but nothing seemed to be forthcoming.

'She likes talking on the phone a lot,' Sarah said with a small smile. 'And shopping. Yep, talking and shopping, that's her main hobbies.'

Becca's eyes widened in horror.

'Mum!' She turned to Aidan. 'She makes me sound like I'm a total airhead. But I'm not, I like reading too. And I like writing stories and stuff, sometimes, although they're not . . . very good or anything.'

Becca faltered to a halt, and Maggie racked her brain for any one of the hundreds of things that should have been obvious to cover the silence.

'I like poetry,' Aidan said. 'Do you write poems? Love poems to your boyfriend?'

Becca squirmed. 'No,' she said flatly. 'And anyway, I'm too young to even have . . . a . . . boyfriend?' she finished uncertainly, her cheeks flushing as she finished the longest speech she had made in front of her father.

Aidan chuckled and leaned a little closer to her. 'Gracie would love a boyfriend, but she's only eight. I wish she were as sensible as you! You know there are two little girls in Boston over the moon with excitement about having a long-lost big sister. They can't wait to meet you, and neither can my wife Fran.' He paused. 'So is there anything you want to do while I'm here?' he asked.

Becca stared at her plate, probably thinking, Maggie guessed, that it shouldn't be up to her to decide. 'Don't know,' she shrugged. 'You decide.'

Aidan glanced at Sarah, who smiled at him. 'What about the London Eye? My guide says it's really something.'

Becca looked up and nodded. 'Yeah, all right,' she said.

'Maybe Madame Tussauds?' Aidan began.

Becca rolled her eyes. 'No way! I'm not queuing for hours with all the stupid tourists!'

Aidan smiled and Becca flushed. 'Where else, then?' he asked. 'Any ideas?'

Becca glanced around nervously. 'I wouldn't mind going to the Tate Modern.'

'Where?' Sarah could not hide her shock. 'You're not interested in art, are you?'

Becca scowled at her. 'I might be. This boy at school said it was cool . . .' She trailed off and all three adults said 'Oh, I see,' to themselves simultaneously.

'The Tate it is, then,' Aidan said.

'Thanks . . . um, Aidan,' Becca said. 'I'm glad you came.'

That hadn't been the end of the awkward pauses or the strained silences, but it had seemed to mark their gradual decline and the beginning of a new friendship.

They said goodbye to Aidan at the hotel. He arranged to take Becca out for breakfast the next morning.

As soon as they'd headed back to the salon, Becca had started talking and still hadn't stopped when Marcus dropped off Sam an hour after they got back. He'd stood and listened as Becca gave him a speed-speak, potted version of her day in a sixty-second package.

'Cool, Becs,' he said with a smile when she'd finally paused for breath. 'I'm really pleased it went so well for you, darling.' He gave her a bear hug, lifting her clear off the floor. Sarah

328

waited for him to tuck Sam into bed and then made them all a cup of tea.

'Sounds like you did the right thing,' Marcus said to Sarah when Becca had disappeared into her bedroom to phone all her friends.

Sarah nodded. 'Yeah, I think it was the right thing, not just for Becca but for all of us. I think we can all move on from this now. I'm just sorry I didn't have the guts to do it years ago.'

Marcus shrugged and, picking up his jacket, leaned in to kiss her on the cheek. 'So am I,' he said just before he left.

'He so loves you *still*, the mentalist,' Maggie told Sarah when Marcus had gone.

'He does not! That was years ago,' Sarah said with a laugh. 'He has girls chase him down the high street throwing their knickers at him. He's a single fireman for God's sake, he has the sex life most men only dream about. He's certainly not pining after me when he could have any passing twenty-year-old!'

'Sarah, he asked you to marry him. You could have married him! Anyway, it's obvious he still feels something for you – it's written all over his face.' Maggie crossed her arms. 'I think he still loves you, and we know he loves your daughter like she was his, and he loves his son more than anyone in the world except maybe you. You were insane for not giving him a chance when he asked you. Maybe now you're so keen on doing the right thing, it'd be a good time to try again with him. After all, he hasn't got anyone serious in his life, has he? He's fair game.'

Sarah shook her head and looked at Maggie as if she were insane.

'You're insane! Even if I was . . . *hypothetically* . . . interested in him he wouldn't be now. He's playing the field, enjoying himself. I mean, even if I did – in theory – think I might care about him, there's no point in thinking about it. You should know you can't go back in life, Maggie – you have to keep

329

going forward even when it hurts you. Anyway, this is me we're talking about. I don't do relationships.'

Maggie shook her head and picked up her bag.

'No, the you who thought some eighteen-year-old kid with spots was the only man you could ever love, *that* you didn't do relationships. The thirty-odd-year-old you with the two kids, the successful business and a new start could do relationships if only she'd give it a go. It might go wrong! So what? You have to give these things a try, Sarah, or you'll regret it!'

Maggie stood up and put her hand on her hips, enjoying having the moral high-ground for the first time in ages. Sarah looked her up and down, clearly unimpressed with her stand.

'I tell you what,' Sarah said with a small smile. 'I'll agree to go out with Marcus the next time I see him if you ask out that Pete bloke. We can double-date.'

Maggie fell off the moral high-ground and sat back down with a plonk.

'I can't ask him out. His fiancée is back. She came back and I went round there to see him and talk to him and stuff and they were . . . in bed.'

Sarah sighed and reached over to pat Maggie's knee.

'I'm sorry mate, but you're not that upset, are you? It was just lust, wasn't it?'

Maggie looked at her hands.

'Yeah, it was just lust. And the way he laughed and the funny feeling I got when he smiled at me and the fact that when I was with him I felt like I was on a first date with someone I'd known all my life. That sort of thing.'

Sarah looked at her. 'Mmmm,' she said.

'Mmmm?' Maggie replied. 'What does Mmmm mean?'

'It means this isn't another double-bluff to get Christian back, is it?'

Maggie looked abashed. 'No it is not!'

She wondered if now was a good time to tell her about Carmen, but decided that best friends didn't need to know everything about each other. Not if there was a chance of her ever having the moral high-ground again. 'No it is not,' she repeated. 'I know it can't happen, but I think that . . . well, I think that it'll take me a long time to stop thinking about that kiss, that's what I think.'

Maggie stood up again. 'I've got to get back to The Fleur, but listen, you never did give it a try with Marcus in the first place. You met him, you had his son and then when you found out he wanted both of you, you ran a mile. You never went anywhere. This is a new beginning for Becca. If there's still a chance, let it be a new beginning for you too.' Maggie gave Sarah a hug. 'Just promise me that if Marcus asks you out again, you won't turn him down, OK?'

Sarah shrugged exactly like Becca would.

'*Promise?*' Maggie pressed her.

'OK, OK!' Sarah rolled her eyes and, raising her right hand, recited, 'I promise if Marcus asks me out again at anytime in the near future I won't turn him down.' She dropped her hand. 'But he won't. No way. And you promise me that if you get the chance to tell Pete how you feel, fiancée or no fiancée, you will, OK?'

Maggie kissed her friend quickly on the cheek and then raced down the stairs two at a time and on to the street.

'OK!?' Sarah shouted after her.

'OK!' Maggie called back, pulling the shop door closed. 'But I won't get a chance, so it doesn't matter,' she mumbled to herself, and then smiled. Marcus was still standing by his car looking up at the flat. Maybe this was her chance to get Sarah going again.

'Trust me,' Maggie said lightly, 'stalking's not all it's cracked up to be – I know.'

331

Marcus laughed and looked at his feet.

'I was just thinking, that's all,' he said. 'About stuff. I don't know, Maggie, I still feel that . . .' Marcus closed his mouth as if stopping a secret from escaping. 'Never mind, I'll get off now. I'm on shift in half an hour.'

As he opened the car door, Maggie put her hand on his arm, deciding that she could try just one more meddle before she gave it up for good.

'You know what I think,' she said, glancing up at the flat window. 'I think that if you were, say . . . going to ask Sarah out again, for example, you know, if you were . . . then I *think* that she'd probably say yes this time. If you were going to, that is. Oh, and we never had this conversation, OK?'

Marcus looked at Maggie and then back up at the flat. Both of them felt the same little thrill of fear.

'Really?' he said.

'Really,' Maggie said, giving him a good luck punch on the arm. She'd left him there standing by his car, plucking up courage. If he did go back up there it certainly would take a lot of courage. She just hoped Sarah didn't back out of her end of the deal.

Maggie stopped short outside the pub, feeling as if she had just been slapped hard in the face by the future. The Fleur, her home and one of her few constants for so many years, had been altered irrevocably in the matter of a few hours. Scaffolding masked the frontage on both corners, and tarpaulin covered that in green swathes of netting. Jim had managed to get the new name sign reading 'Business As Usual' up. She was pleased to see he'd added his own arrow pointing to the small arched side entrance that hadn't been used for God knows how long. He'd managed to open the rusty wrought-iron gate and, Maggie noted, even find a bulb of the faux Victorian lamp that lit the narrow archway. Maggie walked through it in to the tiny courtyard, which had just enough space for one dilapidated picnic table. Only this morning the courtyard had been full of old crates and empty bottles that somehow never got returned, mostly because the brands of beer they once held were long obsolete. Now there was a planted tub of late geraniums in one corner, two outdoor candles glowing softly in the dark and a couple kissing noisily, sprawled across the damp and mouldy table.

'Excuse me,' Maggie said, though she was fairly certain they wouldn't notice her even if her hair was on fire. She felt a little pang of memory as the sensation of Pete's kiss paid a swift return visit. Telling herself it would fade eventually, she took a deep breath and pushed open the door of the pool room bar, The Fleur's only working bar for the next two months.

It was full to the rafters. This wasn't hard as it was tiny, and even if only the five regulars who were usually there had shown up it would still have looked busy. But apart from Mrs Kim, Falcon and his friend (not Pete, Maggie noticed, wondering if he was here somewhere, and then dreading the thought that it might have been him and Stella in the gloom on the picnic table) and the old man, there were at least eight, maybe ten other people in the bar. Jim had somehow managed to move the pool table and squeeze two tables and chairs in its place, both fully occupied. Maggie caught Jim's eyes and headed to the bar.

'Blimey,' she said by way of a greeting, gesturing at the busy bar.

'Yeah, I know,' Jim said. 'I think it's the little side entrance, I think it intrigues people.'

Maggie nodded – it was a possibility.

'So how was your day?' Jim asked her. 'Sarah and Becca get on OK with Aidan? Tearful reunions all round?' He poured Maggie a glass of wine and set it on the bar.

'Thanks!' Maggie was mildly surprised by the gesture. 'Well, it wasn't exactly like it is in the movies, but it was a good start, I think.'

'Oh good, because, look, um . . .' Jim leaned a little closer to her. 'Um, Maggie—' he began.

'All right, Maggie?' Falcon interrupted him, sliding up the bar to stand next to her.

'Not so bad!' Maggie said with deliberate brightness. 'You?'

'Yeah, I'm all right. How's that Sarah?'

Maggie bit her lip. 'That Sarah is fine, really good. In fact, she's got a lot on at the moment with her family and, well . . .' Maggie glanced at her watch and hoped she wasn't totally lying . . . 'she might have just started seeing someone else.'

Falcon shrugged. 'Good one,' he said mildly. He gave Maggie a smile. 'Fancy a whisky with me? The last two singles left in town?'

Maggie was just wondering why ever not when Jim put his hand on her arm.

'Maggie!' he said insistently.

'What?' Maggie looked at him.

'I've been trying to tell you, Christian's here. I mean, actually he's there.'

Jim nodded to the shadowy end of the short bar where Christian sat watching her. His hair was unkempt, his jaw was shadowed with stubble and his eyes looked hollow and dark. Maggie felt a lurch in her stomach and she tried to smile at him.

'He got here just after lunch. He's been waiting ever since. He hasn't been drinking or anything, just sitting there looking like he hasn't slept in ten years. Even Sheila took pity on him and made him two cups of tea, although she wouldn't speak to him. But he didn't touch either one. He's just been waiting.' Jim took in Maggie's blanched white face. 'Do you want to talk to him? I could get rid of him if you want me to.'

'And me,' Falcon said, leaning in on the conversation.

Maggie smiled at him. 'No, it's OK. We've got things we need to say to each other. That's why he's here, I expect.' She took a deep breath and, picking up her glass of wine, walked over to Christian.

'Maggie,' he said, looking at her, his face full of sorrow.

'Are you OK?' Maggie asked him. 'What happened? Is it Louise? Is she OK?'

Christian reached out for her hand and squeezed her fingers more than was comfortable.

'I need to talk to you, but not here. Can we go somewhere?'

Maggie paused for the protracted second it took to pull her fingers from his grip and nodded, leading him through the pool room bar, through the closed-off bar and into remains of the old kitchen where Sheila was already sitting, lighting one cigarette from another.

'Oh, you've found him then, Mag,' she said dourly. 'I'll get back.' She pushed back her chair and gave Christian a long look as she swept past him. 'Don't you let him mess you around, all right? Even if he is sorry,' she said as she exited.

Christian sat at the table and folded his hands in front of him.

'Do you want a drink of anything?' Maggie asked him. 'Tea, chocolate?' Arsenic? She added in her own head. He certainly looked miserable enough.

He shook his head. 'No. Look, sit down, will you. I need to get things sorted.'

Maggie sat down and looked at him, feeling an inexplicable dread.

'I'm sorry that I haven't been in touch, after the other night. When we kissed . . .' Maggie began to tell him not to worry, but he talked over her. 'I hated myself for that, Maggie, for kissing you and leading you on and not letting you go. For lying to Louise about it. But then I realised that maybe there was part

335

of me that didn't want to let you go, that couldn't. I haven't been in touch because I decided to take Louise away on holiday, to try to get you out of my head once and for all. And we had a great time, a fantastic time. Whenever she was by my side I couldn't think of anything else but her. She's so . . .' Christian gestured in the dark air as if he were spreading star dust through it. 'She's so wonderful to be with, she lights me up from the inside, you know? She's a bit fragile sometimes; she's not like you. She's not so self-reliant, but she makes me want to take care of her.' Christian stopped himself. 'But when I was alone, or in the middle of the night, I kept thinking about you, Maggie, kept coming back to you. I kept thinking about everything we'd done together, how much we achieved. I couldn't have built up Fresh Talent without you.'

Maggie wondered if she'd misheard.

'You could have, it was all you, not me . . .' she began.

'No. We did it together. You had just as many ideas as I did, although you let me think they were mine more often than not. I'm not totally stupid, Maggie. Fresh Talent really took off after you arrived. That wasn't just coincidence. And you kept it going, you were the engine room. It's been hard to replace you, really hard.'

Maggie thought she knew what he wanted.

'Christian, look. I'm . . . OK about you and Louise now. I'm fine, but I can't come back to work for you, not now . . . It would be too hard, and I've got to concentrate on the—'

Christian slammed his palm down on the table, making Maggie jump a little.

'No, I don't want you to come back to work for me! You're not listening! Christ knows how long I've spent working out the right thing to do, so please. Just listen to me, please, OK?'

Christian ran his hands through his already dishevelled hair and Maggie nodded, suddenly wishing that the main bar next door wasn't closed and that it wasn't so far to the nearest people.

He took a breath. 'You know me, Maggie. You know where I came from and how I got here. It's taken a lot of blood and guts and a lot of learning. No one, except for you, has ever helped me. Whatever I've got now, I got it on my own. I've learnt that you have to keep building on strong foundations to keep growing. You know I left school when I was fifteen without an O level to my name. You know that. If there's one thing I've learnt, and I've learnt it the hard way, you don't let your best assets go cheaply.'

Maggie shook her head. 'I don't understand,' she said.

'I'm saying that you – you and I. We were the greatest asset I've ever had. We were a team, a great team. And OK, so our relationship has changed over the years, so we don't make each other feel the way we used to, but I still care about you, Maggie. I still love you and I still . . . I still want you to be happy. The way I treated you, you didn't deserve that. It's the worst, most dishonourable thing that I've ever done and I can't live with that. I thought you'd be OK, but then when we had dinner I realised that you weren't, that you were so badly hurt, and I can't bear the thought that I did that to *you*. I can't pretend I'm not in love with Louise, but . . . well, if you're willing to give it another go, then so will I and maybe eventually those feelings for Louise will fade. I just want to do the right thing, Maggie, and I don't think we should throw away everything we had. What we had was solid.'

He looked at her and picked up her hand.

'Maggie, will you come back to me?'

The fridge kicked in, its humming breaking the silence of the room. Maggie sat back in her chair and went over everything he had just said, checking that she hadn't imagined it. And then she thanked God that sometime in the last few days she had realised she didn't love him any more, and hadn't for a long time before

337

Louise – because otherwise right now she'd be dying of a broken heart.

'Are you joking?' she said finally, aware that the anger that had so long evaded her had crept into her voice. 'Are you actually kidding me?' Maggie's laugh was harsh and hard-edged. 'You come in here and you say, "Oh well, Maggie, I'm totally crazy about this other woman, oh yes I love her, but you're ever so good at filing and I really can't cope with feeling guilty so I think we should give it another go. I care about you, Maggie, not as much as I totally love my new girlfriend, mind you, but she's not so good at negotiating with suppliers, so why don't we get back together? Is that what you're saying?'

Christian pushed his chair back a little in surprise.

'No, no. I'm trying to say—'

'That we can't throw what we had away?' Maggie asked him.

'Yes, exactly . . .' Christian stumbled over his words.

'It's too late, Christian. It's too late. You threw it away the day you decided to go to bed with Louise. Maybe you didn't think you'd fall for her, maybe you just wanted a bit on the side, but either way, you threw it away then, and to be honest, I think both of us had been destroying it in little bits and pieces for months. We couldn't go back, even if it wasn't as clear as bloody day that you love her and want to be with her, and I *certainly* don't want to go back for reasons of practicality or because you can't sleep at night. Jesus, how desperate do you think I am?'

'But I thought you said . . .'

'Yes, I did say it, and I did want you back at first, before I realised that you were right. We weren't lovers any more, not really. We might have had all the moves, but it was all so routine, so . . . joyless. And we weren't even that good at being friends towards the end. I hardly saw you, and if I think about it, I didn't actually miss you, not until after you were seeing her when I supposed I must have known something was going on. I was shocked, Christian, that you left me. Shocked out of my routine and my safe, predictable life. Hurt and desperate and a bit mental. But I've had time now. Even if you weren't madly in love with Louise, I still wouldn't want you back. I don't love you any more.'

Maggie panicked as she wondered for a second if that were actually true, but then her heart resurfaced from the depths of her stomach and she felt sure again.

'And you don't love me, so let's just put it behind us and move on. And as for your terrible guilt, what about Louise? How were you going to live with the guilt of leaving her? Or hadn't you thought that far ahead. Look, you go back to Louise, and I'll get on with my life, and we'll both pretend we never had this conversation, OK?'

Maggie was alarmed to see a large tear tracking down Christian's face and her voice softened.

'What? What is it? Come on, babe, you know I'm right, don't you? Louise will make you a hundred times happier than I could,' she told him, still feeling slightly out of sync with the unreality of the situation.

Christian looked at her with bloodshot eyes.

'Yeah, I know. I know you're right, but I . . . I already told Louise I was going back to you.' He broke into a sob. 'Oh fuck, Maggie, what have I done! I've been such a bloody idiot. This thing's just tied me up in knots and I couldn't see what was right any more. Oh God, I've lost her!'

Maggie thought for a moment, trying to see through the mess that was piling up around her.

'It's OK, it's OK, babe. Do you know where she is?' she asked him.

'Back at her flat, I suppose,' Christian said. 'In London.'

'Well then, just go. Go to her and tell her what an idiot you've been. Tell her what you told me, and then tell her you

339

realised that you'd give up everything to be with her, because that's how you feel isn't it?'

Christian looked at her. 'Yes, I think it is, Maggie. I think it is, and I'm terrified that she won't feel the same.'

Maggie felt a tiny pull at the corner of her heart, wishing for one split second that it *could* have been her and Christian. That they *could* have been happy, and that she had never had to take up stalking or double agent spying or kissing Pete for the wrong reasons and getting stuck with the memory. But it wasn't her, and she was mostly glad about it. In a few weeks more she was fairly sure she would be all glad.

'Come on, Christian, just go. Go to her and work it out. You can do it. Don't ask me how, but I just think that . . . well, I just think that Louise loves you as much as you love her. Call it women's intuition. I'm sure she'll be really happy once you've explained it all.'

Standing up, Christian went to the sink and splashed water on his face.

'OK,' he said. 'I'm going.' He turned to look at her. 'I meant what I said, Maggie, about how important you are in my life and how much I hated to hurt you.'

Maggie nodded an acknowledgement.

'I know, and you were a total shit, but I suppose in the end it's not how it happened, just that it did. And I think it was the right thing to happen, I really do.' Maggie shrugged. 'And for what it's worth, it does mean something that you came back to try and make things right. Even if it was for all the wrong reasons and in the wrong way. I still think we'll have each other when this has settled down. Just differently.'

Christian nodded, and, bending down, he grazed his lips against her cheek.

'I'll see you,' he said, and left her again, for good this time.

Maggie sat back in the kitchen chair, tipping it up on its back legs and rocking it as she listened to the hum of the fridge and the ticking of the kitchen clock. Tomorrow, even this old table would be gone and the new stainless steel chef's kitchen would be fitted. It was as if her old life had had its own deadline by which everything had to be changed for ever. The old pub was already gone, and now Christian was too. She just hoped he would manage to work it out with Louise, though if he did, it wouldn't be long before their paths would cross again and she'd have to come clean about Carmen. Maggie sucked in her cheeks.

'Ouch,' she said out loud. Imagine the humiliation. The ringing of her mobile startled her as it always seemed to these days, and she reached into her pocket fully expecting it to be Sarah calling to lambaste her. But the display read 'Home', which meant her old home, Christian's flat. She'd never got round to changing it. How did he get there so quickly? He must have really floored the car.

'I told you to speak to her!' she exclaimed as she pressed the receiver button. It was one thing being all magnanimous about him going off with Louise but another thing entirely if he expected her to step in as relationship counsellor.

'Hi, Maggie,' Louise said. Maggie paused in confusion. Oh flip, she thought, Louise must still be at the flat and Christian's gone chasing all the way to London after her. She must want to talk to Carmen about Christian. Never mind, she'd just talk to her for a bit now. Calm her down and then phone Christian's mobile and tell him to turn round.

'Hi! Louise, sorry about that, I was just telling my brother to get a move on with . . . er . . . something. So how are you?'

Louise laughed, and Maggie decided she was a little drunk.

'Well, Maggie, it started out pretty shit, but it's getting better the more of this bottle of wine I drink. So is he with you?'

Maggie furrowed her brow. It had been a long day and a

341

difficult one, but the sense that something was very, very wrong was gradually beginning to dawn on her.

'Is who with me?' she asked.

Louise clicked her tongue loudly. 'Jesus, considering what a siren you must be, you're a bit slow on the uptake, aren't you? Is Christian with you, *Maggie?*'

It finally clicked. Louise had not been calling Maggie Carmen. Louise was calling her Maggie. Louise knew, and Louise was seriously pissed off.

'Oh shit,' Maggie said. 'No, he's not here, because he's—'

'Good.' There was a pause and Maggie heard Louise swallow loudly. 'Because I want you to come over here now, OK? I think we've got one or two things to talk about, don't you?'

Maggie felt her stomach twist and contort with dread.

'Look, Louise, I'm sorry, I'm so sorry, I really am. I know I've been a cow, and I promise you I never meant for it to get so out of hand, but, well, if you just wait to speak to Christian then . . .'

'YOU WILL GET OVER HERE NOW!' Louise shouted, and Maggie backed away from her own phone before taking a deep breath. Finally all of her cows or crows or whatever the fuck they were were coming home to roost. There was nothing else for it but to face the music. Just hopefully not in person.

'Look, Louise, I'm sorry, but I really don't know what good it will do if I come over there now. Because Christian and I have talked things over and he is trying—'

'I'll tell you what good it will do, shall I, Maggie? It'll give you the chance to apologise to me before these twenty paracetamol and half a bottle of wine that I've had kick in and I'm dead.'

Maggie felt all the breath get sucked out of her lungs.

'What?' she managed to say.

'You heard me. You've taken my boyfriend, you've probably taken my job. You've abused my trust, and when I thought you

342

were a friend, my only friend in this fucking hideous world, you were lying to me, using me to get him back. Destroying me. Well, congratulations. I'm finishing the job off for you. You've won.'

Maggie gripped the edge of the kitchen table. Oh shit. Louise was serious.

'Louise.' Maggie tried to stay calm. 'Louise please, just put the phone down and call an ambulance.'

'Are you coming?' Louise replied.

Maggie watched her knuckles blanch and whiten as her grip increased its pressure.

'Louise, you don't need to do this. Christian still loves you, he still wants you. He's just left here to find you! Please just call an ambulance now.'

'No. You get here now. I want to talk to *you*.'

The line went dead, and when Maggie called it back it was engaged. 'Fuck, fuck, fuck!' she said as she grabbed her bag. 'You stupid fucking bitch, Maggie!' She whirled out of the kitchen, knocking the chair over as she did, and ran through the old bar and into the pool room bar.

'Jim!' She grabbed her brother's arm. 'Have you been drinking tonight?' Jim raised both his hands and shook his head.

'No, gov, honest!' He looked at Sheila rolling his eyes.

'Good. I need you to drive me over to Christian's flat.'

Jim looked at her as if she'd finally lost the plot.

'What? He was just here. What happened anyway, did you guys get it back on?' he said, pouring a pint for Falcon.

'No! No, it's not to see him.' Maggie spoke in an urgent whisper. 'It's for his new girlfriend. She thinks we're getting back together, but we're not. He loves her, not me, and I love . . .' Maggie glanced at Falcon, who was clearly listening in. 'I care about someone else. And now she's decided to take a lot of pills and it's all my fault. I have to get there.'

343

Jim set the pint down and took her by the shoulders.

'Maggie, are you sure? She sounds a bit crazy, don't you think? I mean, why would she phone up Chris's ex to have a go at you and blame you? She doesn't even know you . . .'

Maggie shook him off and headed for the door.

'Look, it's a long story all right, but it *is* my fault. I have to go. Are you driving me or not?'

Jim looked at Sheila, who nodded and picked up his car keys.

'All right,' he said, shaking his head. 'All right, I'm coming.'

Maggie left Jim waiting in the car as she dug into the bottom of her bag and found the flat key that she had never got around to giving back. She took the beige carpeted stairs up to the apartment two at a time, almost tripping over the potted palm that stood to the left of the flat's front door. She knocked on the flat door but then let herself in anyway. She didn't have time to wait – for all she knew Louise could be unconscious by now.

She wasn't, though. She was sitting on the sofa in white linen pyjamas, her feet up, a glass of wine in her hand. She looked serene, Maggie thought, for someone suicidal – although bitterly, icy cold in her demeanour. Maggie cringed inwardly. She had done this. She had made this happen. She had started something that maybe she couldn't stop, that maybe could end as badly as anything could end, and all because of her own ridiculous idiocy over what had turned out to be a pointless obsession.

'You came, then,' Louise said with a brittle smile. 'Do sit down.'

Maggie sat opposite her, leaning forward in her desperation to make things right again.

'Look, Louise, you've got this all wrong. Christian came round to see me today, yes, but it was clear he was crazy about you, madly in love with you. He thought that by getting back

344

with me he'd be doing the right thing, but I told him that you *were* the right thing for him . . .'

Louise lifted an eyebrow and sipped her wine.

'I don't believe you,' she said finally. 'I think you're just saying that so I'll go to the hospital and you'll be off the hook. And if that's true, then why did you do it, *Carmen*? Why *did* you pretend to be someone else? To be a friend? If you never wanted him back, why did you try and mess up my life? You could have just turned up for a good old-fashioned cat fight and sorted it all out fair and square.'

Maggie picked up an empty blisterpack of pills that had been lying on the coffee table and looked at it. She just couldn't believe what was happening.

'When did you take these?' she asked instead of answering Louise. There'd be time to explain later, but not now.

'About half an hour ago,' Louise said, her eyes fixed on Maggie's face, clearly determined not to be deterred or distracted. 'So tell me why you did it.'

Maggie shook her head, screaming inwardly with frustration.

'Louise, please, my brother's downstairs. We could get you to the hospital in ten minutes, *please*! This is all wrong – you've got it all wrong! He loves *you*! Please. You're so young, you don't need to do this, even if Christian had left you, which he hasn't – look at you, you're stunning and talented. You shouldn't throw your life away over a man, or over a stupid desperate old cow like me! I know you want to punish me, I know I deserve it, but what about Christian, what about your mum and dad? They don't, do they? They don't deserve it?'

Maggie thought she saw something waver in Louise's determination and she pressed on.

'Look, let me get you some salt water to drink, make yourself sick. You know it can damage your liver if you leave it too long. Please let's just get you to hospital now and we can talk later.

You can shout at me, call me all the names you want and I won't say anything, just so long as I know you're going to be OK. Please?'

But Louise's mouth was set in a brutally firm line.

'No,' she said with a shrug. 'Not until you've told me why you did it.'

Maggie shook her head in desperation, trying to form a single succinct sentence out of the weeks and weeks of chaos that had brought her to this moment.

'OK!' she snapped. 'I was hurt, OK? I was hurt and I couldn't believe he had left me. I didn't really think he meant it. I couldn't see past what I thought was a perfect relationship. And I wanted to see you, see what you were like, because I thought you couldn't be good enough for him. And I thought that once I'd seen you I'd know how to beat you. Then . . . well, then I did see you, and you're . . . you. You're incredible, and I think I knew then that I was never going to get him back, but I just couldn't admit it. I needed to hope that I would, because otherwise I couldn't see how I was going to carry on.'

Maggie held out her hands in a gesture of exasperation.

'It seems so ridiculous now, but then, in the middle of it all, it made perfect sense. I did something stupid. It wasn't meant to go so far, Louise, it just happened. And I didn't mean for it to carry on, but I was starting to really like you, and I'd more or less decided that I should just give up anyway when Christian took me out for dinner and . . .'

Louise sat up abruptly. 'He took you out for dinner? I knew it! When?' she asked, narrowing her eyes.

'The night he didn't come home,' Maggie said guiltily before adding hurriedly, 'but he wasn't with me that night, he really wasn't, not all of it, I mean. He really didn't know what he wanted and then, after he went away with you, I thought that, well – that was it. The best girl won. You won. And I was OK.

346

Then he showed up this evening. But Louise – he came into my kitchen telling me he wanted me back whilst waxing lyrical about his new girlfriend – you. I knew then that I'd been beaten fair and square. I know that there's no going back. He loves you, Louise. I'm not just saying that – the man loves you. Passionately, madly.'

Although he might not know how much of a mentalist you are, Maggie added to herself, admittedly unfairly. After all, this was all her fault in the first place.

'And he's a good man,' she continued. 'A stupid one when it comes to knowing what he wants, admittedly, but a good one. He loves *you*. And you love him enough to do this! Don't throw your health, your life, away over nothing.'

Maggie paused, trying to read something, anything in Louise's face, but it remained impassive.

'Please let's get you to the hospital?'

'He really does love me?' Louise said, reclining on to the sofa and pressing her palm to her forehead. 'Really?'

'Yes! Yes, he really does! Now can we go?' Maggie asked her hopefully.

Louise shook her head. 'That doesn't change what you did to me. Just because it didn't work, it doesn't make what you did any better.' She shut her eyes and flung her arms above her head dramatically. 'No, I think I've had enough of everything! Of you and your lies, of Christian! It will take me months to get over this, months!'

Maggie frowned. 'It won't,' she said. 'You'll be dead.'

'Yes, that's what I meant,' Louise replied. 'If I stayed *alive* it would takes months. AND I CAN'T STAND IT!'

'But why would you say it at all?' Maggie asked, the wheels of her mind slowly clicking into place.

Louise opened her eyes and sat up.

'Oh for fuck's sake, Maggie,' she said with exasperation. 'I'm supposed to be dying here, give me a break! It's probably the pills going to my brain!' she said distractedly, but somehow the tension in the room was diffusing second by second.

Maggie picked up the empty pack of pills again, turning it over and over again in her fingers.

'OK, I've had enough,' she said briskly. 'I'm going downstairs to get my brother and I'm going to get you in that car to take you to the hospital where they can give you charcoal to swallow and pump your stomach and give you all sorts of other drugs and pray that you haven't fucked yourself up for good, because I'm not sitting around here watching you die. OK?'

Louise set her wine glass down on the glass coffee table and refilled it.

'What I mean is,' Maggie repeated with emphasis, 'is that I'm not sitting here watching you die, am I, Louise?'

Louise pressed her lips together in resolute silence.

'Louise!' Maggie yelled at her. 'What's going on?'

'OK! I didn't take any pills, OK?' Louise said airily. 'All right? I made it up. I thought you deserved it.' She pointed the wine bottle at an empty glass. 'Do you want one?'

Maggie opened and closed her mouth several times before managing to speak. Although she had started to suspect as much, she was still reeling from the shock of what she thought had been happening, added into the realisation of what really had been going on. Revenge, plain and simple, and served perfectly chilled.

'What?' she said pronouncing the 'h' as a mark of her disbelief.

'Well, I wondered how *you'd* like to be messed with for a change. How'd it feel, honey? It's a fucker, isn't it? Fancy a paracetamol? I've got twenty right here in my pocket.' Louise dug into her pyjama pocket and held out a handful of the white pills.

Maggie struggled to find the words. 'You sick bloody insane flipping nutter!' she said at last, in much less obscene language than she felt the occasion merited.

Louise giggled and scattered the pills across the glass coffee table.

'Actually,' she said with a confidential smile, 'to be honest, when I found out this morning I wasn't even surprised. It was like I knew without knowing. It wasn't that hard to work it out.' Louise shrugged and filled up the empty wine glass. 'I just can't believe I didn't find out before. You were crap at lying, total rubbish.' Louise looked rueful. 'I suppose I thought we really were becoming friends.'

Maggie took the wine and, hoping it wasn't laced with arsenic, took a deep gulp. 'Was I really a terrible liar?' she asked, feeling peculiarly offended. 'And why all this? Why couldn't you just, I don't know, throw boiling hot coffee in my face and give me a slap?' Maggie held tightly on to the wine glass, still waiting for the world to stop spinning.

'Because I wanted to know what you were really like. I wanted to get the inside track on you. No offence, Maggie, but I thought when push came to shove I could take you. And by the looks of things I was right. But just when I thought I'd got it all sewn up, and that I'd got Christian for good, he announced he was dreadfully sorry but he had to go back to you – as if he was going to the gallows and not into the arms of the woman he loved. And he's holding a photo, Maggie, of you. Of Carmen.' Louise looked Maggie squarely in the eye. 'Sometimes men want me because of the way I look. Often women hate me for the same reason, and once I enjoyed both of those things. But I *love* Christian, Maggie, and I thought he really *loved* me. And I really liked you, I really liked Carmen. And I thought you really liked me. But all the time you hated me. You must have.'

Maggie shook her head. 'But I didn't, I didn't hate you,' she said. 'I tried to, but to be honest, in the end I was sorry that we couldn't be real friends.' She took a gulp of wine, hoping it would quell the storm of nerves raging in the pit of her stomach. 'I didn't expect this, though. I mean, I don't know what I had expected, but not this!'

Louise shot her a steely look. 'I admit I got a bit worked up, OK? I'm not apologising.'

'You are insane,' Maggie said, sincerely but surprisingly mildly.

'Oh right, yeah. Ever heard of the pot calling the kettle black, love?'

Maggie rolled her eyes and leaned back in the chair. She had to give her that point.

'Why?' she asked the room at large. 'Why do we let ourselves get like this over men? What for? Jesus, I wish I was a lesbian after all, oral sex not withstanding.'

Louise laughed. 'Then you'd be getting yourself worked up over a girl. It's human nature, never mind which side you bat for.'

Maggie remembered Pete saying something similar and she sighed. 'You know what, in the last few weeks my life has been pretty messed up, but this? This takes the biscuit. All that time I'm feeling guilty and manipulative about playing you, and what for? I'd be angry, but I just don't care any more. It all seems so pointless I can't even remember why I started.'

Louise studied Maggie's face for a moment. 'I thought you'd be angrier when I told you I made it up,' Louise said. 'I thought there'd be drama and scratching out of eyes. You seem remarkably calm. It's a bit of an anticlimax, actually.' Louise seemed disappointed.

Maggie found the energy to slightly incline her head.

'It's the apathy. It always gets me at times of megastress. I'll scratch your eyes out later.'

'So he's back with her, then, Pete and his fiancée,' Louise said conversationally. 'I thought you'd made her up, too. I was gutted when I saw them this morning in that cybercafé, because I thought if you were with him you'd send Christian packing and he'd come back to me. They seemed pretty intense.'

Maggie dropped her chin on to her chest in resignation and closed her eyes.

'Fuck,' she said.

'So you do like him, then?' Louise asked her. 'I knew it!'

'Well, sort of, I do. I mean, I never got the chance to find out if I really, really could like him or vice versa. And I never will now Stella's back. Oh well. It's probably divine retribution or something. I deserve it. Right?'

'Right,' Louise agreed with her. 'Still, don't give up all hope. You've never actually met Stella, have you? Maybe you could "accidentally" bump into her and introduce yourself as Carmen again?'

Maggie laughed despite her nervous exhaustion.

'All right, all right. I'm sorry, OK? I'm so sorry. But I think we can both agree you got your own back. Can I stop playing now? Can I just be sorry? After all, you nearly gave me a heart attack. I see the error of my ways and then some.'

Louise pursed her lips thoughtfully and then nodded.

'I suppose so,' she conceded. 'And I'm sorry too. I'm sorry I split you and Christian up in the first place, and I'm sorry it hurt you. But, well, I love him, Maggie, and I need him, and somehow it didn't matter who else got hurt. I feel bad about it now I know you. I quite like you, despite everything.'

'Don't be sorry,' Maggie said, hardly believing her own ears. 'It would have happened anyway one day – we were going nowhere.' She stood up and looked out of the window at the brown Capri. 'Look, Christian really is on his way to your London flat. Why don't you call him and tell him you're here.'

351

'Because then he'll know that I broke into his flat and think I'm a nutter?' Louise suggested with more than a hint of sarcasm.

'Then tell him you guessed that he keeps a spare key under the potted palm in the hallway and that you let yourself in. It's not exactly the world's most original hiding place.' Maggie picked up her bag. 'Look, I hope it works out for you two, I really do, and if . . . well, if we meet each other again through Christian, maybe we could just pretend that we're meeting for the first time and *maybe* we could even have a go at being friends, the traditional way, I mean.'

Louise considered her for a moment.

'Maybe,' she said. 'If you're really not the bunny boiling madwoman you come across as.'

Maggie laughed, aware that she suddenly felt as if a huge weight had been lifted from her shoulders. Tonight had been the single most stressful night of her life, but it was also a beginning. It was the end of the madness and the beginning of a fresh and free start.

'Right back at you, babe,' Maggie smiled. 'Look, if you feel like you have to tell Christian about all this crap then go ahead. I can handle it, because pretty much nothing would surprise me now.'

Louise shook her head. 'I won't. I mean, if I rat on you then I'd have to explain the whole faked overdose thing and . . . well, I just won't.'

Maggie went to the door and then paused.

'You do love him, don't you, Louise? You're not going to leave him or anything?' she asked. 'Not now he's gone through so much to be with you?'

'Yes, I love him,' Louise said. 'And I know that I want him more than anything. I'll try to make it work, and with a bit of luck I will. I can't say much more than that.'

Maggie nodded.

'Well,' she said. 'It'll be nice meeting you. Again.'

'And you.'

Louise watched as she closed the door behind her and then she reached for the phone.

Two Months Later

Chapter Thirty-two

Pete opened the back door and dropped the binbag next to the other three that already languished there. His breath misted in the cold air as he looked at the damp mess of soggy leaves that had piled up on the doorstep over night.

'I can't believe it's nearly November already,' he said to Falcon, who sat at the table enjoying beans on toast for breakfast. 'It's like it was this intense heat day after day, and then bam! A joyless, snowless arctic winter. Is that global warming or what? Whatever happened to seasons?'

'Mmmm.' Falcon shoved the last of his toast into his mouth and wiped his hand across his beard, clearly uninterested in what Pete had to say. 'Not off to work today, then?' he said. 'You've usually gone by now.'

Pete shrugged and sat down, pouring himself a cup of tea.

'No, I've got a couple of days' holiday which, even though I'm only on a contract, I have to take before I . . . Anyway, it's a bit of a lull there now, so I thought I might as well take them before the final push. And I've got things to think about . . . big things.' Pete glanced up at Falcon, testing his receptiveness; after all, in the last couple of months since Stella had moved in, Falcon was pretty much his only local friend.

'Oh yeah?' Falcon said, slurping his tea. 'Planning the big day and all that shite?'

Pete wondered what he was talking about and then remembered that, technically at least, he and Stella were supposed to be getting married. In actual fact, neither one of them had mentioned it since that morning in the coffee shop. In fact, neither one of them had mentioned pretty much anything since that morning, barring basic pleasantries. It was as if Stella was just Pete's lodger, sharing his room and his bed with him and not much else. The day after their 'chat' she'd asked him for some cash and bought herself a small TV, which she'd positioned on its upturned box at the end of the bed. Most days, more or less every day now, it was so cold that she stayed in and watched daytime TV on her own. Sometimes Angie'd come up and they'd watch it together and giggle at the true-life stories of Rikki Lake. When Pete got in from work, which could be any time when things were really kicking off at Magic Shop, she'd already be in bed under the covers, watching the TV and waiting for him to bring her some food. They'd become companionable strangers, existing and coexisting in a kind of suspended animation.

'Um, not exactly,' Pete said to Falcon. 'I've been offered an extended contract, another six months . . .' He sank into the rickety chair opposite Falcon.

'Cool man!' Falcon told him. 'It's all working out for you, isn't it? You must be made up.'

Pete nodded. 'I am, in a way, except it's not at Magic Shop. Well, not in London anyway. They want me to go to LA. There's this new animation technique we worked up on this project, and they want me to go and oversee its implementation on their next film.' Pete couldn't help feeling a little proud. 'Apparently I'm the expert for the job,' he finished.

Falcon nodded with enthusiasm. 'Excellent, and what does the little lady say about that, then? I bet she's looking forward to all that swanky crap they've got out there, right? I might even get out to see you at some point. When are you going?'

Pete frowned. 'Well, it was a couple of months off – a couple of months ago.' Falcon looked bemused.

'I'm supposed to fly out there in just over a week.'

Falcon put down his cup of tea with a thud so that the brown liquid slopped over the sides and spread slowly across the green Formica of the table.

Pete coughed. 'The thing is, I haven't told Stella yet. The thing *is*, I . . . I don't want to take her with me. I know I sound like a shit, but I want to go on my own. I don't want to come back to her, either. We're finished, Falc. I tried to tell her that weeks ago, but she's just clung on, and I . . . well, I haven't been able to really tell her. She's so . . . fragile. It's like someone has come along and let the air out of her. I don't want to hurt her, I really care about her. I still love her, sort of – just not in a way that makes either of us happy any more.'

Pete paused, but as Falcon didn't seem to have anything to add, Pete continued.

'I thought I had a real reason for breaking up to tell her. I thought there was this girl who I'd really like to know better, you know? But then things happened, and when I realised I couldn't go for the girl I wanted, I didn't want to hurt Stella needlessly, so I just . . . didn't. Which makes me a cowardly shit, doesn't it? And an idiot, because the longer I've left it, the harder it is to say, and I can't just sneak out of the house in the dead of night and fly off to the States. Christ knows what she'd do, the state she's in . . .'

Falcon reached over the table and took Pete's last bit of toast without apology.

'Have you sorted out someone to take over your rent while you're away?' he said.

Pete suppressed his exasperation. 'I'll pay it. I'll probably be back in six months. I'll live out of a hotel over there, all expenses paid, and maybe . . . well, Stella might need the room for a while. Now tell me, what do you think, am I a cowardly shit?'

Falcon shrugged. 'You'd have to ask Angie about all that stuff. She's an expert on what makes a bloke a cowardly shit. Although now she's got this new bloke on the go, she's all bloody sweetness and light, and she's got a lot sexier. Have you noticed how much sexier she's got recently? Must be all that shagging. Day and night it's like living above a porn shoot. Don't either of them have jobs? But seriously now, *have* you noticed how much sexier she is? You can tell me, I won't mind.'

Pete shook his head irritably.

'No I can't say that I have, Falc! We're supposed to be talking about me here, mate! Remember?'

Falcon looked at Pete and forced himself to stop musing on the allure of Angie's breasts since she'd started dating that English teacher cretin from the college. It was just that he didn't know why Pete was asking him what to do when it was pretty clear he hadn't the foggiest what to do with his own sex life let alone anyone else's.

'Right, sorry mate.' He tried to focus his mind and review the facts. 'So – you don't want Stella to go to LA with you. You can't bring yourself to chuck her and you can't get the bird you want.' Falcon thought for a moment. 'Which bird can't you get?'

Pete looked at him and then down the hallway for any sign of either of the girls. Angie might possibly drag herself out of Justin's arms, but Stella was rooted to the spot in front of *GMTV*, he was pretty sure.

'Maggie!' he told Falcon in lowered tones. 'From The Fleur. You know, beautiful dark eyes, slim and sort of . . . short? I mean, nothing ever happened between us, not really . . . but I was sort of working up to it when Stella came back – when I really didn't think she would – and then Maggie got back with *her* ex and it all sort of came to nothing.'

Pete sighed. He'd seen Maggie from a distance a couple of times in the last two months. He'd wanted to talk to her, to reinstate their friendship, but it just seemed to be too painful to be around her when there was no possibility of something more happening. Maybe when he was in LA he'd be able to shake her out of his system once and for all.

'Maggie's not back with her ex,' Falcon said, almost to himself, as he admired page three of the *Sun*.

Pete looked at him hard.

'What?' he said, reaching over and closing the paper with a snap.

'Mate!' Falcon gestured at the tabloid. 'I was reading that!'

'Were you? Well let me fill you in. She's nineteen and enjoys hockey and horse riding. Now what do you mean Maggie's not back with her ex. Have they split up again?'

Falcon looked puzzled. 'No! They were never back together! I heard her telling her brother in the pub, in the little bar. You should come up there sometime – it's got a really good atmosphere, really buzzing and . . .'

'Falcon, mate, what did you overhear?' Pete persisted.

Falcon sighed heavily.

'This geezer, Chris or something, was it? Obviously a bit of a twat. Anyway, he came over one afternoon when I was in there. Just after they shut the main bar, so it must have been a couple of months ago. She goes off with him out the back for a chat. Half an hour later he comes running out, blubbing like a bird. A few minutes after that she comes out all in a flap about his *other* girlfriend getting the wrong end of the stick, thinking Maggie and him were getting back together when they weren't, and how she had to go and see this other woman and put her straight and some other stuff. I can't remember it exactly. But anyway, I do know she's not back with that bloke. I mean, I see her at least twice a week. She's as single as I am, mate. Although not

361

really my type in the frontage department, if you know what I—'

Pete stared at him in disbelief. 'But why didn't you tell me this?' he asked Falcon, already knowing the answer.

Falcon shook his head. 'Because I didn't *know* you wanted to know! Shit, I'm not psychic,' he exclaimed. 'I don't have women's intuition or whatever that crap they always go on about is! Sue me!'

Pete shook his head and buried his face in his hands.

'God, I'm such a fucking halfwit,' he said. 'I should have gone round to see her, even if I did think she was with this other bloke. I should have said, "Maggie, I want you, do you want me?" I should have risked it. But no, I had to play it safe, I couldn't put myself out there . . . I should have had the guts to finish it with Stella instead of letting things just drift along. Fuck.'

Falcon leaned back in his chair as he reopened the paper.

'I don't see what the problem is, mate,' he said.

Pete looked up at him in despair.

'What do you mean you don't see what the problem is? How can you not see what the problem is? I'm engaged to the wrong girl, the right girl's been single all along and I'm going to LA in a week!'

Pete ran the sentence back in his head trying to work out exactly what the problem was himself.

'You're worried about hurting Stella, right? And that's what's stopping you?'

Pete nodded. 'Mostly,' he said. 'I mean, I've known her a long time, Falc. She comes across as hard as nails and ruthless, and she is. Sometimes she's had to be. But before all this I saw these glimpses of her through all the show, these little glimpses of a small, scared girl always looking for the best person to protect her from the world she grew up in, the best person to rescue her. Only now it's not glimpses, she's that person all the time – she's clinging on to me like I'm driftwood in a big, scary ocean. I'm frightened to end it with her, Falc, I'm frightened to say the one thing to her I promised I never would say.'

Falcon shifted in his chair and stroked his beard.

'All right,' he said. 'Remember when you told me I had to be straight with Angie? You said I couldn't have sex with her *and* be just her mate?'

'Well, I said you couldn't string her along because you wanted to have sex with her. It's slightly different. For starters, Stella and I haven't had sex since the night she got back.'

Falcon raised a pierced eyebrow which, in bloke's language, said 'Then why the fuck haven't you done this ages ago?' But instead of verbalising the thought, he pressed on with his advice.

'Actually,' he said. 'I didn't want to hurt Angie either. But I only realised that once I had. That night, the night Stella got back and I talked to Angie like you told me, well, mate, she fell to pieces in front of my eyes. Total surprise. I had no idea it was affecting her like that.

'She just disintegrated, and I had to watch her. It was terrible, because it was only then that I realised what I'd done to her. I'd trodden all over her without having the faintest idea what it meant to her . . . or to me.'

Falcon paused, looking inwardly at the memory for a second before sitting up a little.

'She was really, *really* angry. Which was sort of impressive. My point is, she got over it, didn't she? Bloody fucking quickly, actually.' He was unable to hide the offence in his voice. 'And Stella will too. Look, I'm not being cruel or anything, I hardly know the girl, but, well – they're like babies, women. You can drop them on their heads and it won't *necessarily* kill them. Like I said, they're tougher than they look. So I really don't see what the problem is.'

Falcon unknotted his ponytail and then retied it, feeling unusually sage.

'Go and see Maggie. Try it on with her. If she's up for it, you're game on until you go to LA. If she's not, then you're going to dump Stella anyway and you can go off to LA knowing you've got nothing holding you back. American chicks are really classy. I've been to New York twice, I know, mate. Classy and stylish. They manicure their *toenails*. Angie always had a bit of athlete's foot. I bet she's sorted it now she's shagging poncy *Justin*.'

Pete ignored about eighty per cent of what Falcon was saying and tried to concentrate on the nucleus. He *had* to see Maggie. He just had to be in a room with her and talk to her and see if there was anything still there or if it had been in his head. Once he'd done that, everything else would be easier. Telling Stella about LA, finishing with her for good. Even if, as he suspected, Maggie didn't want him, at least he wouldn't always be wondering; at least he could move on. As for Stella, he just had to find a way to separate him and her out for good, without hurting her more than he had to. But he had to do it, because he knew that if they both went on day after day caught in this stalemate they'd smother each other eventually. And he thought that deep down she knew it too.

'You could always go to the reopening of The Fleur tonight. To the party.' Falcon had not stopped talking. 'I mean, after all, we're all invited.'

'What?' Falcon had caught Pete's attention.

'To the reopening of The Fleur tonight. Free booze and canapés, apparently. Maggie told me to ask you and Stella and Angie ages ago, and—'

'When?' Pete asked him, trying to work out if it meant Maggie wanted to see him or if she didn't care about him being with Stella.

364

'Dunno. A couple of weeks ago maybe?' Falcon said with a shrug.

'Why didn't you tell me!' Pete almost shouted.

Falcon just looked at him.

'Do I really have to explain all that crap to you *again*,' he said. 'I thought I had told you. I told Angie, which usually means I've told everyone in St Albans! Jesus, mate, how many times – *I am not a woman!*'

'Sure about that, are you?' Angie said as she entered the kitchen in an exceptionally short T-shirt. As she reached to the top shelf for her guest's coffee Pete noticed that she wasn't wearing pants. For modesty's sake, Pete looked at Falcon instead, whose face had clouded over with a thunderous gloom.

Angie reboiled the already hot kettle and spooned coffee into the cafetière that she kept in her room.

'So are you going to The Fleur tonight? I'm excited, I've never been to a launch party! I expect it'll be all right to take Justin on my invite, won't it?' The kettle boiled and Angie filled the cafetière with steaming water and grabbed two mugs.

'Expect so,' Pete answered when he realised Falcon patently wasn't going to. 'I only just found out about it.'

Angie paused and wrinkled her brow.

'Did you?' she said. 'Because I told Stella about it ages ago. Told her to tell you. She seemed really up for it, asking me loads of questions. I'd have told you myself, but I've just been so "busy"!' She loaded the last word with innuendo.

'Well, I'm off back to bed!' Angie giggled, and practically skipped down the hallway. When she had shut her bedroom door Falcon looked at Pete.

'She's taunting me! She's bloody taunting me!'

Pete grinned, despite the sense of disquiet Angie's information had given him.

'Yep, mate, she is.'

Falcon folded up his paper and shoved it in the bin.

'But what I don't understand is why? What for?'

Pete shook his head and laughed. 'Maybe she hasn't gotten over you quite as quickly as you think?'

As Falcon realised what Pete meant it was like the sun rose over the kitchen table. Perhaps, Pete thought, as he headed up the stairs, there *were* such things as second chances.

Maybe, he thought, in the moment he stood outside the bedroom door, Stella had just forgotten to tell him. Maybe she'd worked out that it was Maggie's party and didn't want them to go, or maybe, and most likely, Pete decided, she just didn't want to go anywhere ever again. Well, there was only one way to find out.

'Maggie.' Jim held both of Maggie's slight shoulders. 'Everything. Will. Be. Fine. OK?'

Maggie nodded and then shook her head. Jim released her and gestured around him.

'Look at this bar! Look at it, it's fantastic, just what we wanted – modern but retaining all its original features and character!'

Jim more or less quoted from Maggie's own design brief, but she had to admit he was right. Taking out the snug seating and opening the space up had created a much airier, lighter feel to the bar, as had replacing the dirty nets with large panels of clear glass windows. The formerly dark bar now seemed twice as big and flooded with light. The ceiling had been painted with a washable white, and discreet extractor fans had been positioned around the room to keep the smoke levels down. The floor was sanded and polished and the bar had been streamlined and moved back a foot or two, which Sheila said meant only skinny people could work behind it, but Maggie still thought it was better than the old one which extended so far into the floor space that it cut down the number of potential customers they could fit in by at least ten. New double doors swung open on to her almost new professional kitchen, which shone like an almost new pin. The place did look fantastic. Now all she needed was the hoard of endless customers to pay for it and it'd be fine. Oh yes, and a chef that could actually cook.

'What about Keisha?' Maggie said to Jim, feeling her confidence wobble again. She was a nice girl, and she certainly had cooked wonderfully for them, but she'd only been a sous-chef before, she'd never yet run her own kitchen.

'Keisha is the best find we've ever made – she's brilliant. If she wasn't, the hotel wouldn't have fought so hard to keep her! OK, she's a bit inexperienced, but with Chris and Louise out there helping her tonight, she'll be fantastic. And don't forget that it was Christian who recommended her, and you said we can trust his judgement, because otherwise you wouldn't have asked him, and that was when I was still at the punching him stage, remember?'

Maggie nodded. It had been hard to explain to her family that not only was she over Christian but she didn't mind his new girlfriend either, as it happened. They'd all treated her like she was Mother Theresa or something for being so at one with it, and her mum had complimented her on her ability to leave the past behind. Little did they know!

Jim examined his sister's still anxious face.

'OK? Do you want to go and see? Let's go and see.'

Maggie nodded dumbly and followed her brother into the kitchen, where Keisha, Christian and Louise all stood over a tray of mini filo tartlets.

It was still a shock, Maggie realised, to see Louise by Christian's side instead of her, and on some deep level it still pulled painfully at her heart. Part of her still wanted to shove Louise aside and take her place, but probably, she supposed, only out of habit. Besides, over the last couple of weeks, when Maggie had finally decided that the relaunch of The Fleur was too important *not* to ask Christian for his opinion and advice, she and Louise had met officially for the first time. Poor Christian had been as white as a sheet and clearly dreading the whole occasion, and Maggie had almost told him that it was OK, she and Louise had been quite good arch nemeses for a while now and there was really no reason for him to worry. But then she had put paid to that impulse and thanked her lucky stars that Louise had just as much to lose from spilling the beans as she did. It had been awkward at first – bordering on catty for a while. But gradually they seemed to be getting more comfortable with each other, and were even approaching friendly. And since Louise and Christian had finally been reunited, neither one of them had shown any signs of psychotic behaviour, which was a relief, frankly, Maggie thought. It took up an awful lot of energy being that conniving.

The trio looked up as Jim and she entered, and Louise took a small step closer to Christian.

'Hello!' Maggie said nervously. 'So how's it all going, then, out here? Everything OK?'

She noticed that her voice squeaked slightly as she spoke, and she struggled to remain calm. She knew what the problem was – this was the one part of the evening she couldn't control. Well, not the only part but the most obvious one. She'd been completely in charge of the refit, made sure all the invites got sent to all the right people (after spending a couple of hours with Mrs Kim choosing exactly the right design). She'd made all the follow-up calls herself (except one) to make sure that the press, the local businesses and public figures would be there. She'd done a great deal on the Veuve Cliquot and had even sourced and checked all the ingredients for the food, sampling each component herself for its taste and freshness. She had organised every single little detail, but she couldn't actually prepare the food herself. She had to let someone else cook for her, and she had to trust them. Keisha was sweet and sort of intense and really into what she was doing, but she was barely twenty, and Maggie was worried that Keisha might get distracted by a boyfriend or a pair of shoes or something – the sorts of things that regularly distracted Maggie until she met Christian, and then . . . well, everyone knew what happened after that.

But on the other hand, that wasn't really a fair judgement. So the only other thing Maggie couldn't control about tonight was a boyfriend. Someone else's boyfriend, to be precise. Stella's fiancé, if she was going to be really accurate.

Maggie had no way of knowing if Pete was coming tonight, and no way of knowing what it would mean if he did come. In fact she'd gone over and over the permutations of her impulsive invite to him via Falcon ever since she'd made it two weeks ago. She bit her lip hard, as Keisha's description of the duck and fig tart filling washed over her.

It was all Sarah's fault. If Sarah hadn't gone through with that stupid deal they'd made in about five seconds flat and mainly only for a laugh, if she hadn't agreed to go out to dinner with Marcus and then apparently had a really good time and agreed to see him again – but only dating him, apparently, not even sleeping with him, just taking things easy for Sam's sake – if she hadn't done all that and if she wasn't still seeing Marcus on a near daily basis and looking all happy and radiant about him, then Maggie wouldn't have to face the possibility of going through with her end of the bargain.

Which was to tell Pete how she felt about him.

Sarah had badgered her. It had started out with casual comments like, 'You were so right about taking chances, Maggie, it's so worth it!' Which gradually escalated to things like, 'You wouldn't want to spend the rest of your life wondering if that kiss was just a fluke, would you?' until it reached a final crescendo.

369

'You're a coward,' Sarah had said over a cappuccino. 'I'm not dissing you, I'm just stating the facts. You are a coward. Now there's nothing wrong with being a coward, I've been one most of my life, but – well, I really think you have to just try and talk to him. The worst that can happen is abject humiliation, and you're getting quite good at that now.' She squinted at Maggie. 'Look at you! You go all stupid whenever you think about him!'

Maggie (who at that precise moment had sort of misted over as she remembered the feel of Pete's touch and the heat of his body) denied it vehemently.

'I do not! And besides, Sarah, he's got a girlfriend, and not just a girlfriend – a *fiancée*. You can't mess with fiancées. I mean, he's marrying someone else! What on earth gives you the idea that I should march round there and say, "Oh, hi – how are the plans for the wedding going? Oh, and by the way, I think I love you!"'

Sarah rolled her eyes. 'Because then at least you'd know,' she persisted, as if that were a good enough reason.

'But I don't want to know! I don't want to know that he's perfectly happy with Stella – and besides, I don't need to know. He's already told me on several occasions. I've had enough rejection to last me a lifetime. Even if I am over Christian, it still smarts, you know, a bit. To have it from Pete would be worse, much, much worse. He's mad about Stella. He never stopped talking about her.'

'Well, evidently he stopped long enough to kiss you – and anyway, you told me she sounded like a total nightmare. And if he was *that* happy, why did he kiss *you*?'

It was Maggie's turn to roll her eyes. 'I don't know what's happened to you recently,' she said. 'You used to be the Hannibal Lecter of dating. Toughest bastard I knew. Now, after a couple of dates with Marcus and a bit of heavy petting on the salon sofa, you've practically turned into Maria Von Trapp.'

Maggie examined Sarah's delighted face. 'You don't even mind that Becca's going to Boston for the Christmas holidays!'

Sarah shrugged. 'She needs to see her dad, and anyway Sam and I will be out there with her for actual Christmas, and we're all coming back together – it will be fun!'

Maggie sulked. It used to be Sarah who was the good-looking one (Maggie was the skinny, quiet one), and then, when they grew up, she was the practical one in control of her life (Maggie was the overambitious one). Now Sarah was the practical, happy, well-adjusted one with a great relationship. What did that make Maggie? The career-orientated one, she decided. Who needs a personal life anyway, she thought to herself. Love just gets in the way, as someone she once knew always used to say.

'I think I liked the old you better. The miserable and bitter one.' Maggie sighed painfully. 'He kissed me, Sarah, because he was a bit drunk and he felt like it. Because he was a man, and that's what men do, don't they? Or don't you remember any of those lectures you used to give me now that you're in *lurve*?'

Sarah shook her head, but she was laughing like her teenage daughter did on the phone.

'I'm not in love! I'm just having a nice time, which makes a flipping change, I can tell you.'

She paused and composed her features.

'What if you invited Pete and Stella to the party?'

Maggie started to protest, but Sarah cut her off.

'Think about it – if he comes alone, well, then, you're in. If he comes with her, it gives you a chance to see them together – study the form, so to speak. If he doesn't come at all, then you'll sort of be back to square one, *but* the first two options could work, couldn't they?'

Maggie looked into the bottom of her coffee cup and thought about it.

'I'm too old for all this planning and wondering and worry. Next you'll be asking him out for me. Or passing him a note.'

'Could do,' Sarah said, only half joking.

'Don't you dare!' Maggie had been unable to prevent herself acting appalled at the idea, even though she knew it would never happen. 'OK, I *will* invite him. I'll ask Falcon to invite the whole lot of them as regulars. After all, I've invited Mrs Kim and a couple of other old customers. But you wait and see. I bet Pete and Stella are all over each other . . . What?' Maggie noticed that Sarah was frowning.

'I'd forgotten about Falcon. He's not the sort of bloke to go up to Marcus and say, "Oh, by the way, I had your date in the ladies", is he?'

Maggie shook her head. Over the last few weeks she'd got to know Falcon quite well, at first as a way of trying to glean any snippet of information about Pete she could (there had been little), but gradually because he was quite a sound bloke and strangely philosophical.

'No, no he won't. I think your little encounter gave him something to think about for a while, but from what he says there's someone else he's into now. Really into as well, I think.'

Sarah nodded gratefully. 'So invite them all. And when you get a chance to talk to Pete alone, Stella or no Stella, just take a chance – OK?'

Maggie had no intention of doing any such thing, but she wanted Sarah to stop talking long enough for her to eat her double chocolate muffin without distraction.

'OK,' she'd said. And Sarah had looked triumphant.

'And then, I thought, we bring round the mini dark chocolate and strawberry cheesecake as a sort of dessert before offering coffee. Is that OK?' Keisha was speaking directly to Maggie.

'Fantastic!' Maggie said, unable to ask her to repeat

372

everything. 'Fabulous. Well done.' She looked at her watch, wondering if she had enough time to go upstairs, sit on her bed and be a gibbering wreck for half an hour.

'So,' Louise said with a slow smile. 'What are you wearing tonight, Maggie? Got your outfit planned?'

Maggie looked down at her somewhat creased and shiny trouser suit.

'Oh, um . . .' She'd actually thought about just wearing this.

'You're not thinking of wearing that old thing, are you?' Louise seemed genuinely horrified. 'You need something glamorous, something the photographer will want to get a pic of you in.'

Maggie mentally ran through the contents of her wardrobe. She instinctively looked at Christian as she panicked.

'Oh God, I haven't got anything to wear!' she moaned.

Louise took her arm and, unnervingly, gave her a little hug.

'Don't worry, there's plenty of time! I'll tell you what – we'll go out now and find something dazzling. Christian and Jim can keep things ticking over here for an hour or so – can't you, boys?'

Christian and Jim looked fairly alarmed: one at the prospect of his ex and new partner being alone together, and the other at the added responsibility, but Louise's smile was like a charm and they both nodded, mesmerised.

'I'll never find anything good in an hour!' Maggie said anxiously. 'Not in St Albans!'

'Don't worry, you will. I know you will,' Louise told her reassuringly.

'How do you know?' Jim asked Louise's breasts with barely concealed admiration.

Louise giggled and fluttered her lashes.

'Because all clothes look good on flat-chested women. Now come on, let's get going, we're wasting time!'

Chapter Thirty-three

Pete looked at Stella curled up on the bed as she ate the toast he'd brought her and carried on watching the TV.

'So anything you want to do today?' he said. 'I thought as I had a day off maybe we could go out or something?'

Stella glanced at him. 'I don't know, babe, I'm really tired. I might have a cold coming on. I might just stay here.'

Pete sat down on the edge of the bed. 'Um, there's this thing on tonight, this party at a pub in town – did Angie tell you?'

Stella shook her head, her eyes fixed on the TV.

'Oh well, she said she did but never mind. Anyway, it's tonight, and I thought I might go. You could come too if you wanted to get out a bit?'

Pete was torn between wanting to go alone and wanting to see Stella in a different environment, anywhere where she might be a little more like her old self again. Stella stretched and pushed her empty plate away from her.

'No, I'll just stay in. You go, babe, if you want to.'

Pete bowed his head. It looked as if she had just forgotten that Angie had told her after all. He struggled with a dilemma, finally deciding that he should give Stella every chance to change her mind.

'Are you sure? It's Maggie's place – remember the girl I told you about? The one I was friends with while you were away? Are you sure you don't mind me going?'

Stella's head snapped up and she looked at him.

'No, I don't mind you going, but . . . well, maybe I *could* come too.' She pulled herself up into a sitting position. 'Maybe we could go out now and I could get something to wear and we could go together?'

Pete nodded stiffly. 'Great!' he said. He picked up a pair of trousers and found his cash card. 'Here, we'll get some money out and get something nice.'

Stella smiled at him and pulled on her dressing gown. She rose up on to her knees and put her arms around his neck.

'Are you OK?' she asked him.

Pete thought about LA. He thought about Maggie. He thought about the stalemate that he and Stella were caught in. He knew that time was running out for him to be able to do something about it. He knew that if he didn't act soon, there was a good chance he just wouldn't go to LA, that he'd stay here with Stella, waiting for her to come back just like he always had. Only waiting for her to come back to herself, this time. He looked at her.

'Stella, I think . . . there are things we need to talk about. I think that . . .'

Stella got up off the bed and went to the door.

'OK. I'm going to shower first, though, and then we can go out. We can talk later. OK?' She looked at Pete.

'We have to, Stella. We can't go on like this . . .'

But Stella had already shut the door.

'I think you should wear red,' Louise said as she ran her finger along a rack of dresses. 'I think you'd carry red off really well with your hair and your eyes. What are you – an eight?' She held up a knee-length red halter-neck dress. 'What about this? Try it on!'

Maggie looked at it; it wasn't something she would have chosen for herself in a million years – altogether too flashy.

'Oh, I don't really think that's me, to be honest. It looks a bit tight!'

Louise put the dress in her hand and propelled her towards the dressing room.

'Just try it on! The whole point of being tiny is that you can wear tight things – you don't have bulges to worry about.'

Maggie glanced over her shoulder as she went.

'I do have bulges!' she protested.

'Not real ones, your bulges are my idea of perfectly toned muscles. Now go on!'

Maggie pulled and pushed and squeezed her way into the dress and then looked at herself in the mirror. Her hair needed a wash and her face looked pale and shiny. She squinted and tried to imagine herself with make-up on.

'It's sort of hard to tell,' she called, 'without . . .'

'The right shoes. Here you go.' Louise's arm thrust a pair of red spiked heels through the curtain. 'I got you a five – you look a five.'

Maggie's eyes widened at the heels.

'I don't know about those! I mean, I have to be able to walk around,' she said, but she put them on anyway, sensing that she wasn't going anywhere until she had. Did Christian know, she wondered, that he was living with a control freak? Another one?

'Mmmmm.' Louise said as she pulled back the curtain. 'It's hard to tell in here. Come out into the shop – the light's much better.'

Maggie resisted growling at her; after all, she was the only person either available or willing to come with her, and she really was trying. She obediently tottered in the shop.

'Very nice,' the shop assistant said. 'Really stunning. Those shoes are a must!'

Maggie looked at herself in the mirror. She had to admit that the overall effect was a pretty good, if slightly slutty, one. It made her legs look great, and the dress wasn't *embarrassingly* tight, more sort of readers' wives tight. With the right underwear, maybe . . . Maggie pinged the material away from where it clung to her body. No, it was the sort of thing you'd only wear to a Vicars and Tarts party.

'I look like a high class – no, strike that – low class hooker,' she said, turning to speak to Louise and coming face to face with Pete. And Stella.

'Oh!' she said, trying not to fall off her heels. 'Hello. Pete.'

Pete swallowed, and Stella watched his jaw muscles tighten.

'Hi, Maggie, it's, er, nice to see you again.'

Pete kicked himself. The shock and surprise of finding Maggie here looking so well, so practically naked, had made him sound utterly insincere.

'Are you going to wear *that* tonight?' he said, trying not to sound as shocked as he felt. 'You look . . . um, really . . . well, I mean.'

'I might do,' Maggie said, looking anywhere but at Pete's face. She had to get out of this dress and out of his sight within the next five seconds or she was going to kill herself by a spontaneous implosion of embarrassment and dismay. 'Anyway, better get on. Lots to do. But glad that you're coming, glad that you're *both* coming.'

Maggie glanced quickly at where Stella had been standing, afraid of her being too beautiful, but she seemed to have gone.

'Bye then!' she squeaked.

Maggie pointed herself in the direction of the changing room and launched herself forward, praying that there was some law of physics that would keep her going long enough to get her there, because what little ability she had to walk convincingly in spiked heels had disintegrated the moment she had seen Pete's face.

It was only when she'd gone that Pete realised he hadn't introduced Maggie to Stella. In actual fact he'd forgotten that she was there.

'Hi again,' Louise said, giving him a sympathetic look.

'Hi. See you tonight,' Pete said. But when he looked round, Stella had already gone.

He found her walking at speed up the busy high street, weaving through the shoppers as she made her way back home.

'Stella, wait!' Pete called after her. 'Stella!' At last she stopped and waited, stock-still, her back still turned on him until he caught her up.

'Stella!' Pete said, slightly out of breath. 'What's wrong?' Pete was aware that it was a facile question, but he thought that if he asked it there was a chance she might tell him.

'What's wrong?' Stella turned on him. 'What's wrong? You couldn't stop looking at her!'

Pete put his hand on her shoulder.

'I didn't, I . . . Stella, I'm sorry. I don't know what to say.'

Stella shook him off angrily and started walking.

'You can tell me *exactly* what happened when I was away. You said *nothing* happened. You said you were just friends and that nothing happened, but it didn't look like nothing in there in that shop. It looked like you were more than "friends". A lot more!' Stella was shouting and tears streamed down her face.

Pete looked around at the faces of passers-by as they watched the ten-second drama on the pavement.

'Nothing happened, nothing except for one kiss. That was all – just that one kiss and . . .'

'And what?' Stella said sarcastically, stopping abruptly. 'And it meant nothing, I suppose?'

Pete looked at her, her upturned face full of defiant anger. This was it, he realised. This was the beginning of their ending.

'Actually it did,' he said finally. 'It did mean something, I think. To me at least. I don't know about Maggie. I haven't seen her since, not until just now. But yes, it meant something.'

Stella stared up at him, her face perfectly still, her eyes brimming with tears.

'What do you mean, Pete?' she said. 'What do you mean it meant something? Did it mean more than us? Did it mean more than everything we've been through? Is that what you're saying?'

Pete shook his head. 'No. I don't know, because nothing came of it, but I wanted to find out, Stella. That's what I tried to tell you when you came back. I wanted to find out if it could go anywhere. I wanted the chance to find out without . . . well, without you.'

Stella crumpled suddenly in front of him, sinking down on to the pavement. Pete quickly scooped her up and held her to him as she sobbed against his chest.

'You can't do this, Pete, you can't do this to me now! I need you!' she cried helplessly. 'Please, please don't.'

Pete put his arm around her and started walking her the last few yards home. When he finally got her into the hallway and shut the door, he'd never felt more grateful to be home in his life.

'Do you want a drink? A cup of tea?' he said, aware that he wasn't feeling this nearly as much as Stella wanted him to. As he wanted to. Now that it was happening it felt unreal somehow, as if it were happening a little distance away from where the real him was actually standing.

Incredibly Stella nodded and, pushing him away, went into the kitchen, taking a seat at the table. Pete examined her closely as she wiped the cuffs of her sweater across her eyes. He set a cup in front of her and, taking a deep breath, began.

'I'm sorry, Stella, all this . . . just took me by surprise. I didn't expect it to happen. And I didn't just stop thinking about you. That's why I emailed you. That's why I told you what was going on, because I wanted to give us every chance to get it right. I'd been so certain that after everything you put me through, what we went through, we'd end up together eventually. I wanted us to, Stella. I wanted that neat, happy ending but . . . I think you and I both know that it was never going to happen. You were never going to be happy with me, not really. If I wasn't good enough for you five years ago, why should I be now? What was going to change that? I don't want to be the man you settle for, Stella. And knowing Maggie gave me this glimpse of how it could be, what it could be like to just be with someone and be happy.'

Pete paused, looking at Stella's tear-streaked face. It was impossible to tell what she was thinking.

'And, well, I asked you to marry me, Stella, and you went to the other side of the world. Both of us should have realised then that what we had between us wasn't enough. It isn't enough for you, and in the end . . . well, it isn't enough for me.'

Stella looked up at last, her light eyes thrown into relief by the swollen red of her lids.

'But I really meant it this time, Pete,' she said quietly. 'I'd really made up my mind to mean it and to be with you and just you. I really had!'

Pete bit his lip. 'Maybe you did. Maybe this time you did mean it, but I'm sorry, Stella, I really am. I think you were too late. I don't think there's anything left for us in the future. I . . . I care about you so much, I can't bear to see you like this, but . . .'

Stella hugged her cup of tea into her body. 'But you want to be with Maggie,' she said.

'No! I mean, I do, but that's not why this is happening. Not the only reason why.'

Pete struggled to say what he had to.

'You are like a firefly, Stella. No, you're like your name, like a star. You burn so brightly. I can't stand to see you so jaded, and I think – no, I know – that it's me that's doing it to you. And that's wrong. Think really hard about it; think about the future we'd have together. Do you really see yourself shining brightly once you'd settled down with me and only me?'

Stella said nothing, only looked at him for a while.

'Are you giving me a choice?' she asked him at last.

Pete shook his head.

'No. I don't think I'm the right man for you, Stella, even if I still loved you like I did once. I'm sorry, but that's the truth.'

Stella nodded and let out a long breath.

'I knew this was coming,' she said. 'I knew it would happen, but I just wasn't ready for it. Not today. I . . . don't want to think of you walking in there tonight and going into someone else's arms, Pete. I can't actually bear that.'

Pete stared at her, knowing what she was asking of him and hating the fact that he had to turn her down, for his own sake. He couldn't pretend for her any longer, he knew that. He didn't want to hurt her any more than he had, but he wouldn't lie.

'I have to go, Stella. I don't know what will happen, but I have to go.'

Stella swallowed, and shrugged.

'You're right, you know, about us,' she said, her tight voice softening a little. 'I do know that, Pete, I just didn't want to face it. Someone hurt me while I was away.' Stella gave a short, bitter laugh. 'Someone totally stupid and wrong, but he hurt me anyway, I let him get to me. And after that I just wanted to be with you until you made me feel better about myself again. But you didn't, you didn't even seem to really be there. I thought if

381

I tried really hard to make you see how much I needed you . . . but you just didn't.'

Stella looked shell-shocked, but calmer at last.

'I suppose . . . I have to try and get along without you now.' She pushed her mug away from her. 'I suppose I'd better fix myself.' She pulled herself up in her seat. 'I'll phone Mum, tell her I'm coming home today,' she said.

Pete reached out and took her hand.

'You don't have to just rush off. You could stay for a bit and I could help you get sorted, and . . .'

Stella shook her head. 'And we could still be friends? I don't think so, Pete. I think I need to go now, while I can. I'll be all right, you know. Mum'll look after me, and before you know it I'll be back largeing it in the Leeds scene, lunching at Harvey Nicks, crowds of men following me around. You wait, it won't take long.'

'I'm sure it won't,' Pete said.

'There's one more thing,' Stella said, holding up her left hand. 'The ring. Can I keep it? I'll need some cash, you see, to get me started again, and, well, you could call it a sort of settlement. Is that OK?'

Pete looked at the ring illuminating the weak afternoon light, and realised that it meant nothing to him now; it was just a cold, hard, beautiful commodity.

'Of course you can keep it,' he said. 'I bought it for you.'

Stella smiled weakly, pulling her sleeves over her knuckles.

'I'll make some calls and then pack. I'll be gone in an hour, all right? Probably best if you go out or something. I don't want to say goodbye to you again because it . . . might be too hard. So just go out, OK?'

Pete looked at her, wondering what his life would be like without her.

'You'll always be such a big part of me, Stella,' he began.

382

'Don't, Pete.' Stella stopped him. 'Don't try and make it all right between us. It won't be, not now, maybe not ever. So please just don't.'

Pete nodded, wishing there was some other way for this to happen.

'Will you call me, though, when you get to Leeds, let me know you're all right?' Pete asked her.

Stella shook her head. 'No, I won't. I'm not your responsibility any more, Pete. And besides, I won't get to Leeds until this evening.'

She raised her chin a little.

'And you'll already be out by then.'

Maggie only let her breath out again about five or ten seconds after Pete had left the shop.

'Oh no,' she said, unable to comprehend exactly how excruciatingly difficult the moment had been, only knowing that it had epic proportions. 'Oh no no no no no!'

Louise looked somewhat bemused by all the fuss and shrugged.

'What?' she said. 'I thought it went really well, myself. You knocked him dead!'

'Oh no,' Maggie said again for the want of anything better. 'Oh no no no . . .'

'Maggie! Enough with the "oh no's"! We all get the picture, OK?'

Maggie sat on the small seat in the changing cubicle and pulled off the shoes, holding them as if at any moment she might convert their spike heels into lethal weapons. Looking up at Louise, she attempted to find something else to say but found that her entire vocabulary had been boiled down to those two words. So she didn't say anything.

'But you're still going to buy the dress and shoes, right? Aren't you?' Louise said somewhat hopefully, leaning against the door of the cubicle and tipping her head to one side.

At last Maggie found the power of speech.

'Are you mad!' she screeched before she could stop herself, causing the woman in the next cubicle to stop talking on her mobile and hurry rapidly out of it. 'I looked terrible in it, cheap and terrible, and . . . he saw me. Oh no!'

Louise gave her own reflection an anxious look and took the dangerous-looking shoes out of Maggie's hands, handing them to the assistant, who had been hovering a few feet away for the last minute or so.

'You can take these back for now,' she said with an abrupt smile before turning back to Maggie. She was surprised to find that she was starting to feel a bit sorry for her. 'He could hardly take his eyes off you!' Louise told her as she began to wriggle out of the dress.

'He couldn't look at me, you mean,' Maggie said through the thin, clingy layer of latex-cotton mix that currently shrouded her head. Maggie yanked the dress off her head, leaving her hair standing on end with static electricity. She glowered at Louise, who she held completely responsible for the entire spectacle. 'He looked everywhere *but* at me!'

'Same thing!' Louise seemed genuinely mystified by Maggie's distress.

'Same thing my arse,' Maggie said as she quickly redressed.

Louise wondered if she should mention she'd buttoned her shirt up wrong, and then decided that now wasn't the time.

'He looked as if the worst possible thing that could ever happen to him in the entire known universe had just happened – and it was me!'

Louise made a gesture that is interpreted the world over as 'Duh!'

'Yes!' she said, 'you're right, but it wasn't seeing you, it was seeing you with his whey-faced misery of a girlfriend—'

'Fiancée!'

'OK, whey-faced misery of a fiancée in tow!' Louise sighed through tight lips. 'No wonder you can't keep a man, Maggie. You can't see what's going on right in front of your face!'

Maggie straightened up abruptly with only one boot zipped up and took a step nearer to Louise, sincerely wishing she still had hold of one of the spike-heeled shoes.

'OK Louise, that's enough,' she said, lowering her voice. 'I've just about taken as much as I can take today, and I'm not taking any more. I've put up with the bitchy comments – I thought maybe I deserved them – but you're no angel yourself, and I thought we were trying to get along with our lives. If you *really* want to go over the fact once again that it was *you* who stole *my* boyfriend right out from under my nose and started this whole thing, then fine, let's do it, right here, right now.'

Louise held up the palm of her hand.

'No!' she said quickly. 'No. Look, I'm sorry. I just . . . well, it is sort of true in a way. I didn't actually mean it to come out sounding so nasty, but I take your point. I'll try and, you know, be properly nice to you.'

Maggie literally backed down off her tiptoes and huffed at Louise's acquiescence.

'Either way, he won't come tonight. She won't let him, or he won't want to, and maybe it's for the best. I was stupidly building my hopes, but it's better to know now and just get on with the whole most-important-night-of-my-professional-career-to-date thing. It's Sarah's fault. I blame her fully.'

Louise picked the discarded dress up off the floor and returned it to its hanger, glad to be off the top of Maggie's hit list.

'So you're definitely sure you're not buying this dress?' she asked.

Maggie looked at her closely. 'Definitely sure,' she said. 'It's just not me. It's too tight, it's too red, it's too much.'

Louise nodded and pursed her lips in thought before saying, 'I'm sorry, Maggie.'

Maggie raised her eyebrows. 'What for?' she said.

'For trying to get you to buy a dress that makes you look like a hooker.' Louise held out her hand. 'There was a little bit of me that thought you might be after Christian, still, with all your niceness and your policy of openness, and it's wrong, but I thought, well, I know how Christian hates tarty women . . .'

'I wouldn't say that,' Maggie said, looking pointedly at Louise's cleavage.

'OK, I deserved that. But now, seeing you . . . I can see there's no way you'd go after him now. So I'm sorry, really honestly sorry. Let's call it a proper truce this time. Can we start again?'

Maggie took her hand. 'Again again?' she said with half a smile.

'Well, if a thing's worth doing . . .' Louise said with a shrug.

'Come on,' Maggie said to her. 'We've been gone nearly an hour. Time's up.'

'But what are you going to wear?' Louise asked her.

'Oh, I don't know. I've got millions of clothes. It just doesn't seem that important any more.'

Pete thought he'd found approximately the same piece of ground that he'd lain on with Maggie all those weeks ago, looking at stars and talking about Stella. It was soggy and damp now, and run through with deep scars of mud where dogs and children had skidded chasing footballs or autumn leaves. Looking up at the same sky, now covered with densely woven cloud leaning low above the horizon, Pete felt that if he could only stretch up high enough he'd be able to touch them, to part the sky and see those stars again.

When he'd been here before with Maggie, there had been not a shadow of doubt in his mind about how he felt for Stella, maybe because her influence over him had burnt so brightly within him that it had chased out any possibility of shadows until finally she was too far away to be able to reach him. In just a short space of time, everything he had imagined he felt, the frailly built construct of her image, had fallen into tiny pieces at his feet. Pete sat down on the muddy grass and, drawing his knees up, dropped his head into his hands.

He was angry with Stella, angry that she had squandered every single chance they had had until there was nothing left. And angry with himself for not seeing a year or two or three ago that there would never be enough chances for them, that 'for ever' wouldn't have been long enough for them to get it right. And he felt sad, incredibly sad. Part of him couldn't help but feel that he had failed her. The first time he had set eyes on her laughing in the moonlight, he'd promised himself that he would be the one to save her, and he had failed.

Large drops of rain began to hit his cold hands and his bare head, and because although he wanted this to happen, he wished it didn't have to hurt anyone, and because the end of this part of his life, though necessary was so painful, Pete began to cry until his tears were lost in the pouring rain.

Chapter Thirty-four

Maggie held her breath and looked around at the newly refurbished bar of The Fleur. It shone and glittered underneath the spot lighting, and shimmered a little, like a mirage. Except that it wasn't a mirage, it was real. It had happened, and Maggie had made it happen. Oh, and Sheila, and Jim, and her mum and dad a bit, and then Christian at the last minute, and ever so slightly Louise. Not to mention Keisha and CMS Commercial Builders and Fitters. But mainly it had been Maggie. It had been Maggie's vision and her ideas, and somehow, though immersed in the mess of her personal life, she had still managed to pull it all together.

'Just imagine,' Maggie thought, raising her eyebrows as the idea occurred to her, 'what I could have done if I hadn't just been chucked by my long-term boyfriend and then immediately spurned by the first other man I met?' Then Maggie realised that if that had been the case, she'd still be sharing a flat with Christian, still doing sex in the same three positions and still filling invoices, and would never even have had the *chance* to be spurned by Pete. For a while now, Maggie had accepted with good grace the changes in her life, even embraced them – but it was only at this moment, standing on the brink of a new age for The Fleur, that she could say that Christian leaving her was the best thing that had ever happened to her.

It had woken her up and shaken a new kind of drive and confidence into her that she thought she had lost, that she'd actually forgotten she'd ever had. Maggie smiled and breathed in, puffing out her chest with pride.

'Are you actually going to say anything, Maggie? Or are you going to stand there gawping like a fish out of water while we stand around like lemons? I'm gasping for a drink!'

Maggie jumped and looked at Sarah, who was standing with crossed arms a few feet in front of her. Oh yes, she was supposed to be making a little speech before they opened the doors on the launch party guests.

'Er, right. Yes, sorry.' Maggie looked around her at everyone who stood in the bar. Her mum and dad stood just to her right, her dad's hand on her mum's shoulder. Jim stood to her left, leaning against the new bar with the same kind of new confidence that Maggie thought she'd discovered in herself. Sarah had come early to do her hair, with Marcus, both of them laughing like a couple of kids the moment they'd got here. Keisha stood by the kitchen doors, her arms crossed across her whites like a gourmet gangsta rapper. Sheila was there, of course, in her best finery, and finally Christian and Louise, dressed in red, looking a million times better than Maggie ever would have.

'Um, I just wanted to say that, well, everyone in this room has been so important in helping us get The Fleur back off the ground. These last few weeks have had their ups . . . and downs.' Maggie tried hard not to look at Christian but did anyway. 'If someone had told me when this all began that all of the people that are standing in this room right now would be here, and what's more would be my very dear friends, I wouldn't have believed them!' Maggie caught the eye of one of the Fresh Talent waiters she'd borrowed for the evening. 'Um, except for the waiters, that is, because I don't really know them. I'm sure they're super, but anyway . . .'

389

Sarah rolled her eyes and performed a theatrical yawn at Marcus as she leaned back against his chest.

'But *anyway*,' Maggie scowled at Sarah, '*none* of this could have happened without all of you. Most especially Sheila. Sheila, my family has known you for most of our lives, and during that time you've never stopped surprising us! Stumping up the cash for The Fleur was the biggest surprise of all, and I really hope you're pleased with your investment.'

Sheila, who was sitting on the other side of the bar for once, took a long drag on her cigarette, which she had inserted into a long black holder for the occasion.

'Ain't nothing, Mag,' she said, with a very pleased smile, through a curl of smoke, shrugging so that the sequins on her black beaded top glittered.

Maggie shook her head. 'No, it is something, Sheila.' Maggie glanced round at her family. 'It's everything, and I want you to know that we love you, Mum, Dad, Jim – all of us – love you very much.'

Maggie smiled and glanced around the room.

'Talking of family, a lot of positive things have come out of my return to The Fleur, a lot. But the main thing is that I've made some really good new friends, friends I think I'll just get closer and closer to as time goes on. I got to make friends with my family again after a very long time, and . . . I'm sorry if that sounds soppy, Sarah, but that's how I feel.' Maggie put her arms as far around her family as they would go. 'Mum, Dad, Jim, I'm so glad that I'm home again.'

'Hip! Hip!' Christian started the cheer and everyone else joined in with the hoorays as best they were able to without laughing.

'Right then,' Maggie said, breaking free from the embrace. 'We're open for business!'

★

'You should drink more,' Sarah said, leaning closer to Maggie so that she could be heard over the hum of the crowd. 'If you drank more and worried less, you'd have a better time!'

Maggie shook her head at her ever so slightly tipsy friend.

'That's easy for you to say. You and Marcus stuck in traffic is your idea of having fun these days. Anyway, this isn't about having fun, it's about making sure everyone else is having fun.' Maggie looked anxiously around her. 'Do you think I should go and say hello to that journalist, or do you think I should just leave her to it?'

Sarah glanced over at the woman who was seriously flirting with Declan.

'I think she'd kill you if you went over there. She's scored!' Sarah leaned her elbows back on the bar. 'Maggie, for God's sake, relax will you? Everything's going really well. The food's great, the atmosphere's fantastic, the champagne's flowing. Everyone turned up! I don't know what you're worried about.'

Maggie took in the scene around her. It was true – everyone was having a good time. In fact, in one corner a few people had started almost dancing to the Latin American music Maggie had chosen as background.

'Not quite everyone came,' Maggie said, sighing under her breath. 'Not Falcon or Angie or . . . anyone.'

'What?' Sarah raised her voice and cupped her hand to her ear.

'I said, what the hell, I'll have another drink!' Maggie called back and, taking the champagne that Sarah handed her, drank deeply, tipping her head back. When she returned her chin to its appropriate position, her head was swimming a little, so for a moment she thought she was seeing things. She blinked again and then once more for luck. No, she wasn't hallucinating. It really was Pete standing in front of her.

'Have you got something in your eye?' he said. 'You seem to be blinking a lot.'

Maggie shook her head, dumbstruck, and looked at the space where Sarah had been standing. She'd made herself very scarce indeed in double-quick time. Maggie forced the muscles in her throat to work.

'Pete, gosh,' she said, wondering when the last time was – if ever – that she had used the word 'gosh'. 'I didn't expect you to come . . .'

'You don't mind, do you?' Pete said anxiously.

'No! No, no. Not at all. I'm . . . glad . . . you're here.' Maggie licked her suddenly dry lips and sipped her drink. 'Um, do you want one? A glass of champagne, I mean?' she asked him.

Pete wrinkled his nose a little. 'Got any ale on?'

Maggie nodded and leaned over the bar, shouting her order to the new barman. Pete moved to stand beside her, seemingly looking everywhere in the room except for the few square feet that she occupied.

'Bloody hell,' he said, 'you've done a really good job in here.' He nodded over to where Falcon and Angie were deep in conversation, probably about Falcon being so rude to Justin that he'd refused to come with them tonight and told Angie he expected her to stay behind with him. Only she didn't. 'I think even Falc likes it.'

Maggie looked at Falcon and Angie, who seemed so intent on each other that they could have been standing in the middle of the M25 and wouldn't have noticed.

'How can you tell?' Maggie asked, because she couldn't think of anything else to say.

'I can't,' Pete said with a rueful shrug. 'I just can't think of anything else to say.'

Maggie smiled at him, and he resisted the urge to either grab her right then or run away for good. He discovered what the expression 'steeling yourself' meant as he felt every sinew and joint in his body stiffen. He had to hold his nerve now, when he'd come so far. And this wasn't something to rush – he had to get it right. He had to be all romantic and say the right thing. Oh bollocks.

'Do you have to be out here?' Pete blurted. 'Being hostess, I mean, or have you got five minutes? Because I was wondering if we could . . . I mean, is there somewhere we could go to, um, talk at all?'

Maggie wondered if she had misheard him over the din of the crowd, but she nodded her head anyway.

'Sure,' she said, impulsively taking his hand and feeling in that second as if she had stepped into thin air as she felt the weight and warmth of it in her own. She led him through the crowd, stopping every few feet to exchange a few half-heard words with someone or to shake someone's hand. They went out of the bar, past the kitchen and into the small, half-lit hallway with the stairs that led up to the flat. Should she take him up there, she wondered? What would it mean? What would he think it meant? She looked at him still not looking at her, and realised she had no idea what he was going to say. She had no idea what she was going to say, only that in the next few seconds each of them would have said everything that had to be said and it would all be over one way or another. Maggie sat down on the stairs, somehow losing the energy to climb them even if she had wanted too. After a second Pete joined her, sitting a step below her.

'I'm glad you came—'

'It's good to see you—'

They both spoke together.

'It's good to see you properly, I mean,' Pete repeated with a smile, looking fondly at Maggie's left ear.

'And you,' Maggie said. 'And how's Stella?'

393

Pete dropped his head suddenly, slumping his shoulders.

'She's gone. This afternoon, after we saw you, we . . . well, she's gone.'

Maggie saw his bowed head and his dropped shoulders and saw how sad he was.

'Oh Pete, I'm sorry. I'm sorry that she's gone,' she said.

Pete shook himself a little and, taking a deep breath, looked up. He looked right at Maggie, right into those huge dark eyes, and felt like he was leaping into the unknown.

Maggie froze under his gaze.

'I'm sad about it, yeah, but I'm not sorry, Maggie. It's been over for a long time, since before she came back. Maybe since before I met you, but I didn't know it because it was only when I met you that I knew I didn't love Stella any more.'

Maggie was afraid to move, afraid that if she did anything to change even the slightest thing at that moment everything he'd just said would disappear without trace.

'Well, if I helped you . . .' she began cautiously.

'You did, you did help me, Maggie.' Pete didn't know what to say next. He ran his hands through his hair. 'Oh fuck! This is ridiculous. I had this all planned out. I practised it and everything on the way up here, but now you're actually there in front of me and we're sitting on the stairs, it all seems to be going pear-shaped.'

Pete stood up suddenly and, taking a breath, pointed at Maggie.

'OK. Maggie, I really fancy you. Oh God, that makes me sound about eleven. What I'm trying to say is that I . . . I think you're great, and sexy, and beautiful . . . and . . .'

Pete realised he was pointing at her and stopped, looking at his offending finger as if it had nothing to do with him.

'And, well,' he continued, feeling suddenly liberated by the truth, 'I wanted to be romantic and sweep you off your feet but

'. . . You might think I'm barmy, but I haven't been able to stop thinking about that kiss we had, and I haven't been able to stop thinking about you.' He knelt down on the stair beneath her, lowering his voice. 'Or your eyes, or your smile, or the way you laugh. I'm crazy, I know, but I just have to know, even if you're not interested. I just have to know if we could . . . maybe go on a date or something. A real one, this time, and . . .' Every muscle in his body tightened as he looked at her. 'Oh God, Maggie, please say yes.'

'Yes,' Maggie said quickly.

Pete stopped talking and almost smiled.

'Yes?' he said.

'Yes. I said yes, I'd like to go on a date with you, and yes, I know how you feel because I felt like that too and I came round to tell you, but Stella was back and I'm sorry you split up, but I'm not at all, you were terrible for each other, and yes, I'd like the chance to get to know you better.'

They stared at each other, studying each other's faces minutely in the half-light.

'Great,' Pete said, and then, because he was tired of being polite and cautious and because he couldn't wait a second longer, he took her face gently in his hands and drew her down to him. 'And now I'm going to stop talking and I'm going to kiss you, Maggie,' he whispered, just before he pressed his lips to hers.

Maggie found herself lying back on the stairs, her back arched over the ridges of the steps, Pete's weight above her, his lips covering her face, his hands in her hair, and she found her winding her arms around his neck, pulling him closer, more tightly against her. The first kiss they had shared had been like a dance, a fragile bridge built across what had seemed like an unbridgeable gulf. This kiss was just as wonderful but completely different – this kiss was about each of them being as close as they possibly could be to each other at last. About touching and stroking and holding each other because they could at last.

Pete groaned deeply and pulled away from Maggie a little, smiling down at her.

'Oh God,' he sighed. 'We have to stop!'

Maggie smiled. 'But why? We've only just started!'

'Because your lipstick's smudged?' he offered.

Maggie laughed. 'That's funny – so's yours.' She tried to pull him back to kiss her more, but he resisted.

'Maggie, *God*,' Pete moaned. 'I want you. I want you so much.' Pete's eyes covered every inch of her face. 'But if we keep on like this then, well, I don't know *what*'ll happen, and on the *stairs* of all places! What I'm trying to say is . . . I don't want to rush you into anything.' He looked at her as if the thing he hoped for most in the world was to rush her into pretty much everything.

Maggie smiled, delighted at the prospect. She sat up, resting on her elbows.

'Do you have to go home?' she said.

Pete smoothed down his ruffled shirt a little. He felt somewhat confused, and realised he was still terrified of all the things that could still go wrong.

'No. Do you mean now? God no, I mean – you don't want me to, do you?'

Maggie laughed and shook her head.

'No, I don't want you to *stay*. Stay for the rest of the party until everyone's gone.' She looked at her watch. 'They'll be out in the next half an hour or so.' She fixed her gaze back on his face. 'I want you to stay while I sort out the waiters for cash and make sure we're straight in the bar. And then I want you to stay the night. With me. I've got a crap bedroom, a single bed and I live with my family, but I want you to stay with me Pete, please. And I need you tonight, because if I wait any

396

longer I'll probably . . . oh I don't know, implode or something.'

Pete laughed and ran his thumb gently underneath her lip, removing the smear of lipstick.

'Maggie, if you want me to stay then I'm not going anywhere,' he said.

It was just over half an hour later that Maggie shut the door on her bedroom and turned on the bedside lamp.

'Try not to look at the wallpaper,' she said, but Pete was only looking at her; now that he'd allowed himself to look at her, he found he couldn't stop.

He crossed the small room in two strides, encircled her waist with one arm and drew her into him, kissing her face and her hair and her lips, kissing her deeply, crushing her against him. Maggie pulled at his shirt, pulled at the buttons until they opened and felt his hands find the zip at the back of her dress, heard it slide down and felt the material of her dress slip off her shoulders until at last her skin met his. She heard Pete's sigh deep in his throat. He held her there for a moment against his chest, and just for a second they were both still.

Then he unhooked her bra, and Maggie didn't know where it went because the next thing she felt were his lips against her breasts, and then she realised he'd picked her up off the floor and was carrying her over to her single bed. Laying her down gently, he drew back to look at her, stroking the length of her body with his fingertips.

'Maggie, you are so beautiful,' he told her, and she knew that she was, she knew that he made her beautiful. She dragged him on top of her, wrapping her leg around his hips, feeling him move against her. At last they helped each other out of the last of their clothing and lay against each other, perfectly close.

'Pete,' Maggie whispered. 'Please . . .'

Pete moved his hand between her legs, but she stopped him, closing her hands over his wrist and pushing it gently away.

'No,' she whispered. 'I want *you*. I just want *you*, now.'

Once he was inside her, everything else, everything that had happened, fell away into insignificance and all that mattered was each second passing, each moment of pure pleasure that came swiftly and then again in waves that might have been endless, if only time had meant nothing.

Finally Pete lay beside her, pressed close against the bedroom wall. He moved his arm under her neck and stroked her hair.

'Thank you,' he said, kissing the corner of her eyebrow.

Maggie giggled. 'I think I should be thanking you at least three or four times as much!' she said.

Pete looked sweetly pleased with himself. And then he sighed, deeply content.

'I can't believe it,' he said. 'I can't believe that we are here at last. That you and I are here at last.'

Maggie grinned. 'I know, it's great, isn't it? And the best thing is that we can just be together. There's no stress, no pretence, no complications. None of that crap. We can just be together and get to know each other and take as long as we like. We've got all the time in the world.'

Pete's heart sank, and reality came rushing back in. How was he going to explain to her? What could he possibly say?

'Oh God,' he said, sitting up.

Terrified, Maggie sat up too.

'Pete, what is it? Look, I'm sorry. If you don't feel like that, then I didn't mean to embarrass you . . .'

Pete shook his head and took her hand, kissing it.

'No, no, of *course* I do. Of course I feel like that. It's just . . . Oh, Maggie, I'm supposed to go to LA next Saturday. For six months.'

Maggie stared at him, speechless.

'Oh,' she said, falling back on to the bed and staring at the ceiling, as she felt the weight of his words sink leadenly into her chest.

Pete lay back down on his side, leaning up on his elbow to look at her. He traced his finger along the line of her jaw and down her neck across her shoulder.

'I never thought this was going to happen,' he said. 'I wanted it to, but I never dreamt it would, or that it would be so . . . wonderful. Just to be with you.'

Maggie tried to smile at him but found that she couldn't. She tried to sound cheerful instead.

'But it's great!' she said as though someone had just told her the world was about to end. 'It sounds great. It sounds like just the sort of thing you've always wanted!'

Pete nodded without enthusiasm. 'It is. But so are you. So is this. I didn't know it until just now, but being with you like this is something I've always wanted too. Oh God, you're going to think I'm an idiot blurting all this out when we've only just . . . for the first time.'

At last Maggie smiled, and reached up and grazed her palm along his cheek.

'I don't think you're an idiot. I think I know what you mean.' She sat up a little and kissed his ear. 'Let's not think about it,' she said, running her finger up into the nape of his neck. 'Let's not think about it now, because it's just us. Two people who've only just met. We don't have to think about that now. We just have to think about each other. Next Saturday is ages away. We've got a week to be together, and that's a week longer than we thought we'd have.'

Maggie sat up, pushing Pete back down on to the bed by his shoulders as she straddled him. 'Let's not think about that. Let's not think about anything.'

Chapter Thirty-five

'I don't know what you're doing sitting here,' Sarah told Maggie. 'He's going in the morning, isn't he? Shouldn't you be round his?'

Maggie shook her head glumly, swinging herself from left to right in one of the salon chairs.

'He had to pick up a few last bits from work and go to some meeting. He'll be back in about an hour and then we're going out . . .' She trailed off and picked up a stray purple plastic roller, sending it scooting across the little shelf that was attached to the mirror opposite her. Maggie raised her head and looked around at the empty salon. 'This place is a bit dead, isn't it?'

'It is now, but we've got a rush on from three,' Sarah said, swiftly detecting Maggie's attempt at a change of subject. She sat down next to her and swung her chair round to face her.

'What are you doing here, Maggie? Why aren't you with him? You could have gone up to town with him. I'd rather you did that than sit here looking all pathetic!'

Maggie picked up the roller again and scooted it across the shelf, from where it clattered on to the floor.

'I don't know,' she told Sarah miserably. 'I thought I'd done pretty well with all this, you know? I mean, I know I went off the rails a *bit* – but then I thought, you know what?, I'm fine, I'm well adjusted and I'm dealing. So what if I've got a thing about Pete, it'll wear off given time. And then he comes round and we go to bed, and then the last week, Sarah! The last week has been . . . totally perfect. Totally, utterly perfect. And now he's going to LA and I want him to go, I'm pleased for him, but . . . I can't believe this has to end after a week. It's just not fair!' She picked the roller up off the floor and rolled it once again, but Sarah's hand slammed down on it with a thwack before it could travel very far.

'He's going to LA, not Jupiter. It's only eight or so hours away on a plane! That's nothing, these days. When Sam and I go at Christmas, you could go too, fly out there and see him.'

Maggie shook her head. 'I can't!' she wailed.

'Why ever not, for Christ's sake!' Sarah asked her sharply, her already thinly spread sympathy fast running out.

Maggie dropped her gaze and picked at the sleeve of her sweater.

'Because he hasn't asked me,' she mumbled.

Sarah rolled her eyes and stood up, pushing her chair back so hard that it skidded across the floor of the salon and slammed into the reception desk with a clatter.

'You two! Jesus! He probably hasn't asked you because he's hoping you'll suggest it, the idiot!'

Sarah paced up and down in front of Maggie, her hands on her hips.

'Maggie, I don't know what it is about you and Pete, but I feel like . . . I know, I feel like I'm watching one of those films, you know – the kind of one where you've been happily involved in the story, you think you've got to the end, you think you've got your happy ending and then BAM! The director goes and adds on an entirely unnecessary extra half an hour for some reason.'

Sarah paused as she stood over Maggie.

'You love Pete. Pete loves you, even if neither one of you has actually said it yet! So he's going away for six months. It's not the end of the world. I'd have thought that if anyone had learnt that hanging about waiting for something to happen doesn't work, it should be you. You need to grab hold of this and *make* it happen, Maggie. You can't leave these things up to men. You have to decide to be happy. Like Marcus and I did.'

Maggie looked up at her Amazonian friend. 'All right, warrior princess, it was me who got you into all this expressing-your-true-feelings milarky in the first place,' she said with some petulance. 'But it's not that simple.'

'Yes it is,' Sarah told her. 'Yes, it is that simple. Now leave here, go and find Pete, and do it now, or else I swear I'm going to kill you, and I think I'd get off on the grounds that you're *such a flipping idiot!*'

Maggie tightened her stomach muscles and looked at Sarah.

'Is it that simple?' she said.

'If you want it to be, it's that simple,' Sarah told her.

Maggie clenched her fists and bit her lip. Sarah was right: there wasn't any reason why she couldn't just tell him how much she cared about him, how she thought she probably loved him. After all, where had beating around the bush got her so far? Precisely nowhere. It was only when she'd made her mind up to do something that anything had happened, and it had been the most wonderful week because of that. And, she thought, she probably *was* in love with him, and she couldn't just let him go without telling him, without him knowing. She had to say something, she just had to. Maggie jumped out of her chair and ran her hands through her hair.

'You're right,' she told Sarah, still chewing her lip.

'Finally!' Sarah exclaimed, rolling her eyes heavenwards.

'You're right. I need to go and talk to him and tell him how I feel, and if he doesn't feel the same then . . .'

'JUST GO!' Sarah shouted, and, grabbing her bag, Maggie

ran to the door, mostly because of her sudden need to see Pete, and only slightly because she was actually a bit scared. Just before she shut the door, she turned back to her friend. 'Thank you, Sarah!' she said, shutting the door just before the purple roller Sarah threw at her hit her head.

Maggie started running. She didn't actually know where she was running to or why, but she knew that when Pete did come back it would be via the station, so she headed there. By the time she got there it wouldn't be long before he got in, and somehow, she had to keep running. Unfortunately, she had hardly got to the high street when she was out of breath and gasping for air. She sank down on to the first bench she found, next to an old lady.

'Miss the bus, dear?' the lady enquired politely.

'No, but I almost missed the boat,' Maggie told her as she gulped down air. Taking a deep breath, she pushed herself off the bench and began running again.

And then suddenly Pete was there. He caught her at full pelt and held her close.

'Oh baby, I was coming to find you! Why are you running? Are you OK? You've not been mugged, have you?' He looked around the street with a thunderous expression.

Maggie gasped for breath and shook her head.

'No, I was running!' she almost laughed. 'Running to find you before you go! Like a maniac! But I had to, I have to tell you something really important. And I couldn't wait any longer.'

Pete took in her flushed cheeks and dishevelled hair and hugged her hard.

'Yeah?' he said. 'And me, I wasn't running but I was looking for you. I was sat in this stupid briefing we've been over a hundred times already with my boss, and I thought, hang on a minute, I'm not having this, I should be with Maggie. I'm going tomorrow, and I don't know when I'm going to see her next, and I need to see her! So I got up and told him it was an emergency and came back. I went to The Fleur and your mum said you'd gone out to see Sarah, and I couldn't wait. So I came to find you.'

Pete took a couple of steps back, his hand still gripping her shoulders, making them an island that the stream of busy shoppers had to flow around.

'And on the way here, I decided something. Maggie, this last week has been the best week of my life so far. I don't want it to be the last week I spend with you.' Pete took a deep breath. 'It's you, Maggie, you are the one. I love you. And I'm not leaving you behind. I decided on the way back from work. I'm not going.'

Maggie was still reeling from hearing him say that he loved her.

'Did you say that you love me?' she repeated.

'Yes,' Pete said seriously. 'Totally and utterly, and if I'm coming on too strong too soon, then I'm sorry, but I just feel like we've already let too much time go by . . .'

'No! No, you're not, Pete, I love you too! I . . . Oh God.' She took a step closer to him and held the lapels of his coat. 'Pete, I'd love it if you weren't getting on the plane tomorrow, but you have to go to LA. It's your dream and I wouldn't – I couldn't – stop that happening. It means too much to you. You *have* to go, you have to go for us both.'

Pete shook his head.

'I can't, I just can't. I love you so much, Maggie, and I'm scared that if I get on the plane you'll forget that, you'll forget how much I care about you and how much I need you. I'm scared that when I'm not here you won't feel the same about me. Look at what happened when Stella left me – I fell in love with you. I don't want to leave you, Maggie. I don't want some other bloke nicking you off me.'

404

Maggie shook her head and smiled.

'There isn't another bloke in the world who could "nick" me off you, you idiot!'

Pete looked at her.

'Not even Christian?' he asked her.

'God no! Especially not Christian!' Maggie exclaimed. 'And anyway, you're not leaving me. You're going to LA, not Jupiter! It's only eight hours on a plane. And I thought that . . . well, if you didn't mind I could come over for Christmas and New Year. I mean, it's a busy time at The Fleur, but we're fully booked already and Jim can more than handle it.' Maggie put her palm on Pete's face. 'Christmas is just a few weeks away. And maybe you could come back for a weekend at some point, and in between visits there's the phone and email.' Her eyes sparkled. 'Hey, I know, we could get web-cams!' she giggled. 'Just imagine how interesting *that* could get!'

Pete began to smile at last.

'I wanted to ask you to come with me. I've thought about it since the moment I told you I was going. But I knew that I couldn't do that, that it would be the wrong thing to do. Knowing how much The Fleur means to you and how hard you're working to make it successful, I knew I couldn't ask you to leave it, or your family.' Pete dropped his chin. 'And I didn't think you would anyway, so I thought, well, I could just stay . . .'

Maggie rested her forehead on his chest for a moment.

'If it was just me, I'd go like a shot with you, I'd go and hang around you and be your FX groupie, if there is such a thing. But it's not just me, it's Sheila, and Mum and Dad – and The Fleur is special, Pete. It's something that I've helped to build, and in a way I feel like it's a part of us, part of what made you and I possible. I can't just abandon that, and even though I want to be with you, you're right, I don't want to leave it, and if you're

405

honest, you don't want to let go of that chance in LA. Not really. You know, all those years of searching, of looking for a place where I really felt at home, where I'm really part of a family, and finally I've found it, right where it's always been. And it's because of you – you helped me see it, and . . .' Maggie shook her head. 'I don't know how to explain it.'

Pete smiled down at her. 'You don't have to. I know exactly what you mean. You've spent your whole life running, and now you want to stop, now you want to stay.'

Maggie nodded. 'And you've spent too long waiting,' she said. 'Waiting for these chances, waiting to move your life on. And I want to help you do that, not prevent it. You have to go, it's your time.'

Pete nodded slowly.

'You're right, Maggie. I really do want to go, nearly as much as I want you, but not at the expense of losing you,' he said.

'It's OK to have both, you know,' Maggie told him. 'This isn't the end of us, Pete! I thought it was for a while, but then I realised I'd just got into the habit of doom and gloom!' Maggie smiled up at Pete. 'This is just the beginning for us. This is . . . Chapter One, page one of The Story of Us. We've got pages and pages to fill yet. And part of that is making sure each of us does the best they can to be happy.'

Maggie wound her arms around Pete's neck and kissed him until the giggles of some passing schoolgirls and the honking horn of a passing lorry made them remember where they were. They were laughing as they parted.

'What do you say,' Pete said softly. 'That we go back to mine and make a start on Chapter Two? I've got some really good ideas about how I want that part to go . . . Listen, did you ever buy that red dress you were wearing in that shop the other day?'

He picked up Maggie's hand and kissed it. And as they walked through the winter sunshine, the spire of the abbey reached into the bright blue sky, and all around them hundreds of different lives were spinning out across the city, across the world, connecting and crossing, each starting their own page.

And on this page, Maggie knew, her life with Pete was just beginning, and knowing that was wonderful.